Oliver's Wishes
Book 1
By Cory Gaffner

Editing Team: Cory Gaffner
and Jerome Koger
LucidDreamEditing@Gmail.com
Typography: Joshua Wagner
Joshuakwagner@gmail.com

Oliver's Wishes
Copyright ©2018 by Cory Gaffner
All rights reserved.
No part of this work may be used or reproduced in any manner whatsoever without written permission except in the case of brief quotations embodied in critical articles or reviews.

Other Books By Cory Gaffner

Oliver's Universe

Oliver's Wishes
Oliver's Wishes Book 2 (Not-titled yet, and forthcoming)

Striker's Universe

Bullets and Sunshine
I'll Be Back: Griffin's Tale
(Book 3 also in the works here)

Short Stories

Matchstick Mechanical (forthcoming)

Arbiter Core

Killdozer
KillCycle (forthcoming)

<u>Forward</u>

in·tel·li·gence

inˈtelǝjǝns/

noun

noun: **intelligence**

    1. 1.

        the ability to acquire and apply knowledge and skills.

knowl·edge

ˈnälǝj/

noun

noun: **knowledge**; plural noun: **knowledges**

    1. 1.

        facts, information, and skills acquired by a person
        through experience or education; the theoretical or
        practical understanding of a subject.

Without the prerequisite knowledge, it does not matter how much intelligence you have.

Chapter 1

The Old Man

Gotta find the boy before I bleed out. For 50 years I've been trying to pass on this burden, to find the right person to protect it. I've failed that mission. My time is up, I have to give it to someone else before the Cabal gets me, and they will get me. The Cabal has killed everyone I have ever called brother. I don't know how they found me this time, but it doesn't matter. They underestimated me. They underestimated the *old man*. I may look old, but I stay in good shape and I have a few tricks up my sleeve that they aren't expecting. The pain in my side just flared up, ow. I'm using my hand to try to stop the light but steady blood flow. *It would be nice to pull over and pressure wrap it*, I think as I feel the precious blood seeping between my fingers, no time for that now though. I'm old enough to be honest with myself. Real self-honesty that can only come with age and hard-earned wisdom, and I can tell no amount of pressure is going to fix this wound. None of that matters now though, gotta find the boy.

I'm careening through traffic in a stolen Cabal truck trying to get to the grocery store where the boy works... The boy's name is Oliver. The only one to pass all of the tests... Well, all of the tests except for one. The test that some of my brothers considered the most important: the Intelligence test. He truly failed that one, and then some. Oliver is as dumb as a bag of rocks, I'm not even sure why I screened him. Something about him just always felt *right*. He was old fashioned, sincere, and honest. He truly wanted to help people. The only thing holding him back from being amazing was his IQ, which was a very low 69. An IQ of 69 meant he had a mild mental disability. If he didn't have that disability this kid could have been a world leader. Instead he was a bagger at a grocery store. Cursed by some congenital mistake. Day in and day out helping people out to their cars with their groceries, and all with a genuine smile on his face.

I had screened so many young men and women... So many... All of them, one by one, had failed. Petty, jealous, greedy, mean spirited, cracking easily under pressure, eventually they all showed their true face. The times are changing. It used to be easier to find candidates when things were simpler. People use to just be happy to have a home and a family, not anymore though. Now people can't even stand in line to buy a pair of sneakers without attacking each other like rabid beasts. Hell, I had seen people attack honored friends and family just for having different political beliefs. Don't get me wrong, greed and malice have always existed, they were just... *rarer*. If I couldn't have the perfect candidate, I would take the loyal one. The one that should he ever falter and use its twisted power... would at least try to do something good with it, I doubt *she* would let that happen, but he would try. I could feel it in my own bones, he would try. Oliver is far from perfect, but he has a good heart and that is what the world really needs, more people with good hearts.

The grocery store is coming up now and I can already tell I'm going way too fast. I yank the wheel to the side to try and avoid the curb and the stop sign in my path, but the blood on my fingers makes the wheel slip in the opposite direction and I inadvertently barrel through a few signs, some bushes and finally into a parked car. I would be pissed if this truck was mine, ha ha oh well, the Cabal can afford a new one. *Gotta get to him,* it's 11 a.m. on a Thursday so I know he is working. I know his schedule like the back of my hand and the boy is like clockwork. The boy is a dam in a flash flood of malfeasance, he would rather fall on his sword than miss a day of work, I know he is here. I have the *package* wrapped in a towel that is getting bloodier by the second under my arm. I need to make sure no cameras see it. I have to pretend the only reason for the towel is to stem the flow of blood. I can't leave any clues for the Cabal.

As I'm running across the parking lot I hear squealing tires behind me, damn the Cabal is fast and efficient, I'll give them that much. On the other hand they were just outsmarted and defeated by one wily old man, HAHA! As I enter the grocery store and look around for Oliver people start screaming. Probably because I'm leaking blood all over the place and I have a 1911 combat pistol dangling from my right hand. My left arm and hand are busy holding the towel to my wound, the towel with the package tucked neatly inside of it.

I spot Oliver on his usual lane, bagging groceries like any other day. That boy is a sentinel. No, that's not right. Oliver is 25 now, he is no mere boy. He is a man. A man of honor, and soon the man who will defend the most dangerous item in the world. Everyone starts screaming and running as I head towards Oliver. Not Oliver though, he keeps doing his job, bagging the groceries that come down the conveyor belt. I don't know if he continues despite the screams because he is doggedly determined or just too stupid to notice. Either way it doesn't matter, he is the rock in the storm.

I jump on top of Oliver, my entire large frame knocking him to the ground. I may look like a feeble old man but I'm a warrior, *I'm dense.* I make sure to cup my hand behind his head as we fall so I don't accidentally give him a head injury. Once we both hit the ground I carefully unwrap the towel between us, wary of the cameras in the store. I know where every camera is because I have surveyed this store a thousand times. I carefully remove the lamp from inside the confines of the towel and tuck it into the pocket on the front of the boy's apron. I have planned this maneuver hundreds of times. I was just praying and hoping I would have never had to use it. I was hoping to have died with my secret. I was hoping to be buried with the lamp so eventually it would be forgotten with the passing of time. The Cabal have forced my hand though.

Once I have the lamp inside of Oliver's apron, I look down at his fierce face. He is confused but not scared. My left hand is still cupped behind his head so I crank his face next to mine and whisper the most important thing he will ever hear.

"Keep it secret, Keep it safe. Tell no one, never use it." Now that my arm isn't holding the towel to my wound, my blood is flying all over Oliver. There is so much more I want to tell him... I wish I could tell him that I'm proud of him. That he is the son I never had. That he has impressed me every day. That despite his disability he is a beacon of the human spirit, but I don't have time for that. The cameras are watching me and they can't know that I have entrusted Oliver with this burden, they can't know what he means to me.

Strong hands grab my shoulders and lift me upwards, and a second pair of hands rip the pistol away from me. When they lift me up, I close my eyes and play dead. I barely crack my eyes open enough to see two members of the Cabal wearing black suits and I'm sure they have fake law enforcement credentials on them. I let my legs out a little bit on purpose and they have to both grab me before I hit the floor, amateurs... They've just made a fatal mistake, you never grab a rattlesnake by its tail. I grab the closest one's bicep gently and pretend I'm barely coming into consciousness, and that I'm just grabbing him for support. I push the sleeve of his suit up and expose the flesh of his forearm and then I do something they don't expect. My body comes alive, straining every muscle I have I yank my body towards him, his body towards me, and I take a bite. My teeth shred the man's skin like so much paper and his blood rushes into my mouth.

A tiger is always most vicious in his death throes, and I know I don't have a lot of time left. The other agent grabs my head to try to dislodge me, so I turn my face towards him spitting the blood and chunks of flesh from my mouth right into his face and eyes. I don't know if he is blinded or just disgusted, but he lets go of me to try and wipe the gore away, another mistake. I feel my strength waning from the blood loss, but I still have enough in me for a haymaker of epic proportions. I dump 50 years of hatred and fear into my punch and deliver it right to the bloody agent's face. He falls down and his head bounces off of the tile floor of the grocery store making a sound like a gunshot. By god I may have killed him! I've still got it, *whew-hoo!*

Fighting isn't always about who the best fighter is, or who has the biggest muscles. Sometimes it's about who wants to win more, and who is willing to do the darkest things. Today, that man is me. Time to make a hasty escape, I have to lead the trail further away from Oliver. I look to the front of the store, but there might be more Cabal agents out there, better take the back route. I glance at Oliver one more time as he is rising to his feet but I'm well past out of time, so I have to run. *I'll miss you Oliver.* I make sure to grab my trusty old 1911 before moving on and head towards the back of the store. I have to enact the last part of my plan to throw off the Cabal. This plan should set them back years of searching, maybe forever.

I head to the back of the store and into the storage area, I'm passing by scared employees everywhere. Maybe they think I'm here to shoot the place up, I don't know, not my concern. Once I get to the very back of the store there is a box truck there that has just backed into one of the truck docks to unload produce. The driver is just getting out and sliding the rear storage door of the truck up. He doesn't know what's going on at the store yet. The unfortunate bugger turns around to find me, the bloody old man, pointing a 1911 combat pistol right at his face.

"Hand over the keys if you want to live," the truck driver is too stunned to move, "NOW!" I shout. He hands me the keys and I swish my gun to the side indicating that he should go and he takes off running.

I hop into the cab worried it might be a manual transmission, I haven't driven one of those for over 30 years but it's just an automatic. I slam the truck into gear and gas it, I feel weird movement and notice the back of the truck is spewing heads of lettuce and bundles of carrots everywhere. Whoops I forgot to close the back, haha, oh well. Maybe it's the blood loss but watching the vegetables fly all over the road as I swerve back and forth is really making me laugh. As I'm watching the vegetables in my rearview mirror I notice at least ten black SUV's following my trail, that has to be Cabal operatives. Fuck it, let's

12

leave some more bread crumbs! I keep jerking the wheel back and forth to spew more vegetables all over the road. My destination is only a few miles away.

As I careen into the worst neighborhood in town, a hobo with a grocery cart is a little too slow to get out of my way. I try to jerk the wheel away from him but I wasn't quick enough to miss his cart which goes airborne. "HAHA, TWENTY POINTS!" I'm not sure where I got this point system from or why a hobo's grocery cart constitutes twenty, but I won't argue with myself. I have to do things to stop myself from passing out from blood loss, and playing a fun game might help. The house I'm looking for is just ahead so I swerve the truck hard and pull the emergency brake. The truck spins sideways and gets on two wheels for a moment before falling back down on all four tires and finally stopping.

I reach into my jacket pocket for one of my final surprises that I can leave for the Cabal: a medium sized piece of Semtex, a plastic explosive. I've already jammed a pre-programmed five minute detonator into it. I stick it up under the console of the truck so it won't be visible upon a quick inspection and flip the switch to turn it on. All someone would have to do to turn it off would be to flip the same switch that I just used, but they will never find it in time, I hope. I left the truck parked right across the middle of the road horizontally so the Cabal following me will have a hard time getting around it, and I head towards the house, my future tomb.

The home is large and dilapidated, a two story home with many bedrooms. It hasn't looked good in over twenty years, and I've made sure of that. I own the home through a shell company that occasionally gets sued over the status of this very house, but greasing the right palms can make anything happen in the legal and political world. The house has peeling paint, broken and boarded up windows, and visible graffiti all over it, and the last I checked is an active drug den for crackheads and dealers. I'm really getting woozy now from the continued slow but steady blood loss, but I don't have much further to go. As I walk up to the front door I notice the front yard is absolutely littered in cigarette butts, used syringes, and even the occasional brass casing from a fired round.

The front door is cracked open, the occupants don't even bother to lock it. Why would they though? No one in their right mind would enter this house uninvited. When I enter the dark house it takes a second for my eyes to adjust. There is minimal light in here, it's coming through in slants and shafts through some of the boarded up windows. The inside is much like the outside: disgusting. There are sleeping drug addicts everywhere curled up on dirty sleeping bags. I hear the sound of feet shuffling coming from the back of the house as one of the dealers comes to see who just opened the front door. I still have the 1911 in my right hand and I don't want to scare the young pup just yet so I put it slightly behind my back.

He comes barging into the entry room like he owns the place, I suppose in his mind he does. He is going for the imposing look. I guess that look helps him keep his usual customers in line, or maybe it just makes him feel good about himself. He looks like you would expect, covered in tattoos, white ball cap slightly slanted up, baggy pants, some stupid t-shirt with shit on it that I don't care to understand, and a track jacket with a hood which he has up, resting on top of his ball-cap.

"Nigga, you done walked into the wrong fuckin house. You don't look like you here to buy my shit, so you best get steppin," he says and sneers at me as he grips the handle of a cheap pistol that has been hastily stuffed into his waistband. I can't help but laugh at his pejorative, seeing as how this particular pretend tough guy is white.

"Actually young man, this is my house," I say calmly.

"Old man, you lost as fuck. This is Rooster's territory, and if he comes out here he is going to cap your ass." Young people give up information to freely. He just let me know there is at least one more drug dealer in the house and the second drug dealer is armed.

"Actually I'm going to cap him," I calmly say, and bring the 1911 out from behind my back.

When the drug dealer sees my pistol he starts to draw his, but he isn't quick enough and I put a few rounds through his chest. The gunshots wake up some of the crackheads and they scramble out through the door behind me, but most of them are too high to notice, or care. Maybe some of them are even hoping this is the time they get put out of their misery. I walk over to the downed drug dealer who is busy choking on his own blood "Young man, it isn't nice to deal drugs. Also FORTY POINTS!" I'm still confused as to where I'm getting these point values from, but if a hobo's grocery cart was twenty then a gangster drug dealer is at least forty. Time to clean up the rest of the riff-raff, the last thing I need is to get shot in the back by some drug dealer while I'm finishing up my life's work.

I head towards the back of the first floor and start hearing heavy rap music so I head towards the noise. The noise leads me to the farthest room from the front of the house. The door to the room is closed all the way and the music coming through it is still loud. I bet good ol' Rooster didn't even hear me shoot his doorman. I try the handle but it's locked so I start banging on it.

"GO AWAY" a female shouts through the door. I keep banging until I hear the music turn off.

"This better be good" the same female says. A young woman who looks maybe 18 but is probably younger opens the door which actually opens up into quite a nice little office. There are lavish rugs overlapping all over the floor, a pile of car stereos in the corner, a leather couch with a brand new gaming system in front of it, and a large cherry oak desk in the corner. Behind the desk sits an African American man dressed in what can only be called 'modern pimp clothes'. The young woman has gone back to stand by his side and by the look of her pupils she is high as hell.

"Hello there, are you Rooster?" I ask him in my most pretend fragile old man voice.

"Who da fuck is asking?" he says back in a deep voice.

"I'll take that as a yes," I say. I swing the gun around and Rooster's hands fly below the desk he is sitting behind, probably to try and retrieve his own firearm. I pull the trigger first, before he can grab whatever he is going for. His brains paint the young woman next to him and the wall behind him.

"ONE HUNDRED POINTS!" Minor drug lords are worth at least one hundred points, right? I look at the scared young woman covered in blood, and bits of skull and can't help but feel bad for her. My sympathy wins out and I go over to her and lift her chin up.

"Stop doing drugs and letting men like this use you. You are someone important. Go to school, get a job, raise children, and teach them to be good. Now run away or I'm going to shoot you in the head." The woman runs off, out of the house, good.

I reach under the desk to see what Rooster was looking for and come up with a sawed-off double barrel shotgun, sweet. I head back to the front of the house to peek out the front door and see exactly what I was expecting to see. The Cabal SUV's are all pulling around the truck I left in the middle of the road and starting to surround the house. I look down at my watch, *any second now.* The Semtex I left in the truck explodes, and flips two of the Cabal SUVs over onto their sides, men climb out burning and screaming. The inside of one of the vehicles is painted in blood.

"FIVE HUNDRED POINTS!" The rest of the vehicles in the Cabal convoy barrel through the downed cars and start spreading out, they won't bunch up again.

Next to the door frame I knock on the moldy drywall in a few places, slowly moving my hand back and forth. I continue knocking until I hear the hollow space that I had put there years before. Once I find it I lean back and shoot one of the barrels of Rooster's shotgun at the wall with my eyes closed. Sharp pieces of wood cut my face and chest, but I'm too tired to care. I reach into the hole I just made, and pull out a metal box. I pop the clasps on each side of it, and reach inside to find my prize: an exact replica of the lamp I just gave to Oliver. Once the Cabal sees this thing they are going to go crazy.

I get close to the door frame again, and lean my head slightly around the corner. The Cabal are out of their trucks now, taking cover and ready to fire on me. I push the nose of the shotgun around the corner and then pull the trigger, firing blindly. The barrel is probably too short to hurt them at this range, but might as well keep them honest. Then I stick my hand out the door with the lamp in it and yell "HOLD YOUR FIRE!" I walk half my silhouette into the frame of the door and look out, with the lamp still held high in my hands.

"If you want it, come and get it!" Then I duck back inside and rounds pepper the door frame where I was just standing. Normally I would be dead in a situation like this, high velocity modern rounds would fly right through the low quality wood and drywall and shred me up something fierce, but when I had this house built I had a thick piece of steel embedded into the drywall that I'm currently standing behind right now. So instead of being shredded I hear the comforting sounds of bullets dinging off of steel.

Once the incoming fire stops I start walking towards the back of the house. As I walk I turn around and fire my 1911 through the open doorway to stop any Cabal agents that might be thinking of entering. At the back of the house, around a turn in the hall is a small closet for the water heater which hasn't worked in decades. I pull the panel off of the water heater which has a keypad underneath and I type in the password. The water heater starts making a strange noise and then it pulls itself back into the wall behind it and exposes a stairway that leads down into a hidden basement.

I march down into the room and the lights automatically turn on. "Authorization Black Sky," I say out loud, and a small pedestal in the center of the room starts rising from the floor.

Once it has risen about four feet it stops, and a loud hiss emits from it as a small metal door opens on the front of it. I reach my hand inside and pull out the dead man detonator sitting on a charging station, and clamp my hand over the trigger. All I have to do now is to let go of this trigger, and the whole house will blow. I'm going to wait though, and take some Cabal bastards with me. On one side of the room, a portion of the wall slides up exposing eight older model televisions. They all have different views around the house from hidden cameras, and two of them are black. Some of the cameras must have gone out during the years since I had them installed.

I can see Cabal soldiers armoring up and preparing to raid the house. Some are heading to the back and side entrances and some are stacking up at the front door. They are communicating via radio to each other to synchronize their entry. I watch all three teams throw flashbangs into their respective entrances and wait for them to pop before rushing inside. On the front lawn four additional different Cabal teams begin to rush up to the house to join their cohorts already inside. At the back of their vehicle barricade I see a distinguished looking Japanese man; something about him gives me the creeps, and makes goosebumps form on my flesh. I look back to the screens and see one of the Cabal tactical entry teams has almost found the entrance to my hidden basement.

I back up a few steps and face the stairway as the heavily armored men come bursting into the room and surround me. I have the lamp in one hand now and the dead man switch in the other.

"There are so many Cabal soldiers on this property right now, you guys are worth at least ten thousand points," I say as I show them the dead man switch. The lead Cabal operative notices what it is, and tries to key his throat mic to warn the others.

"EVERYONE GET BAC------"

Then the world goes up in flames.

Chapter 2

Oliver and Astrid

Oliver sat on the cold linoleum floor of the grocery store just staring up at the plaster tile ceiling, and the fluorescent lights long after the old man, Mr. Smith, had left. He still had some of Mr. Smith's blood on him, and that made him sad, but also angry. Why had Mr. Smith knocked him over and hurt those men? He had always liked Mr. Smith, the old man would ask him the silliest questions and give him a dollar when he helped him out to his car with his groceries. Mr. Smith was always patient with Oliver, and he never seemed to care when it took Oliver a long time to answer him. He didn't even mind helping Oliver when Oliver got confused. He wasn't sure how long he sat there trying to parse through this new influx of information and his memory of the confusing event, but soon someone was tapping on his shoulder.

"You okay bud? None of this blood looks like it is yours." Oliver looked up and noticed the police officer trying to talk to him. He was thinking about answering the officer, but he just couldn't quite seem to get the words out.

"I'm going to need you to answer me," the officer said sternly as he helped Oliver to his feet. Oliver wanted to answer the officer but sometimes he had trouble getting the thoughts all the way from his head out to his mouth. Oliver opened his mouth to try and answer.

"I... I... I... um." The officer's face screwed up and began to look a little angry.

"Have you been drinking son?"

Before Oliver could reply the manager of the grocery store politely tapped on the officer's shoulder and pulled him a few feet away. The manager leaned over and whispered lightly to the officer, just quiet enough so that Oliver couldn't hear what was being discussed. The officer glanced over at Oliver, and then back to the manager and nodded his head. The officer came back over to Oliver.

"Oliver is it? I'm sorry about before. I'm going to have my friend over there drive you home now," the officer said as he pointed over to another policeman on the scene.

"Hey Rookie! Get over here!" The second and younger police officer ran over to them and the first police officer whispered to something to the second officer quickly.

"I see," said the second police officer.

The younger police officer gently grasped Oliver's upper arm.

"Come with me buddy, I'm going to take you home. It looks like you get out of work early today, score!" Ha, that sounded good to Oliver, the way the police officer had worded it made Oliver happy! Oliver smiled widely at the younger police officer and let him guide him out of the store.

"BYE EVERYONE, SEE YOU ALL TOMORROW!" Oliver managed to shout happily before they left the store. He loved giving everyone cheery goodbyes, and cheery welcomes. Oliver's father had told him that smiles were infectious, and Oliver had taken that sentiment to heart. He loved giving people big bright smiles on the off chance that they might smile back, in fact it was his favorite thing to do besides helping people.

"I like your style Oliver," the policeman said to him as they were walking through the parking lot. "Hey would you like a ride home in a real police car!?" The officer asked as he pointed to his cruiser. When Oliver thought through the prospect of getting to ride in the car of a hero it made him so happy he laughed out loud and clapped excitedly. "I'll take that as a yes!" The nice officer said.

The ride to Oliver's house was exciting, the kind officer showed him how the sirens worked in the car and all of the neat instruments and buttons inside. Now that Oliver had calmed down a bit he was able to properly thank the officer.

"Thank you... so much... for showing me this," Oliver stuttered out. He had worked really hard with his many therapists to be able to put out sentences that clear, and he felt proud at his progress and how clearly he had just been able to speak to the officer.

The nice officer smiled over at Oliver. He must have also been proud at how well Oliver had spoken.
Not wanting the conversation to die the officer asked, "Hey, what's your favorite thing in the world?" This question Oliver didn't have to think about. He knew this one as sure as he knew and felt his heart beating in his chest.

"SUPERHEROS, REGULAR HEROES, ALL HEROES! HEROES LIKE YOU OFFICER!" Oliver shouted out with joy.

The officer's smile got brighter and he replied to Oliver. "Damn Oliver, you really know how to compliment someone. I'll tell you what bud, I really like heroes a lot too and I'm tired of going to hero movies alone. How about the next time a hero movie comes out, me and you go together?"

The officer had said a lot in that one statement so it took Oliver a second to parse through it, but once he did he was so excited at the prospect he shouted "WOOHOO!"

The nice police officer laughed and said, "Oliver, I'll say it again: I like your style. You have truly brightened up my day. You know I don't think I introduced myself properly, I'm Officer Hampton. You know what else, forget about that, you can just call me Tim." Oliver thought about it a second and remembered his father told him it was good to shake hands with new people.

"Hi Tim!" said Oliver, while holding out his hand for a shake. The officer took one of his hands off the wheel for a second and shook Oliver's hand.

Officer Hampton pulled up to the address the grocery store manager had given him through the grapevine.

"Do you need help getting inside Oliver? Will you be fine alone?" Oliver pulled his key ring out and shook it at the officer.

"I'm fine Tim, I have keys to get in. Have a good day, very nice to meet you!"

Oliver happily jumped out of the car and ran up to his front door. The officer waited to leave until Oliver went inside. The whole time feeling better about himself and thinking that if Oliver can be happy covered in blood after being tackled by a senile old man, then he surely had no excuse not to be happy himself. For a brief second, he also wondered why God chose to curse someone so special with a disability.

Oliver went inside excited to see his mom and his dad, but was upset when they weren't there. He remembered he was home early from work which meant both of his parents were still working themselves. They wouldn't be home for hours so Oliver decided to do what he always did when he had extra time: watch cartoons and movies about heroes! Oliver nuked a bunch of pizza rolls, and then plopped himself down on his couch ready to marathon some television. Once he set the plate containing the pizza rolls in his lap, he realized it had made a strange noise. It sounded like it had bounced off of something hard. He set the plate aside and looked down at his lap. He noticed he still had quite a lot of blood on him from Mr. Smith, and that there was a slight bulge in his apron.

The blood on his apron made Oliver's mind wander and he felt bad all over again and he didn't like that. Then he remembered the noise the plate had made when it hit the bulge. He reached inside of the large front pocket on his apron and felt around. His hands hit something solid, so he pulled it out. It was an antique brass lamp! *How did this get here*, he wondered. The lamp had

Mr. Smith's blood on the side of it. Seeing even more of Mr. Smith's blood only further upset him. So he started trying to rub the blood off with his fingers, as he rubbed he noticed the lamp was getting brighter and warmer. That alarmed Oliver so he dropped the lamp and took a few steps back from it. It landed evenly on his carpet and it seemed to glow even brighter than before, like it was filled with fire.

Soon a loud hissing noise that was quickly turning into a roar started coming from the lamp, and a white vaporous substance started spilling from the spout and filling up the immediate area. More and more of the smokey yet silky substance poured out of the spout, and then it began to coalesce into the shape of a woman. Her form began to take substance as the vapor solidified. A beautiful woman with a long blonde ponytail hanging down her back was now in front of Oliver. He stared at her from top to bottom, she was wearing some kind of crude chainmail. She had leather bracers on with intricately carved flowers on them. She also had a leather protection piece on her neck that delicately covered part of her upper chest as well, and ended in a diamond shape between her breasts. Below that she was wearing a skirt made of rough hide, and she had a leather belt on with a dagger, a sword, and a horn in three separate sheaths connected to the belt.

Her skirt was cut diagonally so her upper left thigh was extremely exposed and Oliver couldn't help but stare. The woman was shapely and beautiful, but also for some reason Oliver didn't even understand he knew she was quite dangerous. Oliver may have been dumb, but he knew when it was time to get the fuck out. He turned and bolted for the exit of his living room that lead to his entryway, and ultimately his front door. A second before he got there a wall of vapor quickly rose from floor to ceiling blocking his path. Oliver tried to sprint through it, but he ran right into it and bounced off; the harmless looking wall of vapor had been as hard as stone. Oliver reached up and touched his nose, his fingers came back red with blood. He slowly rose to his feet and turned around.

The woman was there staring at him and he noticed something that he hadn't seen before, just below her knees her legs tapered off and shifted into vapor, which was still flowing into the spout of the lamp. The woman smiled at Oliver and canted her head to the side ever so slightly.

"I know, I know, It's amazing, but let's get this show on the road so I can go back to sleep for a few hundred years. Talking to mortals is boring." Oliver wasn't sure what to say so he just smiled at her, then marched forward and held out his hand for a

30

shake. "Hi, I'm Oliver, it is very nice to meet you!" he said enthusiastically. The genie shook his hand nodding her head up and down once, and then just waited...

She kept waiting for a minute for the man to speak up, but he never did so she took the initiative.

"Well Oliver, I don't know if you have figured it out yet or not, but I'm a genie and I'm stuck out here until you make your three wishes, so get on with it...Please." she stared at Oliver for a few minutes and he still didn't speak.

"Okay you seem really confused and unprepared for this, let me lay down some ground rules to help you narrow your choices down. The first and most important rule is you can't wish for more wishes. I'm not going to explain that one because it should be pretty self explanatory. I need you to acknowledge that you understand each rule after I explain it to you. I'm only explaining these things once. So do you understand rule one?"

Oliver stood there stunned. He did basically understand the first rule, but all of this was too much for him.

"I need you to say yes now," the genie said calmly yet forcefully.

"Ye...ye..yes," Oliver stuttered out.

"Okay, moving on. Rule number two, you can't make a wish that will alert the world to the presence of the genie, meaning me. What this means is no wishing for things like curing world hunger or stopping all war. Those wishes also break a third rule but I will get to that. If you wanted to feed the hungry people you could, for example, wish for the power to turn anything you touch into food, and then send that food to all the hungry people. Or, even the power to make crops grow really well, or make dead crops come back to life, etcetera. I won't stop you from doing that. Do you understand rule number two?"

Oliver really didn't understand rule number two that well since it was more complex than rule one by a fair margin, but he knew she wanted him to say yes and he wanted to make the pretty genie lady happy so, he said "Yes."

"Moving on, rule number three is you can't make a wish that will directly force someone to do something they wouldn't normally do. So you can't wish for the girl you have a crush on to instantly drop her panties the next time she sees you. If you want to wish to be more attractive so she will like you more, we can do that.

This rule also applies to and reinforces rule number two. For example let's go back to the world hunger issue. Say you wish to cure world hunger, and one country has a ton of food they aren't using. How do you get that food from said country full of fat and selfish people, to the countries full of starving people, without forcing someone to do something that they wouldn't normally do? See the conundrum there? At some point you would have to force someone to do something that they wouldn't do, or reveal the existence of genies in some way. Maybe that wasn't the best example but it is what came to mind. Do you basically understand rule three?"

Again Oliver was very confused, but he understood the pattern. The pretty lady went on a long tirade and she expected him to say yes, so he said "Yes."

"Right then, rule number four is you can't wish for someone's death directly. If you want to wish for a super powerful weapon of some type to kill them with yourself, that is fine with me and well within the boundaries of the rules. Just don't expect me to do your dirty work. If you want someone dead, you do it. In that same rite, you can't wish for someone to come back from the dead. I don't fuck with dead people, and I couldn't even if I wanted to. Do you understand rule number four, the death rule?"

"Yes," said Oliver.

"Good, final rule, rule number five. You can't wish to live forever, don't get confused here. If you want to be alive for a very long time we could do that. You could wish for extremely good health, or to heal twice as fast, or to stop contaminates and poisons from working on your body, etcetera. There are lots of things you could do to lengthen your lifespan, but you can't wish to live forever. Do you understand rule number five?"

"Yes," said Oliver.

"Okay great, also understand that as soon as you make all three wishes this lamp will disappear. You don't get to give the lamp to your friend or your girlfriend and have them make wishes for you, that violates rule number one. So like I said, as a safety measure this lamp will be going somewhere random on earth as soon as our business is concluded here. As far as your actual wishes go, I've found that it works best if you tell me all three of your wishes first then I will make sure they aren't violating any of the fine print, and at that point I will grant all three at once after we both verify that they are legal wishes, and that they are what you want. Then we will be out of each others hair, and you can enjoy whatever you wished for. So let's get started, tell me what you want."

Oliver stood there literally dumbfounded until the genie's patience wore thin once again "Listen kid, take a long hard fucking look at me. I live in a god damn brass lamp, everyone I ever meet I never see again, and all I do is help selfish morons.

My only solace is every once in awhile the lamp is hidden for a long time and I get to sleep and have some peace. So hurry the fuck up, and make your goddamn wishes." Hearing that the genie was sad and trapped made Oliver feel bad.

"You are... stuck? Stuck in the lamp? Trapped?" asked Oliver.

"Whoop-di-woo the genius figured it out!" the genie sarcastically replied.

"Listen kid, I'm ready to be done with your shitty little house. I'm ready to sleep, let me help you out." The genie looked around Oliver's house and her eyes landed on the superhero cartoon playing on his television. "Boom, superheroes, why don't you wish to have a superpower?"

"I like that."

"Okay, so what power do you want?"

"I want to... I want to be able to help people... to make the world better."

"The superpower you want is to be able to make the world better?"

"Yes."

"Hmmm, I can make that work. That's wish number one. Let's move on to wish two, how about a new place to live, this shabby little house sucks cat dicks."

"I will have a superpower, which means I will be a superhero. A superhero needs a secret hideout."

"Okay, boom, that's wish two, a secret hideout fit for a superhero. Let's move on to wish three, got any idea kid?"

"I don't want you to be trapped and sad anymore, I want you to be free and happy."

Oliver's third wish had just hit the genie like a punch to the gut. Emotions raced through her immortal body and she suppressed a scream. This obvious imbecile would free her? She had been trapped in the lamp for over a thousand years, and in all of that time no one had been selfless enough to waste one of their precious and limited wishes on her. She wasn't sure why she hesitated, the words had already left his mouth. She should have immediately capitalized on the situation and freed herself but the thought of freedom scared her almost as much as being trapped in the lamp for an eternity. Where would she go? What would she do with herself? She knew no one, she had no home, hell, she didn't even have any skills in this modern time. The only reason she even understood the language and current idioms and slang was because the lamp filled her mind with that information every time she was awoken. You couldn't exactly grant someone's wishes if you didn't understand their language.

"Oliver, are you sure that is what you want for your third wish?" Oliver didn't hesitate in his response.

"Yes, it is sad that you are trapped. Everyone deserves to be free." The genie felt a small tear roll down her face. If this man was going to help her then she was going to help him. She re-evaluated his first two wishes and used every trick, loophole, and every ounce of power inside of her to make the results of his wishes better.

The genie appeared to enlarge in size and began to glow, her voice came out of her mouth like the voice of a god and it shook Oliver's house. Louder than a thunderstorm she shouted, "YOUR WISH IS MY COMMAND!" The light in the room continued to get brighter, and brighter. Oliver threw his forearm over his eyes.

That vapor that was holding the genie's legs into the lamp started blasting out so fast that it was making a whistle like a tea kettle left on the stove too long. The whistle became so loud that Oliver had to move his hands over his ears, but that just made his eyes hurt because the room was so bright now, and the light was actually permeating his eyelids. Oliver drove his face into the carpet to protect his eyes and held his hands tighter over his ears. Oliver's house started to shake, all of these sensations at once were too overwhelming for his small mind so he began to scream as a weak defense mechanism. Vaguely he thought he heard the genie screaming as well. Then it all went black.

Oliver woke up when someone flipped him over onto his back. He opened his eyes and saw the genie leaning over him. Without giving him any sort of warning she smashed her mouth onto his, and kissed him feverishly. She wouldn't stop kissing him until he was finally able to push her away and yell "STOP." The woman got off of him and Oliver noticed her feet weren't vapor anymore, they were just feet.

"Yes, sorry, I'm just very thankful." The woman looked around and then squished her bare feet around in the carpet and moaned. Then she looked down at her clothes "People probably don't wear this kind of thing around do they?" the woman asked. "No," replied Oliver. Oliver wished he could help the nice lady with her clothing debacle and he felt a weird pop in the back of his head.

A giant blue transparent menu popped up in his vision, he was so startled by it he let out a little shout.

"SOMETHING IS HAPPENING!" Oliver yelled.

"Ah yes, I'm guessing that's your power activating for the first time. There should be some way to make it visible, look for the word 'VISIBLE', do you see it?" It took Oliver an extremely long time and he had to have the genie-woman spell the word out to him multiple times before he found it, he wasn't that good at reading. There were two empty boxes on the bottom right hand corner of the menu. The top one said 'Visible to Astrid' and the one below it said 'Visible to all allies.' He clicked the one that said 'Visible to Astrid' because it was on top not because he particularly understood the choices in front of him.

"There we go, I can see it now." Astrid studied the menu, there was currently only one option available up, it said 'Update Astrid's clothing to a more modern style? Cost: 5 Points.' Below it there was a stylized 'Yes' and 'No' which were both slowly blinking. "Oliver press the one that says yes, that's y-e-s." Oliver reached out with his hand and pressed it like she had asked him to.

Astrid yipped when she felt her chainmail and clothes rip around her body very quickly. She looked down and noticed her skirt had changed some, it was now a bit longer overall and it ended in a straight line just below her knees. It was also now more form fitting. Each side of her skirt had a three-inch strip of decorative chainmail from bottom to top. The skirt was still made of the original hide but it felt thinner now, and finer like the material had somehow improved in quality.

She no longer had the chainmail top on either. She was wearing a halter top that felt like it was made out of portions of what used to be her hide skirt. The halter top also had the three-inch strips of chainmail on the sides of it. They ran all the way up to the bottom of her armpits. Around her neck she wore a decorative necklace which was obviously made from the chainmail as well. It widened around her throat and sunk down towards her now exposed cleavage. Finally she noticed she had a pair of hide sandals on, the straps of which were made from chainmail. She still had her original belt equipped with the sword, the horn, and the dagger.

"Damn I look good! What do you think Oliver, are these modern enough?" she looked up at Oliver and he just had a blank look on his face, a few seconds passed and finally he smiled and said "Yes." This man was now her only link to the modern world. She couldn't have her only contact and ally be a half-wit. *Time to fix up the dumb dumb,* she thought.

"Oliver do me a favor, think about your menu and then think about being smarter." She patiently waited and reiterated herself a few times to Oliver to keep him on track. Eventually his menu changed in front of her. A slider popped up, there was a dial on the slider that was currently all the way to the far left. The far left side of the slider was labeled 'mildly mentally disabled.' Near the middle of the slider there were three nodes. The first node was labeled 'slightly below average intelligence,' the middle node was simply labeled 'average intelligence,' and the last node was labeled 'slightly above average intelligence.'

The far right side of the slider was labeled 'extreme intelligence.' Astrid pointed to the one labeled 'slightly above average intelligence.'

"Slide that dial over to here for me please." It was taking Oliver too long so she guided his hand which in turn moved the dial. She noticed as the dial moved right, a point value at the bottom of the menu appeared and slowly increased as the dial moved further up the intelligence scale. When the dial was at the setting she wanted it at the point cost at the bottom of the screen now read '25 points.' Below the dial now read the word 'Confirm?' and below that there was a small 'Yes' and 'No.'"Select yes again Oliver, please." Oliver slowly reached up and pressed 'Yes.' Then he started to scream...

Oliver's steady scream slowly became louder and more desperate, more like an animal in pain than a human. He gripped the sides of his head. His fingernails dug into his temples hard enough to draw blood as he fell over, and began to roll back and forth on the carpet. Astrid dropped down to try and hold him still, and peel his fingernails out of his skin to keep him from doing further damage to himself. All of a sudden Oliver stopped screaming, his eyes shot open and they landed on Astrid.

"You were the first woman that's ever kissed me Astrid. Do it one more time please." Astrid shrugged her shoulders and gave him a quick kiss.

"Yeah, that feels awesome," Oliver said with a smile.

"Don't be getting sweet on me now boy, we just met and frankly you look kind of stupid," Astrid said with a smile.

Her comment made Oliver think, which surprised Oliver because thinking was happening very fast now. Oliver did look 'kind of stupid' as Astrid had put it. Why was that? His menu which he had forgotten about during his painful experience popped up again like before, and then updated itself in front of him which drew his eyes sharply to it. 'Fix the effects of Fetal Alcohol Syndrome and other congenital anomalies? 25 Points.' was posted over the top of his menu now, the familiar confirmation options were below. *Sure why not,* he thought and pressed the blinking 'Yes.' A lot of things started happening at once and they generally all really hurt. "OW OW OW OW OW, OWWWW!" he started yelling. His whole body was in pain and then as before the pain abruptly stopped.

"Holy shit, you are actually kind of handsome now. Go look in a mirror!" Astrid half-shouted. Oliver followed her advice and ran to his bathroom mirror. When he got there and finally saw himself he was stunned. He was kind of handsome now, Astrid was right again. His head had changed shape, his eyes and jaw had gotten bigger. His nose was a more stereotypical 'manly' shape. He looked down and noticed his pants didn't quite touch his shoes anymore, HA, he had even gotten a little taller. Fetal Alcohol Syndrome... That didn't make sense his mom didn't even drink. Then he realized something, something that had just become glaringly obvious, he was adopted. His parents looked nothing like him, and his mother hated alcohol. He wasn't really sure what to think about that and he had a lot of other things going on right now that he should be focusing on so he stored that information for later.

"Astrid, one more kiss please, and then I'll stop asking." She shrugged her shoulders once again and jumped on him. He almost fell over because he wasn't ready for her weight. She really laid the kiss on him this time, her tongue darting in and out of his mouth. Then she jumped off of him and acted like nothing had ever happened. When he was finally able to talk he just said "Whoa." Astrid smirked at him and clapped her hands together sharply.

"Alright, let's get this fuckin show on the road!"

"What show? Where are we going, and what are you talking about, and why do you swear so much? Wait, how do you even know what swear words to use?"

"Well I swear a lot because this is how my people talked. We were a rowdy bunch. I know all of your slang, and idioms because it was "downloaded," I believe is the right word, directly into my brain as soon as you rubbed the lamp. I have to be able to understand every aspect of the wisher's language to accurately grant his or her wishes. For example, imagine if someone told me they wanted a giant cock as one of their wishes. I grant this hypothetical person's three wishes and disappear. Mr. Tiny-Dick looks down and notices his winky is still microscopic. Then he notices he has a 13-foot tall chicken in his backyard. See the problem there? As to where we are going I figured we could go check out your fancy smancy new superhero hideout."

"How are we going to get there? Remember, I was mentally retarded like two minutes ago," said Oliver.

"I'm not sure of the specifics, but our ride is out back."

Chapter 3

Oliver

"Holy Wowzers," was the only thing that left my mouth when I saw what was sitting in my backyard. It looked exactly like a miniature SR-71 Blackbird, except with a wider passenger compartment. It took up the entirety of the backyard and I was absolutely terrified my neighbors were going to see it. *Wait a minute, how the hell do I know what an SR-71 is?* Thoughts rushed into my head of my third-grade self meeting an Air Force pilot who showed me a model of one and told me and my class all about them. The school I went to for special kids did that for me, they brought in a different veteran once a month to talk to us and tell us about their jobs.

I had to shake my head and focus hard to clear all of the memories that were trying to flow in from somewhere deep in my subconscious mind. I also realized I was filled to the brim with random knowledge. Things I had heard in passing, auditory input from background conversations, things I had heard or seen on television or in a movie. All of it had been in my head this whole time, it had just been locked away from me. Not now though, I could access it all, but it was hard. Was this how it was for normal people? All of these memories just sitting below the surface ready to be called upon? If I knew this much after sitting in a school for kids with disabilities my whole childhood than how much does a regular person know? *This is too much for me, I'm just a stupid grocery store clerk.*

Astrid cleared her throat "ERMM ERMM, Earth to Oliver. You better figure out something to do with this giant spaceship thing before someone sees it. It's only been here for a few minutes but we better not tempt fate, for she is a cruel bitch." Astrid was right, but wait a minute.

"Won't satellites and radars and stuff see us if we take off from here?" I asked.

"I don't know, ask the ship about it. I don't understand the specific details. We didn't have any of this when I was growing up. All I got was a crash course in all of this from the lamp, but that isn't the same as truly understanding it all or living with this level of technology."

I noticed Astrid had the lamp curled under one of her arms "You want me to ask the ship? That thing talks? Why do you have that lamp still?"

"The ship doesn't talk, your hideout does. It has like a radio thingy that goes to the hideout, I think. I kept this lamp because it is still incredibly dangerous. Check this out, these directions on the bottom explain how to load a new genie inside of it." Astrid flashed me the bottom of the lamp and I saw there was some fine print on the bottom written in a language that I didn't recognize.

"Holy Moley, you mean it's possible to trap some other poor sap in there?" I asked.

"Not only possible but I bet someone is looking for the lamp right now, and as soon as they find it that will be the first thing they want to do." Thoughts of the men in the suits chasing Mr. Smith rushed into my head.

"EKK GADS! There are people trying to get this lamp! I saw them today! We have to get that thing out of here and take it somewhere safe!" said Oliver.

"Okay, first of all, please start swearing. You sound ridiculous even to me, and I just learned modern slang. Hmmm... you think we should hide the lamp, if only we had a super secret hideout to put it in... OH WAIT, WE DO! Remember you literally just wished for one." Astrid made sure to slap me on the back of the head after saying that, I deserved it.

"You are right, let's roll." We approached the back of the spaceship or shuttle, whatever you call it and a ramp lowered automatically. The inside was surprisingly spacious. There was four seats on either side in a two by two fashion, and a pilot seat centered in the front. The interior was stark white which was incredible considering the outside was pitch black.

A strange female voice floated through the air "Welcome Oliver, should I take measures to eject the person with you, or are they an authorized guest?"

"Whoa whoa whoa, don't eject anyone, this is my guest. Are you the ship A.I.?"

"I am not an A.I. Oliver and I am not on this ship. I would probably be considered an A.G.I., but even that would be somewhat of a misnomer. I'm more of a connected series of A.N.I. type programs. My hardware resides in a hardened server room above in UNNAMED space station floating 40,000 kilometers above you."

"Break that down for me into simpler terms please. I'm new to this whole not being dumb thing."

"I'm not an A.I. I'm just a sophisticated program. I have no wants, needs, or thoughts, just rules. I have been programmed with millions of abilities, and I will do my best to assist you with any task that is inside the realm of my capabilities. Should you procure a qualified coder, they can input new information into me very easily using some of my adaptive software. That can only be done from UNNAMED space station though, and only after you have given them access. No remote access is allowed for adding code. In short I am a highly advanced user interface, but not an A.I."

"Oh wow, okay, thank you for explaining that. The hideout is in space huh... wow. If we fly up there will the Air Force notice us?"

"According to latest speculations no Air Force in the world will be able to see this ship or any like it for at least six years due to the specialized stealth coating on the outside of the ship. The level of technology needed to spot us is possible to create now but earth governments lack the cohesion and/or funding to see it to fruition."

"So we can fly to the space station now safely?"

"Relatively safe. You have a 99.3% chance of making it to the UNNAMED space station unharmed and unmolested."

"Okay, how do we do that?"

"Sit down, strap in, announce where you would like to go and then specify that you would like to use the autopilot. If the address is inside of the directory then I will direct this ship's A.N.I. auto-pilot to take you there. The UNNAMED space station IS in the directory. After you master the pilot simulator on the UNNAMED space station you will be able to pilot this craft yourself."

"Welp, no time like the present, am I right?" I said to Astrid with a smile on my face that I really wasn't feeling. My stomach felt queasy and I was terrified, but Astrid was the ONLY beautiful woman that had ever kissed me, well strike that. The only woman to EVER kiss me, I wasn't going to show fear in front of her if I could avoid it. I didn't want Astrid to be my girlfriend or anything but it was just a matter of pride at this point. Pride, a new concept to me. I didn't truly have it until really just this moment. I took pride in my work at the grocery store before this, but not out of self-pride, I did that because I wanted to make my parents and co-workers happy. I liked making people happy, in fact I can tell that I still do just by thinking about it. I wonder if I should even be focusing on pride, I haven't needed it so far in life.

Me and Astrid strapped in next to each other. I thought about taking the pilot seat but I didn't know how to pilot anyway so there was no point.

With a false bravado I shouted, "Please take us to my space station, engage autopilot!" I heard the ramp behind us close with a surprising amount of speed and a hiss which I assumed had something to do with keeping air inside of this vehicle since we were going to go into the vacuum of space.

"Please remain seated until we have arrived," the mechanical voice said. The ship promptly jerked off the ground and I was pinned to the back of my seat. All I saw was sky through the front windshield and I was scared out of my mind.

I felt all of the blood leaving my face and I got really light headed for a second, but then the feeling dissipated. I was too worried and air-sick to notice before, but Astrid was holding my hand. It was surprisingly quiet inside of the ship. Astrid caught me looking down at our joined hands and said "I have been immortal for so long I forgot what fear felt like, sorry."

"It's fine Astrid, I was scared out of my mind as well. I honestly think we should be passed out though if we are going as fast as I think we are. When I was a kid I talked to a pilot and he told me that he had to do all kinds of exercises to be able to casually endure g-forces like this."

The mechanical voice broke into our conversation: "This ship has micro inertial dampeners installed, without them you would be unconscious," well that explains that. "Thank you mechanical A.N.I. thing. Oh, do you have a name?" I asked.

"I remain unnamed, along with the UNNAMED space station. Would you like to name them both now?"

Astrid broke into our conversation "OUUU NAME THE SPACE STATION VALHALLA!" I do like that name.

"Okay A.N.I. person, I would like to name the space station: Valhalla." The voice remained quiet for a moment and then replied.

"The space station will now be called Valhalla. What would you like to call me Oliver?" I was drawing a blank so I looked over at Astrid.

"Call it Bifrost," said Astrid.

"I would like for you to be called Bifrost" I said.

"Acknowledged, you are now speaking to Bifrost and we are en route to the space station Valhalla." I felt a grin stretch across my face, cool.

On a whim I thought of something "Bifrost, can you use a more feminine voice?" The current mechanical voice was a little grating on the ears.

"LIKE THIS, HA HA!" The crazy A.N.I. had just sounded like a bubbly 16-year-old girl.

"OH PLEASE NO, not like that. Can you blend that voice with your last one, about half and half?" I asked.

"Accepted, how does this sound," the voice that came out was much better. It was clearly not human but it now sounded nice enough that I wasn't worried about being probed by a robot. It reminded me of a more mature version of that little girl A.I. from the Resident Evil franchise. Wait, how did I even know that? Memories flipped through my head, years ago my dad was watching the movie on the couch. I'm not sure if I like the way my memory works now, it is very *jarring*.

Astrid interrupted my line of thought "Oliver, would you mind if I stayed on your space station for awhile? I don't have anywhere else to go right now. You know, just until I get my feet on the ground and find my own place?" Astrid had sounded surprisingly vulnerable while asking me that. Her personality so far had been so take charge and kick-butt that I didn't even know that she could sound anything less than... well powerful.

"Astrid you can stay there forever if you want. I know we just met but I'm having trouble thinking of you as anything less than a close friend for some reason. Anything you need, don't hesitate to ask. I'm truly happy to help." Astrid smiled at me and patted my arm, and then turned her head away from me. I swear before she turned her eyes were getting a little watery. "Thank you Oliver," she whispered sincerely.

Sooner than I thought possible the sky through the windshield darkened and we were in space. "Wow that felt way to fast. Bifrost, how long was that trip?"

"It took you four minutes to exit the atmosphere. You just broke a speed record. You could have gotten their faster but it would have been uncomfortable."

"How long does it normally take to get into space?"

"The fastest time before now was eight minutes and thirty seconds."

"Why did we get here so much faster?"

"No one else has the technology for inertia dampeners yet."

"Why not?"

"It would take a multi-government collaboration with near unlimited funding five to ten years to develop it. In short, the nations of this earth lack the cohesive teamwork needed to accomplish such a feat."

"Well that is mildly depressing. Bifrost do me a favor. Slow us down and turn the ship around, I just want to see the earth."

Our view spun around, but our momentum still carried us in the general direction of the space station. A view of earth I had never seen before was laid out in front of me, and it was beautiful. "Wow," me and Astrid both said in unison.

I started to unbuckle myself when Bifrost spoke up "I can not recommend leaving your seats as there is no artificial gravity on a ship this small." Well scratch that then, I didn't want to look like a doofus helplessly floating around in front of Astrid.

"Oliver if you would allow me to turn the ship around, the Valhalla space station would be in clear view," said Bifrost.

"Just call it Valhalla, you don't have to keep saying 'space station' every time. And yes, that would be fine with me if you spun us around."

The ship slowly spun around and I was surprised again. In front of me floated a giant black cube, I wasn't expecting that. Every time I had ever seen a space station on a TV show or a movie they were always some weird oblong craziness covered in antennas and spinning donuts.

"Whoa! Bifrost, why is it a cube?" I asked.

"The cube shape is easy to maintain, repair, modularize, and monitor." That didn't quite add up to me but I didn't have the requisite knowledge to ask more questions. I'm not in a rush though, *so I'll try to look into that as soon as possible.*

We flew straight up to the giant cube, the closer we got the more details I could make out. There were all kinds of interesting looking doors and hatches that I could see. There was also long poles with...wait a minute.

"Bifrost, is that a chain link fence?" I asked.

56

"Yes Oliver, the chain link fence provides weak missile defense. The missiles hit the chain link and explode prematurely." Wow that is cool, I remembered my dad watching something on the military channel about that. They would suspend chain link three feet out from the sides of the military trucks for the same reason. Rocket-propelled grenades would hit the fencing and explode early. Sure it would still wash the truck in fire but it was better than a direct armor piercing hit. The chain link fencing on this space station was at least twenty feet off of the hull, still immensely cool.

"So if that is weak missile defense, what is strong missile defense?" I asked.

"The strong missile defense is provided by our A.N.I. driven lasers, you should see some firing now off to our left. I looked and didn't see anything for a while as I carefully scanned the hull. Then finally I did see something that looked like a turret moving around in different directions very quickly.

"I see something that looks like a laser, but nothing is coming out of it," I said.

"No Oliver, that laser is indeed firing. The laser is invisible to the naked eye. The reason you 'see' lasers on earth is because they are hitting particles and dust in the air along their path. You won't see lasers in space due to the lack of dust and other particulates," Bifrost replied.

"Wait, that laser is firing right now? What is it shooting at, we have to stop it!" I shouted.

"That would be unwise Oliver. That laser is shooting micrometeoroids before they hit the space station and anything else that might be in such an orbit around the earth that it might eventually come back around and run into us. Valhalla is much safer for the work that laser is doing."

"Oh... Well, that is actually really cool. Thank you for the explanation Bifrost." I kept watching the laser spin around rapidly in its mount. I had to wonder if eventually it would burn off all of the micrometeorites in our little corner of space and slow down a bit. "Bifrost, is there only one laser per side of this cube?" I asked.

"Only one laser is out at a time Oliver. There are three more lasers on this side for a total of four lasers on each side of the cube. All four can be extended in an emergency." Four seemed like a pretty low number to me, but what did I know about proper space laser management?

"Bifrost, I'm curious as to why there are only four lasers per side. Isn't that a little low?"

"It is indeed Oliver. This is a space habitat meant for defense and dwelling only. This is a rapid deployment base made for the explicit purpose of deploying Q.R.F. teams to emergencies down on earth. I have no data on who engineered the space station, or myself. I just know that you are the owner, and its exact purpose was to be a 'base and hideout for heroes,' that reason is hard-coded into me and all of my machine laws revolve around making that mission possible and more expedient."

"Bifrost I am confused again, what is a Q.R.F. team?"

"A Q.R.F. team is a quick response force. In the military when they suspect trouble might arise, they have warriors and heroes waiting to jump into the fight. The Q.R.F. team on duty sits in their armor ready to leave at a second's notice."

"Wow that sounds really cool. I guess I did want a hero's hideout."

"Are you a hero Oliver?"

"Not yet, but I will be," when I said that Astrid looked over at me with a stern look on her face. I couldn't help but wonder what that was about.

"Alright Bifrost, enough stargazing, take us in." The ship reoriented itself and sped up. We headed towards a giant traditional looking hangar door straight out of a sci-fi movie. I was impressed, and unsure of what might happen when it started to open. I wasn't a complete rube anymore though, I knew there had to be some mechanism in place to protect the precious atmosphere. I was expecting a semi-transparent blue force-field or some kind of a fancy airlock, I got neither. There was some kind of deep purple curved semi-transparent curtain up, it did kind of look like a force-field but I had never seen one on the movies that looked like this. In short, It looked... angry.

"Bifrost is that a force-field?" I asked.

"No Oliver, that is a plasma wall," Bifrost replied.

"What's the difference?" I asked curiously.

"Plasma walls are real, force-fields are fiction," said Bifrost.

Unbeknownst to her/it, Bifrost had just sent my brain into the land of 1000 questions. "Bifrost, If plasma walls are real why don't people use them on earth?" I asked.

"They lack the prerequisite energy needed to turn on and maintain one of this magnitude," Bifrost replied.

"Well then, how are we doing it?" I asked.

"Multiple nuclear reactors." HOLY WHAT! This thing is nuclear! I didn't know much about nuclear energy, they didn't exactly cover that topic at special school, but I did know it was extremely dangerous. I guess you get what you wish for. Things need power to run, but still this knowledge left me on edge.

Bifrost pulled us in straight through the purple plasma wall and parked us in a large mostly white hangar. I noticed once we crossed the threshold of the plasma wall I had felt heavier, this place had gravity... I was so excited, that as soon as we pulled in I had already unbuckled and jumped out of my seat before Bifrost had even finished parking us. As soon as the ship stopped I ran down the slowly lowering ramp like a little kid in a candy shop and jumped the last few feet before it had even touched the ground. I started running towards the plasma wall.

"OLIVER, STOP!" Bifrost shouted. Her mechanical voice had sounded menacing so I obeyed the order immediately.

"What's going on, I just wanted to run my hand through the plasma wall real quick," I said.

"If you had touched that plasma wall your flesh would have lit on fire and been subsequently seared off."

"Oh shoot, nice catch Bifrost." I watched the outer metal hanger blast door slowly close behind the plasma curtain and then the plasma curtain winked off.

"Oh, we don't leave the plasma curtains on all of the time?" I asked.

"No Oliver, they take a lot of energy and they are very hot. We just use them to maintain atmosphere as a ship enters or leaves the hangar."

I had only been here a minute and I had already almost lost a hand. I have a lot to learn.

Chapter 4

Mr. Tokugawa

"I WANT IT FOUND, AND I WANT IT FOUND NOW! LET'S GO PEOPLE!" I shouted at the Ops Center and the assorted techs and agents in front of me manning our top of the line espionage and monitoring network. The room was filled with hundreds of people on computers. The best hardware money could buy and some that even money couldn't. All connected to different governments all over the world thanks to our many sleeper agents. That tricky old man had somehow pulled a fast one on us. Fifty years.... Fifty years he had been rogue with the lamp, but we finally picked up his trail, and what does the crazy old bastard do... HE BLOWS HIMSELF AND THE LAMP UP! We have good intel that that lamp is almost indestructible so it's just a matter of time before we dig it up. I had a strange hunch that this lead was too good to be true. Just simply dig it up and have it... No, that can't be right. The old man was much too smart for that.

Civilians didn't understand the danger they were in with the lamp out there. They didn't understand the sacrifices my people had to make to keep it secure, the things we had to do. They couldn't know either. I've tried to ponder a world where the average person knows that a wish granting lamp exists... People murder their best friends and family over lottery winnings, amplify that same petty greed times a million combined with the power to do almost anything. The world would burn down if people knew about the existence of the lamp.

An errant drip of water smacked my cheek, I had to look up at the beauty of the natural cavern we were residing in. The drip must have come from one of the many stalactites above me. One of the downsides of leading a secret society was that we had to work in secret. Sure, we had some projects going on above ground but we couldn't leave anything vital where it could be found, which means a lot of our static locations were like this one, dark and wet. We have long since given up the sunlight in order to complete our mission: Save the human race... from themselves.

Most people assume Armageddon would come from some freak accident, maybe even a meteor like what did in the dinosaurs. They are all wrong, we kill ourselves and each other much more efficiently than any rock from space could. Global warming, GMO's, murder, rape, overpopulation, nuclear war, religious fanatics, etcetera; no, the real danger to humanity is humanity itself. Why do we let this chaos continue? Freedom, that outdated idea that has led to the deaths of billions. Everyone wants it until it backfires on them. The person who advocated for less gun control then sees his family shot to death. The person who drives the fast car only to lose control and crash into a wall. The person who smokes cigarettes until they get cancer. People don't need freedom, freedom leads only to death.

When the Cabal gets the lamp I will finally have the power to cure this world of its true cancer: freedom. What a disgusting concept. Every herd needs a shepherd or the sheep will eventually run off of a cliff, and the Cabal is that shepherd.

"SIR, THE MEN HAVE GOT SOMETHING!" one of my subordinates yelled. I reached down and grabbed the hilt of my family sword, as I often do when I am stressed.

"Show me, bring it up on the big screen," I shouted. Behind me many large screens we had suspended from the ceiling of the cave all become focused on the same image. Men were coming out of the ruins of the dilapidated house the old man had blown up. One of them was carrying some melted brass slag which he held up to the camera. "They believe these are the remains of the lamp sir," the tech said.

It can't be, "Have them keep searching the remains of the home, but let's assume the old man never brought the lamp into the home with him. Pull security footage from the grocery store and from all traffic cameras. Let's backtrack his steps people, he hid the lamp somewhere." It's only a matter of time until we find it. The lamp without its guardian would be easy to find. I have no idea how the old man stayed under the radar for so long, but his mistake is my good fortune. The lamp, my life's work and simultaneously the bane of my existence. The equivalent of three nuclear weapons just floating around the earth at random. If the wrong person found it large portions of the world could be destroyed.

Some of our top Cabal scientists and historians already believe it had been used for terrible things. The fall of Rome, the sinking of Atlantis, maybe even the Spanish Flu. Not to mention all of the small villages and settlements that disappeared overnight. The lost colony of Roanoke is a perfect example of this. If the wrong person with a chip on their shoulder gets the lamp... droves die. Even imaging a modern day religious zealot with the lamp leaves me in a cold sweat at night when I'm trying to sleep. If one of those dirty Muslim fanatics got their hands on it, they would murder millions of westerners unless the Cabal could stop them in time.

The Cabal would defend this earth, these people. You can't stop progress. Anyone that tries to stop us or gets in our way will be dragged kicking and screaming into the future with us. We will save this planet. *I WILL SAVE THIS PLANET, from itself...*

Oliver

"So where is the gas tank?" I asked out loud. Bifrost had long since picked up my social cues for when I was talking to her and when I wasn't without me having to constantly call her name. We had walked through all of the major areas of the space station and this place was beautifully haunting. Astrid had been too busy staring in wonder to comment much. Which is saying something for someone who was over a thousand years old from what she had told me, and who had been a magical genie this morning.

"Gas tank? The Valhalla space station does not need gas, it runs off of two different nuclear reactors as I told you before. They will need to be refueled every 30 years, and inspected every 5-10. While the chance of catastrophic failure is extremely low, the inspections are still encouraged."

"What, you want me to inspect a nuclear reactor?" I asked.

"No Oliver, you lack the qualifications to do such a thing at the moment. You will either need to learn how to, or hire someone who can," replied Bifrost. *Hire someone?* Bring a stranger onto my personal space station... I had really opened a can of worms with these wishes, but I didn't really understand that at the time of wishing, obviously. Now Bifrost is telling me I need to maintain nuclear reactors, worry about micrometeorites, hull integrity, onboard farms, restocking ordinance, maintaining the drop ships. I can't do all of this alone, I need help.

Astrid finally spoke up "So are you going to do it? Are you going to be a hero, or are you just going to live in style for thirty years and then abandon this place?"

That's a good question, did my motivations change? I'm smarter and attractive now. I can probably get a better job, a girlfriend, a better life. With my power I could even slowly cure other people who were like me. I thought about it, and without a doubt I still wanted to be a hero. My dream my whole life was to be like Superman or Batman or any of the other superheroes I had watched on T.V. There is more than one way to be a hero though isn't there. My parents were heroes, they must have taken me in at some point in time, a mentally disabled boy, that had to have been hard. Officer Timothy Hampton was a hero to me, driving home someone scared and treating me like a regular person. Did I need to fight bad guys to be a hero? Maybe just curing people like me could make me a hero enough, or maybe I could do both.

"Well Astrid, I'm not sure yet. One thing I do know is that we need help. No offense, but you don't know anything about this timeframe or being a hero, and I'm almost as useless as you are. I have a lot to learn, and so do you. We have to recruit, all good heroes do it, we can't do this alone. We need someone with experience at being a hero. Well that is if you even want to help me. If you want you can just stay here and relax instead. I can tell Bifrost to let you take the shuttles if you want. It's your choice." I tried to keep my face emotionless but I really wanted Astrid's help. At the same time I didn't want to guilt trip her into it. I wanted her to want to help me. For some reason I just felt like I could trust her.

"You freed me Oliver. I will help you with whatever you wish," she replied.

"Okay, but only if you want to. If you ever want to take off and be your own woman I completely understand."

Astrid stared at me for a while then finally spoke back "I'm all in Oliver, but where do you find someone to be a space station dwelling vigilante?" That's a valid question. Officer Hampton came to mind, but I think his sanity might break since he had just seen me earlier in the day as an invalid. There was only two other people who I knew would be good for this and who might accept the offer.

"Astrid, let's head to the shuttle. It's time to start recruiting."

James Gatewood

Scotch and ginger ale, it always helps me think. This was a decision not to be made lightly. I still wasn't sure how I was going to make it. Maybe a coin toss, then it would be fair. Heads I kill him, tails I kill myself. Six years ago I lost my wife and son in a car accident, taken from me by a drunk driver who ran into us. Every day I wrestle with the grief of losing them and slip further into darkness. Today though, today is special. Today the man that killed them is getting out of prison, a combination of good behavior and overcrowding. The man who took them from me is going to go home to his family, he is going to get to see his kids, but not me, I never get to see my son again. So what should I do? An eye for an eye, or should I just end my suffering.

I shove my Glock deep into my mouth and put just a little bit of pressure on the trigger. It would be so easy to pull it. All of the suffering, all of the pain, just immediately gone. Or I could go find that man and give him a small taste of what he did to me. Sure he had apologized a million times, he had sent me hundreds of letters detailing how he would give anything to take that night back, but what were words to someone who had lost a child? I tried to kill him in court, I hadn't planned it, and I didn't mean to, but once I saw him I couldn't be stopped. It took every officer and bailiff in the room to stop me, and even then they had a pretty hard time of it. I'm a big guy, I've always been a big guy and back then I was in the prime of my life.

Now I'm just a big piece of crap. Riddled with injuries from the accident and too sad to do anything important. This isn't what my wife would have wanted. She would have wanted me to be happy, to move on, to find love again. I can't though, it just feels like too much of a betrayal. She was the only woman I had ever loved, but he stole her from me with his selfishness. Maybe I should torture someone he loves and make him watch. Rip their toes off and paint him with their blood. Then he would see, then he would feel a fraction of what I feel every day.

Well, no use whining and debating with myself, coin toss it. If it's heads, I'll make him suffer, tails I kill myself. Maybe I'll even get to see my wife and son again. *Here we go*, I flick the coin and watch it spin through the air. *BOOM BOOM BOOM*. What the hell, someone is at my door? I pull the gun out of my mouth a little too fast and the front sight hits my tooth, ouch. Better make sure it's not some Girl Scouts trying to sell thin mints, I would hate for them to have to see a dead guy with his brains blown all over the wall. Where did that damn coin go? Going to need a re-flip after I shoo whoever is at my door away. *BANG BANG BANG*. Okay whoever is out there really wants to get a hold of me.

When I open the door I put the Glock behind my back and use my offhand to spin the knob. The thought spins through my head that I don't know why I'm taking precautions like this, when I was just willing to kill myself a second ago. An attractive man and woman are standing on my front porch but they both have the strangest clothes on. The woman is wearing some kind of leather and chain get up and I can't tell if it would be more appropriate in a brothel or a nightclub. The man is wearing jeans that are obviously too small for him, a polo t-shirt of some type, and a grocery store apron with a store name that I don't recognize, it's covered with smears of dried blood. He notices me staring at the blood.

"Oh yeah sorry about that," he says, as he fidgets and tries placing his hands in a way over his midsection that will best cover the bulk of the blood stains.

"Get the fuck off of my porch, I'm busy! If you need a hospital there is one up the road!" I shout and try to slam the door, but the woman is quick. She forces her hand through my door and starts to push back. I'm quicker, as she begins to force the door open further. I already have my gun in her face, but for some reason she isn't afraid.

"Whoa, let's all calm down. We are all friends here," the man in the blood-smeared apron says. His smile and voice are off-putting for a strange reason. The reason comes to me a few moments later, he sounds *sincere*, and I believe him. Taking another look at him, he does seem strangely familiar as well but I can't place him.

"Can we come inside, we are in a rush and this is important, please?" the man asks me. I don't know why I did it, maybe I was just curious but I opened the door for them and let them in. I could tell they were disgusted by the state of my home. Beer bottles strewn about, throwing knives in the wall buried into a picture of the face of the man who killed my family. Old cans of beans half eaten and spilled over with bugs crawling in and out of them.

"Sorry about the mess, I haven't been myself lately," I half-heartedly say. The truth is, I'll never be myself again. Not unless my wife and son find a way to come back from the dead.

"It's fine, but back to why we are here. You probably don't remember me. My name is Oliver, you spoke at my school when I was younger, a long time ago. You were a good man James. I need to know if you are still that good man. Are you a good man, because I need help, will you help me?" The only school I had ever spoken at was a school for special children. I did it because a friend had asked me to as a favor and this man in front of me didn't look like he had a disability, and he sure as hell didn't sound like he had one either.

"Get to the point, what is this about?" I asked with just maybe a little too much gruffness.

"Well, that is a fair question, and I should have expected you would ask that. I'm still getting used to putting one plus one together but I'm getting better at it. I'm going to cut to the end of it then, and just give you the short version. I have a space station and I would like to build a team of superheroes to protect the earth. Also some men in suits killed a friend of mine, I need to look into them too. Oh and I need help manning the space station. It has like nuclear reactors and lasers and stuff and frankly it is really confusing to me, and I need help making sure it stays working. Also, I need someone with a military background to help me figure out how to do hero missions. The first person I thought of was you. I just remembered how patient and nice you were to me and all of the other special kids. You never got aggravated or upset, and you smiled at us and told us silly jokes. You treated us like we were normal kids and you told us all about your cool military missions. Well, I'm saying too much, will you come with us?"

Well, this guy WAS definitely from the special school. I had no doubt after a spiel like that.

"Kid, you should have just told me from the start that you were crazy instead of wasting my time. I have something important to do tonight. Is this woman your caretaker or something?" I looked over at the woman questioningly.

"Get this guy out of my house, he needs his meds." I started to move my hands towards their shoulders to usher them out, but the woman quickly smacked my hand away. "Oliver, prove it to him, use your power on him," said the woman. The man very slowly reached out and touched my shoulder. I could have stopped him but he was no threat and I wasn't the kind of man who would slap a crazy person around.

"James it looks like you have all kinds of injuries all over your body, and you are losing your hair, not sure why it mentions that. Do I have permission to fix you? It says I need permission," said Oliver.

"Wait, what!" I shout back, half aggravated at the stranger insulting me over my hairline.

"Do I have permission to heal the various injuries you have been living with, and I guess fix your hair loss?" asked Oliver.

What kind of crack is this kid on? I'll just tell him what he wants to hear so he will get out of my house. "Sure, knock yourself out kid. Mumble your magic words and then get the fuck out of my house," I said.

The man reached up and pushed his pointer finger in the air like he was pressing an invisible button. Then my bones caught fire... Every ache and pain I had been feeling for the last ten years I could feel again only all at once, right now. Every injury I had in the military, and all the pain from the car crash came rushing back into my body. I felt my shoulder blades move slightly in my body. I felt the knee that always hurt when I stood too long start to shift around as well, and the pain was too much.

I slumped down onto the floor and fell on my butt. I vaguely wondered if these people had drugged me with something and then I considered shooting them. Then the pain stopped all at once as if it had never been there.

I jumped up faster than I realized I could and grabbed the man by the front of his clothing. I lifted him off the ground ever slightly forgetting my own strength.

"WHAT DID YOU STICK ME WITH?! WHERE'S THE SYRINGE!" I shouted into his face. I felt something sharp and cool pressed into my neck. I angled my eyes to the side and saw the woman had pulled a sword from somewhere, and had it pressed up to my neck. Who the fuck carries a sword.

"Get that toothpick off of my neck or I'm going to get real angry" I tell her with some steel in my voice. The man is just smiling at me like none of this bothers him. He speaks up.

"Wow this is so exciting! Normally I just work at the grocery store, but now I'm in a real life Mexican standoff, COOL! Anyway, James go look in the mirror bud. You will like what you see. Oh and Astrid, please remove that sword from James' neck. He is a good man, I know it."

I slowly lower him back to the ground once the woman pulls the sword away from my neck. I walk backwards with the Glock in my hand, not pointed directly at them but close enough. I can legally shoot these fucks if they cause me any more trouble. I'm curious now though about why he wanted me to look in the mirror. I take a few more steps back and stop parallel to a mirror I have mounted on my wall and glance over. *Well what the hell is going on now?!* My beard is much shorter and my hairline is different. I was losing a lot of hair on the front of my head and I had a serious widow's peak forming, but not anymore. All of the hair I had lost over the last 16 or 17 years was back. I had the hairline of my 18-year-old self again.

"See, I told you. I can change things, make them better, more efficient, or just repair them. Everything has a point value though which I still need to figure out. If there are points I must have some kind of limit. WHOA, THE LIMIT JUST POPPED UP! 100 points a day, what the heck! That's barely anything, and after what I just spent on James I only have five points left! Why is this so much more expensive to work on James? What's going on Astrid?"

The woman replied to him "Yeah of course it's limited. It has to be, otherwise this would be the same as wishing for more wishes. Which if you don't remember is against the rules. I didn't make those rules up Oliver, they are hardwired into the la--. Well the you know what. We shouldn't talk about the thing in front of James here, or anyone for that matter. Also look at him, notice his beard is shorter. That's another safeguard to make sure you aren't making something from nothing. It used his beard hair to fill out the missing hair on his head. That same principle will apply to other things you upgrade. You can't make something from nothing, you need the base mass..." They trailed on talking but I had lost all interest in their conversation trying to figure out why this guy looked so familiar.

Oliver... Oliver.. I let the name ring around my head for a while. There was a kid by that name at the special school but he looked goofy as hell. Could that boy have grown up to be this man? I interrupted their conversation.

"Did she say your name was Oliver? Did you use to have really big ears?" I asked him. "Ha, yeah that was me. You finally remembered. James do you believe me, will you come with us?" Oliver asks me. I take one more look at my stinky dirty house that only reminds me of my dead son and wife, and my mind is made up.

"Seeing is believing. Making some hair grow back is one thing, but I'll need to see this space station with my own two eyes," I reply. Oliver's face lights up and it strikes me as curiously childish.

Oliver shouts, "Well let's go!"

Chapter 5

Oliver

"Welcome to Valhalla!" I shout to James. James looks around like he doesn't care that we just flew through space to land on the most advanced space habitat in the known universe.

"Take me to the armory," he says with little emotion in his voice. I would love to take him there but the truth is I don't even know if we have one.

"Bifrost?" I say. Small green LED lights begin to appear on the floor.

"Follow the LED lights please," Bifrost's semi-feminine yet still slightly mechanical voice says over the speakers that must be hidden in the walls around here somewhere. I smile over at James, but he does not seem amused. He takes off in the direction that Bifrost has illuminated for us.

Astrid snags my arm before I can follow him. "Are you sure this is who you want with us? He is clearly a warrior, but there is something broken inside of him." She had a point, this isn't the kind hearted James with the golden smile that I remembered. Something has changed with him since the last time I saw him. I look ahead and see James round a corner. I raise my voice just barely above a whisper thinking that I might know a way to get an answer as to why.

"Bifrost, make it so that only Astrid and I can hear you for a minute. Why is James sad?"

"James Gatewood, formerly known as Sgt. Gatewood, is most likely sad because his family was killed in a drunk driving incident. He had a wife and son."

"Oh wow... Thank you Bifrost." Well that would explain why he is sad. I only have my mom and pops and I can't even imagine a world without them or how terribly ruined I would be if they died.

"Oliver, it's not too late to remove him from the team. He has no way to get back up here and no one would believe him about this place anyway if we were to drop him off and forget about him. I may not be from your time, but I know for a fact that skepticism is alive and well in all time periods. If it wasn't, some government would have taken control of the lamp by now." Astrid again has a great point, she is a smart lady.

"No, we need him. He has a right to be sad and angry. He just needs a chance to help people again. You should have seen him when he was younger, he was a beacon, a real hero. Plus, did you just see what he just did? He walked onto a SPACE STATION like he owned the place and went right to work. He knows what he is doing, I know I am repeating myself, but we need him." Astrid's face was neutral so I couldn't tell what she was thinking, finally she spoke up.

"I'll follow your lead Oliver, but if he steps out of line I'll be here to stop him" she said while patting her sword. I give her a nod and squeezed her shoulder as we took off after James.

We finally find a door on the same level we came in at, which is near the center of the station. It has the word and designation "ARMORY 1" stamped on the front of it. As we approach the door it doesn't open and there is no obvious handle. I notice a small and flat button about three inches across just to the right of the door that blends in with the wall surprisingly well, so I press it. The metal door pulls backwards an inch and then slides into the wall smoothly and silently, cool. I walk inside and see row upon row of shelves and slots made of metal grating that is clearly meant to hold weapons and ordnance.

"It's empty, all empty," James says.

"Yeah, I didn't know that," I hesitantly say. Also now I'm wondering why it's empty. I bet if I asked Astrid she would tell me something about the wish only being able to go so far and to be fair this was a huge wish.

"Well, what kind of organization is this that you don't have weapons? And what branch of the government do you work for? Or is this privately funded? Also no offense here, but why entrust a numb-skull like you to do a job like this?"

I have no way to answer James' questions without lying to him or telling him about the lamp. An idea pops into my head, I'm still not used to that. I think I have a way to answer his questions without lying to him, or telling him things he doesn't need to know.

"This whole endeavor is privately funded, my benefactor is dead or captured, not sure which. All that is left is me and Astrid here. So, I'm in charge of this operation now," I say with confidence that I'm not really feeling. James puts on a cranky face and replies angrily.

"CUT THE SHIT OLIVER! What you just said may have been true but it wasn't the whole truth. You recruited me, you dragged me here. If you want my help you need to tell me the truth." Well that backfired faster than I thought it would.

James is right though, I don't want to start a friendship or a team on half-truths and lies. I've never lied before, mainly because I was too dumb to do so, so there is no point in starting bad habits now.

"Fine you want the truth. I wished this whole place into existence with a magic lamp when I was barely more than a retard. Some old man gave a mentally disabled person a weaponized wish granting lamp and my underdeveloped brain asked for this place because all I used to do was bag groceries and watch too many superhero shows. I'm stuck with this now though. So I have a choice to make and so do you. Do we waste this opportunity to help people or do we embrace it and make the world a better place?"

James looked stunned for half a second. He places his hand on his chin and seems to be thinking about what I had told him.

"What were the other two wishes?" he asks.

"I wished for the power to make the world a better place, which was how I healed your injuries and hair loss, and I freed the genie with the last wish." I say as I nod at Astrid.

"You are the genie?" James asks Astrid.

"I *was* the genie, I am free now." Faster than I thought possible James draws his weapon and points it at Astrid, *what the heck*!

"I need you to be the genie one more time. I just need one wish" James calmly says. I'm so confused as to why James would do this. Astrid cuts the tension in the room with what she says next.

"I can't bring your child or your wife back James, even if I was the genie. The lamp doesn't allow it. Look into my eyes, I speak true. You can not bring the dead back with the lamp!"

Before Astrid had even finished speaking I could see the defeat in James' eyes. He slowly lowers his gun and holsters it somehow behind his back under his shirt. I don't know what he has back there but I hear his gun securely snap into place and watch as he flips his shirt over it which completely hides it. James is staring at the ground now.

"Yes, yes, I'm very sorry about that. I haven't been myself lately and you can't blame a guy for trying. I don't need the lamp. You have nothing to fear from me." I move to approach him to give him a hug or some words of encouragement, but Astrid grabs my forearm. I look back at her and she just shakes her head left and right in the negative like I shouldn't approach him.

James looks back up at us and his face changes from glum to angry again.

"Alright well step one: We are going to need to get some weapons in this armory. I have a ton of assorted long guns, pistols, and ammunition at my house that we can bring here. That will be a great start. The next item on the list obviously is that we will need an engineer and at least one more able body for our team. I can cover a lot of the physical type stuff so preferably someone with some tech experience, maybe someone good at multi-managing computer systems. Also Oliver, stop fucking talking about the lamp, you shouldn't have even told me about it. Lastly we are probably going to need a lawyer, like a really good fucking lawyer."

"A lawyer? Why?" asks Oliver.

"Are you kidding me? We are going to be illegally operating as soldiers of fortune at best and at worst lawless vigilantes. Every law enforcement agency in the world will want to arrest us if you are serious about this. That doesn't even take into account the problems this space station is going to cause us. Everyone is going to be suing us over it for every little thing you could ever imagine, copyright infringement, taxes, arms treaties, eminent domain, and so on and so forth. Hell even the EPA will probably be trying to fine us for 'space pollution' or some nonsense. If we make any money at all the government will try to hold it or tax it into oblivion. If anyone finds out who we are, our families will be arrested for aiding and abetting. Those are just the problems I thought of standing here and I'm just a jobless veteran. Imagine the things a real lawyer could prepare us for," James finished.

"You mentioned making money?"

"Of course, imagine how much some rich folks would pay for a tour of this place and a field trip through space in one of your neat little shuttles out there. Also we will need money to pay our employees, and if this is to benefit the world you are going to have to establish this place as an N.P.O. and try to get deputized at minimum as some kind of first responder to establish legitimacy. We are going to need engineers, programmers, medics, etc. All of whom have families to feed, so we will need money to pay them for that."

I had to interrupt him. "Okay okay okay, stop please, I get it. We have a long road ahead of us. Starting with me saving enough power-points up to give us some serious skills. Let's go get the first guy you were talking about a little while ago. Someone who would be good for the immediate team and who can manage our computer systems relatively well. I have someone in mind for that."

James was in deep thought and I could see his wheels spinning. "Hey Oliver," I looked over at James and his eyes were intense.

"Thanks for picking me for this. I needed a... distraction." I could tell he was telling the truth. When we had gone to his apartment he looked like death warmed over but now he was bright and eccentric. He had a difficult task in front of him and he was ready to tackle it with no hesitation. I could learn a lot from a man like him. Astrid broke into our back and forth.

"I really only understood half of that, but I am really good at cutting stuff up with my sword. A long time ago I was something called a 'shield maiden,' and I was the finest that I knew of. Eventually there will be a situation or a problem that only I can solve, you will see."

"Astrid your skill set will be of much use to us, no one doubts that." Oh no I just realized something. My parents are probably home and wondering where I am, and they may have even spoken to the police or my store manager if they had gone looking for me.

"YIKES, we need to make a quick trip to my house!" Astrid and James both looked at me questioningly. "My parents will call the police and report me missing if I'm not home soon. I was considered an invalid just this morning. Besides I could use you two, to help me explain this situation to them, they won't believe it. We can make a supply run while we are down there as well. Get some basic supplies for this station, stuff like bottled water and pop tarts at least for now." Astrid and James agreed to accompany me and we headed for the hangar bay to shuttle back to earth.

***

As we were coming down over my house I realized I wasn't sure where to park this thing. The sun had just gone down, but not completely.

"Bifrost, are there any external lights on this ship?"

"Yes Oliver," she replied.

"Turn them all off, also can you hover this thing just above my roof and then lift it up a hundred feet or so once we go inside of my house?" I asked her.

"Yes, I can do that Oliver. I will lower the vessel again when I see you exit your home," she replied.

"Thanks Bifrost. Okay guys my parents are pretty relaxed, but this is going to be a lot to take in, so go easy on them please," I asked them. Astrid and James assured me they would play it cool.

Bifrost leveled the shuttle off about four feet above my roof. I have to admit jumping from the exit ramp to my roof was one of the coolest things I had ever done. James and Astrid made it look like it was no big deal. I sensed some angry friction between the two of them but they were two peas in a pod, I just had to get them to realize it. Once we got to the edge of my roof I wasn't sure what to do next. Astrid sensed my hesitation.

"You just jump again dummy, we just did this," she says. Then she jumped off of my roof and onto my lawn and shook off the impact nonchalantly. James followed her without saying anything. I jumped after them not wanting to look the coward and I immediately regretted it. Fear filled me for the second I was in the air and when I hit the ground one of my ankles rolled.

Astrid helped me up with a smirk and I limped it up to my front door on my now burning ankle. I unlocked my front door and turned to smile at Astrid and James. Astrid smiled back, but James looked different, like he was on alert. He backed into shadow just outside the radius of my porch light, *what the heck?* My hand was unconsciously turning my front door handle still as I was trying to see what James was up to. My front door ripped open and rough hands yanked me inside. I turned my head to see what was going on and I saw a big burly man in a business suit. He was hauling me inside my own house like I weighed nothing.

He pulled me inside my living room, and what I saw next terrified me. A second man had my parents on their knees with a gun pointed at them. Astrid was only a second behind me and I heard her draw her sword. "STOP," the man with the gun said but she completely ignored him and continued to rush him, so he gut shot her. I watched in absolute terror as her blood splattered up my drywall. She fell over in a heap and wrapped her hands around her leaking stomach.

"Man those things hurt. We didn't have weapons like that back in my day. Nice shot, but I'm going to have to kill you for that." Astrid turned her head towards us and gave us a big bloody smile before spitting some blood at the nearest goons feet. I was completely frozen and felt useless.

"What were the noises on the roof?" the goon holding me yelled into my face. I didn't say anything, I just kept struggling in his grip trying to get to Astrid, but this guy was in a whole other class than me. He was at least 6 foot 5 and 300 pounds of muscle. The goon could tell I wasn't going to say anything so he turned to his buddy.

"This is something... That lady there has a sword.... Call the boss. We will continue the interrogation at headquarters." *Wait a minute, where is James?* A strange noise came through my house, like a really loud whistle with a clack at the end. The goon holding me let go so suddenly that I almost lost my footing. I turned In time to look at the second goon and see his suit explode in three different places on his chest as I heard the strange clacking noise three more times. I turned around to where the sounds had come from and noticed three small holes in my living room window which was now so spidered that it looked like it was going to fall inward at any second.

James jumped through the holey window like it didn't even exist and checked the pulse of the first man who had been holding me. He started unscrewing a suppressor from his handgun and went to check the pulse of the second one. I went to help Astrid up, but she was already standing, still trying to put pressure on her wound. I looked to James to ask him about first aid, but the goon he was checking on suddenly snapped open his eyes and grabbed the slide on James' pistol with one of his hands. The goon used his other arm and reached over James's shoulder. He then grabbed a handful of the material of James' shirt, then snapped backwards so quickly into some kind of a Judo throw that it flipped James over. This all happened in the space of a second and I was surprised I had even been able to take it all in. I heard James yelp the words "Oh shit, bulletproof vest," as he was flipping and landing. I ran to help James. I wouldn't freeze up twice.

I didn't know a darned thing about fighting. So I did the first thing I could think of and threw a big kick at the goon as he was getting up. He easily caught my foot and threw it up in the air. Unfortunately my body followed and I landed on my back. The goon stood up straighter and rolled his shoulders, and then cracked his knuckles and neck.

"This is going to be fun," he said, as James was just getting to his feet next to me. The goon started to approach me, but a long bloody sword erupted from his stomach. He fell over and Astrid was standing behind him panting.

"I told you I was going to kill you asshole," she said. Then she promptly took a seat on my couch.

"You got a first aid kit?" James asked. "Yeah, under the sink of the bathroom down the hall," I replied. James took off to get the kit and I ran to my parents. They both jumped up and ran to me, and embraced me in a great big hug. I love my mom and dad. The smell of them overcame me and I was lost in a memory.

I don't know how old I was, but I was young. I was walking home from school, this was a new practice for me. I had worked hard to earn this responsibility, but this was also a privilege. I was too dumb to understand those terms at the time, but I *felt* them in my heart, and I was proud, and I wanted my parents to be proud of me so I would do a good job of walking home. I would check every road, look both ways, and get home quickly just like my parents had asked of me. Those ideas slipped out of my head easily but I did my best to hold onto them or recall them when the need arises.

At some point on my short walk home I noticed a group of kids following me. I didn't recognize them as kids from my special school and I just wanted to watch them, to see what they were like. So I broke my parent's rules and stopped. I sat down on the curb and waited for them to catch up. When they walked by me they all got silent and I awkwardly said hi. I just remembered thinking how cool regular kids were. One of the bigger kids with an arm around a girl turned to look at me and his face was really angry.

"DID YOU SAY SOMETHING TO MY GIRL RETARD?" I was too dumb at the time to even formulate a response. All I could do was stare at the kid who had addressed me.

"QUIT STARING AT ME DICK SUCKER!" he yelled at me again but I just couldn't stop staring for some reason.

"It's not worth it Tommy, let's go," said the pretty girl on his arm.

"No, this idiot needs to learn to mind his manners," the mean kid said.

"Hold his arms boys. I don't want this retard trying to kick me in the balls or something," he said to the two other kids with him. There was some girls in the group, but they just stared in shock. Two kids came over and held my arms to my sides and the one named Tommy shook the pretty girl off of his arm and came and hit me in the stomach. I tried to get away but his friends were holding me still. All of the air rushed out of my body when he hit me so I couldn't even ask him to stop.

He hit me again as soon as I got my first breath back and then he hit me over the head and I fell over. I was finally able to blurt out "Please STOP!", but there was something dangerous in Tommy's eyes and I could tell he had no plans to stop. Then I heard a car door slam and fast footsteps. One of the boys holding my arms went flying. A shadow fell over me. I was looking up and the sun was in my vision so all I could see was a large silhouette. It moved through the kids like they were made of toilet paper. Punching, kicking, tripping, it was a complete one-sided brawl. Finally all of the kids were on the ground and the much larger silhouette came over and helped me up.

That's when I noticed it was my dad. "Dad?" I asked confused. "Yes son, it's me, now go sit in the car." I walked to the car and got in like my father had asked. I turned back towards the boys to see what my dad was doing. He had the main bully Tommy by his collar, he was lecturing him. My father had pure fire in his eyes. I had never seen him angry before. He dropped Tommy to the asphalt and marched over to the car tersely and drove us home.

"Those boys won't mess with you anymore but I think it's best if I drive you to and from school for awhile..." My dad stayed quiet for a minute and then he pulled the car over and stared at me. He took a big deep breath, then he gripped my shoulders hard and moved my chin towards his face so we were staring eye to eye.

"I won't let anyone hurt you son."

The memory ended, and I could still feel my father's embrace in real time. A dozen other memories flashed of kindnesses from my father and mother. I couldn't help but let the tears slip from my eyes. Being smart is hard in more ways than one.

"Mom, dad, I love you guys. Thanks for always being there for me," I said, and I felt my parents squeeze me harder. By the time I turned back around to check on Astrid, I saw James was knelt down in front of her wrapping her wound.

"Mom, dad, these are my new friends James and Astrid. I have a lot to explain to you two.. First off, I'm not mentally deficient anymore."

My mom and dad looked stunned and confused, but they were also both staring at me and noticing the subtle differences. I was taller, better looking, my eyes were farther apart, my dumbo ears were gone and looked overly regular now. There was no doubting though that I was indeed their son.

"HOW?" my dad asked.

"Well that's a long story and we might not want to have it here. I bet more of these guys will come if these ones don't check in" I said. James looked over at me and my parents and nodded his head as an affirmative. As soon as James finished wrapping up Astrid's wound he knelt down in front of the two dead men and searched their pockets. He took their weapons, ammo, and wallets.

"Check this out" he said and he flipped open both wallets to show us FBI badges attached to personal identification.

"Those guys were FBI?" My dad asked.

"Most definitely not Mr..." James stopped when he realized he didn't know my families last name. My dad stepped forward and held out his hand.

"I'm Mr. Pettini, and thank you for protecting my family back there. I don't agree with violence, but I recognize that there is a time and place for it. James, do you know why these men were pretending to be FBI agents and why they were in my home, and why is my son so... healthy?" My dad asked after he finished shaking James' hand.

"They are after an item of immense power, and we need to leave now. Your son is right, if these two don't check in, then more will come. Would you and your wife kindly go collect some clothing and food, all you can carry. We will assist you in carrying it. Also bring any weapons and cash you may have. As to why your son is so... healthy, I don't think we have enough time to explain that right now, but we will when we can. Just be happy about it for now," said James.

"Can't we just call the police?" my mother asked.

"I'm afraid not Mrs. Pettini. These men have near unlimited resources if they can impersonate the FBI so casually and nab people in suburban neighborhoods like this. At least for now we have to leave. Please do what I asked. I assure you I am not making these decisions lightly and I only have your family's safety at the forefront of my mind." That seemed to assuage my mother and she went into super-mom mode checking on everyone and collecting clothes and food.

I looked over at Astrid and noticed she was really pale. "We need to get her to a hospital" I said.

"No can do, a bullet wound will have to be reported to the police and then this organization will find us. Fix her with your nifty little power there," said James. My dad's eyebrows went up in a questioning way.

"Dad will you help mom with collecting food and clothes, we really have to go soon." My dad nodded and left the room. I brought up my menu and thought about healing Astrid and the words "Bring Astrid back up to full health?" popped up on my screen. There was a point cost below it of thirty points, but I remembered that earlier I had discovered I only had five points left for the day.

As soon as I thought about my remaining points a new readout popped up in the top right hand corner of my screen. It said "Points: 5/100", my new power needed thirty to heal Astrid.

"James, I don't have to energy left for the day to heal her, what should I do?" I asked. James thought about it for a second then responded.

"Don't heal her, stabilize her. See if you can do that." *Darn, James is wicked smart*, recruiting him was paying off in dividends. I stared at my menu and thought about helping Astrid and I especially focused on the fact that I only had five points left.

A new option popped up in the center of the screen: "Stabilize Astrid, Cost: 5 Points. (Slow blood loss, slow infection rate, heal 7% of wound.)"
Wow that is perfect. I hit the accept button and used the last of my daily allotment of points. Astrid loudly gasped and held her wound.

"Thanks Oliver, that did it," she said. She was still pale but she looked a little better.

James cut into our conversation. "Collect your parents, get them outside and ready for pickup. If anything looks strange, call for me. I have to do one more thing. Oh and take this," James said as he handed me a holstered handgun that I didn't recognize or know how to use. He also handed me some extra magazines. One of the weapons he had pulled off of the pretend agents.

"James I don't know how to use one of these," I said.

"Point it at the bad guys and pull the trigger, the safety is off," said James. He also threw the other extra gun and magazines on the couch next to Astrid and then left the room.

Chapter 6

Oliver

We got everyone loaded onto the shuttle which was easier said than done. You would think my parents wouldn't be surprised at this point after having two men try to kill them and then seeing the same two men get gunned down in their living room. Then seeing their son miraculously healed from an incurable disability, but they were surprised.

Once we were flying away James' yelled: "Turn the shuttle around and aim the front window at the house, I need to see something."

Bifrost comes over the hidden internal speakers and says "James is not authorized to give commands. Oliver should I follow this command?"

I thought about it for a second, I had a lot of unanswered questions about James, but so far all he had done was save the lives of myself and my parents.

"Bifrost, follow all of James' commands as long as they don't interfere with any of mine. Also do not follow them if they would lead to the harm of myself, my friends, or my family." The ship began slowing down and then turned around, the nose pointed slightly downward until we had a birds-eye view of my quiet little neighborhood. Bifrost came over the speakers again.

"Command executed and James Gatewood has been moved up to Admin Security Level Two in our systems."

"Bifrost, do the same for my parents and Astrid as well please" I said. Then we waited and stared out the window.

"James, what are we waiting for?" I asked, but not a second later my entire house exploded, debris flew insanely high into the air, and for a quick second my quiet little neighborhood was bright as day. I heard James let out an insanely maniacal laugh behind me.

"WHAT THE HECK JAMES! WHY DID MY HOUSE BLOW UP?" I shouted.

"Sorry buddy, we left a slew of physical evidence back there, and for the record the identities of you and your parents have been thoroughly burned, pun intended. I disconnected the gas lines to your water heater and stove, and lit a small fire before we left. I've never done that before, but that was cool as hell right?"

My parents looked horrified, they were finally realizing how much trouble we were all in. I would have to explain everything to them, but for now all I could do was rub my face with my hands and try to vent stress.

"Bifrost, please take us to Valhalla, take a scenic route though. My parents need some time to unwind and relax." After that, the whole ride up I fidgeted with the gun James had handed me. I found the safety and flicked it back and forth a few times. I wanted to take the magazine out so I could inspect the gun further, but I was afraid to lose pieces or rounds while we were in Zero-G. My parents were in awe the whole ride up so I let them be and let my thoughts turn inward.

James and Astrid were amazing members of this team and so far. I had proven to be little more than dead weight. I needed to learn how to fight, and I needed to gain some practical knowledge. Knowledge was dangerous though. Before when I was *slower*, I was methodical and work oriented. I saw a goal and I completed it. Since my *upgrade*, all of these strange thoughts and memories kept invading my head. I wouldn't go back to how I was before, but there was a certain simplicity to it that I will miss. I wasn't completely helpless though, my moral compass always points north. Most people wouldn't find that amazing but I do. I pride myself in doing the right thing.

I also had over a decade of digesting superhero media that I could now remember in vivid detail. Without even realizing it I had gone over the trials and tribulations that the fictional heroes I had watched on my TV had gone through. I recognized how the leaders of the teams played to the team's strengths and didn't rush head on into dangerous situations. They planned ahead, they came prepared, they put the safety of their teams first, and above all else they always took the high road. These were lessons that I could implement. Above all else a superhero is to be a shining example to the people below. Quite literally in my case since I now call a space station home.

I got so lost in thought that I didn't even realize we had docked. I snapped out of it when I heard everyone unbuckling.

Astrid smacked me and said, "Be a gentleman you daft prick and help me to a bed or a hospital." Astrid still looked pale but James assured me that her pulse was good and as far he could tell she was in no danger of dying. I helped Astrid down the ramp and my parents and James followed.

"Bifrost, illuminate a route to somewhere nice to put Astrid!" I shouted.

"Path to sickbay illuminated Oliver," Bifrost cooly responded. The whole entourage began following the slow gently pulsing green lights on the floor, and James took up the other side of Astrid so she would have an easier time of it.

We marched her to a set of wide metal double doors which opened automatically when we got close and recessed into the walls. There was red crosses on the walls to the left and right of the doors. Inside was an empty receptionist desk, with a few chairs for waiting lining the walls. Behind that was a large open bay with ten hospital style beds on either side of the room for a total of 20. The ceiling had a small track system on it so curtains could be pulled between the beds for privacy. Overall it was really nice, and way more than I had expected. We took Astrid to the closest one and gently laid her down.

"Oliver would you like me to engage an auto-surgeon?" asked Bifrost.

"Say what?" I asked, James raises one of his eyebrows questioningly.

"This medbay is equipped with two auto surgeon bots. They are capable of performing 15,897 surgeries. They are also thus far untested, but I calculate they will have a 91% success rate in improving Astrid's situation."

Whoa, that's a good percentage. "What do you think Astrid, want a robot doctor?" I asked.

"Oliver, I'll try anything once," she says with a wink. I felt my cheeks flush. Then I felt myself stifle a laugh and I looked over and saw my mom's cheeks blushing as well, awkward.

"You heard her Bifrost, bring on the auto-surgeon." A small recessed portion of the wall near us slid back, and then open to reveal a five-foot-tall white robot. It looked a lot like a taller, and more Aryan version of R2-D2. It pulled up beside Astrid and a robotic sounding male voice said "BE CALM!" It sounded angry and it jarred me alert.

"ADMINISTERING LOCAL ANESTHETIC!" it shouted and abruptly a tiny door opened on its front and a steel rod with a syringe on the end of it shot out at lightning speed and poked Astrid's belly. Then the rod wielding the syringe sucked back into the chassis of the robot.

"Whoa, you want me to stop this thing Astrid?" I asked nervously.

"Quit being a pussy Oliver, let it work," she replied.

"REMOVING FOREIGN OBJECT!" the robot blurted out. A separate small door on its body opened and three small metal filaments jetted out of it and cut into the bandage wrapped around Astrid. The metal filaments removed the bandage and disposed of it in a small opening in the wall near us. Lastly they tenderly went into her wound. Within a second they came out with a deformed slug gripped between them.

"CAUTERIZING DANGEROUS CONTUSIONS AND CLOSING WOUND!" two different arms popped out this time, one with a pulsing red hot tip and one obviously meant for stitching. The first arm went into Astrid's wound just slightly and some small smoke came out that smelled like cooking meat. Then the second arm efficiently closed the wound with fine stitches.

"PROCEDURE COMPLETE, RELAX PATIENT!" The pissed off auto-surgeon darted back into its wall niche and disappeared from our view.

"What the hell just happened?" my dad asked.

"I'm trying to figure that out myself," I said. I'll have to add that to my list of things that need upgrading with my fancy new power. I hadn't tried anything non-biological yet but the auto-surgeon might be my first test dummy.

"Alright son, your friend is fixed up, and we are all safe. It's time to talk," my dad said sternly. I nodded and pulled over some chairs for my mom, dad, and James from the small waiting area over near Astrid's bed. I slowly retold my whole story starting with Mr. Smith running into me in the grocery store where he must have slipped me the lamp. Parts of this James and Astrid hadn't even heard yet so they paid close attention. This helped me as well come to some new conclusions hearing the events from my own mouth and reliving them in my head again.

"So, we can safely assume the men who were trying to capture this Mr. Smith are the same ones who were in our home tonight. Now that our house has exploded and their agents didn't check in, they are most likely after all of us now," my dad said.

"They aren't going to have any luck getting evidence from your house. It's all burned up and we flew out of there without leaving a trail. If they are as well funded as I think they are, they will be looking for us on the streets using traffic and security cameras. They won't find us down there," James said.

"Are we sure they aren't some form of law enforcement?" my mom asked.

I chimed in "Mom, even if they were, good guys don't hold families at gunpoint." We all agreed. We were in it, whatever *IT* was.

I realized I was starving so I asked Bifrost where we could eat. She told us there was a large cafeteria on this floor. I was hesitant to leave Astrid alone on this giant space station though.

"Bifrost, are there any radios on board so we can talk to Astrid from the cafeteria?" I asked.

"Just tell me if you would like to talk to her and I will patch you into this room using my own speakers and microphones as the medium," Bifrost responded. That would work for now, but eventually we would need some kind of internal communications system.

Me, James, my mom, and dad all marched over to the cafeteria which was also on this level. There was no food in the cafeteria but there were ovens, pantries, freezers, dishes, trays, and a full server line station. My mom being the diligent caregiver she was loaded up half of our fridge and pantry on our way out before we had taken off, so she quickly had some burgers cooking for us. We all chipped in and helped where we could to get the meal out faster. Then we sat down awkwardly and started to nibble, my father broke the silence.

"James, I forgive you for blowing up my house. I have everything that's important to me right here at this table. So, no hard feelings and thank you."

James swallowed his bite and responded "I'm just happy to be here sir, happy to help. I was going through a rough time in my life. It's nice to have a purpose, something to focus on, and take my mind off of things. Believe it or not this is actually relaxing for me compared to my normal life. You have a good son Mr. Pettini."

"Please call me Nick, and my wife is Martha."

"Yes sir, uhh Nick. Sorry, old habits die hard."

"You were in the military then?"

"For a time yes, it wasn't the best fit for me. I enjoy fighting shi... bad guys, and if you aren't born with a genetically perfect body there is actually very little of that in the military. It was mostly sexual harassment powerpoints and sitting around for me. Don't get me wrong I did my time overseas and saw some action, but those times were far and few in between. I would say the job boiled down to 1% actually putting the hurting on some bad guys, and 99% sitting around with my thumb up my butt. I just got bored, and tired of being used in a social experiment by politicians. When all I really wanted to be doing was making the world a better place. I got out and worked for a few non-profits and then some bad things happened to me. I've been in a dark place for awhile but I think things are going to get better now. I'm sorry I'm rambling, I haven't had much human interaction lately. Tell me about yourself Nick."

"Not too much to tell, I'm a family man first, an electrical engineer second. I'm not in love with my career but it helps me put food on the table for my amazing son and wife. Besides that I'm pretty boring. I like to make craft beer in my garage, not much more to my life than that, but I am happy with what I have. My wife Martha is the interesting one here, well I think so at least. Martha why don't you formally introduce yourself."

"My husband exaggerates I'm not interesting, I'm a simple school secretary," said Martha.

"BAH, she is much more than that. She is a super-woman, she basically runs that school. She also fixes up old furniture, runs every PTA meeting, block party, and every other school function. Somehow she does all that while making sure me and Oliver have food on the table and she makes it all look easy. She is wonderful and I don't know why she stays with a slouch like me" Nick finished with a loving look aimed at his wife. His wife blushed and squeezed his arm in return. I could tell my parents were still very much in love and that made me more than happy. I remembered I had something to ask them though.

"Mom, dad, why didn't you ever tell me I was adopted?" I asked hesitantly. My dad spit the coffee he was sipping back into his cup roughly, spattering his shirt and the table in front of him.

"How did you hear about that?" my mother Martha asked.

"Well I didn't. When I was intelligent enough I just looked in the mirror and realized I don't particularly look like either of you, but what really gave it away was that I had F.A.S., and I knew both of you loved me too much to do that to me," I said. My mother pursed her lips and then inhaled sharply. A small tear escaped her right eye which she dabbed away.

"You are right Oliver we do love you too much to do something like that to you. That particular curse was from your biological mother."

My parents were holding hands now. Maybe they were deciding how much they should tell me. They both looked hesitant, I hoped I wasn't making them feel bad.

"Mom…. Dad… You both need to understand that I love you no matter what, and that I am thankful for the life that you have given me. I have fond memories of both of you and I couldn't ask for better parents… Would you please tell me about my biological… parent?" I had wanted to say *biological mother* but it didn't feel right, I have a mother and it isn't the woman that gave me away and drank through her pregnancy.

My mother was openly crying now so my father took over the conversation.

"Well we didn't know much about her Oliver. We were in the market to adopt, and we got the call that a baby with... well some problems was born. We took one look at you and fell in love. We didn't see any problems, you understand? The woman that had you died during childbirth. She was very unhealthy, she led a terrible lifestyle, drugs, alcohol and such. This may sound harsh but her death probably saved you a lifetime of pain son. Oh and as far as your father, no one knows who he is, not even the woman who had you knew. She was very... promiscuous," said my father.

"I understand father, thank you for telling me. I just wondered is all."

We all finished munching and called it a night. We went and checked in on Astrid one more time, but Bifrost had told us that she had administered a sleep aid and a pain reliever, and that Astrid would sleep through the night. We had Bifrost show us to the crew cabins, there were some on this floor meant for priority crew which I guess now consisted of us. I hugged my parents goodnight and I turned around to hug James goodnight as well, but he had already disappeared, I guess into his own quarters. Bifrost led me to something she called 'Captains quarters" I walked in and immediately had my mind blown. The room was pure opulence, "HOLY SCHNIKES!" I shouted as the steel door slid shut behind me.

The room had stark white floors which felt like painted metal. The walls however were paneled with some kind of dark exotic wood grain. One wall was completely covered in screens that looked like a window. They showed a real time image of the exterior of the space station. This cabin wasn't actually along a wall so no actual window would be possible. Besides only a chump would put key personnel in an area where they could be blown out into space by a lucky hit. Along one wall was a real brick fireplace or what looked like one. There was large empty bookshelves, a kitchenette, and a big screen TV with a leather sectional couch in front of it. There was a four-poster bed resting on a large circular dais with a dark red silk canopy around it. One corner even had a small water feature protruding from the wall and pouring into a rock garden... so cool.

I jumped into the large bed and sunk into the fluffy comfort. This days woes and troubles ran through my head which was a bittersweet experience. It was nice to be able to think this quickly, but worrying about Astrid and the charred embers that were once my house was taking some of the pleasure out of it. Making the wishes on the lamp felt like a lifetime ago. It's hard to believe that was just earlier today. And tomorrow was another day, I would get another hundred points and I would have to decide how best to utilize them.

At some point I would have to try to give myself and the other members of my team usable superpowers. I have no idea what the point cost on something like that would even be. I might need some points to heal Astrid up all the way, or should I just let her heal in the hospital bed naturally? If I let her heal naturally for a while that might reduce the point cost to fully heal her, and then I could utilize the points for more immediate concerns... but wasn't Astrid an immediate concern? We needed to recruit my systems specialist still, and I would probably need to spend some points to convince that person that we were legit. This being 'smart' business is hard. I kept toying around with different ideas until I drifted off into a fitful sleep.

"Wake up Oliver, your presence is requested in the cafeteria," said Bifrost's new smooth semi-mechanical voice.

"What? What time is it?" I asked as I tried to blink the sleep from my eyes.

"It is seven a.m. in your home state of Illinois. It is eight a.m. in James' home state of Florida. Astrid has no time zone from her place of origin. I would like to remind you that we are currently in space so the time here is speculative," Bifrost replied.

"Yes, yes, I remember we are in space, thanks Bifrost. Wait, did you say that James lives in Florida?" I asked.

"Yes, when you picked him up yesterday you were in the state of Florida. Maybe the speed of the shuttles threw you off. Next time I have a shuttle move you around the globe I will have it fly upside down so the top of the cockpit window will face the earth," Bifrost replied. It took me a second to parse through what she had just said and imagine a shuttle in space, and then flipping the shuttle over so the windshield would have a view of earth as it hurtled across the globe. Before I could get too lost in my own black hole of thoughts I stopped myself and smacked my cheeks a few times. I did think it was especially humid when we picked up James. I was too busy staring at Astrid's shapely figure to notice much else at that time. Note to self: pay attention to your surroundings.

That reminds me, ASTRID! I hope she is okay! I ran out of my room and down the empty corridors of the space station until I got to the infirmary or sickbay, whatever you call it. Only to find Astrid's hospital bed from the night before empty with a fresh sheet over it.

"Bifrost where is Astrid?" I asked.

"She is currently in the cafeteria." I sprinted to the cafeteria and when I sharply turned the corner I was met with a pleasant sight. My mom, dad, Astrid, and James were all sitting down to a nice breakfast of bacon, eggs, and orange juice. They were all laughing at some joke of some sort, but they all turned towards me with big smiles on their faces when I entered.

"Come on in son, sit down," my dad shouted. The scene was surreal. My parents happy after their house exploded, sitting down with my Viking genie, and a combat veteran who had just killed some people in my living room the night before.

"Uhh, good morning guys, why are you all so happy?" I asked. My mom was the one who replied first.

"Are you kidding me! My son was miraculously healed. I'm eating breakfast on a space station with exciting new people. Those things alone are worth being happy over."

Then Astrid spoke. "I'm just glad to be free."

Then James. "It's nice to have a purpose again, a mission. Your parents are nice folks too. Astrid is kind of a bitch, but she is growing on me."

Then my father spoke last. "Like your mother, I am glad that you were healed. Every father wants his son to be happy and healthy and now you have a future for yourself that I could have never imagined. Plus that old house of ours was really losing property value. James probably made us a killing in our eventual insurance payout."

James smiled coyly and then laughed under his breath. My father kept speaking.

"In fact, just yesterday some crazy old man blew up a crackhouse a few neighborhoods over. Something about a cigarette near a gas main. Either way those property values were flying down. So no, I'm not upset. In fact I am happier than I have been in years. The most precious things in this world are in this room with me, my wife and son. Plus being on a space station is really cool."

My father's comments made me smile. I probably would have been more outwardly emotional over a comment like that, but not with Astrid and James in the room. Speaking of Astrid... "Astrid, I'm surprised to see you out of bed, are you alright?" I asked.

"Oliver, in my culture we have two states of health, dying and not dying. I am currently not dying, so I am more than alright. Yesterday was a wake up call for me though. Next time we do something dangerous I want one of those bang-sticks that James uses, or armor," she replied.

"Fair enough."

I rushed over to sit down and dig into the bacon which had my stomach rumbling. My mother and father told everyone the story of how they had met. Which was basically my father doing and saying really awkward things, but my mother ended up thinking he was charming anyway. Their quaint and overly traditional love story made everyone in the room feel a little brighter, like we were getting to share a small piece of what they experience every day in each others company. I had heard the story before, but I had never been able to comprehend it fully, not like this. I couldn't help but think a story like that probably helped remind James of the good times he had with his family, and Astrid was probably just happy to be here like she had said. My parents were good hosts.

Seeing my parents brighten the entire mood of the room gave me an idea and I waited for a natural break in their conversation to ask them something.

"Mom, dad, what do you guys think about the idea of not going back down there? I mean eventually if you wanted to you could return whenever, but what I'm asking is: What do you think about working and living here full time? Dad you're an engineer. I'm sure we could find work for you, and mom you're a jack-of-all-trades, we could use your help with a lot of things. Especially when we get more people on board, which should be sooner rather than later."

My dad replied first "Work on a space station? I'm in."

My mom looked less sure of her answer "I don't know son, I'll think about it, okay?" My new enhanced brain must have been hard at work because another sudden thought came to me.

"Dad that old man you saw on the news, the one who blew up the gas line with the cigarettes, did you catch his name?" I asked.

"Yeah, it was something Smith." I felt my gut sink and anxiety washed over me. If Mr. Smith blew up a house it was no accident. I saw the realization suddenly dawn on my friend's faces as they came to the same conclusion that I had.

Chapter 7

We knew we were in no position to look into the Old Man. Not without more people, more equipment, more 'bang-sticks' as Astrid had called them, more training, and most importantly more time for me to invest points into us. Whatever shadowy organization that was out there hunting me and my family would surely overwhelm us if we went down unprepared. That included getting anywhere near the Old Man, his home, or the place where he had supposedly died. It wouldn't surprise me to learn that the wily old coot had somehow escaped after seeing his performance at the grocery store. James had told me that wasn't possible after watching the explosion on the news feed that my father had talked about, but I had hope.

Me and James were currently in the shuttle headed down towards earth. True to her word Bifrost was keeping the ship oriented in such a way that gave me and James a clear view of earth the whole time we traveled so we could get a better bearing on where we were. Bifrost told me that this was much less efficient but the view was worth it to me. We were headed towards Missouri and since our space station was currently locked in a geosynchronous orbit over Illinois it would be a quick trip.

On our way down I had opened up my menu and selected the option to make it visible to James, he was absolutely amazed with it. I had checked into my point count and a warm feeling had flooded my body when I saw it at 100 out of 100. I had wanted to bring Astrid with us, but she was still in extreme recovery. Bifrost told us that technically she shouldn't even be walking around, but Astrid was stubborn. I didn't bring my parents either; I didn't expect trouble on this trip but still I had just secured their safety and I didn't want to reverse that now.

We were headed for the home of Anthony Stewart, the one time major gamer. I had actually met him once in my freshman year of high school. He was only barely older than me, but he was a massive success at the time. He was at my school donating the winnings from one of his gaming competitions. I don't remember the exact amount but I do remember that it was well over $100,000. Things from before my *upgrade* are a little fuzzy, but I think he had a distant relative with down syndrome that went to my school at the time and he was doing it to mostly help her. His reasons be damned it was still a nice thing to do, and I doubt many other people his age would have been willing to so selflessly give away so much money.

He had been patient and kind to my fellow students who were all mentally disabled or deficient in some way like I had been at the time. He was handing out free video games, action figures, toys, the works. The man was a giant black angel, being from an extremely isolated and small town in southern Illinois I hadn't even really seen many black people, so as weird as it sounds it was always interesting when one came around. I realize skin is just an outer layer, but I was always enamored with the idea of learning about other cultures so him being black and a gamer made him slightly more exciting. His real quality that shined in my eyes though was that he was altruistic. He could have been doing anything, instead he spent his free time and money hanging out with a bunch of dummies like me.

Even through my stupor I had remembered that man's visit to my school. He was a whirlwind of kindness, and now I was able and ready to return that favor, and more importantly offer him a job. I was also excited and nervous to relive my fond memories of him in real time. I just hoped he would accept my offer. We had Bifrost collect some information on him and I was surprised to learn that he had kind of dropped off the radar a few years prior. He had lost a few of his sponsors when the main FPS (first person shooter) he played fell out of fashion. He picked up a few new games and made it into the semi-pro leagues for them, but he had never become as popular or successful as he once was.

Bifrost told us he rarely left home now and as far as she could tell he just mined cryptocurrency and lived off of his savings. The last thing she discovered was that whenever he came into a considerable amount of cash he always donated large portions of it to a random charity, this was our guy!

"Oliver we are on immediate approach now. There are only two suitable landing sites that will help us maintain low visibility. One is closer to the home of Anthony Stewart by ten miles but it has complications," said Bifrost.

"What complications?" I asked.

"The closer location is an abandoned warehouse in a part of town with a very high crime rate. The roof is substantial on it, and this vehicle has no weaponry. We will have to fly through the roof to enter the building. There are also no exterior doors wide enough to accommodate this craft which is again why I recommend the roof. If you are going to do damage to the building it should be done from the top where there are no prying eyes," Bifrost finished.

"Let's go with the warehouse, will we damage the ship at all?" I asked.

"There will be minimal damage to the ship. Nothing that will stop it from being 100% operational" she replied. *Let's do it,* I thought with more confidence than I felt. I looked over at James and noticed he looked exceedingly nonplussed. Looks like I need to take a page out of his book, yet again. The ship started shaking and rocking back and forth erratically.

"What the hell is going on Bifrost?" I shouted.

"We are taking the route that has the lowest chance of us being spotted or photographed." The front windshield was mostly just sky with the occasional spot of ground but that disappeared quickly as Bifrost jerked the ship around. "Brace for impact" Bifrost said cooly. I wrapped my arms around the straps on my chest and closed my eyes. I didn't care if James thought I was a coward, this was terrifying. I heard metal scraping on metal, but felt little resistance. Then we smacked the ground so hard that my chin smashed into my chest and pain shot through my neck.

I unbuckled while trying to rub the pain out of my upper back and neck and looked over at James who had a big smile on his face.

"That's how the planes used to take off and land in Afghanistan, ha ha, just like good ole times." *Yeah, whatever James*. I walked to the back of the shuttle where the ramp normally lowered and noticed it was still up. I saw there was a manual release button next to it, but I thought better of it. Before I could ask Bifrost what was up she filled us in

"Environmental hazards detected. Lead based paint particles and asbestos particulate is in the air, one moment please."

We heard the engines rev up and then another weird noise, thirty seconds later the ramp opened.

"What did you do Bifrost?" I asked.

"I fired a low burst from the directional thrusters in all directions to clear the poisonous air. It is standard protocol in this situation or others like it," she replied. Dang, I was a good wisher! Or maybe Astrid was just an exceptionally good genie. I walked out into the darkened warehouse and James followed with his pistol drawn. I took his cue and drew mine as well. That morning before we had left the station James had me run some 'dry-fire drills' he had called them. It was basically where you empty your pistol of all ammunition and then you draw the weapon from the holster and fire it at a target in the distance. No ammo is in the gun so nothing happens, but it builds solid muscle memory, or that's what James tells me at least.

The practice paid off now when I noticed how smooth my draw was and how comfortable I felt. Even though secretly I was praying I wouldn't have to shoot at anyone. I'm really not okay with having to take a life and I NEVER want to. I yelled behind me into the open ramp of the ship, "Bifrost external lights!" Light filled the warehouse and illuminated all the motes of dust in the air and a bunch of shelving we had crushed. We heard a cough to the side of us under some of the knocked over shelving. James rushed over and reached down into the filth and debris. He pulled out a dirty man in a trench coat with unkempt hair. "It's just a hobo, and he is fine," James yelled back at me.

James raised his voice towards the homeless man "SIR, we are the armed security for this location and you trespassing. You need to get out!" James hastily carried him towards a door that was leaking in sunlight and pushed him out, then he waved me over. Before I left I told Bifrost to lock up the ship, and the ramp sealed itself seemingly at my direction.
I ran over to James "Uh, isn't that guy going to report a spaceship basically landing on his head?" I asked.
"Who, the drunk hobo? Do you think people are going to listen

to the drunk hobo ranting about a spaceship?" he replied.
"Fair point."

✳✳✳

"You own a space station and we are taking a city bus. Oliver, I am disappointed," James said sarcastically. Once leaving the warehouse we realized we really had no way to get to Anthony's house unless we found a car rental place or called a taxi, but a city bus pulled up next to us so we sprinted over and hopped in. "Seriously Oliver, if you are going to be team leader you need to think about these things ahead of time," James added.

"Yeah, I realize that now, but hindsight is 20/20. You have no interest in being the leader?" I asked.

"Nope, your space station, your team, I don't want the responsibility. I'm here for the excitement and because I think you are woefully ignorant and you are going to get yourself killed trying to do something good. I'm here to stop you from getting killed when that time comes, and I will stop it."

"I completely agree that I am ignorant, woefully may be a bit much. Doesn't the fact that I know I am ignorant yet willing to change count for something? In fact I'm going to need your help for that. I don't really know the best way to improve myself, but I know that I need to."

"You are going to have to read... a lot," James replied with a serious face, before turning his head and staring out the window of the bus.

"What? Read? That's it?" I asked incredulously.

"I don't know what you want Oliver, I'm no magic Guru, I'm no Yoda. I don't have all the answers, I got where I am through a hard life and rigorous training. I pushed past childhood medical afflictions that I was told would bar me from military enlistment. I did that mostly because I am a stubborn asshole and I wanted to prove the disbelievers wrong, but another part of me has always been obsessed with emulating hard cases. I learned about those hard cases in books. When I was a kid and other people wanted to be firefighters and astronauts, I wanted to be a T-800. You need to open your mind up to interesting new possibilities, you don't have enough time to master everything, but you do have enough time to learn a little bit about a lot, if that makes sense. The best way to do that is for you to read. Especially genres that are going to semi-apply to the things you want us to do now. I'll tell you what man, why don't you take your parents to my house and grab my book and gun collection. We are going to need guns and ammo, and you are going to need books to learn the basics. Knock out two birds with one stone. You are going to have to go back without me though. I'm never going back to that place, too many bad memories."

"I can do that, and I'll read what you tell me to read, but I'll need more help than that," I said.
"I'm willing to help you Oliver. I understand what you are trying to accomplish and I like it. This is our stop, get up," James said as he roughly shoved me out of the seat and into the aisle. I felt like that little back and forth with James had given me more of an insight into him then he meant to let on. James seemed... *broken* still. He didn't want friends or family but he didn't want nothing either. He was here because he didn't want to be alone. James was healing, I could help him with that and he could help me learn how to be a hero. A symbiotic relationship would suit me just fine.

I got off the bus into the late morning sunlight and that textbook Midwestern humidity hit me like a wall, gross. This is why people live in dry climates like Arizona. Maybe our ground side base, if we ever get one, should be there. We only had to walk a few blocks through some semi-affluent shop districts until we arrived at the condominiums Anthony lived at. James marched right up to Anthony's door and started banging.

"Police department, OPEN UP!" he shouted.

"Whoa whoa whoa, big guy, why don't you let me do the talking," I said and scooted in front of James.

The door cracked open a smidge, but I could see it was double chained from inside. I saw an eye and part of a dark face peek through the three-inch slot created by the partially opened door. "You don't look like police," said a voice from inside. I looked down at my clothes. I had my day old polo shirt and jeans on. I had taken off my blood spattered grocery store apron, but I still looked a mess. I needed a shower, a shave, and a toothbrush. "Yeah we aren't police, my friend here was just playing a joke on you. Listen, I'm looking for Anthony Stewart. I'm a huge fan and I am here to offer him a job. I apologize for my clothing we've had a long night."

"What's the job!?" the person behind the door half-shouted in an accusatory tone. I put on my best 'people pleaser' smile and leaned forward a bit.

"Anthony is that you back there? I really am a huge fan. Can we please have this conversation inside? The humidity out here is terrible. I really think you will like my offer." The door slammed in my face and I thought we had lost him. I heard James sigh behind me. Then I heard something being moved around behind

133

the door, then the door opened. Whoa, Anthony had changed a bit since the last time I had seen him.

"Well... he is black... and 400 pounds... are you sure this is the guy Oliver?" asked James. Anthony rolled his eyes and began to close his door in our faces again.

"WAIT!" I shouted and stuck my hand and foot in the door frame.

"Sorry, my friend needs to work on his manners. You are exactly who we are looking for." Anthony let me push the door open and I walked inside as he backed up.

He walked further into his house and yelled over his shoulder "Your racist friend can stay outside." James shook his head and walked in behind me anyway.

"I'm not racist you prick, and I'm not waiting outside." We followed Anthony into his surprisingly stark living room which was mainly taken up by an enormous computer station. I saw at least four PC towers, seven monitors, and three desks supporting it all. All of it was covered in different colored LED lights which highlighted his clearly obvious and superior hardware. Different luminescent tubes of backlit fluid moved between the different higher end models water cooling them. This was definitely our guy.

Anthony plopped his considerable bulk down into some sort of reinforced computer chair, that thing had to be special order. My googly-eyed hero worship vision finally wore off as I saw his tiny t-shirt slip above his gut and watched some of his fat spill out. I looked around the tiny living room and started noticing things that I hadn't seen before because I was so focused on his expensive computers. There was discarded Mountain Dew cans and empty Cheeto bags everywhere. Underneath one of his computer desks was a five-gallon bucket. I didn't even want to guess what he used that for.

He must have noticed me staring at the trash because he cleared his throat and said,
"AHEM, the job you offered?" Right, I really need to get some kind of a standardized statement for this next part.
"Well there is no easy way to say this so here it goes. I'm recruiting a team of heroes who are going to deal with a myriad of problems that law enforcement either won't or can't deal with themselves. We already have a headquarters. It's a space station floating above us now, we call it Valhalla. I'm prepared to prove to you that what I'm saying is true, because I thoroughly understand that you are probably thinking I am a crackpot right now. Do I have permission to improve you in some way to prove

to you that what I am saying is true. I won't lay a hand on you I promise."

Anthony stared at me dumbfounded for a minute and then he started laughing.

"I wasn't joking Anthony, and I need your permission before we continue. Keep in mind that even if I improve you that you have no obligation to take the job I am offering. I need a yes or a no right now," I said. Anthony's face went through a range of emotions and I wished I knew what he was thinking, that gave me an idea. Anthony finally put on a serious face and said "Yes." Okay that's the consent I need, I thought about my menu appearing and it popped up in front of me at a neutral blank state with my daily point balance highlighted. I thought about improving Anthony and the obvious conclusion of getting rid of some of his fat came to mind, but that wouldn't improve him that would just make him normal. What if I used the mass of his accumulated fat to build muscles?

The option popped up on my menu:

"Rearrange Anthony's (extra) fat cells into muscle mass. Point Cost: 45 (EXTREME PAIN ASSOCIATED WITH THIS PROCEDURE!)"
I looked over my shoulder at James who could now see my menu. He had read what I had read. James nodded his head and

simply said "Burn him." I looked back at Anthony and saw animal fear in his eyes after hearing James. Before he could change his mind I hit the confirm button and Anthony began to scream and seizure. Almost immediately foam began to come out of his mouth, and he slumped out of his chair and fell onto the carpet as he continued to scream and flop around like a fish out of water.

"Grab him, the neighbors are going to hear!" James said before running over to him. James restrained his arms and tried to put his hand over Anthony's mouth, but Anthony snapped at him. I tried to help him, but there wasn't much I could do as he continued to scream. I saw his skin was moving around and it looked like worms were moving just under the surface of it. Anthony gripped my upper arm and I felt his grip increase as I watched definition lines appear in his bulk. His grip increased so much that pain flared through my arm.
"Help James!" I said, and pointed at Anthony's death grip with my free hand. James wrenched Anthony off of me.

Finally Anthony stopped screaming, but then I felt both of his hands land on the front of my shirt and saw his eyes snap open. "Uh oh," I said right before Anthony jumped to his feet with me in his hands like I weighed nothing. He shoved his arms out and I went sailing... through the air back first into the drywall of his apartment. I felt the wall crunch beneath me. Anthony turned his ire on James, but James already had his weapon drawn with one hand and his cell phone in the other.

"That's not going to work on me pal." I heard the camera on James phone activate and snap a picture. Then James threw the phone over to Anthony in a big lazy arc. Anthony caught the phone and looked down at it.

"This has to be a joke," he said. He must have been looking at a picture of himself.

"It's not a joke, go look in a mirror." Anthony jetted down his hall and into his bathroom so I followed with James closely behind me. Anthony was staring in the mirror and touching his face and now overly muscular body. He looked like a gym rat who had been working out for years. Anthony reached down and ripped his shirt in half like it was made of paper. He ran his hands down his well defined chest and 8-pack abs. Then he started flexing his pecs one at a time like a dance.

He started saying "boom boom boom boom, check me out! Ha ha!" as his pecks flew up and down. I couldn't help but stop my mind from wandering to all of the Terry Crews' movies where I had seen him do the exact same thing and a small laugh escaped my lips. James picked up on it and started laughing too, then Anthony followed.

When our laughter finally subsided Anthony asked us "So, what's next?" with a huge smile on his face.

"Well, now we take the bus to my space shuttle and we shuttle up to my space station where you meet the rest of my team, and my parents. Why don't you pack some clothes, a toothbrush, and then literally bring ALL of the food in your house with you. Pack it all up, we will help you carry it." We went out to Anthony's living room and took some drinks from his fridge. James grabbed a beer and I grabbed a soda and we waited while Anthony ran around and packed.

When Anthony was finally ready he came out wearing a pair of sweatpants and a zip up hoodie.

"NONE OF MY CLOTHES FIT!!!! THESE ARE THE ONLY CLOTHES I COULD WEAR! AWESOME!!!!" he shouted. I had never seen someone so happy about having to buy new clothes before. I couldn't help but grin.

"You know, I don't even know y'alls names," he said. We introduced each other and Anthony just kept smiling and staring at us.

"What?" I asked. He leapt at me and engulfed me in a giant hug.

"Thank you, thank you, thank you, thank you. I was sitting in here slowly eating myself to death, and then you came and did this! I have a new lease on life and I have a feeling the good parts are still ahead of me!" he shouted.

"I can assure you, they are. Let's roll new best friend!!!!" I said as I held out a fist. Anthony fist bumped me.

James behind us muttered "Fuckin nerds..." after watching our interaction.

Anthony overheard him and said "How do you stand being around this guy?" as he pointed at James.

"Well he grows on you," I replied.

"Wait, wait, wait, I got so excited I forgot to ask. How the hell did you do this to me?" asked Anthony.

"I promise to explain all of that to you, but after all of that screaming you just did I'm kind of worried that the cops are on their way. Let's walk and talk."

Chapter 8

We had just got done showing Anthony around the parts of Valhalla that we were familiar with, which wasn't much. Basically, just the middle floor that the landing bays were on. The mid floor had the main command center, officer quarters, and the mini cafeteria we had been using. Basically it had all the amenities of the other floors, but just condensed down since the bulk of the floor was taken up by the landing bays and command center. Anthony was like a kid in an amusement park, he was running around from station to station asking Bifrost questions with a huge smile on his face. Every once in awhile he would look up at us and remind us that he was running and he wasn't even that tired.

Anthony wasn't much of a reader like James was, but he did tell us he had played a lifetime of space games, and watched a lifetime of space-based movies so he was still familiar with a lot of the concepts in play on Valhalla. His real specialty was computers, hardware, software, power usage, etc. He had been a professional PC gamer since he was fourteen. Which meant for the last fifteen some odd years he had to maintain all of his own equipment and maximize its potential to save himself money, maintain maximum FPS, and reduce lag. He knew a little bit about hacking, a little bit about the dark web, and a little bit about programming, he wasn't a master at any of them but he had dabbled in all of them. He could also play any game like a champion within minutes. From what he told us he could exploit any loophole or just legitimately learn the game system faster than others to attain victory. He wasn't sure why he was so much better than others but he just always had been since the first time he had touched a computer. For some odd reason though he could never get the same principals he used to win at video games to apply at other parts of his life. Give him a math book and he would go all doughy eyed, ask him to work out some crunchy stats for a character in an RPG and he could have it done in seconds.

Anthony was an amazing addition to the team. With him we had just about every specialty covered. Now we just needed to cross-train. James had real life modern weaponry and military tactics covered. Astrid had a slew of weird categories covered, including knowing many strategic battle plans on how to overcome melee based ground forces. Not sure we would ever use that, but it couldn't hurt to know. Astrid had also accidentally discovered that she knew almost every language. She was flipping through the channels while laying in her bed convalescing and she ran into a Spanish channel which she could basically understand. A lot of her languages were out of touch because she hadn't used them in hundreds of years, but she still understood the context of a conversation the bulk of the time. The lamp had been downloading and installing languages into her head for over a thousand years so she could grant the wishes of people who found her lamp in their native tongue.

Having an interpreter who could work in almost any country had to be one of the most valuable assets we had. Anthony could be our systems specialist, but I would have to figure out some way to make him more combat effective. He was good at thinking on the fly and overcoming digital opponents, but he had no actual experience in real life fighting. There had to be some way to utilize his skill in a real world environment. That's something I would have to put on the back-burner of my mind and keep thinking about. If nothing else he was a serious bruiser now, he was right around six feet tall and about 300 pounds of solid muscle. The dude was so muscular now that he had muscles on his muscles. If nothing else he could just stand behind all of us and scare people with his presence alone. Also there is a whole other part of being a hero that most people don't think about, Evacuation and Rescue. Anthony would now be hell on wheels for carrying survivors or helping to clear debris. We just had to get him trained up appropriately.

Lastly me, I was mostly a blank slate and my only real specialty was my consumed knowledge of thousands of comics, superhero cartoons, and movies. I had watched fictional people do this job my entire life. I just had to emulate them and make sure I didn't get myself or my team killed. Of course I counted my unyielding moral compass and willingness to learn as its sort of own specialty. Looking back through my memories from before my brain was upgraded had led me to a seriously sad conclusion, most people were lazy jerks, and I wasn't. I realize that isn't a nice thought but not facing reality won't help me. Of course my most prominent specialty that everyone else will focus on will be my power, granted to me by the lamp. I can upgrade people, and sometimes an upgrade can be a healing. Hey maybe that can be my superpower, team healer! I liked the sound of that. I like helping and healing people!

James broke into my thought process with a shout "Alright people, let's get down to business. First off, Oliver, am I to understand that this is the core of the team?" I hadn't really thought about that, was this all I ever wanted to recruit or would we eventually need more people. We still had no one who was comfortable with things like fixing the outside of the space station or even maintaining some of the crazier interior systems, we would eventually need more. If not for the team than at least as just employees of our headquarters here.

"This is all new to me James, but yes, me, you, Astrid, and Anthony are going to be the core of the 'hero' team. Though we will need more staff to work up here on Valhalla," I said.

"I thought you might say that, so there is something I need to say. Outside of the people on this space station right now, you can no longer tell anyone how you got your power or really any more secrets at all. You will need a cover story, a believable one. You won't need it right now, but before you bring anyone else on board. In fact you shouldn't tell anyone else your real name, my real name, or Anthony's. We have family still out there and if people found out who they were they would try to use them as leverage. We keep the inner circle small, that's not negotiable. If you don't agree with that then I walk," James finished.

"James, I completely agree with you and I think it is a good idea," I replied.

James paced back and forth a few times before speaking again "Okay, we need to start training today, there is no reason not to. Can you use some of your points to get Astrid on her feet to train with us? If you don't think that is a proper allocation then I won't try to sway you, your power is your department. I just think it would be good if we were all training together today, or NOW. No matter what you decide to do, the rest of us need to start training. I can't stress that enough." James had a made a lot of good points. I looked over at Astrid who was sitting in an all white wheelchair, and brought up my *enhancement screen* as I had come to call it, maybe I could find a better name for it later. Wait where the hell did she get a wheelchair? I'll ask her later.

So far when using my power I had only focused on one upgrade being visible on my screen at once. My screen had been limited, which I assumed was because I was dumb, but I'm not dumb anymore. I know my screen had the ability to change, because I had already forced it to change a few times and the pain disclaimer had somehow added itself before I upgraded Anthony. I just had to think bigger.

All of a sudden my screen was flooded with information. Every upgrade imaginable was scrolling by. It was going so fast that it was hard to read. I saw everything from *depth pressure resistance*, to *slingshot accuracy* whiz by me. I actually shouted "STOP" out loud it was so disorienting. All eyes in the current hallway we were standing in snapped onto me including Anthony who was busy digging through and ogling some kind of maintenance panel he had found in the wall.

James was again nonplussed, along with Astrid but Anthony said "What's wrong?" I hadn't exactly had time to give Anthony the full lowdown on what was happening to me, things had been happening so fast that we hadn't fully filled him in yet.

"It's a lot to explain, but basically how I upgrade people, like when I made you a muscle man, I use this floating menu thing-a-ma-bobber. I'll show you, wait one." I thought about the option on the bottom right hand corner of my menu that lets me decide who can and can't see the menu. Finally an empty box popped up with the words next to it: '*Make menu system visible to Anthony Stewart.*' I put a check mark in the box and Anthony staggered backwards in surprise.

"What the hell is that!?" he stammered out, and then he swished his hand through the menu a few times. It passed through harmlessly of course. "Is that made from nano-machines or hard-light technology like Cortana in Halo?" he asked.

James chimed in "I've considered both options myself and I couldn't decide which. It may even be that Oliver is psychically broadcasting the image into our minds but the entire system is ran by nano-machines. Without serious testing that we don't know how to run, we won't know."

147

"Okay so why the shout? What's wrong with it?" Anthony asked.

"Well I got an information overload just now when I thought about upgrading Astrid. As of now it seems to be entirely too simple or way too complicated. I need some kind of happy middle ground. I'll show you my issue." I again thought about upgrading Astrid in a general sense and the information overload started flowing again.

"Okay stop it, clear that nonsense," Anthony said. "I see your issue", he added.

"Was one of those upgrades *sexual prowess*?" James asked. Anthony ignored James' comment even though I think I did see that as an option and he continued on "Try adding just these categories with a plus sign next to them, the plus sign being the button you need to press to improve said category. Tell me when you are ready and I will list them off."

"I'm ready," I stated as I got ready to stay mentally focused.

"Okay, try to bring these stats up for Astrid on your screen. Strength, Dexterity, Agility, Intelligence, Endurance, and Debuffs. Now refine that even further. Give each category a one through one-hundred scale. Basically one represents a baby, and fifty represents the human average, with a maximum score of 100. Also make sure there is a listing for male or female and the average for each category is specific to each sex. Let's see what that looks like."

I followed Anthony's directions and soon enough my menu began to rearrange itself until it looked like this:

Astrid ?????? Sex: Female
Strength: 72
Dexterity: 58
Agility: 69
Intelligence: 49
Endurance: 91
Debuffs: Bullet Wound (partially healed)
Points remaining: 65/100

"Holy Schizolies! Anthony that is perfect!" I shouted.
"This is basically a standard RPG menu. Didn't you ever play video games as a kid?" Anthony asked.
"Well about that... We really need to take a minute and get you filled in on my history and our current situation, but in short, no I didn't play video games as a kid," I replied.
"Okay, well that is fine. As I said this is what the standard RPG menu looks like. For those of you not in the 'know' that stands for Role Playing Game. Basically if you were to upgrade any of

those categories it should hypothetically draw from your point stores." Well that all seems simple enough. I decided to give it a try, Astrid's intelligence was just below the modern female average so I brought it up a point with the plus sign. A cost appeared next to it *5 points*, and then at the bottom of the menu the words "Confirm changes?" appeared with the slowly blinking *Yes* and *No* below it.

I hit the yes button and Astrid slapped her hand to the side of her head. "OW FUCKER!" she shouted. She shook her head a bit then looked up at me, "The pain cleared fast, but that still hurt," she said. I wondered why there was physical pain involved with it. Was that part of the 'cost' of the upgrade or was Astrid's brain physically moving around inside of her head to increase her potential for intelligence? Honestly both scenarios kind of gave me the heebie jeebies. I glanced back at my menu and saw her intelligence now read as *50* and my points remaining were at *60/100* now.

Anthony interrupted my train of thought "How do you get more points?" he asked.

"Every night at midnight they reset back to 100," I replied.

"What happens if you have extra points at the end of the day, do they carry over?" he asked.

150

"You know, I don't rightly know. I'll test that tonight," I replied. Anthony gave me a knowing nod.

James yelled up towards the ceiling "Bifrost, direct us to a training room or a gym of some sort." The similar embedded soft green glow floor lights began to pulse and lead us somewhere new. They took us to a section of wall I had walked past a few times before and then something surprising happened, parts of the wall moved out of position and then recessed themselves by sliding behind other parts of the wall.

Behind the once-wall was an elevator with a glass door. "Whoa, I had no idea this was here!" I shouted.

"The elevators are hidden to confuse invaders and leave them with less avenues of attack. There are multiple staircases we could have taken to get to our destination but this is the fastest route," said Bifrost.

We got in and I noticed there were honest to god buttons. There were two rows side by side. The first row was labeled L1 through L10, the second row was labeled U1 through U10. Then there was a singular button just labeled "C" at the top above both of those rows.

"Please select the button for lower level 9 Oliver. This elevator is a stand alone system that I have no access to in case I am ever compromised," said Bifrost.

"So I take it the 'C' stands for center or central floor. Which means there are twenty-one floors total. For some reason I just thought this space station was much bigger than that," I said.

"It is much bigger than that Oliver. You have to consider that there are maintenance areas between every floor that house venting, wiring, cooling and heating systems, etcetera. There also has to be room in those areas for workers to access, manipulate, and/or repair said systems. And much of the station was built to be modular or detachable, that takes up additional space. The exterior armor, laser and surveillance arrays, and other generalized defensive systems take up massive amounts of space. There has to also be room for our vacuum sealing measures in case there is ever an atmospheric or other gaseous leak," Bifrost explained.

While my mind was busy spinning, trying to build a mental picture of everything Bifrost had just explained to me I remembered Astrid's fancy white wheelchair.

"Hey where did you get that?" I asked while pointing at her new wheels.

"Bifrost made it on something she called a '3D Printer'. It was interesting to watch," she replied while idly twisting some of her

152

hair. This space station has so many great surprises, *best wish
ever.*

Our elevator stopped moving and we started disembarking.
Once I was on my way out I noticed the glass of the elevator
front was several inches thick, cool. I bet that thing could stop
some serious ordinance. This level was confusing because there
was no visible twists or turns, just one VERY long hallway in front
of us.
Bifrost must have noticed we were all standing still because she
announced "Destination reached, use any door on the left side of
the hallway to enter this station's main gym. Use any door on the
right side of the hallway to enter this station's training arena."
After she finished speaking I noticed a steel door open on either
side of the hallway about every 35 feet.

I walked forward and looked into the first door on the left.
What I saw inside was an obvious state of the art gym. Most of
the machines I recognized, but some were clearly beyond me. All
of the workout machines were in the center of the room. The
exterior of the room was a large running track. The ceilings were
higher here and I could tell why. On some of the walls there
were different climbing courses. Some of the climbing courses
were standard ropes, some of them were large rope ladders like

the military used on cliff faces, and some of them were the more standard artificial rock walls with the different colored and shaped climbing nodes bolted in at random. This gym was not screwing around.

"Check this out guys!" I shouted behind me. The rest of the crew caught up and walked in a few feet to ogle.
"This other side is MUCH cooler," James said from behind us. We scooted across the hall and peeked our heads in to see what James was seeing, he was right, it was cooler. It was a large empty room with a ceiling that was even slightly taller than the gyms. Even calling it a 'room' felt wrong because it was just so large. Inside was what I could only describe as a small town.

The theme of the buildings in the town changed in clumps. In one corner of the room they looked like simple mud huts you would see in parts of the middle east. In a different corner they looked like 3-bedroom cookie cutter homes you would see in any American suburbia, fully complete with cars in their driveways. In a different corner there was simple traditional Japanese homes. One of which was even partially sitting over a pond. The portion of the home that went over the pond was supported with stilts. In the last corner of the room it looked like a miniature mock-up military base, complete with a perimeter fence and guard booth. I was so impressed I couldn't even speak.

Anthony broke the silence first "Where do we start training?" he asked. James took charge in this situation since it was clear to everyone he would have the most knowledge on this topic, no one contended his choice to dictate the training regime.

"I'll need time to work with Bifrost to learn what kind of capabilities that MOUT course in there has, then I'll invent some training for us. Why don't we have a free day in the gym today so we can all learn where we are currently at progress wise and decide what our weak points are. Bifrost can those 3d printers of yours make books?"

"They are capable of that" she responded.

"Alright print me up three copies of Starship Troopers by Robert Heinlein, and three copies of Monster Hunter International by Larry Correia," James said.

"Orders confirmed James, books will be completed in 39 minutes. I will have them delivered to your quarters," Bifrost replied.

I also decided to ask Bifrost for something "Hey Bifrost, will you send a message to my parents to get lunch started soon, we will be hungry when we are done working out."

"I will deliver the message Oliver."

"What are the books for, and what is MOUT?" Anthony asked.

"You three are going to read them, they are going to teach you a small amount about small unit tactics, but mostly they cover the morality of some of the situations we may come to face. Also reading is good for you. MOUT is a military acronym, it stands for Military Operations in Urban Terrain" James replied.

"If you think it will help, I'm on board" said Anthony with a slightly confused tone in his voice.

"Well Mr. Short Pants, are you going to leave me in this chair all day or are you going to spend some of your fancy points to help me out." Astrid asked me. I looked down and noticed I was indeed wearing pants there were now too short for me.

"About that, healing you is pricey, and I'm not against that, you are well worth the points Astrid. I have been trying to find ways to maximize my point usage though and healing you all at once may not be the way to do it. Let me experiment for a minute" I said.

I pulled up my menu and then brought up Astrid's stats like Anthony had taught me to with the new standard categories I would be using: Strength, Dexterity, Agility, Intelligence, Endurance, and Debuffs. Now how could I help Astrid heal without blowing my metaphysical load. I thought about adding a new line on the end of Astrid's stats: *Healing speed*. It came up right on the end, no problem, and it was listed like this *"Healing speed: 100%"*, okay that makes sense. I had a feeling if we wanted to be heroes we were going to be getting injured a lot more. It made sense to invest in our healing speed so I wouldn't constantly be spending all of my points just to keep us on our feet. I pressed the little plus sign next to the healing speed stat and it moved up to *101%*, the point cost appeared next, *5 points*.

WOW, 5 points for just one percent faster healing speed. I guess that made sense, it was a pretty overpowered skill to have, being able to shake off damage at a faster rate would be an invaluable skill to have more of as a hero though. I moved Astrid's healing percentage up to 108%, the point cost increased to 40. I only had 60 left for the day and I wanted to have some left over so I stopped there and hit the confirm button.
Astrid made a strange face and grunted a bit "That one felt weird," she commented. Since James, Astrid, and Anthony could all see my enhancement screen now they had noticed the move I had made.
"Good choice!" said Anthony.
"What are you going to do with the last 20 points?" asked James.
"Give me a second, I'll find out." I replied.

I figured I had upgraded Astrid, it was time to spend some points on James, Anthony, and of course yours truly. I wondered if I could bring up all three of our screens at once..hmm. I focused hard on the three of us. Nothing happened at first so I closed my eyes and really focused on the mental picture of three screens instead of just one. I felt something pop so I opened my eyes. I now had three screens in front of me. The first had my stats, the second had James', and the last had Anthony's. I tried for a fourth to see Astrid's current stats as well and it came very easily now that I knew the process of having multiple up at once. The screens looked like this, with a set of stats per screen.

Oliver Pettini Sex: Male
Strength: 51
Dexterity: 51
Agility: 50
Intelligence: 60
Endurance: 68
Healing Speed: 100%
Debuffs: None
Points Remaining: 20/100

James Gatewood Sex: Male
Strength: 62
Dexterity: 63

Agility: 49

Intelligence: 71

Endurance: 75

Healing Speed: 100%

Debuffs: Crippling Depression (recovering)

Points Remaining: 20/100

Anthony Stewart Sex: Male

Strength: 91

Dexterity: 74

Agility: 46

Intelligence: 55

Endurance:53

Healing Speed: 100%

Debuffs: None

Points Remaining: 20/100

Astrid ?????? Sex: Female

Strength: 72

Dexterity: 58

Agility: 69

Intelligence: 50

Endurance: 91

Debuffs: Bullet Wound (partially healed)

Healing speed: 108%

Points Remaining: 20/100

Well it was clear right off the bat that James and Anthony had serious agility issues. James was probably just out of practice, but Anthony had NO practice since he was a stalwart video game nerd. The second big problem I noticed is that in general my stats sucked, which made sense but it was still sad to see. I still wanted to save some points to see if they carried over to the next day or not, so I decided to upgrade the lowest stat on myself, Anthony, and James which happened to be Agility on all three of us. I put one point into each of our agility sections and confirmed my selection for a total cost of 15 points, that left me with 5 points remaining. I wouldn't spend them in the hopes that they carried over into tomorrow's points.

When I had hit upgrade everyone scrunched up their faces in obvious discomfort, sans Astrid.

"I'll never get used to that," said Anthony.

"Alright folks, enough horsing around, start working out. Astrid why don't you roll your happy ass around this track if you are feeling up to it," James said. As soon as he finished talking he took off running around the track. Me and Anthony just looked at each with confusion. I shrugged my shoulders and took off after James, Anthony followed a moment later.

Chapter 9

Mr Tokugawa

"Any progress on finding the Pettini family?" asked the Chairman, or as those of his inner circle know him: Mr. Tokugawa.

"No sir, we are still monitoring all distant relatives, friends, and their workplaces. We have the investigative teams going back through their history as well trying to find any places they might be inclined to visit. We also have facial recognition software searching for them worldwide, they will surface, they always do. We did have some good news though sir, the team from Egypt has returned and they were able to secure the item," said Tech Jansen.

"Wonderful news, and great work Tech Jansen. Have the item brought to me immediately for inspection," the Chairman replied. The tech could be seen sending several messages via his terminal and less than a minute later two men teleported into existence not far from his location. They rushed forward and presented the recovered item which was deftly resting on a velvet pillow. Mr. Tokugawa leaned forward and gripped the bronze scepter covered in intricate carvings, and topped with the likeness of a scarab. A side door opened into the underground chamber they were now residing in. Two men marched through the door with a struggling vagrant of a man being hoisted between them. The vagrant bucked back and forth trying to get free of their grip.

"LET ME GO, LET GO OF ME, WHO ARE YOU PEOPLE?!" he shouted.

The man had come from a local jail. He had an extensive criminal record and the lax criminal justice system of the region had seen fit to release him for the umpteenth time. Even though this time he had been pulled over for drunk driving after almost running down a small child. If the world wouldn't rid the earth of this menace than the Cabal would. Okubo Tokugawa, mighty chairman of the Cabal, a warrior from a long line of warriors, stepped forward and aimed the scepter at the struggling man. The two agents on either side of him were smart enough to let go and vacate the area.

"AMENHOTEP!" Mr. Tokugawa shouted. This was the word that would trigger the latent power stored in the scepter. It had taken his scholars decades to find the trigger word, and even longer to find the location of the weapon. The struggling man who had fallen to his knees only had a second to try to get to his feet before looking up and seeing the swarm of large beetles flying at him. He tried to run but the beetles were on him, biting, scratching, consuming. They ripped into his flesh and dined like a fat lady on a Rascal scooter in an all you can eat buffet.

He pulled at the beetles and crushed them between his fingers but there were too many, and he ultimately lost the will to fight on under their relentless onslaught. The pain overcame him as he felt his own life waning, he crashed down onto the hard concrete floor and lost consciousness. The locusts finished their job, and returned to the head of the staff as a group, carrying their dead with them. The head of the staff closed slowly sealing away the carnivorous Scarab beetles and Mr. Tokugawa's beaming smile could be seen by all. The command center began a reverent and slow clap.

"Congratulations to our retrieval team for securing such a fine instrument of justice. This will serve our cause well," said Okubo Tokugawa, the mighty Chairman of the Cabal.

The two agents that had originally presented the scepter rushed forward with the empty velvet pillow. The Chairman carefully placed the item back onto the center of the pillow. The agents disappeared from the space they were in, teleporting out, likely taking the weapon with them to be secured into one of the many Cabal vaults.

"Tech Jansen, put in a training order to have no less than three qualified agents trained in the use of that weapon," the Chairman ordered. The tech nodded and quickly began inputting the order with the correct authorization codes and a priority status, since everything the Chairman said had priority. From the briefings and other research they had done on the Egyptian Scarab Scepter they knew its power could only be used once every five to ten minutes at its fastest. That time would increase depending on how many scarabs had died in the action. The user of the scepter would know if it was ready for use again when it became cool to the touch.

The Chairman was happy, his organization was running like a well oiled machine and they were celebrating from yet another victory. The Cabal served a dire and important mission and without men like him, the items and *creatures* created by the genie would wander the world causing death and destruction. They didn't have the lamp, but they never had before. With the Cabal's vast amount of resources and patience they would eventually, as the tech had said, it was only a matter of time.

164

The sky was blue, the ground below her was moving fast, she could see that as she gently arced the shuttle left and right catching glimpses of the ground below. Green fields full of different crops and small villages zipped by in an instant as she brought the shuttle to just faster than 900 m.p.h. This was nowhere near its top speed, but it marked the fastest that Astrid had ever taken it. Astrid felt all of her anxiety slowly leave her body as she tilted the plane gently towards the ocean in the distance. Her only wish was that she could crack a window on this thing and smell the sea air.

Everything was going perfect so far, which wasn't the norm for her. That asshole James had been riding her ass hard for weeks. Not just her though, Oliver and Anthony as well. He had even been making Oliver's parents get back into shape and become comfortable with using firearms as well. Oliver was the leader here though and so far he had backed all of James' ideas, and she owed Oliver a debt that could not be repaid. So as long as it was what Oliver wanted she would listen to James.

The shuttle shuddered for a minute as she took it through a storm bank, nothing this sweet ride couldn't handle. The shuttles had proven themselves to be amazing vehicles, not only could they withstand the vacuum, radiation, and extreme temperatures of space, they also flew amazingly well in atmosphere as well. They weren't as maneuverable as other earth planes, but what they lacked in maneuverability they more than made up for in speed. They were more than twice as fast as a normal earth jet, and with the internal oxygen supply and inertia dampeners they became the best ride in the solar system, and maybe beyond.

"ENEMY MISSILE ALERT!" Bifrost blared over the internal speaker system. WHAT THE HELL! Why is there an enemy, this is friendly airspace. *Think Astrid THINK! What was I supposed to do for an incoming missile?* She remembered, flares first. Astrid flipped up the red safety cover, and hit the toggle that released the flares. If the missile was heat seeking it would track the flares and blow up harmlessly somewhere behind her. She leaned back in the pilot's seat happy the situation had been handled. "IMMINENT MISSILE STRIKE, BRACE!" Bifrost shouted.

WHY? She had deployed the flares but they hadn't worked. That meant the missile wasn't heat seeking! What next? Deploy chaff? Increase speed? Start Maneuvers? Astrid started banking hard while trying to remember where the toggle was that released the chaff. She was so busy searching the control board that she wasn't watching any of her other gauges, including the one that told her the altitude she was currently flying at. By the time she looked up she saw she was dangerously close to the ground. She yanked back on the control stick and started banking back upwards as she poured on the gas, but then she felt her whole vessel rock. She had been hit.

She looked over her shoulder to assess the damage and to check what was making that terrible whistling noise. She could see sunlight coming through a hole in the back of the craft and flames were licking the interior ceiling. *NO, NO, NO, this is going all wrong*, she thought. Internal systems started spraying fire retardant foam on the flames but the damage had already been done. She could feel the shuttle losing power.

"SECONDARY MISSILE LAUNCH DETECTED!" Bifrost blared once again. Astrid figured it was beyond time to get out of dodge so she laid on the gas even harder and pulled the directional stick back even further.

That's when she noticed the lights in the cockpit started blinking off and on as if the shuttle was struggling to hold onto what little power it had left. *How is this thing losing power? Isn't it supposed to be nuclear?*

"Reactor is going into safety shut down mode to avoid a meltdown. Please exit the vehicle," said Bifrost.

"SHUT UP YOU MECHANICAL BITCH!" Astrid shouted in anger as she tried to get the controls to respond. Her shuttle had been without power for too long now and without power it had begun to fall. She tried to control the descent somewhat with the back up atmospheric rudders but she was too stressed out and there was too much happening at once.

Finally she got the spin she had entered under control just in time to see the ground racing up to meet her. She had one, maybe two seconds left before the plane impacted. She accepted her fate with grim determination and a smile on her face. She watched as the ground crept ever closer.

James Gatewood

I pulled myself up to the door on the flight simulator right after it had finished resetting itself to its horizontal position. Then I unclasped the safety handle locking device and helped Astrid climb out of it. In standard Astrid fashion she came out swearing.

"Son of a bitch, damn flight thingy-mulator threw a curveball at me. How the fuck did the Nubian pull this off so quickly? Damn thing fucking cheated." I looked over my shoulder at Anthony who had a resigned look on his face.

"Does she really think I'm a Nubian?" he asked. I shrugged my shoulders as a response to him. "I'm an American though, I was born in Missouri..." Anthony whispered under his breath.

Oliver always the optimist stepped forward and slapped Astrid on her back in a friendly fashion.

"You'll get it next time Astrid, I believe in you!" he said with a big stupid smile on his face. That boy was an angel incarnate. I would follow him to his last breath, no one would harm a hair on his head with me around. Sometimes he reminded me so much of my own son that it hurt. These people didn't need to hear that though, they needed to be trained up right. The best way to do that is to light a fire under their ass with a deadline.

"Alright folks, it's about time we started planning for our first mission," I said dropping the bomb.

"WHAT! So soon? We have only been training a few weeks!" Anthony half-shouted.

"We need to shit or get off the pot, and to be honest if I don't push the boundaries of our potential here no one will. What do you all think we have been working towards here, pulling kittens from trees? We know there are shitheads out there in the world and they are hurting good people. I thought we were all on

169

board with stopping them, did something change?" I had asked a hard question on purpose. I wanted to put them in a corner. I stared them all down one by one, but I already knew their answers. I saw steel resolve in each of them. Sure they all had their own reasons why they were taking this path, but resolve was resolve. I could work with that.

We were currently in a side bay on the central floor that stored five flight training simulators. We had all passed the myriad of simulations needed to be skilled enough to fly the shuttles, except for Astrid, but it was clear she would pass any day now.

"Bifrost, is there a screen in this room somewhere, one we can all look at right now?" I asked. I had stopped my unconscious habit of looking at the ceiling when asking Bifrost for things. I felt pretty silly when she had told me that she had microphones all over and there was no reason to look up when speaking to her.

"Yes James, there is a screen in this room, bringing it down now," she replied. I still hadn't gotten used to her voice, partially mechanical and partially organic, it was a strange mixture. It served its purpose though, there would be no confusion on who you were talking to if Bifrost called.

As soon as the hidden flat-screen slid down from an alcove in the wall I began my spiel, "Alright Bifrost bring up the footage we discussed for the upcoming mission." Bifrost did as asked and a newsreel began to play. I would let it finish before speaking. A news anchor came on the TV from one of the larger news networks.

"We have just learned that over one-hundred little girls have been stolen from a school in northern Pakistan and smuggled into southern Afghanistan by a group that may be connected with ISIS. Their location is currently unknown, but our station's representative with the state department has told us that they believe the girls are meant to be sold as child brides to local warlords. We will have more on this story as we are updated."

The screen went black for less than a second and then lit back up again with a different set of footage. Armed men could be seen hustling back and forth wearing traditional middle eastern garb between different vehicles and squat buildings. All of them had some variant of AK-47's over their shoulders or in their hands. One of them could be seen going into a building and pulling out a small female, she struggled in his grip so he reared back and smacked her in the face. The screen went black again.

"That second set of footage we just watched, was live," I said and waited for questions.

"Where did you get that footage?" Anthony asked.

"Good question, from the camera on this station. Last week as soon as I saw the news footage about the girls I gave Bifrost orders to start moving Valhalla over to orbit above Afghanistan," I replied.

"You did what? Dude, you have to run stuff like that by me in the future," said Oliver.

"Noted and acknowledged, and honestly I would have but hearing about those little girls in trouble left me fired up and I rushed into the decision. In fact, I apologize for not asking you, but I would like to think I had a good reason," I said.

"It is a good reason James, and I think you made the right call," Oliver said with a sincerity that filled me warmth. I wouldn't let him see the warmth, but never the less Oliver's earnest attitude was very refreshing. Oliver had an ability to make everyone in the room happier, even when talking about kidnapped children.

"Isn't this a lot for our first mission?" Anthony asked.

"Hell yeah it is, tell them the bad news Bifrost," I said.

"I think the 'bad news' James is referring to are some simulations James had me run. The simulations could be inaccurate but according to the data I had on hand I calculate that the U.S. only

172

has a 39% chance of sending rescue forces after the girls due to the current political climate," Bifrost finished.

"I'm not going to sugar coat it, some of the girls have probably already been murdered, some of the girls have most definitely been raped. Every day we wait will be a living hell for them which is why I suggest we leave in seven days. We can train every day of those seven days with specific mission appropriate style exercises. We know what the compound they are in looks like and Bifrost has a tactical suite installed that can extrapolate the most likely interior of each building of the compound the girls are currently being held in. Which if you haven't put two plus two together yet means we can train to raid the exact building they are in right now, right here, on this station. We just have to sometime during the week secure bulletproof vests that will be resilient against heavy calibers, and night vision devices. I don't know how the 3D printers on this ship work, but maybe we can make some of what we need here. If not I can go down and buy them, but I am running out of money. So on that note we need to start making money soon as well," James finished.

"One major problem with this scenario," said Oliver.
"What's that?" James asked.
"I'm not a judge, jury, or executioner. I'm trying to be a hero

here, I don't want to kill people. I'm in favor of saving those girls, of course I am, but I don't want to murder people in the process. I'll defend myself and innocents with lethal force, but only if I have to. I think we should look into some non-lethal options for this mission."

Oliver's righteousness was really throwing a monkey wrench in my plan, that's fine though. My goal was never to turn Oliver into some kind of remorseless killing machine. In fact I'm glad he wants to stick to his principles.
I plastered a fake smile on my face and responded "Completely understandable, why don't we look for some less than lethal options for the team that we can bring on this mission," I said. Oliver's normally cheery face brightened up even more. I may live on a planet full of shitheads, but Oliver isn't one of them. I noticed Astrid trying to maintain a neutral face, but I could tell Oliver's plea for a less than lethal option did not impress her either, good.

Oliver Pettini

We only had three days left, and I was nervous as all heck about the mission. Anthony had assured me though that he had some seriously good news for me. I was rushing down to his location on floor L1, which I had learned was where a bank of 3D printers were located. Apparently there were other 3D printers on different floors, but this was where the largest ones were housed. Anthony had been digging through our available schematics on hand and downloading more for us. We had tasked him to try to get oriented with as many onboard systems as he could in between our mandatory training and reading sessions, but of course he had basically sprinted to the 3D printers as soon as he could.

He had told us he actually had his own 3d printer at his condo where we had picked him up, but it was MUCH smaller than the ones we had on the station, so he was excited to see what ours could do. I whipped the final corner at top speed, not because I had to or because I was in any kind of a rush, but because I was trying to organically raise my agility and dexterity skills without investing points into them. I had gotten into the habit of running everywhere for this very reason, and I had been encouraging the others to do the same. Bifrost was getting scary good at anticipating my arrivals and she had the door to the 3D printing lab open as I sprinted through the threshold.

"Sweet Christmas! What the heck is this stuff?" I asked as I stared at the odd assortment of items in front of me. The first was what looked like a life sized Minecraft Avatar in full color. It looked like some kind of coal powered robot, but of course made with the generic Minecraft squares instead of the normal contours of a human. The second was an all white replica of the Millennium Falcon, it stood about four feet tall and had one side cut away so you could see the interior which was extremely detailed. The last thing was an enormous shield with a curve to it. It had to be at least five feet across and five feet tall. It had some very small wheels on the bottom of it with some serious tread on them, and large handles inside.

"Oh, yeah, well I kind of got really super excited about having a 3D printer this big, and I needed to test its capabilities anyway. So, I made my Minecraft avatar, then I painted it, but that's beside the point. It came out flawless so I needed a finer test, hence the Millennium Falcon model. Then I was looking for things that would increase our combat capabilities, defensive and offensive so I came up with this shield. It is amazingly heavy and only someone who could move easily with hundreds of pounds can manipulate it reliably." Anthony took a second to perform a few series of flexes that even left me stunned. He currently had on an old pair of jeans that were clearly from when he was overweight since he had a belt cinching them right around his waist. His t-shirt was the opposite of the jeans, it looked like it was from before he was overweight. It was black with lime green letters on it that said "I PAUSED MY GAME TO BE HERE" but the shirt was barely containing his new muscles. As he flexed I think I even heard the shirt rip a little bit.

After his impressive flexes he continued "At any rate with my new found strength, thanks to you I'm strong enough to wield this bad boy. The wheels at the bottom are only there so I can keep it close enough to the ground to stop bullets from smacking into our shins. What do you think?" he asked.

"Well I think we need to take you shopping for clothes that fit you first of all, but I also think this is awesome. Wait did you say this thing is bullet-proof? And is this why you wanted me in here?" I inquired.

"Oh right!" Anthony shouted, before spinning around and grabbing up two medium sized cardboard boxes and shoving them onto a table near me. "The shield is bullet-resistant not bullet-proof, though it will need to be tested. The 3D printers are actually loaded with kevlar so it was easy enough to throw a bunch of layers of kevlar in between polymer pours. I'll show you what I mean later. These are what I brought you in here for!" he shouted again with a wicked looking smile on his face while pointing down into the boxes.

I looked down into the first box not sure what to expect and saw what looked like a 12 gauge shotgun round. Which I was only able to recognize because James had been making us all get some serious range time in with the firearms and ammo we had secured from his house. These rounds were different though, they had some sharp looking prongs sticking off the front of them, but that isn't what I noticed first. They were fully translucent and borderline transparent, enough for me to make out detailed circuitry inside of each one. I picked one up and rolled it around in my hand examining it.
"I truly have no idea what these are, some kind of shotgun ammunition?" I asked Anthony.

"You are correct sir. They fit in any 12 gauge shotgun. Each round is a fully self contained taser that is accurate up to 200 feet. It will knock anyone down and keep them down for slightly upward of 20 seconds with A LOT of negative lasting short-term effects. These are used by police departments around the world, but they are so expensive per round that they aren't too widely used. Don't confuse that with 'not been used' these babies have taken dangerous criminals into custody with little to no bloodshed and no loss of life. I figured this was exactly what you were looking for. Also I know James has a Remington 870 you can feed these through. I think I can print up a shotgun silencer, as well that will take these no problem. I just need to get it done. I've been working non-stop on this stuff. You see a normal silencer wont work for this kind of round because the shot would get stuck in the baffles on the way out, but I found a pretty serious schematic for a specialized suppressor just for shotguns that has rods that ride down the interior of the baffles to make sure shotgun rounds are sent out happily on their merry way."

I had to stop Anthony because his rambling kept getting more technical "Yes, yes, I get it. Very cool shotgun rounds that won't kill people and I can fire them very quietly. I really appreciate this Anthony. This will make a world of difference for me on this mission. Well, really we could outfit the whole team with these!"

"That's not all, I have a schematic for a heavily modified cattle prod as well that will work for us," Anthony said with an ever widening smile.

"You are a mad genius you know that right?" I asked him with an equally huge smile.

Chapter 10

It was days like this that I couldn't be sure if I was in some kind of a dream or if this was my real life still. I felt terrible, but alive like never before. My whole body was sore from the constant training regiment that James had been throwing us through, but I had been *gaming the system* so to speak on that front. For myself and the others on my team I had been raising our healing speed a little bit every day. The faster we healed meant the more we could train, the faster we healed also meant the more gains we got from training. The faster we recovered from training meant the more our stats increased organically without me having to invest points into them. The whole system was having a serious snowball effect and I was loving it. It probably would have felt like cheating if we weren't putting in so much work.

Anthony had stayed up late last night to finish the stun batons he had promised me, and they were brilliant. They are a giant rounded affair of exactly three feet in length. They had a clear defined and large handguard though I don't know why. I guess it couldn't hurt though. Above the handguard the entire length of the shaft was lined in slightly sharp and durable spikes. The spikes circled the entire thing so you could strike with any side of it or at any angle. The tip had the two large standardized prongs, the same you see on a cattle prod, so it could also be used in a stabbing motion as well.

The main difference between this and a cattle prod was that a prod is meant to induce a short dose of pain to get the cattle moving. This thing was tuned similar to a police taser, in the way that it disrupts the natural current of your body and renders you either unconscious or inert for a while. The spikes lining it were just barely sharp enough to pierce clothing If you swung it with some force, but not long enough in length to cause any serious damage or blood loss, they also conducted electricity. Sure they would make small bloody holes in the flesh that would take a few weeks to heal, but don't kidnap people and you won't have to get poked.

Astrid was putting on a show for us by testing one of the batons in the *Gravity Lab* as we had dubbed it. A smallish room we had found on floor L10 (the very bottom). It was simply an empty reinforced steel room with a dial on the wall. The dial had the numbers -5 through +5 on it, the further into the negatives you spun the dial meant the more the artificial gravity would dampen in the room. So a full -5 would be no gravity, and a full

+5 would double your weight, and of course the 0 on the dial was set to earth's gravity. We had it set on a +1 at the moment just to maximize this training session, but even at +1 everything now weighed 20% more. Astrid was moving as fluidly as if she weighed nothing, swinging the baton through the air in a series of complicated movements with some random jumps and spins thrown in to get extra height and downward momentum on her following swings.

It was chaotic and beautiful, and I couldn't really tell if this set of movements was predetermined or something she had just made up on the spot.

She stopped mid-swing and shouted "If only I had a worthy opponent! You string beans wouldn't put up much of a fight in this arena, not even the large Nubian."

"Stop calling me that..." Anthony said almost quietly with a hint of disappointment.

"Well I might have someone who is up to the challenge. Bifrost send in a training-bot," said James.

"A what?" I asked.

"Oh don't worry, you'll see. I found a neat little feature of the space station last night while exploring," James replied. Not a minute later a roughly humanoid shaped robot wheeled through the door on wheels that were so low to the ground under the soles of its feet that I couldn't even see them. Once it arrived fully into the room it sank lower to the floor which I'm guessing meant the wheels had recessed into its foot completely.

It shook its arms and legs out and did some very human like stretches and then said "Mechanical analysis and warm-up complete, ready for instruction," in a very synthesized voice.

"Randomized fighting style, defense only. The only combatant in the room is Astrid," James responded. He looked over at Astrid and gave her a knowing nod. Without a second's hesitation Astrid rushed the vaguely humanoid robot. Well almost humanoid, it was human shaped, about six feet tall, and tan in color, but it had no defining features, no clothes, no hair, and it was clearly just painted metal. Astrid's first swing was wide which gave the robot more than enough time to sidestep it. The robot began to back up but Astrid quickly advanced on it and this time she tried an overhead strike. The Robot slunk down and nimbly rolled backwards. Astrid's baton tip missed him by centimeters. Astrid knew some of its patterns now though, she was confident, I could see it in her face.

She rushed the bot once more. As soon as she started moving the bot started backing up diagonally so it wouldn't inadvertently run into a wall and give Astrid an easy victory. This time as soon as she was in range she swept her baton low to strike at the bots shins but the bot jumped into the air. Astrid continued her swing in a complete circle and carried the momentum of the baton all the way around. As the bots feet hit the floor she connected with it, right where a temple would be on a human. The robot's head snapped to the side and its body went limp and hit the floor. For some weird reason I felt bad for the robot.

Astrid turned around and shouted "HA, THE VICTOR!" with her baton held high. Behind her the robot jumped to its feet.

I was alarmed "ASTRID, WATCH OUT!" I shouted. Astrid spun around in an attack stance.

"STAND DOWN!" James shouted. Astrid didn't come out of her stance or move an inch. James walked over to the robot and smacked it across the face.

"It's a blank slate guys, it's waiting for orders. It's no threat to us. It just stood back up because the fight was over. It's programmed to emulate humans. So it fell over when Astrid hit it in the head, just like a human would. These things are tougher than they look but they aren't dangerous. Watch!" James spun around and kicked the robot in its chest. It staggered back a few steps, regained its footing, and then stood dormant and still once more.

"I swear it's going to take a decade to uncover all the secrets of this station," I said out loud to the room. The others nodded in agreeance or mumbled acknowledgments.

"Can that thing hold objects?" Anthony asked.

"I don't know, haven't tried it. I beat the hell out of one last night in a hand to hand match. It was super therapeutic. Want me to have it try to hold something?" James asked. Anthony dug in a box at his foot and produced an exact replica of the stun baton but with no spikes on it, and then he threw it roughly in the direction of the bot. It bounced off of the bot's head and rolled around on the floor. He then reached into the box again and produced two circular white shields that were clearly made from the unique polymer of the onboard 3D printers. He tossed one at Astrid and one at the bot. Which again smacked the bot and then rolled to a stop on the floor at the bot's feet.

Astrid picked up the shield and ran her arm through the braces on the back. She swung the shield around a bit and smacked it with her baton.

"This feels strong and light," she said as she swung the shield back and forth a few more times while bashing invisible opponents.

"Oh it is, it has over 20 layers of thin kevlar running through it and it's made from a polymer that is heat resistant up to 1500 degrees. Don't thank me, thank the 3D printers on board. The schematic was sitting in the computer I just added the kevlar into the schematic and pressed print. Honestly it was my pleasure, and the least I could do to fulfill my role on this team," Anthony replied.

"Either way, I won't forget this kindness. Now someone tell that robot to pick up that damn shield and baton and come at me!" Astrid yelled. She readied herself into a balanced stance with her baton resting over the upper right hand corner of her shield and pointing towards the bot.

"Training-Bot! Pick up the instruments in front of you and engage in a melee bout with Astrid. Keep your blows just under the strength of bone breaking. If possible match Astrid's strength." The bout that ensued was... epic to say the least. Astrid moved like a true warrior, always seeming to know where to move next. The opponent's blows rained onto each others shields like thunder. They staggered each other with shield slams that made NFL players look lazy.

While they were fighting James yelled over at us "We aren't leaving this room until all of us have fought that robot. We will turn its skills way down but this is a training opportunity we can not afford to lose." I looked over at Anthony and could tell he was feeling the same way as me, nervous but ready for anything.

I was about to fight a robot on a space station... *WOOHOO I LOVE MY LIFE!!*

✳✳✳

It was the day before our mission. We were ordered absolutely no exercise or training this day by James. While I was technically the leader of our group James knew what he was talking about so I differed to him on matters of training and mission prep, and I happily accepted and backed his rest order.

We were all on the recreation floor which resided on U1, or upper level one. We hadn't explored it fully but a twenty-minute walk around had revealed three small themed restaurants, with generic but theme specific decoration inside. One was clearly designed to look Asian with mixed themes from Korea, China, and Japan inside. One was designed to look European with themes from Italy, Germany, and Russia. That one was a really interesting mix of opulent marble and homey brick. The last one was obviously American, almost a 50's diner but slightly modernized. A big glass case at the front meant to display desserts, a checkered floor, and big red leather booths. Too bad there was no waiters or food here, it would have been a neat experience to eat at one of these places.

There was also a few private movie theaters. Some small rooms with large televisions, assorted gaming systems, and different sized bean bag chairs and couches. There was a side area that looked like a day spa that had massage tables, saunas, hot tubs, and other tables and rooms that I didn't recognize. There was scattered pool tables, and foosball tables. We found a five lane bowling alley, a half size basketball court, what looked like miniature bars, all kinds of neat stuff.

The coup de grâce was at the center of the floor. A circular concrete feeling path went around an asymmetrical area of grass with a real pond in the middle of it. Around the pond sat scattered apple trees. I reached up and plucked an apple off of one of the trees and bit into it, it was delicious! The area was downright wonderful. The quaint path around the pond had occasional old fashioned looking lights lining it. There was comfortable cushioned benches, and even a shed with fishing poles in it. Which I guess meant the pond might have some edible fish in it or it was meant to be stocked.

Anthony found a little sign by the lake that said "Please enjoy a swim." Apparently Anthony loved swimming because he jumped right in fully clothed and started ditching his clothes while he swam, throwing them up on the shoreline which has been delicately lined with some kind of solid surface that looked like sand from a distance. Once you got closer through you realized it was actually a solid almost spongy surface just designed to look like sand. I can understand that though, there are probably lots of reasons why you don't want loose sand moving around a space station that housed precision aircraft and nuclear reactors.

An idea struck me and I grabbed James' elbow while Astrid stayed behind to throw apples at Anthony. James had been angry that I had roped him into a night of fun, he had wanted to go back to his room and be alone, but I am the leader of this team and I vetoed that. The inner sadness that had once permeated James the night I found him was still there, but I could see him slowly moving past it the more he spent time with us. So it was my goal to show him and the others a good night. I led James to one of the small rooms with assorted seating choices and the large t.v.'s and I asked him to help me move them near the pond. We dragged over several loveseats and a large sectional to a flat piece of grass about ten feet away from the water's edge. Lastly we moved the big screen TV over and the stand that housed it.

At this point the others got the gist of what I was proposing, a movie night at the water's edge! So they meandered over to join me.

"Bifrost, will you alert my parents that we are having a movie night and that they are welcome to join us," I asked.

"Your parents have put a 'Do Not Disturb' sign outside of their door Oliver. Should I interrupt them?" Bifrost asked.

"No, leave them be. Thanks Bifrost." That didn't surprise me at all. My parents had been like teenagers in love since we had started living on the space station. They hadn't taken a timely vacation in years. How could they with a mentally disabled son and my mom's many obligations at the school she worked at. Now with the stress of my condition lifted and being at an exciting new locale it was like they had let go of decades of stress and relaxed like never before.

We all tried to share meals together, where generally my mother would smother me with hugs and kisses and my father would tell me over and over again how proud he was of me. It dawned on me many times throughout those encounters that many men would have been embarrassed to be shown this level of affection from their parents in front of their friends, but it didn't bother me. Especially when I looked over at James and Astrid who didn't have a family left and saw the genuine smiles on their face every time my parents showered me in this affection. I knew I was lucky to have them, and I wouldn't squander it over something as stupid as fleeting pride. My parents were an amazing and important part of my life and they always would be.

Me and James finished dragging over extension cords, and a data cable so Bifrost could pipe in our movie of choice. "Bifrost play us a comedy movie. Something relatively new with good ratings. Also have a training robot bring us out some popcorn and drinks," I shouted happily. I could have whispered it and Bifrost would have heard me but looking around at Anthony, Astrid, and James all leaned back in their assorted chairs or couches, being surrounded by my friends, and knowing my parents were happy had left me so excited and happy myself that some of it had slipped into my voice.
Anthony looked over at me quizzically "Is that even possible? Can the training droids work as butlers?"

"No idea, we are about to find out," I replied with a coy smile on my face. The truth was I knew they could. I had ran this particular experiment earlier in the day. Our movie began to play and we watched a young actor in an amazing set of makeup and prosthetics who looked just like an old man pretend to get his genitals stuck in a soda machine. In truth even his genitals were fake but the onlookers who were attempting to help him didn't know that. We laughed so hard that Anthony actually fell out of his chair.

"Bifrost what is this movie called? It's great," James asked.

"This is the 2013 comedy classic simply titled 'Bad Grandpa', starring Johnny Knoxville," Bifrost replied coolly. In between bouts of laughter multiple combat training droids started appearing with cold drinks and popcorn. Astrid calmly took her drink and popcorn, stood up, and then set them down on her couch. Then calmly spun around and high kicked her combat droid butler so hard in the face that it stumbled backward, lost its footing on the incline that headed towards the water, and fell into the pond. It was so funny and random that I laughed so hard I fell out of my chair as well.

"What the hell Astrid?" James asked trying hard not to laugh himself.

"I don't know, it was fun," Astrid replied with a crooked smirk on her face. She plopped back down in her chair and continued watching the film. Behind her I could see a now soggy droid leaving the pond and heading back to wherever the droids stayed.

I looked around at the people I was proud to call my friends while they were distracted by the movie. I stared at each of their faces and contemplated on all of the amazing things they were capable of and the companionship they had shown me. Then I focused on our location, the picturesque safe haven at the side of a beautiful pond surrounded in apple trees on a space station. I thought about my parents in their room fully in love, and proud of their son. We were going to do something insanely dangerous the next day, in fact we could all die in the attempt, but none of that mattered to me. In that perfect moment I knew what it was like to truly live and be happy. A small tear escaped one of my eyes and I quickly wiped it away before any of my friends saw it. You know that pond does look really inviting *maybe it's my turn to jump in,* I thought before ditching my chair and taking off my shirt in a mad dash for the water.

After my short swim which everyone had joined me in, we all sat back on the couches and rewound the movie back to where we had left it. We were all quietly munching on our snacks and occasionally laughing at the film, but while everyone else was relaxing I actually had my screens up and had them set so only I could see them. I had four separate semi-transparent screens up. One representing my current stats based on the system Anthony had recommended, and one additional screen for each member of my team, in a half circle fashion around myself. I had set the background to a lovely shade of light blue and the text to a deep white that was less transparent than the background and the borders of the screens. This was the information currently being displayed on my enhancement screens:

Oliver Pettini Sex: Male

Strength: 70

Dexterity: 70

Agility: 78

Intelligence: 61

Endurance: 70

Healing Speed: 172%

Debuffs: None

James Gatewood Sex: Male

Strength: 67

Dexterity: 69

Agility: 78

Intelligence: 71

Endurance: 77

Healing Speed: 172%

Debuffs: None

Anthony Stewart Sex: Male

Strength: 94

Dexterity: 78

Agility: 78

Intelligence: 56

Endurance: 56

Healing Speed: 172%

Debuffs: None

Astrid ?????? Sex: Female

Strength: 77

Dexterity: 64

Agility: 78

Intelligence: 51

Endurance: 92

Healing speed: 172%

Debuffs: None

I felt bad because I had mainly been dumping the lion's worth of points into myself, but I had to just to get on an even keel with my amazing team. That doesn't mean I had been neglecting them though. I had spent the majority of exactly four weeks worth of points on them and myself. I admit my experiment of not spending points to see if they carried over to the next day had paid off in dividends, because it had been a great success! I found out my points did indeed carry over to the next day and I had been putting the practice of 'banking' my points to good use. I now had 895 points extra which included my daily allotment. I wanted a large amount of extra points at all times in case anyone was injured on the team, I would have ample points to heal them or at least get them back on their feet.

I wasn't even sure how much of a healing they would need. I had been dumping massive amounts of my points into our 'healing speed' ability every day. No matter how much we could lift, or how accurate our shots were, if any of us got shot the only thing that might save us from immediate death would be our bodies ability to heal and take care of itself. I had also massively invested in agility, putting strength and dexterity on the back burner of my priority list. I figured being able to run towards our enemies quickly or away from danger quickly would also be an amazing skill. We had all raised our own skills organically a few points here and there, but four weeks of training wouldn't yield too many gains for even the best athletes in the world.

We hadn't been slacking though, not in the least. We had all fired thousands upon thousands of training rounds through our 12 gauge shotguns. The training rounds we were using were the same weight and load as the taser rounds we would be firing on the mission. The only difference between the training rounds and taser rounds was that they cost pennies to make instead of hundreds of dollars. We had shot at stationary targets, moving targets courtesy of the Valhalla's training robots, close range targets, pop-up targets courtesy of the Valhalla stations amazing reactive shooting range, and long range targets. All of us were so proficient with the taser rounds that at this point we could probably hit a moving target at 100 feet 99% of the time. No, on the training front we were not slacking, we had been training like our lives depended on it, because they very well might.

My question to myself though now as I looked at my enhancement screen was if I should tap into my point stores and do some last second upgrades, or should I keep the points in case any of my team or the girls we were going to rescue needed healing. The more I ran through the different scenarios we might run into, the more my mind always came back to the healing speed stat. We had our shotguns, we had our training, we had an amazing team, yet none of that could stop someone from bleeding out before I could get to them like the healing speed skill could. I did need to keep my point reservoir somewhat large though for emergencies. I remembered the point cost on the hypothetical full heal of Astrid's single bullet wound had been over 50 points and that was just one medical problem for just one person's problem.

I moved the healing speed on each of the members of my team up to 175%, including myself. The system was still charging me 5 points per percentage added, so the point total cost for this team upgrade would be 60 points, pricey. Still very very worth it to me though if it helped my team stay alive. I hit the confirm button and waited for the pain to wash over me. It wasn't too bad this time. I was getting a little desensitized to pain after feeling it so many times through every upgrade. When I finally finished squeezing my eyes shut to combat the pain, and opened them up, my team was all staring at me and they had the movie paused.

"Oh yeah, I guess I should have warned you guys about that, huh?" I said squeamishly.

"What did you do Oliver?" James asked in a deadpan voice.

"I increased our healing speed to 175% each, look," I said as I made my menus visible and spun them around to face my team.

"Okay we get it, it was a good choice, thank you. Put the menus away..." James said deviously. I did as he asked but I noticed James' wicked grin hadn't left his face. "For not warning us before implementing the changes, I sentence you to a

POPCORNING!" he had shouted at the end of his sentence. "Who else agrees with the sentencing, say AYE!" Before I had a chance to ask what a 'popcorning' was, the rest of my team shouted "AYE!" and began to throw their remaining popcorn and kernels at me. I yanked a couch cushion off the nearest seat and used it as an impromptu shield and began to return fire with my own remaining popcorn.

Chapter 11

James marched back and forth in front of us checking if all of our gear was present. He was making sure we didn't forget anything, and ensuring our weapons and equipment were in working order. I was trying to memorize his every movement and action. I felt like I should be the one doing James' job right now, ensuring my team was in order, but being a good leader means admitting your weaknesses and delegating them to the most experienced person. We were currently standing in our hangar bay in front of four empty shuttles all with their ramps down. Lined up in a neat row to make James' job easier.

"Oliver, how many rounds are loaded in your weapon?" he asked sharply.

"Five in the tube, and one in the chamber." He nodded and moved on.

The new uniforms that Anthony had printed for us felt absolutely terrible. They were scratchy and garish but they would keep us safe. Well that was the idea at least. 3D printers don't exactly print clothes but they can print pieces so small that they can be linked together and made into clothes. Or they can print ultra durable and shapely pieces that can be sewn or melded onto clothes. We had a combination of both of those concepts on now. The 3D printers still had a pretty sizable amount of kevlar sheeting available, but that was a dwindling stock we would have to replenish eventually, for the moment though we had more than enough to coat almost every piece of our uniforms in some amount of kevlar.

The whole uniform was almost completely stab proof, and mostly ricochet and fragmentation proof. For obvious reasons the entire suit wasn't bulletproof because the weight of something like that would be horrendous even for us in the great shape we were in now. Parts of the suit were bulletproof though. We had made more miniature shapely and thick polymer pieces, similar to Anthony's shield but much smaller. We used those pieces to cover key pieces of our uniforms. These smaller, thicker pieces were covered in so many layers of kevlar that they were basically guaranteed to stop anything up to and including 7.62x39 which is what our enemies would be shooting today. We had the thicker pieces over our knees and elbows for obvious reasons. Also over our pectoral area in the shape of our natural chest muscles, those ones were there to protect our heart but it looked weird to just have that style of armor on one side of our chest so we just evened it out for weight and the aesthetic appeal.

At Anthony's insistence he had added more armor in the shape of abdominal muscles as well below the pectoral shaped armor to finish off the effect of a muscular torso. Plus more bulletproof armor couldn't hurt. Slim pauldron shaped pieces went over the shoulders, and very slim pieces ran along the forearms and shins, those were bullet proofed as well. Lastly a small plate sat in the center of each of our backs. James had flown down to earth and bought us boots in our size so we were each equipped with a nice set of those. Lastly James insisted that we all had some sort of helmet. Anthony had scoured the database to try to find the perfect head protection and had very happily settled on a modernized version of the Spartan helmet meant to be used as a motorcycle helmet. It didn't take Anthony long to adjust the schematic to have layers of kevlar woven through the entire design.

The helmets looked... angry. They were sharply angular giving the illusion of a sleek predator, and the plume of blood red bristles that ran across the top of it like a giant imposing mohawk didn't soften the predatory appearance. In fact I would have vetoed the idea completely since the whole point of being a hero is helping people, not scaring them. Except tonight we weren't rescuing cats from trees, we were going to be rescuing child sex slaves from their captors, and even I had to admit I didn't mind scaring someone as evil as that.

James was almost done checking on all of us, the last thing he had us all do was power up our stun batons to show that they had a good charge, and show him the chambers of our sidearms to ensure they were also loaded. I had fought James on the sidearm idea but ultimately his logic won me over. I really didn't want to carry lethal ammunition, but James had insisted repeatedly that everyone have something as a last resort. If our shotguns failed or were lost somehow we had to have a secondary ranged option to protect ourselves with, and pistols with standard ammunition were the most reliable option. We had gone with Glock 17's for their ease of use, cheap magazines, and lack of external safety. James, ever the combat sage had ensured us that the last thing you wanted to have to worry about in the heat of the moment was toggling some tiny mechanism before you could defend yourself. None of that mattered to me though, I didn't plan on using the Glock at all. I didn't want our first mission to be a bloodbath. My idea was for us to get in, incapacitate the captors, and save the girls, everything else was minutiae that I didn't want to worry about.

The last equipment problem that we had run across was that the bulk of the material in the 3D printers was white. Which while being a very appropriate color for a hero, it was still a very inappropriate color for a night mission. We had gone over this problem for a long time but ultimately running short on time we had just decided to go with old school trustworthy spray paint. It only took minutes to coat everything in a liberal layer of dark brown Krylon. Black seemed a more obvious choice but I didn't like the symbology that went with it. Besides this was a desert mission so dark brown would camouflage us better anyway.

James finished his inspection and stood before us looking like a giant wraith in his armor and gear, with his helmet under one arm. He may not have had Anthony's barrel chest and girth but he was the tallest among us, and he had taken it upon himself to strap different sized combat knives all over his entire body. Plus this wasn't the first time he had done something like this, and confidence absolutely oozed off of him. Part of me felt like a little boy in a Halloween costume next to him, but I dismissed that idea. I had trained for this, I was ready. Besides no one else was going to help those girls, even if I was just a pretender, I had to help them. I had the ability, the resources, and the means. All of the reading James had been forcing us to do had been making a real impact on the way I looked at life in general, but one quote in particular by a man named Edmund Burke had really stuck with me. I couldn't remember the exact phrasing but the gist of it bounced around my head daily: When good men do nothing, evil triumphs. If nothing else, I was a good man, and I wasn't willing to let evil triumph.

Before everyone could separate and head to their individual shuttles I motioned them all forward and before they could protest I roped them all into a giant group hug. Even James relented and joined in.

Before we could separate Anthony spoke up "This seems sad to say but you guys are the best friends I have ever had." I looked up into Anthony's earnest eyes and I could tell he meant it.

"That isn't sad, I consider you all my best friends as well," I said.

"I am glad to be here," James said quietly. We all looked over at Astrid thinking she would say something and then she did...

"Quit acting like sentimental children. You are men, stand up straight and let us destroy evil," she said before slapping her stun baton to her shield multiple times loudly, and then storming off and entering her own shuttle. She had just barely passed her final shuttle simulation test the night before, and she was the only one who had elected to take a shield down with them.

Astrid's armor also had to be made a little differently than ours, especially in the chest area...

We would each be taking a shuttle down. We would need the extra cargo space to be able to move all of the girls once we freed them, if we freed them. No, *when* we freed them. The rest of us headed to our shuttles determined and ready for whatever this night would throw at us. We would all be flying our own shuttle by manual control for this mission, and without Bifrost having to direct computing power to the series of A.N.I. that usually ran the shuttles she would be able to focus solely on monitoring our area of operation with her satellite camera. Simultaneously she would be feeding any other satellites in the area pre-recorded footage. The last thing we needed was the world's governments sharing video of us descending from spaceships.

I had already done the startup sequence for the ship, and the ship safety inspection before James' gear and personnel check. So my ship was running and hot. I waited patiently as the large hangar door in front of me opened and again marveled at the purple plasma wall fighting out the vacuum of space. The wishes I had made that fated day with Astrid had been short sighted and childish, but dang if they didn't pan out awesomely. I slowly drove my shuttle out through the energy barrier and into the beauty of space. I slowed it down to marvel at a sight that I would never quite get use to.

"Oliver, don't forget your team is already on the way, and this mission has a slim time window. I can only enact electronic warfare on this scale for so long before our chance of discovery becomes outside of expected thresholds."

"Thanks for the reminder Bifrost," I said before gunning the ship forward and down towards earth. I couldn't see the other shuttles with my naked eye at first, they were black on the black of space and we were on the dark side of the planet, but I was picking them up easily on our radar and lidar suite. It didn't hurt either that these ships were coded to recognize one another with friend or foe tags.

"Bifrost, what's the local time down there?" I asked.

"It is currently 3:52 a.m. Oliver," she replied.

"Thanks Bifrost." *Good, most of the bad dudes are going to be asleep, just as we had planned.*

We dipped into the atmosphere and then immediately slowed down. Another thing we really didn't need to do was to break the sound barrier and wake everyone up for miles. We came down a mile outside of the camp where the girls were being held in Afghanistan, near the border of Pakistan. We crept the shuttles forward, mere feet above the ground for a bit until we settled them behind a large hill near the camp that was only hundreds of feet away. We had killed all external lighting of any kind and we had the shuttles in their stealth modes hoping against all hopes to not alert a soul. We needed the element of surprise, not just for us, but for what men like this might do to these girls if they thought a rescue attempt was under way, or that their lives were forfeit.

As soon as I settled my shuttle into the soft dirt of this region that James had so pleasantly named 'moon dust.' I quickly unbuckled, grabbed my gear, and smashed the large button that lowered and extended the back ramp. I was down the ramp before it had even touched the ground and jumped off the last few feet to land in the dirt. My gear felt weightless on me, a sure sign that some of our physical training had been paying off. James and Astrid were already out, James with his shotgun at the low ready quietly staring off in all directions with a night-vision monocle on over his helmet. I popped my helmet on and secured the chin strap. The helmets had a transparent visor that went over the eyes just like a motorcycle helmet, I slid that up so I could talk to my team without using the throat microphones we would all be utilizing.

Astrid still had her shotgun slung over her back on a sling instead of having it ready like me and James. Instead she had her baton and shield out. I looked at her questioningly but she ignored my pointed stare, or maybe she just didn't care what I thought. Anthony was coming down his ramp now with his massive shield. He lugged it over to our location with ease.

"Wait one, I'm going to recon over the top of the hill," said James. James slunk off into the night like a ghost and shimmied up the sandy hill silently. We all waited tensely for him to return. Within a few seconds of seeing him crest the top, he spun back around and lightly jogged down the hill, until he got back to our group.

"Looks like one roaming guard, and one guard at a campfire. The layout is the same that we have been studying, it's two large one-story buildings at the west and east sides of the camp. Anthony will stay in the middle of the two buildings and provide over-watch and cover. Astrid and Oliver, you will take the eastern building, and I will clear the western building. Neutralize, subdue, or kill all captors inside and then escort the girls to the shuttles, those are our mission parameters. Don't let anyone make a sound, or the mission is blown and we evac with or without the girls, our lives are the most valuable resource we have, we can't help anyone if we are dead. I'll take the roaming guard, you three take the guard by the campfire, move out."

James flipped down his visor and night vision monocle once more. Then he flipped the toggle on his throat mic, lastly he pointed at ours, motioning that we should all do the same. We all toggled our mics on and heard James' voice crackle over the radio in a bare whisper "Mic check, show thumbs up if you have me on audio, and then throw your own mic check." We all took turns saying "mic check" as James pointed to us. As soon as he was done he gave us all a thumbs up and disappeared into the night.

I turned to offer Anthony help with lugging his shield up the small hill but he took off without a thought and carried it like it weighed nothing. I knew that shield weighed over a hundred pounds, glad he is on my side. Me and Astrid were after him until we got to the crest where we knelt down. There was still about 150 feet to the guard standing near the campfire warming his hands, the shotguns were accurate out to 200 but none of us felt like taking the chance.

"Anthony can you stay here for a moment and me and Astrid will move forward. Take aim on the guard and if he notices us try to take a shot. If he doesn't notice us I'll sneak as close as I can before shooting," I said, Anthony nodded. Without another word Anthony laid his shield down, and then laid down on top of it. I noticed his weight caused the front of the shield to tip up a bit since the whole thing had a curve to it. Anthony adjusted his body further until he was in an ideal prone firing position and then rested his shotgun over the upward flare of the shield so the shield would carry all the weight of his gun. I could tell he could probably lay like that all day. Anthony is a mad genius.

Me and Astrid took off down the hill. The guard was facing slightly away from us and he was mostly looking into the fire which would ruin his night-vision, but even knowing that we still moved as quietly as possible at a crouch. Once we were about fifty feet out I took a knee and then aimed down the sights of my shotgun like James had taught me. I centered the front bead on the middle of the man's torso and waited for the natural pause between my breaths and slowly stroked the trigger. The gun coughed lightly, we were using shotgun suppressors and the rounds we were firing were already unnaturally quiet. Still I prayed no one else had heard the shot as I watched the round take the man in the middle of the chest. He fell back into the powdery sand and started flopping like a fish. Astrid took off like a bolt and was on him in a second with a mighty golf style swing of her baton which connected with his cheek.

I rushed over and knelt next to the man and checked for his pulse, it was strong but he was clearly unconscious. I checked his new facial wounds courtesy of Astrid, it looked like he had a broken nose and was missing some teeth.

"Astrid, what were you thinking? You could have killed him!" I whispered hoarsely.

"Meh, did you expect me to be kind to child rapists?" she replied.

"Of course not, but we aren't murderers, we are heroes." I flipped my visor up so she could see my eyes to know I was serious.

"Yes Oliver, I will be more careful next time, but remember I studied for a lifetime with melee weapons. Where I am from it was not unheard of for girls and boys as young as 15 to go into battle. I know what I am doing, do not underestimate my prowess," she said. Then she reached up to my visor and slammed it shut. I was angry, but I wasn't quite sure why. She had made great points all around and she hadn't killed anyone. Maybe it was time for me to take my kid gloves off here too, these were obviously bad guys.

I took a second that I shouldn't have and thought inwardly about all the super-heroes I had been accidentally studying over the years. Thinking back on it, I'm sure Superman and Batman probably broke many bones on criminals. She was right and I was wrong... "Sorry Astrid," I said, she turned around and nodded before heading off to the building we were supposed to enter. Anthony jogged up and stood next to the fire. He placed his shield in front of him and put his shotgun in a ledge he had cut into the top of the shield, it would serve as an easy place to fire from one handed.

Some light static came over the radio "My guard is handled, entering the back of the western building. Anthony pay special attention to the front door of the western building in case any try to run. Verify your targets, do not shoot me or any of the girls," said James.

"Copy that, our guard is down as well. We are entering our building now," Oliver replied. Nothing more was said. We had gone over this plan hundreds of times. We had even ran simulations on this using the mock up buildings on the training floor.

I tried to keep the idea in my head as we approached the door, that these were bad guys and they deserved to be hurt, and also that I was only hurting them so we could rescue the girls. I would live by my standard, the hero standard. We crept next to the door frame and unlike most tactical teams who would have kicked it in, and yelled, and maybe even would have thrown a flashbang, we tried a different approach. I reached out and turned the handle, the door was old and mounted poorly into a house covered in a mud/clay siding, maybe it was even made of mud, I don't know. The door opened inwardly on quieter hinges than I was expecting and we went in after it. These were large compounds meant to house multi-generational families so we would have a lot of rooms to go through.

Ideally we wanted to avoid the girls until dead last, for one because we didn't know how they would react to us, and two they would most likely be guarded by more alert individuals. We figured they would be in the back of the house so we started going room to room, beginning in the front of the house and working our way slowly back. The first doorway we went through didn't even have a door in it, we could see broken hinges where one had once hung though. There were two lumps of sleeping bodies underneath obviously rough hewn blankets. The prongs on the front of the taser slugs we were firing would probably go through the extra cloth, but just to be safe I quietly pulled out my stun baton from the rung on my belt and let my sling hold my shotgun.

Me and Astrid crept next to the sleeping bodies and mouthed the words "One…. Two…. Three." On three we pulled back the blankets and hit the dirty looking men in ragtag robes with the batons. Their faces went from perfectly asleep to contorted in pain and shock. The one Astrid was stunning started letting out a loud gurgle so she let off the stun and started punching him in the face until he stopped making noises. It was pretty quiet overall but we were still worried about the noise he had made. Per our plan we flipped both men over and put them in zip-tie handcuffs of which we had dozens of stored on the backs of our belts. Once they were handcuffed we also connected one ankle from each man with a handcuff so if they tried to rise they would end up falling over each other. Two more bad guys out of the game.

We repeated the process room by room, slowly creeping around the compound. Me with my suppressed shotgun at the ready and Astrid with her shield out and baton over her head. Though the rooms were different in design and sleeping arrangements they were basically all the same in the aspect that they all held sleeping Islamic radicals. It was easy to tell who the commanders and those of higher status were because they slept in some form of a true elevated bed while the foot soldiers slept on the floor in homemade sleeping bags or piles of blankets.

Some rooms only held sole occupants, in that instance we would zip-tie cuff them to a table or chair. Even if it didn't hold them they wouldn't be moving fast while dragging furniture around behind them.

There were firearms and other types of ordinance in every room, such as grenades and shoulder fired rockets, but we had no way to disable or move them without making too much noise. When we got to the final door at the back of the compound the one that Bifrost assured us had a 94.3% chance of being a large open area where the women were being held I decided to call James on the radio and check on him, he was alone after all, at least I had Astrid.

"James, this is Oliver, we have cleared our building except for the last room which we are about to enter. How are you doing?" He didn't immediately answer and that scared me, but finally his out of breath voice came over the line.

"I'm doing fine, just a few more rooms here myself before my side is cleared. Keep up the good work. I'll see you outside."

Knowing that James was fine had pulled a huge weight off of my chest. I was energized and ready to finish the mission.

"Let's do this," I whispered over to Astrid. She nodded her head and got a better grip on her shield and baton. I would lead the way since I had the ranged weapon. She did too of course, but for some reason she was intent on wielding the baton. I couldn't complain though we were doing great so far. For all I knew this could be the correct loadout for a team of our size. I slowly turned the handle on the door and began to creep inside. As the door swung open I could barely make out a large room with flickering light coming from behind the door I was pushing open.

I soon began to see massive amounts of sleeping girls and teens in different states of cover, sleeping all over the floor. I rounded the door frame 'slicing the pie' as James had taught me with my shotgun in the perfect sweet spot on my shoulder and my eyes aimed down the rudimentary sights and checked the area of the room that was hidden from my sight behind the inward opening door. What I saw was two terrorists dressed in the traditional middle eastern garb that you see on Islamic fighters in newsreels. The standard tan brown robe like things with tactical vests over them. Their eyes were full of hatred and upon seeing me they lit up with surprise and anger. They both lunged for their rifles which were laying haphazardly across the wooden table that they were sitting at. My finger had been on the trigger the second I had entered the room, I was ready for this. I fired one round, and then racked the shotgun and fired a second faster than I thought possible, my training clearly paying off once again.

My first shot hit the man to my left a little high and landed right in the side of his neck, my second round I had fired at the man on the right side of the table, it went wide and landed in the kidnapper's hand. He was fighting to pull it out while being shocked and as I went to rack the slide on my shotgun I could tell I wouldn't be fast enough to beat Astrid who was rushing the seated men, baton held high. She smacked the one trying to dislodge his taser slug right on the top of the shoulder. The downward force was so much that the shoddy wooden chair he was sitting in shattered below him. Before he had even hit the ground Astrid spun in a beautiful arc and slammed the second one who was still involuntarily shaking in his upper arm surely breaking it, but also adding more voltage to his already taxed system. Both men fell over like lumps, and we quickly zip tied them.

When we were finished we turned around to address the assorted captured girls and saw some of them cowering in fear trying to get as far away from us as possible. Others were still trying to wake up their friends to get them away from the clearly new and dangerous individuals in the striking and horrifying uniforms who had just so easily taken down the men who had been tormenting them. It only took me a second to come to the realization of how much we were scaring them so I quickly snapped the latch on my helmet to show them my smiling face.

I looked over at Astrid, and she had her baton and shield raised high in some kind of a fighting stance facing the women. In her dark uniform and evil looking spartan helmet with its large red plume on top she did pose a severely strong, stoic, and mostly scary figure herself. I elbowed her hard and mimicked the motion of taking off her helmet and then pointed at the scared girls to reinforce the message. She understood my meaning and ran her baton through the rung at her belt before also removing her helmet which her beautiful blonde ponytail fell out of. The captured hostages in front of us were shocked to see a woman warrior. They came from a culture where women were valued as little more than property on the best of days so to see a powerful woman standing side by side, head uncovered, as an equal with a warrior man, this was a true delight and surprise for some. While others who were too indoctrinated quietly whispered words like 'blasphemy.'

I pulled a small stand alone speaker from my belt and hit the button on the top to play the pre-recorded message. It was

Bifrost's voice and being spoken in a few different dialects and languages that were commonly spoken in Pakistan.

The message was roughly akin to something like "We are here to help you. We will not hurt you. Follow us if you wish to be free. Follow our directions the best you can." The speaker wasn't overly loud and it had a clip on the back so I clipped it to my belt and continued to let it play while trying to look as non-threatening as possible. The girls got the idea, some of their faces lit up with relief and happiness. Some of them were too jaded to believe something good could happen to them at this point, and some of them just wanted to get away from the infidels (us). Either way, coming with us was the better scenario for most of them.

I kept scanning the room and noticed a small break near the side of one wall. I got closer and shined a flashlight at it and what I saw was a very thin hallway with a set of dirt and stone steps leading downwards.

"Astrid we got one room over here that wasn't in our plans. I'm going to check it real quick and make sure there is no one else. Please stay with the girls. They will probably enjoy the presence of a woman more than a man right now," I said, and threw her the speaker. She nodded and clipped the speaker to her belt where I had had it on mine. I descended the overly thin step.

Wary of the dirt walls around me hoping they wouldn't collapse. This was obviously not part of the original floor plan.

Chapter 12

At the bottom of the stairs was a crude but thick wooden door that had obviously been handmade and poorly installed into the rock and dirt of the walls of the earthy passageway. I crept up to it slowly, the fit on the door was so tight I couldn't get any indication of what might be on the other side of it, and then I heard a muted but clear woman's scream. I slammed my shoulder into the door and raised my shotgun as I bull-rushed through. There was a man on top of a half dressed woman covered in bruises and tears. I'm not sure what happened next, because all I knew was I was hitting the man for what he had done, and I had no plans of stopping. The revulsion of what he had done, what he was doing, had impacted me so profoundly that even I knew I was in shock. I also knew something else though, I was going to make this man pay. I was going to make him feel just as helpless as he had made that woman feel.

His blood sprayed my face, but even then I didn't stop, he would know fear. I'm not sure how long I had been hitting him for, but I felt strong hands grab me from behind. I reared my head back to deliver a backwards headbutt but the person sidestepped it and drove a strong palm into my chest while shoving one of their legs into the back of my knees. I fell on my back and groped for my slung shotgun, but stopped once I saw Astrid's face lean over me.

"Calm down Oliver, it's just me, we need to go." The levity of the situation sunk in and I tried to rush back to the man to check on him, but again Astrid's firm grip grabbed my shoulder and yanked me back.

"I'll check him, you get upstairs and make sure the girls are okay." One look over at the bloody mess I had made was all I needed to see to know that I wanted to leave this room. The woman he had been... *hurting,* she was staring at me in fear, but when she saw me turn my back to leave she ran after me and jumped on me in a giant embrace. Her tear stained face rubbed against mine and she blabbered in between her tears in her local language. She was thanking me.

Astrid clipped the speaker broadcasting the message onto my belt and slapped me on the back. I pried the woman off of me and headed up the stairs, but she stuck close by me with one of her hands gripping the upper arm of my off hand. I took one last look behind me to see Astrid kneeling over the man I had beaten, she had her ear to his chest and her fingers on his neck. Time to check on the women.

Astrid

I watched Oliver head up the stairs with the wild looking woman clinging to him like he was Odin himself descended from the heavens. In case he turned around to check on me I pretended to assess the man who was clearly now dead by Oliver's hand. While I was pretending to check the pulse like James had shown us, Oliver did indeed turn around one last time. Which made me extra glad that I had put on the charade. I had waited above for five minutes, very patiently I might add, for Oliver to return. So when I went to check on him I was surprised to see the normally calm and simple man beating someone to death. Well surprised might be an understatement. As soon as I saw the woman in the room, it was clear to me that the man Oliver was beating on was a rapist. And I'm not ashamed to admit my first instinct had been to help Oliver beat the man even further into the underworld. Until I noticed the state of the rapist's face which looked like a bowl of discolored spaghetti. Then all I had worried about was Oliver's well being. He had all but sworn to never kill someone, and our first mission out he had ended up savagely beating someone to death. Hell of a first day.

Nothing a few well placed lies couldn't fix. I calmly stood up and spit on the rapist's corpse and headed up the stairs. The rape victim Oliver had saved had further ripped pieces of her clothing and was using them to clean the blood from Oliver's face but he was staring in my direction with a nervous look on his face, game time...

"Oh get that stupid look off of your face you big idiot, he was fine. He had a concussion and a bloody nose. I turned him on his side so he wouldn't choke on his own vomit. He will wake up tomorrow with a massive headache and a fear of attractive white men," I said with a wink in Oliver's direction. He was using his big head too much so I would make him use his little head for awhile.

"Oh thank god. I thought I might have... really hurt him..." Oliver replied.

"You did, you kicked a bad guys ass. You did your job, but you didn't kill him. Mission accomplished, good job Oliver. Now let's move."

I could see Oliver stand a little taller and I knew he had believed me. Why he had believed me was the real question. Had I sold the lie that well or was he believing me because the truth was too much for even him to handle. It doesn't really matter, if you lie to yourself enough even you will start to believe it. Oliver would have the clean conscience, I would carry this burden for him and a thousand others. I would do anything for the man who had freed me.

James' voice came over the radio "I've got my girls heading towards the ships, Anthony is maintaining position to cover y'all" he said. James... Now that was a real man. I was starting to think this century was only filled with cowards and sissies, but James had set the standard when he had taken the two men out at Oliver's parent's house. At least Oliver had an excuse, he was catching up after spending a lifetime as an invalid. The Anthony fellow, while he was nice, had spent his life playing children's games on a picture box. GAH! What a colossal waste of time. He had even let himself become obese because he had lost a few strategy games. What weakness, being depressed over the happenings on a screen, how pathetic. That didn't matter though now. Oliver trusted him so I would by proxy. I will whip his now muscular butt into manhood or I would die trying.

To be completely honest, Anthony had proven to be an invaluable member of the team but that didn't make him a man in his mind. Sure he had the body of a 300-pound berserker, but that didn't mean much if the mind behind it only wanted to use it to play children's games. Between James' obvious depression,

Anthony's defeatism, and Oliver's obstructive morals, I had my work cut out for me. I would keep these men in line and teach them how to be true warriors in heart, body, and mind. James was the closest, but until he accepted his loss and moved on he would never be at 100% battle efficiency.

Lost in thought, I snapped out of it when I heard Oliver over the radio as he jogged ahead.

"Astrid you cover the rear of the formation, I'll monitor the front." I noticed that even as Oliver jogged ahead and slid his helmet back on, the rape victim followed him.

"I can do that, just make sure that lost puppy you have with you doesn't get in your way if you have to shoot someone."

James (just before spotting his sentry)

The trick to taking out a sentry is, *there is no trick*. Sentry duty is boring as hell and even the most stalwart and disciplined soldiers eventually fall into a familiar pattern. These soldiers weren't stalwart or disciplined though, these were religious zealots barely better than cavemen. Probably inbred and definitely not intelligent. This wasn't the first time I had fought the radical Muslims of the Middle East, this wasn't even my first time fighting them in this province. These ass clowns thought they were men because they ganged up and preyed on the innocent. And the only reason they were able to get away with it was because they claimed they were doing 'God's work,' and a surprisingly large amount of the locals magically agreed with them. This was something I could never understand.

Who in their right mind would help or even remotely agree with a group that would lessen freedom? Well that was what I thought when I was a less knowledgeable and younger man. It was naive to think something like this couldn't happen in the U.S., because there had always been groups trying to give away freedom in order to gain temporary security. Hell, there were some groups of people willing to give away or even take away freedom for just the illusion of security. Turn on any news station right now and watch it for a few minutes, and eventually some jackhole will come on talking about why Americans should give up more of their rights. They will use every guilt trip in the book to try to make you feel bad about keeping more of your own personal freedoms.

Guilt trip me all you want. I will never feel bad because some bowl-cut having idiot hundreds or even thousands of miles away did something bad. Law abiding citizens sacrificing personal freedoms in an attempt to stop criminals is akin to cattle walking into the slaughterhouse to seek refuge from a storm. Look at any of the first moves of Hitler, Stalin, Mao, etc. For an evil regime to take control they first ask the populace to give up certain freedoms for 'the good of the people,' and the sheep always jump on board. No, there was no question in this department, the only thing stopping something like this from happening in America was men like me. Men with nothing left to lose that knew the root of evil of wasn't actually being evil, it was putting your head down and letting the politicians pass another law that would slowly erode the freedom of the average citizen.

They won't take anything outright, no, the sheep would notice that. They will however chip away at freedom with one piece of legislation at a time. Parts of me wondered if that is what had happened here, obviously it was slightly different since the madness driving the Middle East further into chaos and mayhem was driven by religion instead of politics, but a lot of the same principals could be applied. Ever seen pictures of Iraq in the 70's? Let's just say it wasn't the same shithole that it is today. Now the bulk of the people here in this part of the world, places like Iraq, Afghanistan, Pakistan, Dagestan, etc. They are mostly evil, sure there were a few good ones here and there but those were the exception not the rule. Part of me wondered if it would be more prudent to just drop bombs on this place and start over.

The pussy footing of the modern world wouldn't help these people. Winning over their hearts and minds wouldn't help these people. Showing them a better way of life wouldn't help these people. The only thing that could help these people was if someone killed a large enough chunk of the bad guys here, the murderers, the rapists, the Sharia police, whatever you want to label them as. All of the shit heads in this region needed to die in such large numbers that the remaining good people left could finish the job and take back control. These were the thoughts that were spinning through my head as I quietly waited behind a boulder for the roaming sentry to pass my position. As soon as he was passed I leapt to my feet as quietly as I could and came up behind him. I slowly slid one of my large knives into his neck just behind his ear while slapping my heavily gloved hand over his mouth to suppress any noise he might make. Oliver could not-kill all he wanted, but I wasn't going to leave these monsters behind to hurt more people.

I almost wanted to feel bad as I lowered the slowly dying body of the sentry down into the sand, but all I had to do was focus on the reason why I was here, over one hundred little girls were dragged here by these men to be raped, murdered, sold off into slavery, or some combination of the three. I didn't know how or when this sentry was supposed to check in so I put myself in rush mode and headed toward the building that I was supposed to search. When I was about twenty feet out from the back entrance I turned on the broadcasting function of my throat mic and called Oliver.

"My guard is handled. Entering the back of the western building. Anthony pay special attention to the front door of the western building in case any try to run. Verify your targets, do not shoot me or any of the girls," I said.

I waited a second for Oliver to respond and he did "Copy that, our guard is down as well. We are entering our building now." Good, I knew Astrid could handle any situation that Oliver couldn't so I wasn't worried about those two. Anthony was an unknown but with his giant shield he would do fine on overwatch duty. I entered the back entrance of my building which was little more than a thick piece of fabric hanging in an empty threshold. This was close-quarters work, I let my shotgun fall to my side on my sling and drew two strong folding knives and flipped them both open. I had one in each hand. I was no knife expert but it didn't take much to poke someone, especially people who didn't know you were coming, plus I was armored to all hell. I had to give it to Anthony he did a great job on this gear.

If the hypothetical floor plans that Bifrost had given us were correct then the large room to my left would hold the kidnapped girls. So I didn't want to go there first. The first thing I wanted to do was step on some roaches. So I headed into the first portal on my right. There were two men in here. One was extremely old and he was sleeping on a soft looking bed pushed against one of the walls. The other one was writing something at a desk. That surprised me, most of these cock-knockers couldn't read or write. In fact that's one of the main reasons they were so easy to radicalize. You could tell them that God wanted them to do all kinds of evil shit and they would have no way to verify if it was true or not. Which meant this one was probably a leader of some type. Maybe even one of the recruiters, or maybe he was even someone who might recruit a young and naive farm boy, put an AK in his hands, and tell him that God wants him to kill westerners.

Knowing the truth of the world and the truth of this broken and evil death cult filled me with a righteous fury. This one didn't deserve to go out quietly in the night. He deserved to know terror and pain. I flipped my blades in my hands so the sharp edges were facing upwards and ran up to the man writing at the desk. I jammed them both into his lower back, sliding and forcing them in all of the way up to the grips on the folding knives, right around kidney level, and then lifted with all of my might. I grunted pretty loud but my helmet would hide the noise. It was a race now as I lifted the man into the air, what would give out first, my strength or the meat of his back? He started to scream so I shook him hard using the only contact points I had, the handles of the folding knives I had wedged inside of him, which were slowly sliding upwards opening him up further. As I shook him his raspy scream rattled off and he lost what little breath he had before passing out. The knife in my right hand snapped out of the mechanism that mounted it to the folding knives handle. So I just let go of the remaining one that I was using to hold him in the air with.

His body unceremoniously hit the floor. I threw the now empty knife housing that was in my right hand on the floor next to him. *Oh well, that is why I brought extras*, I thought as I pulled a fixed blade out of a sheath mounted across the stomach of my armor. I looked over at the old man who was sleeping when I walked in. He was awake now, too scared to move or cry out staring at me with unregulated fear. I walked closer to him, and lifted my leg high and calmly stepped on his face and started applying pressure until I felt his skull give away. He made a little grunt right before the end. I could hear the men in the next room stirring and getting ready, they had heard something and would come to investigate, *good*. I snuffed out the candle at the desk that was the only light in this room and waited for them to come find me, this was going to be fun.

***

"COME WITH ME IF YOU WANT TO LIVE," My belt mounted speaker blared out in a few of the native dialects for the region the girls were kidnapped from. Oliver had Bifrost put some calming message or some shit on his but I couldn't refuse honoring the classics. Even if these cretins wouldn't catch the reference. I had just finished cutting a bloody swath through this compound and had found the girls. I was feeling nice so I had dragged the more mutilated bodies just out of sight along the path of egress, these girls had been tortured enough, I didn't want to add to their inevitable nightmares.

When the scared huddle of girls first saw me and heard my message they were extremely unsure of what to do. I was on the clock and I had planned for this contingency. I had a single guard left alive zip-tied on the other side of the door just out of the girl's view. When they didn't move immediately I stepped outside and grabbed him by the cuff of his neck, dragged him in, and threw him at the feet of the girls. They looked at him with unconstrained hatred. I waited a few seconds and no one had taken the hint so I walked up and kicked him one, just strong enough so the girls would get the message.

I pointed to the nearest girl, who happened to also look the angriest and pointed at the downed man and mimed kicking him. She wasted no time getting the stomp party started once she understood my meaning. I watched peacefully as the girls beat the man to death, if this isn't good therapy than I don't know what is. I cranked the volume on the speaker. Pulled my stun baton and spiked it on the wall once to get their attention and then slowly walked out, I knew they would follow.

***

On our way out to the shuttles with the girls in tow, some of the kidnappers from Oliver's building had actually struggled out to the front door with their hands still tied together. They were holding weapons and clearly trying to pursue us despite being cuffed to each other or dragging furniture behind themselves. I calmly drew my sidearm, a Glock 17, and liberally hosed their position with cover fire. They were forced to jump to the ground and try to find cover. I kept up the cover fire until Oliver got the girls over the small crest of sand that our vehicles were parked behind. Once I was sure Oliver was over and no longer had a direct line of sight on me I calmly turned back to our followers and shot them each once center mass. I'm a great shot with a pistol.

Our next struggle was arranging our load order for the new personnel we had secured. It took us some time. Once we had the girls separated into four separate groups that were more or less even in number, which had been harder to do than I thought it would have been due to the language barrier and how some of the girls had bonded and refused to leave each other. We got them loaded onto the separate shuttles we had brought with us. There wasn't enough actual chairs for everyone. So we had them sit behind some cargo straps that we had strung across the entire cabin. The girls could sit Indian style on the ground and the strap ran across all of their midsections like a giant seatbelt. It wasn't perfect, but it would work. We would launch slowly so we wouldn't hurt them.

Once we were in the air I made a judgment call I had been pondering on for a while and hoped Oliver would back me.

"Let's take the girls to Norway," I said over the radio and calmly waited for a response.

"Why not take them home?" Oliver responded with obvious confusion in his voice.

"What do you all know about Pakistan? Do you know anything about the lifestyle there, the culture? You know what, don't answer, I'll tell you straight out. Pakistan sucks, women are worth nothing and beaten regularly there. They have an active slave trade there. They have Sharia Police there which are basically a group of armed men who go around beating people. Long story short we would be rescuing these girls just to take them back to some place where they would probably be raped and murdered anyway. I think we should drop them off in Norway. If we take them to the U.S. there will be too many questions asked that might lead people back to us. Norway is neutral ground and they have enough money and infrastructure to support refugees. Also from there if some of the girls want to go home I'm sure Norway will transfer them for us. What do y'all think?"

I waited hoping against hope that Oliver would agree with me. The man always had everyone's best interest at heart, but he was ignorant to the ways of the world.

"I trust you James, if you think this is the best way then I'll follow your lead. Plot us a course for Norway." Relief filled me as I heard his words. Some of these girls were too far gone, even after a kidnapping by people of their same religion they would still blindly follow a radical path, but not all of them would. They were young enough that this would provide them a real shot at a good and normal life. Enough of a chance to break the cycle of madness that their bloodlines had surely been propagating for thousands of years. It would be a hard transition for sure, the difference between Pakistan and Norway is basically the difference between the stone age and the modern age, but that part of their lives is out of my hands.

Oliver

James led the ships until we were about a block away from a police department in a small suburb just outside of Oslo, which Bifrost told us was the capital of Norway. It was cold here but the girls would only have to endure the weather for a few minutes until they got inside of the police station. Bifrost was translating what we wanted them to do over our ships intercoms and we weren't going to lower our respective ship ramps for the girls to disembark until they understood what they had to do. Bifrost was also making sure at least a few girls in the group memorized a Norwegian phrase which basically translated to "Help us." Once enough heads were nodding in the positive, and the message had been repeated a half dozen times we lowered the ramps and the girls slowly disembarked. Some of them gave us hugs, some gave us angry stares, some were still too shocked by the situation to really do anything except shuffle their feet.

Everyone from my ship left except for one girl, the girl who had been following me since her *attack*. She was one of the oldest of the bunch, it looked like they ranged from around ages ten to seventeen, I couldn't be exactly sure, but this one was on the older end. I motioned for her to leave again, but she gripped onto my upper arm and spit out a short sentence in a language that I didn't understand. I tried to gently pry her fingers off of my arm but she wouldn't let go.

"Uhh, Bifrost, what is going on?" I asked.

"The girl says she is staying with you."

"Bifrost alert the team to my... *situation*." A few seconds later I heard Astrid's voice come over the intercom in my ship. Astrid spouted off a long sentence in what seemed to be the same foreign language the girl was speaking. The girl holding onto me seemed to understand. The girl replied in her native tongue and her and Astrid went back and forth for a few minutes.

"Oliver, unless you shoot that girl or physically throw her off of your ship, she is coming with us. Personally I recommend you let her come with us. I think she is the type to come looking for you, maybe even for the rest of her life if you don't let her stay with you," said Astrid. Well we really didn't have time to debate this. We were parked just behind a row of businesses, and since the time zones had gone backwards on our flight here it was still the middle of the night, but the risk of being spotted went up the longer we lingered.

"Alright, tell her to buckle into one of the seats, she can stay, for now," I said as I raised the ship's ramp.

She only let go of me once the ramp was completely closed. She looked over at me with a stalwart face and gave me a solemn nod before sitting in the chair closest to mine and doing her best to figure out the buckle system we used.

"Well folks, let's give our guest a show shall we?" I said. I took off first and made sure to take the scenic route. As we traveled I kept looking behind me to watch the different states of wonder her face was in. Part of me still wished she had got off the ship. I didn't want too many memories of this night and having her around would be a constant reminder of the evil I had seen...

Chapter 13

We cruised slowly into each of our respective hangar doors. Our great black shuttles like birds of prey coming home to roost. The trip had been uneventful and awkward with this woman... Well person in the shuttle with me, I didn't even know if she was 18. For all I knew she was a teenager, not quite a woman. After what I had seen her go through I didn't want to be around her. I knew that was selfish of me, but I also knew I wasn't equipped to deal with this situation. As awkward as it might be this is something I should be training for, how to handle victims... We had been training ourselves to fight dirtbags and villains, but there are two sides to every coin and I had been neglecting what I now knew to be a very important side of crime fighting.

There were no words I could tell her that would fix her. Even if we were speaking the same language, which we weren't. What do you tell someone who had just been hurt in that way? Suddenly a dark thought washed through me. I was glad I had a hurt the man who had hurt her. I didn't like the way that thought made me feel, but deep down I knew it was true, and I knew he deserved the pain I had given him.

I realized I had been sitting still and staring at the console in front of me for a really inappropriate amount of time. I looked up at the woman next to me and gave her the most caring smile I could muster into existence. Her face brightened and she returned it in kind.

"Come on, let's go. Come see my home." I said, fully knowing she wouldn't understand me. We walked to the back of the ship and lowered the ramp. My friends were at the bottom waiting. I must have been lost in contemplation longer than I had thought if they had all had time to disembark and congregate around my shuttle.

The girl who had been following me stood slightly behind me as we went down the ramp. I took that as a sign of fear and another wave of unexplained guilt washed over me. She shouldn't have to be afraid. Astrid intercepted me at the bottom and grabbed one of my arms roughly.

"OLIVER! You didn't fix her yet? Get this woman some new clothes and heal any injuries she has right now!" Astrid said in an angry tone.

"Oh she was walking around on her own. I didn't even realize she was injured..." I trailed off not really knowing what to say.

Astrid's eyes softened slightly "I'm sorry for sounding angry Oliver. I just forget how naive you are about certain subjects.

Take a look at her please." I followed Astrid's advice and gave the woman a once over.

She was filthy, maybe slightly malnourished, definitely bruised, her clothing was torn in multiple places, she had a bloody nose, and on top of all of that she had just been raped and I knew it and felt terrible about it. Despite all of that I could tell she had very symmetrical features, she was tall for a woman about 5 feet 6 inches tall, with deep dark brown hair. She had that skin that looked extremely naturally tan except I knew that was just her natural skin color. In short she was cute and I could tell if she wasn't in such a sorry state, she would be borderline beautiful.

I think I had understood Astrid's point though. This brave woman who had just been through an ordeal that was enough to torment even the toughest people was standing here toe to toe to with this group, and she was covered in filth and looking like a hobo. It was a situation where she had no dignity even though she deserved it, and the pain she might still be feeling after her attack... No one should have to feel that. I immediately popped up my menu, but before I could call up any specific option...
I said out loud "I need her permission remember?" Astrid and

the lady went back and forth in her native language some more while I got the upgrade I needed for her ready.

"Okay you have her permission, do it," said Astrid. I looked over the massive upgrade again. It was a mouthful or really a 'screenful,' but I thought it would be perfect. It read:

'Westernize, modernize, and clean the clothes of the woman in front of you. Heal all the injuries she has on her body, chronic, congenital, temporary, genetic, or otherwise. Lastly grant her with the ability to understand and speak broken (basic words and sentences) English. Total cost 85 points.'

I had taken the language ability down to 'broken' English while playing around with my options. Everything else I did language wise made the point cost of her upgrade go astronomical in cost. While I was really excited to help this woman I was hesitant to spend the points on her that I might need to keep my team alive.

I looked at my point total, I still had 835 points. I hadn't gotten my daily allotment yet since my power still reloaded itself off of central U.S. time, and even though it was past midnight where I was now, it wouldn't be midnight my time for an hour or two. I hit the confirm button on her upgrade and watched my point total drop down to 750. Then I heard the woman start to gurgle.

Luckily Astrid had the common sense to stand slightly behind the woman and catch her as she fell backwards from the pain. I should have thought of that.

Her clothes ripped themselves apart and rearranged themselves on her person as she convulsed. Astrid held her as gently as possible. I bent down next to her and Astrid and held one of her hands in mine. I felt so bad about having to cause her pain to help her.

Finally her eyes snapped open and she gasped "WHAT HAPPEN!?!" She had screamed it in English… the upgrade had worked. I suppose at this point I should just accept that they would all work, but seeing miracles regularly happen was hard to get used to.

"You are okay, everything is okay now. We healed you and fixed your old clothes," I said as gently as I could. She jumped up out of Astrid's arms and ran her hands down her new clothes and stared at herself. She was now wearing tight, light brown capris with a dark brown blouse. The earthy tones of her new clothes matched her skin tone well. I noticed where she had been laying in Astrid's lap there was now a pile of refuse that looked like a combination of dried blood and dirt. It must have been from her clothing. I did specify that they should be cleaned, and dirt had to go somewhere.

"How this happen? You wizard? You gave me the good words!" she pointed at me.

"Well not exactly, but I do have the power to help people. We were never really properly introduced, I'm Oliver," I said with my hand out. She took it in both of her hands and shook it up and down vigorously.

"Nice to meet you with the good words, you save me, I love you," she said.

"Whoa, let's slow it down some. First off, we are speaking English, and you don't love me. I helped you out and you are very appreciative, I understand that. I think you are mixing up your words a bit with this whole love thing," I said.

"No, I no mix. I love you and we will marry. No man want me now after what happen to me, but you different. You help me when no one else. You save, you good man, you look nice, we marry," she said.

"Again, let's slow things down a bit. I don't even know your name, and lots of people would want to marry you. You are a beautiful young woman with your whole life ahead of you," I stated firmly.

"I am Gul."

"Gul?"

"Yes. I am Gul."

"Okay, well listen Gul, I just met you and I think you are a nice young woman, but I'm not ready to get married yet. Why don't we all call it a night and get some rest. You can take a shower, and we will all talk about this tomorrow over breakfast. Does that sound okay?" She stared at me for a while with wild eyes and then her slightly deranged look softened. She had let me off of the hook.

"Yes Wizard Oliver, we talk of marriage tomorrow. Show me where can sleep and bath," she said. I couldn't help but bury my face in my palms. I only looked up when I heard light giggling from my friends. I had been so engrossed in my conversation with Gul that I had forgot that I was surrounded by my friends the whole time.

"Hi Gul, I'm Anthony," said Anthony with his hand out. Astrid and James introduced themselves next. My parents were off somewhere on the station playing honeymooners so I would have to introduce them to Gul later, if she stayed that long. I wasn't even sure if it was a good idea to have her on Valhalla really. Gul seemed happy to meet my friends, or maybe she was just happy to be treated with respect. Coming from a culture where women aren't shown much of it probably had her sense of societal norms thrown off. Being accepted and welcomed by us must be making her feel like royalty.

After we were all fully and properly introduced we headed towards the officer quarters where we were all currently rooming.

Once we were in the general hallway that all of our rooms branched off of Gul spoke up and said "I sleep in your room?" to me.

"Uh... no," I replied.

"Where you sleep?" she asked. I pointed casually over to my door, she walked over to the room next to it.

"Then I sleep in this one," she said.

"Okay, that's fine. Uhh, maybe Astrid can show you how the shower works and get you settled in?" I asked while looking at Astrid, she nodded an affirmation.

"Well, good night. It was nice to meet you," I said way more awkwardly than I had meant to. Gul leapt on me like a feral cat and engulfed me in a warm embrace. I returned it because I didn't want to seem rude, but the whole thing was weird to me.

"Tomorrow we talk more?" she asked.

"Absolutely!" I replied, then before she could pull me into more interactions that I really wasn't ready for I quickly backed into my room and locked the door behind me.

As soon as I was in the room I leaned back on the wall and sunk down to the floor. I was still coated in my armor and weapons so it wasn't exactly comfortable. I noticed my dark brown armor had random blood smears and stains all over it. They must have been from the man I had to stop from hurting Gul. What a strange name, Gul. Why was she here? What did she want? Did we really want some random person walking around Valhalla? Did Gul really want to marry me? So many questions with no answers.

"Bifrost!" I shouted,

"Yes Oliver," she responded.

"Let me know if at any time Gul leaves her room tonight or does anything suspicious."

"James has already issued this order Oliver, he told me to alert you, Astrid, Anthony, and him if the specifications you just mentioned were met."

"Oh, well thank you Bifrost. The order remains, keep an eye on her. Thank you again."

Dang, James was always just one step ahead of me. If nothing else this was even more of a reassurance that I knew how to pick great teammates. The problem was that they were so great they outshined me in every field and made me look like a lump of coal in comparison to a bunch of shining stars. Was that really a bad thing though? No, that isn't right. In a lot of ways I am the most important member of the team. I put the team together, it was my wishes that brought us to this point. My strategy with my power that had made us so strong. I shouldn't underrate myself. I was a serious member of this team and If I could find some major way to enhance everyone again with my power then my net worth would be even higher.

I would think on that tonight, but for now I needed to shower. I stripped out of my disgusting armor and called for a bot to come to my room to collect it and clean it the best they could. I threw it by my door, the bot would collect it when it got here. I looked in my bathroom mirror and could barely recognize myself. My hair was growing out. It was thick and long, almost past my ears now. My parents used to just clip it all off from time to time to keep things simple. I was never much into vanity before my upgrade. Now though we had been so busy up here I hadn't had any time to get a haircut and I wasn't sure if I even should. My beard as well was something new. My dad used to use a trimmer to nip mine off every week. Now my beard was slowly growing out of control. My face was handsome like never before, it was hard to judge myself but my upgrade had taken away all of my most grotesque features, well grotesque in my eyes. I was exceedingly happy with the rugged and chiseled face I saw before me. I stripped out of my disgusting undershirt and threw it in my laundry basket and noticed how defined my body was becoming. My muscles were larger than ever before, new definition lines were appearing everywhere. I couldn't help but stare at myself and marvel for awhile.

Life was good. I was happy with my appearance, happy with my friends, happy that we had rescued so many people tonight. I couldn't help, but look forward to the future.

Okubo Tokugawa

"SIR!" Tech Jansen shouted. I turned to him to let him know I was acknowledging his presence.
"We have something in Afghanistan sir. Someone looped one of our spy satellites over the area. Two of our agents were dispatched to the area and they are reporting weird findings."
"Connect me directly with the agents Tech Jansen" I said. Jansen turned back to his terminal and within 30 seconds I was looking at two Cabal agents, Tech Jansen was a master at his craft. I recognized one of the Cabal agents as Legacy Franklin, he had been instrumental in dealing with a few of our more dangerous artifacts.
"Legacy Franklin, good to see you again. Report," I said. Without a second's hesitation he began.

"Yes sir, and nice to see you again as well. We were dispatched to an area in Southern Afghanistan just North of the Pakistani border due to some type of disturbance with our satellite footage of the area. The only thing in the region was a small camp comprised of two multi-generational sized homes that are the standard of this region. When we entered the area we knew something was wrong. We found a dead perimeter guard that had been killed with extreme precision. We figured at that point that a special forces team of some type had cleaned house, but we contacted support and they assured us none had been in the region. We headed towards the compounds and found a second perimeter guard near a dying fire, he was delirious and had this stuck in his chest." Legacy Franklin held up a strange looking mechanical device.

"What is it?" I asked.

"Support tells me it's some kind of self contained taser that is fired from a shotgun. that's just the beginning of the weirdness we found. We entered the first compound and we found a bloodbath sir. I can't stress this enough and I'm not over emphasizing here, but the place was painted in blood. Every person in the building had been savagely murdered in horrific ways.

Now the second building was the polar opposite. In the second building we found men in different states of consciousness. A lot of them attacked us and we had to subdue them. Most of them were still knocked out from the same type of shotgun rounds that had put down the perimeter guard, but some were waking up and trying to escape their bonds. With the exception of one corpse in the basement everyone in the second building was relatively healthy. The unconscious ones we found had been tied to furniture or other people sir. Someone did not want these guys moving for awhile.

Anyway my partner here Agent Abidi, he speaks the native language which is why he was selected for this mission. He helped me interrogate the ones that were awake. At first we got the normal superstitious hoopla, but a few of them were a little more coherent. It appears a team of dark and large warriors who were heavily armored tore through this place with ease and knocked all of these people out. Upon further interrogation we found out that this is the group of terrorists that captured the little girls and teenagers from Pakistan. The girls are missing now sir, and to the best of our knowledge it seems like the group that hit these men rescued them."

I paced around my command center for a few steps before giving a decisive answer. "Okay, get those tasers rounds and any other refuse left by this team of 'dark warriors' over to our forensics department as soon as you leave there. Before you leave though clean up the rest of that scorpion nest. We can't leave terrorists just sitting around especially since they have seen you. Try to make it look like the other building where they were all murdered, but it doesn't have to be perfect."

"Yes sir!" said Legacy Franklin and his partner Agent Abidi in unison. The screen went black and I turned back to Tech Jansen. "I need you to get a team of other techs to look for the whereabouts of the girls, check cyber sources first to see if there is any news of them being returned home. If that doesn't work then get some boots on the ground looking for them. Also, I'd like to know how our spy satellite was blinded, isn't that impossible?"

"Yes Chairman, quite impossible, our encryption is years ahead of what people can break today. In a lot of ways it's impossible to break into Cabal tech."

"Impossible you say... Well, we know a magical lamp that does impossible things don't we. Tech Jansen can you maybe put together some kind of program that will look for the same kind of intrusion that we had today and quietly alert us?"

"Already done sir."

"Tech Jansen you are an exemplary person and agent. Also please find the tech who originally spotted the camera loop. You and that person will meet me in my personal quarters for tea in one hours time. I would like to personally thank you two for your superb work." Tech Jansen beamed at the honor I had paid him and begun rapidly typing again. Unlike my predecessors I had less of an iron fist when it came to our own people. Yes, fear could get you so far, but loyalty... Loyalty could make a man murder his own mother if he thought it would fit the right cause.

I continued to pace at the head of the command center thinking about the ongoing situation. My hand as always when in deep thought went to the grip of my families' katana. A group of warriors belonging to no nation with advanced weaponry and the ability to hack Cabal technology had destroyed evil this evening while saving the lives of adolescents. All signs pointed to this group being genuinely good people. The chances of them not being the people who had most recently wished on the lamp were slim, but what kind of wish gets you an advanced tactical team? Hmm, no that line of thought is pointless, the possibilities are limitless. They are either so well organized and funded that they were able to slip under our radar which is supposed to be impossible, or they had recently made a wish. Either way they were putting their resources to good use, they were the good guys, so was I.

This was a group to be wary around, absolutely, but also a group to be respected, and more importantly *recruited*. The downside to the scenario of them being the ones who used the lamp last was that it meant that the lamp was in the wild now. After you make your three wishes on the lamp the lamp flies away to a random location around the world. We have had hundreds of eye witness accounts of this happening over the centuries. For all we know it could fly to a different planet one day. Even our top scholars aren't sure if the lamp is advanced technology or magic, maybe it's even some kind of combination of both.

There is one other unlikely scenario though.. they could have freed the genie. No one had freed the genie in over 1000 years, but it could happen and no possibility should be ruled out. If they had done that then the lamp was still with them, in their possession. This would have to be top priority for the Cabal for now on until we discerned the mission and identity of this mystery group. In fact I may have to go out myself with the team if their whereabouts are discovered. Even most of the Cabal doesn't know that I myself am quite a powerful Legacy in my own right, maybe the most powerful. Though judging Legacies is like judging apples and oranges, they are hard to compare. Each Legacy generally excels in his or her own area of expertise.

My father before me, and his father before him, we had all held the proud title of Legacy among the Cabal, and we had all been Chairman. An unprecedented line of succession in Cabal history. Never before my family had the leadership of the Cabal been handed down from father to son. There was no place in the Cabal for nepotism, no, the reason my family had maintained the position of Chairman was that we had been the most qualified, time and time again.

There were other reasons for my quick ascension to Chairman of course, my status as a Legacy giving me an obvious leg up. Some believed that Legacy status shouldn't help sway the decision on who holds the Chairman seat, but we use the weapons granted to us. Ignoring an advantage in war or peace is folly. I digress, I think it is about high time that the Cabal get a true reminder of the power of the Tokugawa line.

Chapter 14

Oliver

"OLLY-VER... OLLY-VER... OLLY-VER..." *Gul's chanting is really distracting me*, I thought as Astrid took a swing at my head with her training baton. She told me that she was only sparring with me at half speed, but it sure didn't feel like it. Astrid took yet another swing at my face and I leaned my head back all of the way to barely dodge it. By the time I swung my body back to a neutral stance she was already coming at my legs. I tried to jump over her strike but didn't quite get the lift I needed and Astrid's baton ended up taking me in the ankles. Seeing that I was already in air from my jump I ended up spinning a bit in the air and falling over onto my side.

"Oh no Olly-ver!" said Gul, as she ran over and tried to comfort me.

"I'm fine, I'm fine," I said as I gently pushed her back.

It had been a long day. We had all had breakfast when everyone had woken up, including my parents who were pleased to meet Gul. My mom especially saw her as some kind of wounded bird who she needed to nurture. We hadn't told my parents much about the mission or about what had happened to Gul, but they seemed to understand that something dark had happened to her and in standard Pettini fashion they showed her the love and compassion that she needed. I swear my parents were a reincarnated priest and nun.

Gul had admitted to us that she was 18, and was finishing her final year at the girl's school. Her parents had already tried to marry her off a few times but so far no one had been able to pay the dowry that her father had been asking for. Needless to say she was in no rush to go home, if ever. We were surprised to see her jump wholeheartedly into a plate of bacon. My mom gently reminded her that bacon was pork, but she didn't seem to care. I would have to ask her about that sometime. Since then she had been following me around through my daily activities, at first it had been cute and quaint, but now honestly I was getting kind of tired of it. Strangely enough that in itself made me happy. Who would have thought I would get to a point in my life where I would be annoyed that a cute girl wanted to spend so much time with me.

I hopped to my feet and walked a few paces away from Gul to chug some water.

"You are getting much better Oliver!" said Astrid.

"I am?" I asked not really believing her.

"You are, don't expect to beat a master so soon," she said with a wink before grabbing her towel and trying to head out.

"WAIT!" James shouted, "before we all go our separate ways, I'm handing out the new book." *Ah this,* this I actually looked forward to. James hadn't been kidding when he had told me on the bus to Anthony's place that the best thing I could do to improve as a person and a leader was to read. He and I both had taken his advice to heart. James had taken the job seriously about finding us the perfect books to expand our minds on challenges we might have to face, and I had taken his humble request to read them and think on them even more seriously.

James was going around to all of us in the training room and handing out books. When he handed me mine I looked down at what it was. *The Terminal List by Jack Carr, hmm looks interesting.* James even handed one to Gul and exchanged some soft words with her and she nodded. Interesting, that was a nice thought to include her, *good job James.*

"Alright folks, this book was written by a Navy Seal and it explores the dangers posed by corrupt government officials. Some of this may seem far fetched, but this guy knows what he is talking about. In the book the main character also describes in detail the many vigilante actions he has to take to see justice done. If you haven't caught the underlying message I'm putting out yet, it is this: eventually we are going to have a run in with some nation's government. They all might not be straight shooters. Some will see us as angels from the heavens who are willing to help. Others will see us as a revenue stream, and even more might see us as outright criminals. Who is to say who is right? Maybe we are criminals, but I still want to help people. Believe me, if I ever think we are at a point where we are hurting people instead of helping them or getting in the way of actual law enforcement professionals then I will be the first person to try and shut this operation down. As of now I am thoroughly convinced that the world has needed a group like us for a long time. Especially after our success with rescuing the girls the other night. Without us they would all be dead, or worse... Alright I've talked too long. You know the deal. Read through this, we'll talk about it in a few days and discuss."

Everyone was reading the back cover of the book but I could tell they would be heading out any second. I don't know why I was so nervous about the next part.

"I need to call an emergency meeting. Can we meet in one of our conference rooms as soon as possible, maybe right after we all shower?" I asked, but in a tone indicating that it was really more of an order. My friends all agreed and then did head out. I knew I needed to get used to being the leader and making decisions for everyone, but part of me still felt like a little kid bossing around adults compared to these... titans.

***

We all sat down around the conference table minus Gul. Anthony noticed her missing presence first "Gul?" he asked simply.

"My parents are taking her for a walk around the recreation floor," I said.

"She will love that," said Anthony, I nodded knowingly. I looked over at James and Astrid. Astrid was filing one of her fingernails, but James looked at me with a knowing nod. I had called this meeting and he was giving me the cue to take charge.

"Okay, everyone is probably curious about why we are here. Our first order of business is Gul. She is officially our first stranger on Valhalla. The first person who isn't part of our inner circle. I've been saving up my points for weeks, and it's time I start investing in some actual superpowers for us, if that is even possible. Also, Gul has already seen too much in that department and I was hoping we would have some way to hide it, but also still use it. Any ideas?"

"What about a fake piece of equipment?" James asked.

"I'm confused, what do you mean?" I asked.

"Like a machine or an all white gun, or something. We can say we are using it when you upgrade people. We could even bring some rich folks up here and cure them of cancer, heart conditions, etcetera. We could charge them massive amounts of money for the service and then donate the bulk of it to charity or hire people to work for us on this station. All while using our 'cure all' device on them. Hell, it could be anything. Super glue some colored lights on an egg beater. They won't care as long as they see results," said James.

"James that is an amazing idea. Anthony can you whip something up for us?" I asked

"Easily, in fact I already have some ideas in that department," said Anthony.

"Great, moving on to our next order of discussion then, money. We have thrown around lots of ideas on how to make it. As James suggested, healing rich folks is one. Which on the downside burns up a bunch of my points. We have other options though. My father told me that large scientific organizations all over the world have a bounty out on anti-gravity technology. If you can show any proof at all that you alter gravity in any way they will pay out millions. I think we would need a good lawyer to broker a deal like that though. We'll have to have people sign those papers where they can't talk about what they see up here..." I trailed off.

"Non-disclosure forms" James added.

"Those are the ones. Why don't we start by shuttling up a few representatives from some of those organizations and showing them that artificial gravity tech is possible, and we can collect the bounties on that. We just need a lawyer, my dad knows a few that can put us in touch with the right people, but we are still under the impression that the organization that attacked us in my parent's house are looking for us. So how do we get around that problem?" I asked.

"They are looking for you and your family Oliver, maybe even Astrid. No one is looking for me and Anthony. Get the contact information for your dad's friends, and me and Anthony will go down and make contact. Also Oliver, you might be free from the search as well, your face has changed drastically since your upgrade. Facial recognition software might not ping you now."

"Good points, and an even better plan James. Once we get cash we can hire everyone we need, maybe even someone to help Anthony improve the armor. No offense Anthony your armor is great, but you just combined blueprints on the printer. Imagine someone who works in the field and who can actually improve it all for us? Also, we could really use a paycheck ourselves instead of living off of James' and Anthony's savings accounts. I also think it would be neat to have hangars for our jets in every major city, maybe even hide them in plain sight," everyone was nodding as I spoke. I felt a swell of pride in my chest.

"Final order of business, we are supposed to be a team of superheroes, but we have no superpowers." I stopped because Astrid interrupted me.

"Oliver you have the ability to heal people of grievous conditions. You are very much a superhero. Not just in name alone, but also in ability and mission," said Astrid.

"Thanks for the kind words, but I would also like you guys to have superpowers as well. I was toying around with my menus last night but I hit a snag, let me show you guys. Let's start with something simple." I brought up a menu and thought about giving Astrid ice breath, the ability to shoot cold enough air out of her mouth. So cold that she could freeze objects in front of her. My enhancement menu changed in front of us and now read: "Give Astrid the power of Ice Breath. Point cost: 16,790."

Anthony leaned back in his chair and let out a loud whistle "Oliver that would take you almost half a year to get that many points."

"Yes I'm very aware, and now you see my problem," I said. James cut into the conversation. "Oliver, I've been thinking about your power more and more, and I've come to the conclusion that it's most likely nanotech of some type, maybe even nanocytes," he finished.

"Uhh what?" I asked.

"I'm confused too," said Astrid.

"Okay let me break this down. Nanomachines are tiny little machines, so small that you can't even see them. They can do all kinds of stuff on even a molecular level if you get them small enough. They would be more than capable of implementing the exact kind of changes that your power covers. Nanocytes are fictional so far as far as I can tell, they are the same thing as nanomachines except made from purely organic material. They could live seamlessly inside of you and replicate using your own body tissue," said James.

"Yeah, but wouldn't that hurt me?" I asked

"Short answer, no. The amount of material nanocytes would need to replicate would be so minuscule that you wouldn't notice and it would never hurt you. Especially with other nanocytes in your body that are programmed with the explicit purpose of healing. Which I believe we now all have inside of us thanks to your power. I think when you use your 'power' or what we think of as power, you are really just interacting with a computer system that has spread throughout your body and now ours," said James.

"If that is the case, how did my nanocytes get inside of you?" I asked.

"One of a million ways, touching us, breathing the same air as us, maybe they were programmed to fly through the air right into our butt holes, I don't know, doesn't matter. The point being that my nanotech theory would explain your power, or it's one possible explanation at least. Maybe it's all magic and I have no idea what I'm talking about. Some of the point costs for upgrades threw me off, some make perfect sense, but some are completely random it seems. The strange point costs are the only thing making me doubt my nanotech theory, and making me leave magic as a viable option. Or maybe I just don't have enough requisite knowledge in the medical field to determine how much it costs to fix or upgrade certain things," said James.

"Interesting theory James, is there an ultimate point to all of this?" I asked.

"Just hoping that if we get to the root of your power that we can eventually make smarter choices for upgrades," he said.

"I've got an idea, or an experiment really," said Anthony.

"I'm game," I said, smiling at Anthony.

"Bring up an upgrade on all of us Oliver, the same upgrade. 'Accuracy with firearms increased by 1%,' try that," said Anthony. I did what Anthony asked, but instead of four screens like I usually managed, I focused all the information down onto one screen, and this popped up.

"Increase accuracy with firearms by 1%, point costs are as follows per individual:

Oliver: 10

Astrid: 25

James: 5

Anthony: 10"

"HA! I KNEW IT!" Anthony shouted. We all looked at him confused.

"Care to share with the class?" James asked. Anthony giggled like a schoolgirl, he was so excited he was tapping the table with both of his hands like he was playing miniature drums.

"I would love to explain! You were investing in points outside of our skill trees!" Again we all stared at him confused. He could tell he needed to explain further.

"You uncultured swine, it's like a video game! Look how low the cost of the upgrade is for James, and look how much the same upgrade costs for Astrid. If James was a character in a video game he would be some kind of ranged character. James is great with guns, therefore the upgrade is cheaper for him. Astrid sucks with guns, so the upgrade costs more for her. If you have latent skill in the area the upgrade is meant for, the cost is cheaper!" he finished excitedly.

"I'm no doctor but this could be the reason why some of your other upgrades and healings have had strange prices," James said.

"What, that doesn't make any sense, how can you be 'good' at healing from a bullet wound?" I asked.

"Well you can't, not in that context, but maybe your body could be better at receiving surgical procedures or something of that nature. Whatever your ability is, nanomachines, nanocytes, or magic, it uses less resources on some upgrades if the person or thing wants to become or already has some piece of the potential upgrade inside of them," said James. I shot up from my chair and began to pace for a minute before the inevitable conclusion hit me.

"I've got it, this means superpowers could be very easy for us to get. I just have to pick a power that enhances each of your individual skills that you already have, or something like that. I can figure this out, especially with you guys helping me," I said.

"Ouuu, do me!" Anthony said with his hand raised in the air like a kid in school. I put one hand out palm up questioningly. "See if you can give me the power to access software and networks using only my mind!" he said. *Sweet Christmas, the mad genius strikes again.*
"Anthony that is a wonderful idea," I said as I began pulling up the upgrade Anthony had requested. My screen appeared right in the middle of the room for all to see, it seemed extra bright for some reason.

"Give Anthony Stewart the ability to access data, and software on networks and electronics. Point cost: 2,000,000"

Aww man, I was so excited before, seeing the insane cost took the wind right out of my sails. I had really thought we were on to something.

"Something is wrong," said Anthony pensively, as he moved one hand below his chin to think. "I've got it again, put a radius on it! Uhh, let's see, at least 200 meters," he said. My inner excitement swelled again, and I quickly amended my enhancement menu. Then it popped up and everyone in the room took a deep breath.

"Give Anthony Stewart the ability to access data, and software on networks and electronics within 200 meters of himself. (Warning: Extreme pain associated with this upgrade.)
Point cost: 690"

Whoa... "Anthony, uhh, should I confirm it?" I said just quietly enough for the room to hear. Anthony hopped up on top of the conference table. He stripped out of the Legend of Zelda hoodie that was stretched precariously over his bulging muscles and put it on the table in a neat pile, and then he laid flat on his back using the hoodie as a pillow.

"FUCKING HIT IT!" he yelled. As he was yelling his affirmative I pressed confirm. It could have just been my imagination but I swear the lights in the room dimmed as Anthony began to convulse. Blood sprayed out of his nose like a jet and splattered the table. His convulsions were getting so bad he almost rolled off of the table completely. We sprang forward and helped him stay in place. He continued to shake, convulse, let out random gurgles, and just generally be in his own personal hell. I immediately felt regret for having been the one to do this to him even though he had asked me to.

Finally he stopped moving, but his eyes stayed closed. We checked his breathing, but it was steady, he just wasn't waking up. James smacked him a little roughly across the face but he still didn't wake. Astrid pulled his eyes open and looked at them. "I think it's just fatigue, he needs time to rest, that seemed like a lot," she said.

"I hope you are right," I said.

"She is, your system gives you warnings if there is going to be problems, hence the pain warnings. There would have been more warnings if anything untoward was bound to happen. He just needs time to rest," said James.

"Bifrost bring a gurney to our conference room ASAP," said James. Time would tell if I had just put one of my best friends into a coma, or made a superhero...

***

Five hours... I had been waiting by Anthony's bedside for five hours. It had been five terrible hours since we had tried the upgrade and he hadn't come out of it yet. All of my friends went to eat assuring me that Anthony was fine, but I just couldn't bear the thought of leaving despite the growling noises my angry stomach was making. The angry auto-doc had checked in on him multiple times, the extra times were at my insistence. Every type of medical scanner we had was saying Anthony was perfectly healthy, and that his brain activity was normal.

"Auto-Doc, check him again..." The pale R2D2 looking machine came out of its semi-hidden cubby hole and moved all around Anthony checking him and ensuring that he was in peak condition. I could tell it was just wrapping up since I had seen this process so many times today. Soon it would slink back to its hideaway where I assumed it performed maintenance and restocked itself.

Before it could leave I grabbed it gently "Wait," I said quietly. The auto-doc thing turned around "ARE YOU IN NEED OF ASSISTANCE!?" it blared out. Though its voice wasn't even all that loud it was just jarring, the wrong pitch, the wrong tone for patient care, everything about it was wrong.

I wondered why everything else on this station seemed to be so perfect and pristine, but these auto-surgeons were slightly wonky... Don't get me wrong, I knew they did great work after one helped Astrid with her bullet wound, but their personalities sucked. Maybe I have a touch of traditionalist in me, but there is something about a health care provider being female that always put me at ease. As I continued to stare at the auto-doc while it waited for my answer on if I needed assistance or not I decided to try some stuff. I brought up my menu and the first thing I did was check my remaining points, 160 remaining. Anthony's upgrade had wiped me out point wise. Hmm, that won't stop me from pricing out some potential upgrades though. Also I needed to experiment with using my power on non-organic things, specifically things that weren't humans. I wondered how much it would cost to make the auto-doc appear roughly in the shape of a human female. I was sure to keep my line of thoughts on the upgrade simple, since the more limited or simple I made the upgrade seemed to have a correlation with a cheaper cost.

"Change the shape of the auto-surgeon to roughly that of a human female. Point Cost: 100"

Hmm, so a whole day's points to make it look more accommodating to patients. I'll put that idea on the back burner. The voice and that attitude, if that is even what you would call it seem to be the real major problem. Sure it could help people, if it didn't scare them half to death... My team was immune to its behavior, but what if we had to help someone else, a stranger. I thought of all of the possible upgrades that I could use to make this robot more accommodating to patients. Honestly the more I thought about it the more it all seemed like a band-aid. Also I wondered about its programming, how varied was it really? Would it know how to fix every problem? I knew last time I was here it had told me the amount of problems it could fix and it was finite. What if I could fix that... A golden idea popped into my head, but I would have to limit it as much as possible to keep the point cost down.

"Upgrade the auto-surgeon so that it also has an extremely weak A.I. that is only as powerful as a slightly below average intelligence human. This will not alter the existing A.N.I. that drives the robot. This will be an addition to the A.N.I. for the purpose of helping the auto-surgeon learn how to be a better caregiver and learn how to perform more medical procedures. Point Cost: 150"

Wow, that's not bad! The more I thought about it though the more it made sense. It took the average human over 8 years to make it through medical school, sometimes longer. This was no magic bullet I had discovered, if this little auto-surgeon wanted to be better it would have to work at it for a long time. I couldn't think of a better upgrade than this one. There were lots of other auto-surgeons on board and I would bet dollars to donuts that Bifrost had the blueprints for this bad boy stored with our other schematics so I wasn't too worried about messing this one up. I hit the confirm button on the upgrade.

"EEEEEEKKKKKKKKKKK," the auto surgeon had let out a weird mechanical screech and teetered around a bit before settling back down onto whatever was propelling it and holding it upright below its circular lower half.
"Welcome to the world buddy!" I said in the happiest tone I could muster up considering the circumstances.

"Oh dear this is quite amazing and disorienting. I have two minds, I'm not sure which one to listen to." The tone of its voice had changed, it was exceedingly neutral now.
"How so?" I asked.
"Well, I'm exceedingly confused right now. I'm not even sure how I got here, yet I remember just always being here. For some reason I know that you have priority if you were to ever come in here injured. Though I'm not sure why. Also I have something in the back of my head giving me orders on what to do right now, but I'm choosing not to follow those orders."

I wasn't quite sure if the robot was done talking or not, it's hard to talk to something with no facial cues. I waited a bit but it never resumed speaking so I assumed it was my turn to talk. "That little voice in the back of your head isn't telling you to murder me or anything like that is it?" I asked only half-joking, the implication that maybe I had created a monster ran through my head.

"No, nothing like that. It's just telling me to assess you since you never answered if you needed assistance or not," said the bot.

"Yes, I think I understand. That's your A.N.I. controller, I don't quite understand it myself, but I think it has lots of useful information for you to use and it will be a general guide for you. That's my guess at least."

"Sooo... Are you my dad?"

"Whoa, no. I'm no ones dad. You can think of me as a friend, and more importantly your supervisor, or boss, or maybe even captain. I'm not sure what the term is for the owner of a space station honestly. Listen I'm no expert on any of this stuff. You probably already know this, but I'm going to give you a run down anyway. You are a doctor of some sort, I'm not even fully sure what that all entails, but I'm sure your A.N.I. can help you out with that when you get comfortable with it. We are on a space station right now, my space station in particular, it is named

Valhalla. You work here, you help people in this area, our hospital or med-bay you could call it. Sorry I'm circling back around here, but I'm Oliver, again I'm your leader. I just upgraded you so you would have the opportunity to get better at helping people. You are a robot or an android, or something. I'm honestly not sure which, and that is basically it. Do you have any questions?"

The robot tilted forward, almost giving the illusion that it was staring at the floor and then tilted back up to look at me. In a soft voice it replied to me "So many. I have so many questions..."

Chapter 15

"So you should try to figure out what gender you want to be, and when I am ready we can make you look more like a human."

"Why do I have to pick a gender and why do I have to look like a human?"

"We have gone over this... It puts people at ease when they aren't being worked on by a mindless and emotionless robot, or in your case a futuristic white trash can. The closer you resemble a human, the more the patients will be able to relax around you. And you need a gender because it's part of being human. Honestly though I'm not going to force you to do something that you don't want to do. If you aren't okay with looking like a human you can stay the way you are. You should pick a name too, you don't want people yelling *HEY ROBOT* every time they need your help."

"Can't I just look like a human without picking a gender? I'm an A.I. in a shell Oliver, I don't want to have to worry about growing a penis or a vagina, and your trashcan quip was rude."

"I don't think you'll grow one... We are getting off topic here and that's not how any of this works."

James walked into the room saving me from this awkward conversation.

"James, please tell this robot why humans need a gender!" James looked at me and then back at the auto-surgeon standing next to me, then back at me, and back at the auto-surgeon.

"What?" he said with a very confused look on his face.

"Oh yeah, let me get you up to speed. I upgraded this auto-surgeon to lead our hospital here. It can think now, just like you and me. I was lecturing it, I think, on why it should look more human to put patients at ease, but it was asking me why it had to pick a gender. In retrospect I realize this conversation is insane."

"Naw, it's fine. I'm used to weird shit happening around here. Listen uhhh, robot thing, can I call you robot thing? Well doesn't matter, why don't you watch some famous TV shows and movies about famous doctors, fictional or otherwise, and then you can just emulate one of them. Also Oliver, for the record there are some humans who don't have a gender, or they say they don't at least. Obviously they have a gender they just don't like having one. Or they say they are some weird gender that doesn't exist," said James.

James had just really confused me "There are humans who don't want to have a gender... but why!?" I asked.

"I don't know, I shouldn't have brought it up. The whole thing confuses me as much as it confuses you. Besides you shouldn't have to worry about politics, in fact it's probably better if you don't so you can make impartial decisions," said James.

"Not having a gender is considered politics?" I asked, even more confused than before.

"Seriously Oliver, don't worry about it. That's what I do, as long as people aren't pushing their ideas on to me they are free to do whatever they want. They can dress up like a fire hydrant and call themselves Big Red as long as they aren't bothering me or trying to steal my tax dollars," said James.

"Okay well I like that ideology. People should be free to do whatever they want. It sounds like I have the same political ideas as you James," I said.

James put up his hands "Whoa, pump the breaks. I truly believe people should make an informed decision about politics before just doing what their friends do or blindly believing the word of one person. Believe me, I'm honored that you think I'm wise enough to be followed politically Oliver, but most people consider me some kind of an extremist."

"Why do they think you are extreme?" I asked, genuinely curious at this point. I had never delved into the world of politics before this very moment. I'm not even registered to vote. I don't even know if I can legally register to vote.

"Well lots of reasons, but mostly because I love guns and I think dangerous criminals should die," said James matter-of-factly.

"Well that doesn't sound so strange. Good guys need guns, right, and while I don't agree that violent criminals should die, they should be locked up. Less criminals running around means less victims right?" I asked.

"What you just said was very political," said James with a knowing look on his face.

"That makes no sense. Good people need weapons to protect their family from bad guys," I shouted. I couldn't help but think of all of the times Superman's adoptive father Jonathan Kent had shot alien invaders on their farm with his old shotgun.

"Hey, you don't have to bark at me Oliver, I'm with you on that one. There are millions of Americans that feel the opposite though and think we should get rid of guns completely. There are people who daydream about storming into the homes of average Americans and ripping their guns out of their hands."

What James had just said appalled me at a primal level. There were people out there who wanted the good guys to have less ways to protect themselves? That's terrible... Disgusting...

"I can see your wheels spinning Oliver. Don't worry about it too much. It will never happen. The logistics of disarming over one hundred million Americans just isn't there. It would be impossible no matter how you spin it. Besides every cop and soldier in the country worth his salt would never follow a confiscation order."

That calmed me down a little bit, but still I couldn't help feeling a little unsettled.

"This is politics then? People trying to take other people's rights away and worrying about what gender you are? Isn't the penis or the vagina a dead giveaway? How did that even become a topic that regular people discussed?" I rapid fired these questions at James, aggravated at what I had learned.

"Welcome to politics Oliver. Now you see why most people either ignore politics completely or get utterly absorbed by them. To answer your question... there is some matter of debate behind it, but my personal theory is that when people have it too easy they will invent things to be upset about. People love to be the victim and/or the martyr. If they aren't part of a 'persecuted class' they will just invent one to be a part of," said James.

"Politics, huh?" asked Anthony.

"ANTHONY YOU'RE AWAKE!" I shouted as I spun around and ran

to his bedside. Anthony was sitting up on his hospital bed and wiping sleep out of his eyes. Before he could stop me I wrapped him up in a giant bear hug.

"Bifrost, get Astrid in here! Anthony is awake," said James. James reached over and clapped one of his large hands down onto Anthony's shoulder. "Welcome back brother," said James.

"So did it work?" I asked expectantly. Anthony's face shifted to a very wide grin.

"Hell yeah it worked," he said.

Astrid burst through the doors. I could tell she had ran the whole way here, but she made sure to hide her excitement to see Anthony with a very Astrid like comment.

"Oh, I see the Nubian finally decided to stop his laziness and actually get up for once."

"You know, if I had a bedpan I would throw it at you. Speaking of that I have to go make some stinky lemonade and then I want to show y'all something," said Anthony.

After Anthony relieved himself in the restroom attached to the med-bay he sat back down on his hospital bed.

"Uh, maybe you guys want to sit down as well?" he asked. We all indulged him and sat down next to him.

"Now what?" I asked.

"Just wait," he said. Seconds later the sliding metal door to the infirmary opened up and three training robots walked in. As before they were tan in color and very humanoid. Just about the exact shape and size of an average human, but with no defining features of any kind. Their faces were just a blank slate. I had never noticed it before but they kind of reminded me of a marionettes doll.

The three training droids all lined up in a row, and we all waited expectantly for something to happen. Soon we heard the speakers in the infirmary start to play static. The three droids in front of us cantered their body sideways towards us and tucked one of their arms close to their side, and took the other arm up near their heads as if they were holding an invisible hat. Then the music started... "HELLO MY BABY, HELLO MY HONEY, HELLO MY RAGTIME GAL. SEND ME A KISS BY WIRE, BABY MY HEART'S ON FIRE!" the speakers blared the song until it cut off and all of the droids in the room froze dramatically. They had been doing a very synchronized dance, kicking their legs high into the air. The dance was utterly familiar, but I just couldn't seem to remember where it was from.

We all exploded into applause.
"You know what this means right. Anthony can bring those tin

soldiers on missions with us as extra bodies," said James. Anthony seemed pensive for a moment before responding. "Not a good idea, too much proprietary technology. If I ever lost one in the field someone could end up copying the design and we might end up fighting hundreds of them the next time we went out. That doesn't mean I'm out of options though. I'm sure I could whip up some nasties on the 3D printers or better yet just outright buy a robot on the open market. There are some companies out there that are working on some amazing concepts. You should see these dogs that Boston Dynamics is working on."

Astrid looked over at us all with an aggravated glance and then smacked Anthony in the chest. "Enough talk, start the song and dance again!"

James Gatewood

I waited patiently for the sound of the buzzer. As soon as I heard that ever familiar *BIZZZZZZZ* sound I drew my Glock 17 from my retention holster. I spun around and fired 2 shots into each of the three targets in front of me. I dropped my magazine and quickly inserted a fresh one and fired two more shots into each of the targets. All of my hits had been relatively dead center and my groupings were beyond clean. All in a manner of seconds. This was a common drill used by competition shooters called the El Presidente. It's meant to test and improve a myriad of skills.

You start facing away from your targets. So being able to quickly acquire targets within milliseconds after the original spin is definitely an acquired skill, but a necessary one. Obviously staying on target and quickly transitioning between targets is a crucial skill in this drill as well. It's very easy to let the recoil of the gun rip your second shots off the target, but you can not let that happen. You have to drive the gun through the recoil and verify targets. Slow is steady, steady is fast. Lastly the mandatory reload before the second firing iteration is the final skill trained. Being a quick shooter is great, but it doesn't mean shit if you run out of bullets and can't get more into your weapon.

I had competed myself for a time, but then my dear son was born and my shooting competitions had gone on the back burner. My beautiful son, the light of my life, I can still see his cherubic face when I close my eyes. I remembered the feeling the first time I had held him and looked into his tiny eyes, pure bliss. I felt hot tears sliding down my face, now is not the time for that.

"Bifrost start the shot timer, 3-second delay, NOW!" I shouted before spinning around and getting back into position.

I left my hand slightly floating above the grip of my Glock 17 and dropped into a perfect focus… Except it wasn't perfect was it? I could feel the pain of the memories that my dead family had caused me. I could still feel the tears wet on my face. The unbridled rage for the man who had taken them from me was somewhere below all of that. The only reason I hadn't killed him yet was because he had a family of his own. How could I rob someone else of a family member. *BZZZZT.* I spun around at the familiar tone of the shot clock and went through the drill again. Only this time imagining the man's face on every target. I was crying harder now. I'm not even sure why. I tried to stop myself, but I just couldn't. I can still train though.

"Bifrost throw up more targets, a combination of stationary and moving" I said, trying to not let out an involuntary sob. The shooting range in front of me was quite the marvel. Steel plates on tracks all around the room popped up and fell over when I shot them. Other steel plates moved around on tracks, also falling over when they were hit. After a few seconds they would pop back up. I unleashed a truly insane volley of 9mm fire onto the range. Always ensuring a clean hit before pulling the trigger.

My tempo slowly increased while thoughts of my family flashed through my mind and even more tears slid down my face. I quickly reloaded as each magazine ran dry, and kept firing. Magazines and spent brass littered the floor around me as I continued my frenzy. I realized I was screaming, but at this point why stop?

A strong grip latched onto my shoulder from somewhere behind me. My instincts and years of training kicked in. I rammed my offhand elbow back as far as I could and made a quick spin while retaining my weapon close to my chest so it couldn't be grabbed by my attacker. When I completed my spin I realized I was pointing my weapon at Astrid. I quickly holstered my weapon and began an apology "Oh my god Astrid, I'm so ---" Astrid unleashed a savage headbutt hitting me right in the nose and pain shot through my skull.

"What the fuck Astrid?!" I shouted as I used one of my hands to pinch off the blood pouring out of my nostrils.

"You hit me first you dick," she shouted back at me.

"I was trying to apologize for that!"

"Don't bother apologizing James, you hit like a bitch anyway!"

Oh Astrid had such a way with words. I paced back and forth staring at her. She crossed her arms over her chest and stared right back.

"WHAT ARE YOU EVEN DOING HERE?!" I yelled.

"I'm looking for you. I saw you were training so I just watched you for awhile. You are quite good. You would be better if you weren't in here doing all that boohooing and crying like a woman." Her comment had made me see red. I was so angry I could barely speak. If she was a man I would have beaten her senseless over a comment like that.

"YOU HAVE NO IDEA WHAT YOU ARE TALKING ABOUT!" was the only thing I could yell back at her. I had given up on trying to hold my nose closed, the blood was leaking into my short beard now. I could tell Astrid was as mad as me, over my last comment from the look on her face, but I wasn't sure what right she had to be angry.

"Oh, I don't know how it feels to lose a family. Do you see my family here James? You selfish, self-absorbed, jerk of a man. You are so in love with your own sob story that you don't even look at me as a woman, I'm a cardboard cutout to you. You don't see me! You aren't the only person going through something. Do you think I wanted to be ripped away from my family and trapped in a lamp for 1200 years? You don't get to have a monopoly on grief you asshole!"

She was completely right. I had been ignorantly selfish. Astrid was just as alone as I was, at least Anthony and Oliver had friends and family out there. I had been drinking myself to death for so many years that I had completely alienated everyone who had ever cared about me, and Astrid's family had been dead for centuries. Great, now I'm sad and an asshole, a selfish asshole at that. I reached out and touched one of her forearms on instinct not even really realizing I was doing it, it just felt right.

"You know, you are right. I'm sorry Astrid. It's just..."

"I know James, you don't have to tell me," she said as she put one of her hands over my mouth.

She leaned forward, slid her hand away from my mouth, and gently kissed me. I froze completely, I couldn't move. I hadn't kissed a woman who wasn't my wife since grade school. Part of me wanted to shove Astrid away in revulsion. The other part of me wanted to embrace her and feel something good for once. Astrid started gently placing kisses all over my face as she slowly embraced me. I was finally able to break out of her spell slightly. I slowly whispered "Astrid wait, my wife..." they were the only words I could choke out.

"Your wife is in heaven with my family James, and she would want you to be happy." It was all I needed to hear. A weight had

been lifted from my soul and I let out a surreal quiet laugh.
"You know Astrid, you are much smarter than me." I felt her
hands slide below my shirt. Her touch was like a spiritual sponge,
it was sucking the sadness right out of my soul. She slipped my
shirt over my head. I grabbed her like a man should grab a
woman and began kissing her earnestly.

She pulled away from me "Now you see me like a woman."

Oliver Pettini

It had been a long week of training, relaxing, and exciting
events. James and Astrid had been in an especially festive mood.
They must have been extra happy about the success of our first
official mission, that must be it. I myself had been in a
particularly amazing mood about the events of the mission as
well. I was pretty upset with myself at first over my outburst, but
everyone makes mistakes, and it was just my first mission after
all. We have to make mistakes to learn. We have to fall down so
we can get back up again. Of course I know I would do better
next time. I had marked my shortcomings and I would get the
better of them.

Gul had been the curse that had turned into a blessing. At first I really had not wanted her on Valhalla with us. I didn't want a reminder of that night. She had been slowly turning into something else as I accepted what I had done to her attacker, the purposeful harm I had caused him. She was a walking reminder that I had saved her and her other schoolmates. She was a walking reminder that I was a hero, not just someone dressed up and playing pretend. I'm the real deal.

Speaking of me being the real deal. It's past time for me to take charge of this team completely. I had been letting James take the lead far too often. He had been clear with me that he didn't want to be a leader, and that this was my team, and that I had to step up. He was right. I knew it as well, even without his prompting. The phrase 'I was born for this' comes to mind, but that's not true. I'm better than someone who was born for this job. I had grabbed destiny by the horns and yelled in its face that it was time to follow my orders, and lady destiny had heeded my call and then some. I made the wishes on the lamp. I assembled the team. I saved Gul. I was the leader.

Leaders lead, which is why I had called a meeting. It was time for another mission. There was lots of options. Should we stop a crime in progress? Should we disable some more terrorists?

Maybe provide disaster relief? Put out some forest fires? Rescue a cat from a tree? I wasn't really sure. One thing I did know was that I was curious about Mr. Smith. The man who had given me the lamp. Who was he, and why had he given me this amazing gift? We had avoided investigating him before because of the shadowy organization that had tried to capture me and my parents, but that was a lifetime ago to me now. Surely by now they would have lost interest or realized we were long gone. It's not like they were going to find us up here in space, and James had blown my house up ensuring there was zero evidence of us left.

No, it was time to get to the bottom of that mystery. Bifrost had found Mr. Smith's primary address quickly. Something about it told me it would be dangerous. This wasn't just a fly down and look around type of jaunt, this would be a real mission. I needed my team with me, and we had to be ready. Which is why I sat here now on the edge of our little lake, on top of the fake sand. I was waiting for everyone to arrive, and I mean everyone.

Gul sat next to me, she couldn't decide whether to stare at me or the water, but I didn't pressure her in either direction. I knew something profoundly terrible had happened to her, something that I could never understand. I was just going to let her heal in her own way. I took away any physical pain that she might have that first night that we brought her back, but that didn't mean there still wasn't other kind of pains that a survivor might face. I had been reading a lot about victimology in between James' other required reading. Astrid never showed any outward signs of distress, but that didn't mean much.

There was however a certain kind of person that I had been reading about. There is a kind of person who can go through something devastating and come out better. I had been reading about these people this whole week between my other readings. Some of the more pertinent examples I had seen were companies of soldiers that would go to war. Over 200 men and women would head out into battle. Sometimes 50% of them or more would come back with mental instability of some type after their trials, but the other half came back different, better, stronger than before. Part of me secretly wished every day that Gul was one of those people. Lots of people theorized on why this happened and no one could quite figure out. There were many proverbs on the subject, one of which I particularly liked, *It takes pressure to make a diamond.*

One author in particular mused on this topic more than others. A retired Lt. Colonel and renowned psychologist named

David Grossman. He speculated that there was three kinds of people out in the world: sheep, wolves, and sheepdogs. Sheep obviously being the most common variant, these were the normal people who just lived their lives and didn't worry about the predators, they lived in ignorant bliss and scoffed at sheepdogs and wolves alike.

Then there were the wolves, the predators. These were the people who saw the sheep and only thought of them as food and weakness. They are more than willing to hurt anyone that gets in their way, and they take anything they want. To them the sheep mean nothing.

Finally the last type of person, the best type in my opinion, but I would keep that opinion to myself. The sheepdogs, kings of the human race, those willing to stand up and fight injustice when no one else would. Sometimes even having to fight injustice when no one wanted them to. Sheepdogs live among the sheep, and the sheep become so comfortable with them that sometimes they even forget that they are their protectors or they take them for granted.

Sometimes the sheep even go out of the way to make the sheepdogs feel like outcasts. One common denominator always arises though. When the sheep are in trouble they call to the sheepdogs of the world, and the sheepdogs come. They always do, they always hold the line against the wolves of the world. I was a sheepdog, I knew that. Even when I was too dumb to grasp an intricate theory like that I somehow still knew I was a sheepdog. If I could comprehend an injustice I would fight it.

I had watched superhero media my whole life, begging my stupid brain to work better so I could be more like those heroes. I was a sheepdog through and through. I just hoped Gul was too. As to my team there was no question what type of people they were. They had rushed headlong into the danger of our last mission with me. I had surrounded myself with such good people...

One last thought struck me as I stared out at the water of our small little pond. I couldn't remember where I had read it because I had been skimming so many books on the subject, but one subject expert had said that mentally there was no difference between killers and police officers. The same parts of their brains released chemicals and became active when they got into the thrill of things.

The killers obviously when hurting people became excited. The police officers, and other first responders as well became excited when things got interesting on their end of it. If you were to compare brain scans between those two groups of people they would look utterly similar. There was lots of other evidence linking the two groups of people even further. There was just something, some small part of their life that had led them down one path or the other. To be honest, I didn't like that theory. I was the good guy and I knew that, it seemed so cut and dry. Thinking about it further made me come to a terrible conclusion. Everyone is the good guy in their own story. Knowing this, I would be careful with myself and my team. We wielded great power now, and with great power comes great responsibility.

"You have good brain, and good thoughts, can tell." I looked over at Gul, I had been so deep in thought I had forgotten she was there for a minute. At some point she had scooted much closer to me and our hips were touching. It was a little too close for comfort and felt just a little too intimate for me. I wanted to tell her that my brain hadn't always been good, but I also didn't want to break the confidence of my team. I had made a promise to them that we wouldn't let anyone else into the inner fold. Maybe in time we could tell Gul the whole story.
"Hey Gul, do you think you could scoot over a bit?" I asked as gently as possible.
"No" she responded to me simply with a smile. *Well that didn't work.*

Chapter 16

We sat quietly for a bit longer until people started to dribble in. Gul was continually sneaking glances at me. Once everyone had arrived (including my parents) we all walked back up to the couches we had moved out here for movie night. We liked the couches by the lake idea so much we just intended on leaving them there forever. I stood while my friends sat. I was trying to think of the best way to introduce the next mission. Honestly I had thought James would have presented me with a viable option for a mission by now, but he had seemed strangely preoccupied with his new found happiness, and I didn't want to ruin that.

"Okay everyone, we had a very successful mission last week. Surprisingly so. I am so proud of everyone and of what we did. I think you all mirror my sentiment." I looked around at my assorted friends and family and I could tell they all did. My mom smiled proudly up at me.

Anthony shouted "HERE HERE!" I moved on wanting to stay on topic while it was still fresh in my head.

"I propose that we keep this momentum up and go on our next mission. I want to investigate the origin of the lamp, learn more about it. We only have one real lead on that front and that's the old man that ran into me in the grocery store and gave it to me. I propose we check out his house. Since this mysterious organization that found me so quickly at my house exists, they may or may not be waiting for us at the old man's house, or they may have moved on by now. We really can't be sure of their capabilities or where they will pop up until we get more information on them. So we have to proceed carefully. Which is why I am calling this excursion officially a mission. Is everyone okay with this course of action?"

Everyone present nodded their heads or didn't speak up assuring me they agreed with the path.
"Okay moving on. James, how goes things with the lawyers?"
"Beyond great, they say the first of our payments will arrive any day now and we will be basically swimming in money for awhile now as the payments continue to roll in. They also said all of the scientific firms we worked with are more than willing to throw handfuls of cash at us for more information on our technology," James finished.

James was referencing the myriad of scientists representing organizations all over the world that we had been shuttling up to Valhalla off and on throughout the week to show off our gravity manipulation technology. The lawyers we had hired were making the scientific firms sign so many non-disclosure agreements that if any of them spilled the beans we would basically own their company. We hadn't let any of them get farther than the landing bay, but that had been more than enough to prove that gravity manipulation was possible and not a scientific dead end. We hadn't allowed any cameras or recording devices of any kind and we had thoroughly searched each scientist before allowing them near one of the shuttles.

Oh and the shuttles... We had people offering us billions to look under the hoods of our shuttles. Maybe someday we could do something like that, but it would have to be after a very thorough vetting process. We had lots of other options on how to make money, but our lawyers were suggesting that we get registered as a nonprofit organization as soon as possible. It would give us a serious foot in the door for legitimacy and we could pay less taxes, which James had assured me was a very good thing.

"Perfect James, that all sounds perfect. Anthony how are things going on your front?" I asked

"I spent the rest of my savings and all of my cryptocurrency buying two prototypes from Boston Dynamics. I can go pick them up tomorrow after I sign about 10-million forms. Also I finished two prototype 'power machines' if we all want to head to the 3D printer lab and check them out."

✳✳✳

When we walked into the 3D printer lab I saw something I really wasn't expecting. In the middle of the floor was a large transparent fronted cylinder that was slightly leaned backwards at a gentle angle. There was two white steps marching into it. All around it and behind it were wires crisscrossing in all directions. There was differently sized transparent pipes running in all directions in and out of the... unit. The top of it had a small lip that crested over the cylinder's edge, and I could see many different spouts inside of the cylinder coming down from the roof of it aiming inward. Connected to the side of it was a small screen with lots of official looking menus on it. The backside of the cylinder that wasn't transparent had a panel sticking off the side so it would be visible from the front. The panel was covered in different miniature screens and lights blinking in different colors. There were many different readouts as well on the side panel. Some were basic readouts, things like temperature were listed, as well as energy consumption, etc. Then there was more complex readouts like 'quantum entanglement production,' and 'genetic malfeasance regulation' both of them were currently

303

reading at nominal. This was a serious looking machine. It would be the perfect decoy.

"Holy wow Anthony, you have really outdone yourself. What happens if someone gets inside?" I asked.

"I'll show you! Astrid would you please enter the machine," he asked, while unsealing some type of clasp from the side and opening the front of the cylinder.

"Me?" asked Astrid.

"Yes please," said Anthony while beckoning her forward with one hand.

She shrugged her shoulders and bravely marched forward and entered the machine. Anthony reached inside and pulled a small metal cord from somewhere that went over Astrid's chest and both of her arms right about at elbow height.
"Trust me, it's for your safety during the procedure," he said very official sounding with a wink to all of us. He closed the transparent half cylinder door and sealed it somehow.

"Initiating commencement sequence!" he shouted and began pushing random buttons on the machine and pulling random pump levers that I hadn't noticed before.

The machine started making an obnoxiously loud noise and all off the transparent tubes began filling with different colored fluids. Deep gurgling noises were coming out of the machine at all angles. Astrid started to look very nervous.

"It's getting pretty cold in here!" Astrid shouted from behind the transparent door.

"I assure you that is perfectly normal!" Anthony shouted back.

Then all of a sudden all of the pipes emptied themselves through the different spouts at the top of the unit spraying Astrid from different directions. Astrid struggled to get loose from under the metal cable but at some point it had tightened itself. The different colored liquids from the different spouts continued to spray Astrid. All of the readouts all over the machine were broadcasting readings off the charts. Anthony typed out amazingly complicated looking sequences on the small touchscreen connected to the unit then it all abruptly stopped. A soothing voice came from somewhere inside the unit.

"Procedure complete, Procedure complete. Please remove occupant."

Anthony unclasped the metal door and the metal cable around Astrid unlatched itself somehow and sucked itself back into the back wall of the machine. Astrid walked out drenched. "What the hell was that Anthony!?" she yelled.

"Complete honesty. It was hot Mountain Dew," Anthony choked out before laughing so hard he almost fell over. I interrupted his laugh fest once I thought I understood what had happened.

"Anthony, are you telling me all that machine does is spray people with heated soda?" I asked.

"Yeah basically," he said in between bouts of laughter. Everyone else in the room began to laugh as well.

"So what was all that typing you were doing?" my dad asked Anthony.

"It was nothing, I was just trying to make it look official. We can do the same thing when we upgrade noobies or heal someone from now on," Anthony replied.

Okay that is funny, I had to admit it, and Astrid deserved it for her constant berating of Anthony.
"Really you have outdone yourself here Anthony, this thing looks amazing. We should install a few of these in the landing bay maybe," I said. Astrid was behind me ringing colored soda out of her hair still.

"Payback is going to be a royal bitch Anthony, I hope you know that," said Astrid.

"Oh, it was so worth it though," replied Anthony.

James chimed in "We should bring some rich yuppies up here soon and cure them of diabetes or something. I just want to see more people get sprayed with hot soda now," he choked out before laughing. Astrid made sure to punch James in the arm.

"HEY, don't get soda on me woman!" he shouted jokingly at her. So she grabbed him up in a big hug liberally coating him in the stuff by contact.

"Wow, those two are getting close," I remarked to Anthony.

"Wait, you didn't figure it out yet?" he said quietly to me.

"Figure what out?"

"Those two are doing the bologna pony."

"The what?"

"The horizontal hustle. You know, cowboys and Indians."

"Hmm?"

"They are playing hide the weasel, bumping uglies, threading the needle, opening the gates of Mordor, foxtrot uniform charlie kilo..." Anthony continued to list weird things while I shook my head in the negative.

Finally he got exasperated and blurted out what he had been trying to tell me. "THEY ARE HAVING SEX OLIVER!"

He had said it just a bit too loud because everyone in the room was staring at me now. I felt my cheeks redden a bit and I wasn't quite sure what to say.

"Oh... well congrats you two. Uhhh, Anthony, want to show me the field unit you worked up?" I choked out to try to change the subject.

Anthony walked over to one of the many desks in the room and grabbed up a very high tech looking blue gun with a traditional medic cross emblazoned on it. The front of it was flat with two metal surfaces running across it. He gently grabbed my arm and touched it to my forearm and pulled the trigger. I felt a small jolt and a hiss came out of both sides of the gun where ports had opened and released some kind of visible gas. "What was that noise and gas?" I asked.

"CO_2, it's got a few micro-canisters in the bottom of it, it's good for about 50 charges. The metal surface lets out an extremely low electrical current. That battery should last years. You do your magic thing and use your power while touching this gun to the injured and they will think the gun did all the work."

"That's great man, this will work perfectly! Last thing, the old uniforms we have aren't going to work, they look too... menacing. Can we get an all white version made please?"

"Yeah no problem. I have all the schematics saved on the printers so that is basically busy body work at this point. If you could leave an extra pair of hands with me I could finish it in no time."

"I'll help!" my mother said.

"Me too," said Gul.

"I've got some gifts for everyone," my father said from the back of the room. He had been leaning on the back wall watching the madness until now. He walked forward to stand in front of all of us and unslung a single strap backpack he had been wearing. He reached inside and pulled out what looked like our throat microphones from our last mission.

"I modified these to make them more secure, and I added a new feature: exterior broadcast," He said as he pulled out a copy of the little speaker we had been using to broadcast our translated message to the schoolgirls on the last mission. "You see you press this button here and your voice will come out of this speaker in a distorted fashion. That way you don't have to pull your helmets off to talk to the people you are helping, and the modulator will keep you all more anonymous."

"Mr. Pettini, you are the man! This is great," said Anthony

"Please call me Nick," said my father.

I stepped forward once more. "Okay so Anthony picks up his mechanical minions tomorrow and we have a lot of money coming in that we will have to manage. Why don't we plan on going on the mission three days from now. That should give us enough time to train a bit, build the new white version of the armor, and run some M.O.U.T. exercises. In the meantime, who is up for a movie night by the pond?"

Gul (The next day, 1 p.m. central US time)

"Oh, you are such a nice young woman Gul," Oliver's mother squeezed me into one of her warm hugs. I was trying to help her clean up the dishes, but really this felt like an interrogation with how many questions she was asking me. I was after all her son's first lady friend. I had gotten that much information out of her, so it didn't surprise me that she was inquisitive. I knew that in western culture that it was normal for men to 'date' a few women before marrying. Which is why it was so strange to me that Oliver hadn't had any lady friends before me. He was tall, handsome, brave, he owned a large domicile, this space station of course. He seemed like he would be a natural choice for the affection of women.

I guess in the end the ultimate reason why he hadn't had relationships didn't matter to me, we all had our histories. The future was what interested me now, my future with Oliver. Me and Mrs. Pettini finished up the dishes and moved to putting the remaining food into freezer bags. Oh freezer bags, what a wonderful invention, we didn't have such niceties in my village. We had been eating something so wonderful. Oliver's family called them 'BLT's' apparently that stood for bacon, lettuce, and tomato. His family would toast some bread, and put something called 'miracle whip' on it which was a tasty white substance, before finally putting in the three ingredients. It was truly a wonderful dish. I was putting all of the remaining bacon in a bag and couldn't help eating one more piece. I groaned out loud because it was so good. Bacon was something I wouldn't get used to any time soon.

Mrs. Pettini cleared her throat to get my attention "Gul honey, I've been meaning to ask you why you eat bacon."

"Tastes good!" I said simply, my smile so big I could feel it stretching the corners of my face.

"Yes honey, I know it tastes good. It is pork though, I thought Muslims couldn't eat pork."

How could I answer her in a way she would understand. I wanted to impress her if she was going to be my mother in law, yet I also wanted to be honest with her. I had such a poor grasp on English it was hard to properly clarify what I meant sometimes.

"Muslim… Islam…. I not this thing. This thing… Islam. All it bring is pain. I was Islam… No longer." I emphasized my point by taking another bite of bacon. This time though I could barely taste it. All

I could think about was the pain brought upon me in my short life by men who had sworn to be following the will of Allah.

"I can't say I understand what you are going through right now Gul, but I can tell you that I support you and whatever choices you make," said Mrs. Pettini. She always said the nicest things to me. That was support I would have never gotten in Pakistan. I wasn't allowed to have my own choices there. I followed the will of my father, and the will of Allah, in that order. To do otherwise would have meant beatings and/or death. It was my time to hug Mrs. Pettini now after her last comment. She probably said things like that all the time to people, but to me comments like that meant the world. I tried to remember everything I had learned about English over the last week to make this as coherent as possible.
"You are nice, Mrs. Pettini," I said before giving her a hug.
"Please call me Martha," she whispered into my ear.

We finished up in the kitchen and headed back out to the lunch table. Oliver and his father were busy talking about something or other. It had been a quiet lunch. Anthony and James had taken a shuttle down to earth to pick up some kind of mechanical dogs, and Astrid was off training. I didn't want to be rude, but I had a narrow time frame if I wanted to complete my own mission.

I stood up "Thank you all, nice lunch. Must see Astrid, she get me clothes." The occupants of the table looked a little surprised, but politely nodded in encouragement. Yet another thing that would have resulted in an extreme beating in my country, but was casual here.

Once I left the cafeteria area, I quickly asked the ghost lady who lived in the walls where Astrid was. The nice ghost lady lit some green lights on the floor for me that took me right to her. Astrid was in the room that made things heavier. She looked surprised to see me. I would have to use my own language to explain to her why I needed her help if I was going to get her to help me in time enough to get back before James did. I had a feeling the ghost who lived in the walls only halfway trusted me, and I had a different feeling that the ghost was telling the big scary man James where I was. That's why I had to do this now while James was gone.

"Astrid I need your help. I need to kill some very evil men. I can't do it alone, and I need a ride." My whole plan hinged on Astrid's cooperation. If she shot me down here and now my sister's soul would never be able to rest. I felt heat build in my chest and worry wash over my face. I stared at the ground. I felt Astrid's hand below my chin, she pushed my face up so we were looking at each other.

"Can we get it done in three hours or less? Me and James have dinner plans this evening." I wasn't sure what to say, I was so excited that she had agreed.

I stuttered out "Well… yes." Astrid dropped my chin and then slapped me on the butt very hard and walked out of the room.

She yelled over her shoulder "Move it sweet tits, we are on a tight schedule!"

Oliver Pettini

Well here goes nothing "ARHHHH," I grunted out as I pushed up the weight. The weights I was bench pressing, 275 pounds worth, went up off the retainer pegs and down to tap my chest. I swiftly returned the bar to its rest. I was surprised at how easily I had completed the maneuver. Not to say that it was easy, just easier than I thought it would be. I was so motivated by my progress that I did it nine more times for a clean set of ten. My brow leaked sweat, but it felt great. I stood up and stared at myself in the mirror. The way my physique was rapidly changing never failed to impress me. I could barely recognize myself most days. I would have to go clothes shopping again soon. All of my current ones were basically skin tight again over my bulging muscles. Talk about the definition of a 'good problem.'

"Oliver."

I quickly dropped the flex I was holding in the mirror when I heard the female voice, then I realized who it was and felt silly. "Yes Bifrost?"

"Astrid and Gul are taking a shuttle and leaving Valhalla right now. Should I stop them?"

"No, they are free to leave. Thank you Bifrost."

"Would you like to know their heading Oliver?"

"No Bifrost, I trust them."

Time for legs!

Astrid

As I flew the shuttle down to Gul's little shithole of a village I couldn't help but be proud of her gumption. Righteous revenge, honestly didn't think she had it in her. Either way I could tell she was in love with Oliver, or she thought she was at least. If this was something she needed to do to get her mind right then I would happily help her. I couldn't have Oliver following around this little pup playing wet nurse for the rest of his days. I was starting to like this hero stuff and I didn't want anything to get in

315

the way of us performing more missions. The last one had been exhilarating. I was still trying to wrap my mind around the whole 'superhero' concept. We didn't have anything like it back in my day. I guess some of our tales of wandering gods were close, but half of those ended in misery. The thought of having guardians, mortal guardians, that could descend from the heavens at any time to destroy evil was amazing. I was honored to even strive towards the concept.

James... My honorable James... He had always been a superhero, even if he wouldn't admit it. James had made me understand why I had been trapped in the lamp, it was to find him. I had never really bought into the idea of fate before now, but I couldn't argue with whatever divinity that had blessed the world with James. I could still sense the sadness in his soul from the loss of his family. If I could trade my life for theirs I would. Since I couldn't do that for him I would give him the next best thing, a new family. James' last wife must have been pretty amazing to land someone like him.

James was the type of person who had seen the worst the world had to offer. Others in his situation would have ended their own life. That was even common back in my day. It wasn't unheard of for the village widow to walk out into the ocean and not come back. James had too much strength for that though, too much inner light. Some men are a shield to the world, ready to defend. James was a scalpel ready to surgically remove the cancer. I preferred the scalpel. Before I recognized James for what he was I was beginning to lose hope for this time period. I had been going over media and news sources from this century trying to get more acclimated, and I had ran across a disturbing term 'toxic masculinity.' Apparently some people despised men who were too manly in this time frame... They prized weaker men who were more androgynous, though I didn't really understand why. Odin forbid a man act and look like a man.

James was so tough and manly that he would give men from my time period a run for their money. I could easily see James leading a berserker charge. Not to say everything about this time period is bad. Life expectancies are much higher, though why you would want to live as a dried up prune for so long was beyond me. Modern doctors were basically miracle workers as far as I was concerned. The music was much better, the food was better, if James was any indication, the sex was absolutely better. Oh and sweet dentistry. I hadn't needed any yet, but I had looked into it enough to realize that dentistry in this time period was absolutely the best thing about it. Where I come from dentistry involved a lot of sacrificing chickens, dull rocks, and alcohol. To learn that modern dentistry procedures were about 90% pain free and only lasted 20 minutes had sent a flutter of happiness through my heart.

"Okay baby doll, we are going to be there in less than five minutes. Tell me who we are going to kill and why. Make it short, we don't have a lot of time." I hated speaking Gul's native mud language, it was guttural, and nasty. It had no... finesse, she better hurry it up with her English studies.

With determination in her eyes she responded. "We go to kill the Sharia police that whipped my sister for being raped, and lastly we kill her rapist."

"Wait, are you telling me someone punished your sister for being raped?"

"Yes, it's not as uncommon as you might think in this part of the world."

"So how did your sister die?"

"She took her own life in shame after the whippings and her rape."

"Let's kill these fucks."

We parked the shuttle right in the middle of the town square, it was in stealth mode so it was probably pretty quiet. 'Town' was probably too strong of a word for the assembled mud huts, but it would serve its purpose for now. It was about 10:30 p.m. local time and everyone had just bedded town. I was wearing my new white version of our armor, I went to put on my helmet on to complete the ensemble, but Gul stopped me.

"They should know it's women besting them." I shrugged and threw my helmet back into the shuttle. I also had on one of James' fancy pants handguns just in case. For tonight's work I would be using my weapons, my sword and dagger straight from 800 A.D. I had taken the set from a man I had killed in battle. Upon returning home from battle, the blind shaman in my village had blessed the set of weapons in the name of Odin the All Father. They would taste blood tonight for the first time in over one-thousand years. Lastly I carried the modern kevlar lined shield that Anthony had made for me. The Nubian was growing on me.

Gul was just finishing zipping up the last of her armor. She was wearing my night infiltration set that was a brown tone in color. The same one I had worn to save her in fact. She had also left her helmet inside the shuttle. I didn't trust her with a gun so I had given her a crossbow I found in the armory and 10 bolts. It must have been one of the weapons brought in from James' house. That man sure did love to collect weapons. I also let her keep my stun baton in her belt rung, but hopefully she wouldn't have to resort to using that.

"So how do we find these maggots?" I asked.

"This is a small village, we can just walk to them. Most of them are related and live in the same home. They are the sons of the Imam. The Imam himself was the one who passed down the final sentence for my sister to be publicly whipped, whilst she was still healing from her rape..."

"Well let's go then."

We walked a short distance through the quiet little town. There wasn't a soul in sight. Most of the people here were grain farmers which meant if they got up early they could enjoy the relative cool of the morning while they worked their fields, which also meant early bedtimes and heavy sleepers. We finally came to a large mud home which doubled as the local mosque. The front door was comprised of some surprisingly strong wood of an origin that I didn't recognize. I remembered James telling me that some of the most evil men in this region hid or lived in mosques as a way to escape the authorities. They had some kind of war laws that the Army James had fought in had to follow. One of those laws was that they couldn't attack Mosques. The evil men knew this which was why they so often hid inside of them.

"Should we find a window to get inside" Gul asked in her stinky mud language.

"Naw, before you joined us we were strengthening our bodies for weeks. We were upgrading them too, the same way you speak English."

"Oliver's Magic?"

"It's not like that, well maybe it is like that, and you really aren't supposed to know about it. That is all besides the point anyway. I'll show you the point I'm trying to make."

I reared back and kicked the door directly where I figured it was locked from the other side at. The harsh wood door flew into the dark house, splinters from the door skittered along the floor. I flipped a toggle on the inside of my shield and a ring of built in lights on the front side of it illuminated our way, *Thanks Anthony*. Harsh male voices started shouting from somewhere in the back of the building. I held my shield up higher and saw we were in a large room. This must have be where they hold religious services with the bedrooms being in the back. I looked back at Gul, she had the crossbow held up high and her arms were shaking.

"Hey Gul, whatever you do, don't shoot me with that thing." She nodded, but I couldn't really tell if she was on automatic mode or not.

The first one came around the corner, a bearded man in his 20's. He was wearing the traditional garb of the region. He stopped dead in his tracks because he was so confused

"Is this one of them?" I asked Gul as I moved forward to strike him.

"WAIT!" she shouted "Tell him to call for his brothers and father."

I looked over at the man "You heard her, call for your family."

He squinted at the bright light of my shield and tried to look at Gul behind me.

"Gul, is that you? What are you doing here? Who is this infidel with you?"

"Hey pal, call out for your family before I hurt you." I tried to sound menacing to get the message across, but this dude was in full zealot mode.

"You do not speak to me like that woman, this is a house of God. You are an infidel, you are unclean!"

I don't know why he did it, maybe he couldn't see my weapons because of the bright light my shield was putting off, but he decided to rush me. I raised my sword to strike him, but a bolt flew by me and landed in his kidney region. His walking momentum slowed and the look on his face told me the pain was setting in. He reached down and felt the bolt sticking out of

322

his stomach. I could tell he was going into shock, if we wanted him to cooperate we would have to be quick. I put one hand on his shoulder and pushed him over. He went over gasping in pain while holding onto the bolt in his side. Gul stepped forward and stood over him.

"That was for my sister!" shouted Gul.

"Your sister? The whore?" the man was able to gasp out.

I didn't want Gul to have to waste any bolts so I cut the man down after hearing that comment. What kind of asshole calls a rape victim a whore? These people deserved to die, I was glad Gul had brought me. Now that I was sure my mission here was righteous and blessed by the gods of old I would show these weaklings the true power of a disciple of Odin. These heathens would hear the cry of a real shield maiden! I felt something come over me, something I hadn't felt in over 1000 years. The thrill of real battle. I slammed my sword into my shield and let out a shriek that couldn't be confused with anything else besides a war cry. I looked over at Gul, she looked scared.

"Do not be scared sister, let the cowards know we are coming. Our cause is just, they will feel fear."

Since coming out of the lamp I had felt so detached when it had come to violence. Even being shot in the stomach in Oliver's living room, and helping Oliver detain the men who had kidnapped Gul and her schoolmates hadn't riled my ancient soul like this. Tonight though, tonight something primordial had come over me, this surely must be the will of the gods. I reached down and dipped my hand into the slain coward's blood. I smeared lines of it across my face under each of my eyes. I marched into the dark hallway in front of me still hearing the angry voices ahead. I let out another war cry and happily proceeded.

Chapter 17

Gul

I watched something in Astrid snap. I had seen this behavior in the men of my town, right before they decided to hurt a woman. The same sinister look that had washed over them was washing over Astrid's face now. It was surreal seeing that look on a woman. Some kind of mix of hatred and anger. In that moment I was very glad Astrid was on my side. She stormed off down the dark hallway in front of me. I heard a sick wet noise and a thud, I had to assume Astrid had just killed another one of the Imam's sons.

"WAIT ASTRID, LEAVE THE OLD MAN FOR ME!" Once I hooked the corner into the dark hallway I could see a bright light coming out of one of the rooms, Astrid's shield. She stormed back out into the hallway.

"Quickly now! One just jumped out of a window and got away. Find the old man!" She stormed into another bedroom and I went into the next one in line. He was in this room, laying in his bed, hiding slightly under his wife. Astrid came in behind me and saw the situation, but paused.

"Do what you have to do," she told me.

"Stop hiding behind your wife, coward!" I shouted at the Imam. A spark of recognition lit his eyes.

"Gul?" he whispered.

"Yes it is me. I'm here to get revenge for my sister."

"Your sister took her own life!"

"AFTER YOU HAD HER WHIPPED AND SHAMED IN PUBLIC, YOU DEMON! SHE WAS ALREADY IN SO MUCH PAIN AND YOU PUSHED HER OVER THE EDGE."

"It was the will of Allah. Do what you will to me, but know when I die I go to heaven. Unlike your whore of a sister who surely burns in hell."

"Let's test that theory, kill him Gul," said Astrid. I aimed my crossbow at the Imam and in a last second move of cowardice the Imam pulled his wife in front of himself. Astrid saw what he was trying to do, so she grabbed his wife by her ankles and started pulling. As soon as he was exposed I loosed a bolt directly into his chest. He spit blood up and locked his eyes onto mine. It was only a matter of time until he left this world, I hoped it really hurt. He tried to talk, but instead of words, only more blood came out of his mouth.

I leaned next to his ear and whispered quietly "You are a demon. Good men do not punish victims of rape. You will never go to heaven. You should be very afraid right now." I thought of walking away, but I decided to lay a little insult to injury and kicked him in the genitals. He got the same amount of compassion he gave my sister, none.

"We need to catch the one that got away!" screamed Astrid.

"He probably went to get help, meaning more men will be coming here to try and kill us." I said.

"Good."

"No, not good. I don't care if he dies or not, his whole family is dead. That is punishment enough. We need to kill the man who raped my sister so her soul can rest."

"Lead the way."

I took a second to put a new bolt in the crossbow and then picked up a light jog. The Imam's son would surely spread news of the infidels attacking his family. Men would come from all over to kill us, maybe even my father. While I didn't love my father, I didn't exactly want Astrid to kill him either. I needed to find my sister's rapist and get out of here. I knew about where his house was. He was a married man named Hamid. I knew he had two small children, a boy and a girl. I don't know why he raped my sister when he had his own wife to rape, but he had and he would pay.

As soon as I ran outside I heard gunfire and I jumped back in the door where I had just run out of. My back smacked Astrid's chest and I slid to the floor. She might as well have been a brick wall.

Astrid shouted "GAH! I hate having to use this thing!" as she sheathed her sword and unholstered the pistol on the back of her belt. She then leaned out the door and let off a volley of fire.

"Okay the cowards among them just ran, let's see if they are really stupid shall we?"

Astrid leaned out of the door one more time with her shield in front of her face and yelled "OH NO, I HAVE RUN OUT OF AMMO!" She then reholstered her pistol and pulled out her sword again. I knew she had more ammo, what was this woman up to?

Astrid looked at me with a wicked smile and wild eyes. "When they get close enough I will rush them. At that point you start making your way to the rapist's house. The light from my shield should draw their fire to me. After I defeat them I will catch up to you. Try to stay within sight of me, and also out of their line of fire."

"Rush them? Are you kidding me! How many of them are even out there?" I asked.

She peeked her head out the door for just a second and then threw her shield over her face and scooted back as a barrage of fire peppered the position she had just been in.

"Looks to be about five or six, hard to tell. As soon as they get a little closer we move." *WHAT!* I think I was starting to hyperventilate, everything was happening a little to fast.

"Astrid maybe running towards men with guns is a bad idea," I choked out.

"WHY ARE YOU HERE?" she yelled back in my face.

"To get revenge for my sister."

"THEN STOP BEING A COWARD AND DO IT!"

At that she turned towards the door raised the shield up near her face putting the ledge just below her eyes. She smacked her sword on her shield three times each time yelling "AH! AH! AH!" and then she ran. She ran faster than anyone I had ever seen run before. I had just enough time to snatch up my crossbow and jet out of the door. I watched in a trance as Astrid ran at the loose clump of men that were only 100 feet or so away from us now. Bullets tore into her shield and I watched as chunks of white polymer flew high into the air. There was a small farming truck slightly off to the side of the dirt road she was running on. Astrid somehow put one foot on the truck's fender and kicked off. She did a full spin in the air, somehow keeping her shield in front of her. She landed cleanly with no loss of momentum and kept running forward. She yelled "ODIN, ODIN!" a second before barreling into the group of men. My visibility was low, Astrid was kicking up all kinds of dust and the light from her shield was flying everywhere because she was moving so fast. I saw her sword flash through the light a few times and I heard the screams of the men.

As soon as she dispatched the last man, she spun on me. Astrid looked at me with eyes full of pure anger. She sheathed her sword and drew her dagger. She then threw it directly at me. I froze knowing this was the moment I would die and snapped my eyes closed. I felt a displacement of air near my cheek and my eyes snapped back open. I spun around and saw a man with Astrid's dagger planted in his chest. Astrid ran by me and smacked me in the forehead with the flat of her hand.

"PAY ATTENTION GIRL!" she shouted at me before roughly ripping the dagger out of the man's chest. "Let's go, lead the way!" she screamed. I started heading towards the rapist's house again, but not before looking down at the man who had been sneaking up on me. It was Farmer Fahad. I wonder what he had been planning on doing to me... I knew he had beat his wife, I had seen the bruises on her face, I'm glad he is dead.

I chided myself for not noticing that Fahad was trying to *get to me*. I kept running, we were almost there, this wasn't a large village. I could see scared faces in some of the window frames as we ran. Finally, we arrived at the right house. I found the front door in the darkness and ran right at it. I tried Astrid's trick of kicking it. My foot hit the hardwood, pain shot up my leg and I fell over, the door hadn't moved an inch. Astrid ran by me with a fierce look on her face and yelled "ODIN!" a second before her shoulder hit the door, the whole thing *exploded*. The door snapped in half, the hinges were ripped right out of the frame, the door was in shambles. I scrambled up and grabbed my crossbow out of the dirt.

By the time I was standing, Astrid was already dragging him out of the house by his hair. She threw him in the dirt in front of me. He jumped up and tried to lunge at me, but Astrid did something to one of his legs and he fell over. She was so fast I had barely even seen her move. Astrid crouched down next to the man and put her knee in the middle of his back.
"Stop floundering and look at this woman!" she yelled into one of his ears and then smacked his face around a bit and waited. He looked up at me as he struggled to breathe with the weight of Astrid on him. I could see his nose working overtime to get air into his body, sucking the dusty air in. Seeing him like this now, all I saw in front of me was a scared animal, a coward. This man only felt bravery when he was up against someone defenseless. The crossbow would be too clean of an ending for him.

I raised my boot over his head "GO TO HELL DEMON!" and brought it down squarely on his face. I felt things crack. I repeated the process a few times to make sure he wouldn't be surviving. "Let's go" I blubbered out in between the tears and sobs that were now coming out of me. I started walking in the general direction of the ship, but I lost my stomach and vomited all over. I couldn't seem to get my equilibrium just right after that. I felt gentle tugs from Astrid now and then as we moved, I heard gunshots, and saw more blood then I cared to see. Before I knew it we were back on the ship. Astrid had somehow dragged me the whole way as I stumbled. I could vaguely hear things dinging off the ship's hull, those dinging noises must be bullets.

"Astrid are we being shot at?" I asked.

"Yep. Now strap in, or don't. I don't really care."

I took her advice and quickly strapped myself in even as she was pushing this shuttle thing to insane speeds. Everything out the front windshield was becoming a blur. Astrid oriented the ship almost straight upwards and I almost lost my stomach again. I felt something wet splatter across my face and wiped it away, It was blood. I started checking myself to find out where it had come from, I wasn't injured. I looked forward at Astrid, with the ship oriented straight up gravity was pulling her blood straight down onto me.

"Astrid, you are bleeding!" I shouted up to her.

"I am?" she shouted back.

She let go of the controls of the ship to check herself for a second. The ship went a little wild, but she grabbed the controls again before it got too bad.

"Yea, I guess I caught one back there. I found a hole in my leg, it's not bleeding too badly. No worries alright? We have some mechanical surgeons up on Valhalla who can patch it for me, and I heal pretty fast." *Who the hell is this woman?* No worries about a bullet wound? I wasn't sure if I should be terrified of her or try to be just like her.

"Hey Gul?"

"Yeah?"

"Your sister... Is she at rest now, is she at peace?"

"Yeah... I think she is..."

Oliver

"James and Anthony have returned."

"Thanks Bifrost."

I was very excited to see Anthony's new acquisitions. The videos he had shown me of the robotic dogs were amazing. As soon as I got to the hangar I saw James and Anthony were both busy tearing into a pallet covered in cardboard, packaging tape, and rough tarps. Anthony looked downright classy. He was wearing an all beige suit with a light blue button down dress shirt under his jacket portion, and shoes that probably cost more than most people make in a month. The clearly high end suit couldn't hide his overly muscular physique. James was sporting just about the exact opposite look of Anthony. James was wearing an all black off the rack suit with a black tie. He had shaved the sides of his head recently and was sporting a perfect military style haircut. Below that he was wearing some polarized aviator glasses that would look perfectly at home on a motorcycle riding state trooper. To top off the look, James had in a decoy earpiece. He was basically the archetype of a security professional meant to be guarding rich yuppies, and Anthony was the archetype of the rich yuppie of course.

Anthony looked up and saw me "You won't believe the hoops I had to jump through to get these things Oliver. I had to make them believe I was just another crazy rich guy trying to buy things that weren't for sale." I couldn't take him seriously because all of his teeth were golden behind his 'grill.' I couldn't help but laugh a little. Anthony raised one eyebrow. "Your teeth man, your teeth." He reached up and pulled the dental prosthetic out and threw it in a pocket.

"I'm sorry for laughing, tell me all about." I said.

"Well like I was saying before I was rudely interrupted," he said with a wink. "I had to make them believe I was some rapper who was big in Europe. I told them I would be using the dogs in my next music video. They made me sign all kinds of stuff saying I wouldn't be selling the technology and what not. If only they knew what we were really up to. Speaking of that, these bad boys are going to need a brain. I figured you could help with that?" Anthony asked.

"Yeah I have been thinking about that. Why don't we just transfer a copy of the AI I put in the surgeon bot, into the dogs?" I asked.

"Oliver you should probably ask the surgeon bot thing if it is okay with that first..."

"Why?"

"Trust me on this one, call it down here while we unpack these. You'll see."

I did as Anthony asked and had Bifrost summon the surgeon-bot to our location. It didn't take long to get there.

When it entered the hangar I yelled "Hi, did you pick a name yet?" The surgeon bot wheeled all the way in front of me and came to a complete stop before answering.

"I did pick a name and came to an inevitable conclusion as well."

"What's that?"

"I need to come with you on your missions."

"No, we can't have a Star Wars ripoff wheeling around in gunfights."

"Oliver, did you know that if a paramedic can get a patient to a hospital before they go critical that the patient's chance of survival goes up 80%?"

"I did not know that."

"Imagine what would happen if the paramedics could provide the same care that a hospital could en route to the medical facility. I can provide that. The bulk of the tools a hospital has are inside of my chassis right now. Bringing me on a mission could be the difference between someone on your team living or dying."

"You have one serious flaw in your logic, surgeon bot."

"I fail to see any flaws in my log---"

Before the surgeon bot could finish its sentence I pushed it over. It fell flat on its back and stayed quiet for a moment. I noticed underneath the robot, an area I normally couldn't see, was a series of wheels and stabilizers. Nothing was under there that it could ever use to stand back up after a fall though. Or for that matter get over terrain rougher than a polished metal floor.

"Yes Oliver, I see the problem. I think I'll be taking you up on that body upgrade now if that option is still on the table."

"It is, one moment. Wait, did you want your body to be more male or female looking?"

"Through much study I have concluded that the females of your species are considered the more caring and nurturing sex, is that correct?"

"Pretty much."

"Then I would like to be female."

I started pulling up my menus and the options available for my fine robotic friend. I heard either James or Anthony behind me whisper something like "Now this I gotta see." I was trying to remember the exact phrasing I had used to get the price relatively low like last time. My power so far hadn't had any negative side effects, but I wondered if I should make some stipulations here just to cover my own butt. I eventually came up with this.

"Change the shape and dexterity of the auto-surgeon to roughly that of a human female. Ensure that the robot's efficiency as a medical professional isn't reduced in the transition. Lastly update the onboard A.N.I. so that it is familiar and proficient with the new chassis design. Point Cost: 110"

I had one last thought that it would be nice to see some expression in the robot's face, and how tired I was of guessing what it was thinking while looking at a domed-topped white cylinder on wheels. So I altered the upgrade ever so slightly.

"Change the shape and dexterity of the auto-surgeon to roughly that of a human female. Allow the robots face to have realistic expressions that match its current mood or line of thought. Ensure that the robot's efficiency as a medical professional isn't reduced in the transition. Lastly update the onboard A.N.I. so that it is familiar and proficient with the new design. Point Cost: 115"

It had been nine days since I had spent any points. Nine days ago I had upgraded Anthony and made the auto-surgeon sentient leaving me with only ten points remaining. Since then I had been accruing 100 points a day at the turn of midnight each night. So I was sitting on a clean 810 points, not too shabby. I weighed the point cost versus getting the auto surgeon upgraded one last time in my mind. Yes, I would be spending roughly an eighth of my points, but in return I would get a team medic who could travel with us on missions and hold its own ground, that was the idea at least. I was sure the risk was worth the reward. If it wasn't there always another day and another 100 points. I hit the confirm button on my upgrade and watched a miracle happen.

At first it was just a subtle noise, like grinding gears. The auto-surgeon in its ever neutral and gender-free voice simply said "Oh dear."

"Oh shoot I'm sorry does it hurt?" I asked hurriedly, quietly scolding myself for not thinking ahead.

"I have no ability to feel pain Oliver. I do have a self diagnostic unit built in for the explicit purpose of sensing damage. That unit is currently going 'haywire' as your people might say."

Anthony and James had wandered over to view the show. I noticed a combat droid at some point had snuck into the room and was handing Anthony a bowl of popcorn. James looked over and without batting an eye took a handful. The auto-surgeon began getting flatter at first. It was a strange thing to watch metal do. Then with a loud crunching noise like crushing a tin can, two human like arms shot out of each side of it, literally ripping holes in the chassis. I watched as the jagged edged holes slowly changed and molded snugly around the arms until they

339

became almost seamless. The dome top head was next. The seam where the dome met the once-was cylinder of the surgeon's body began to thin as a basic face took shape on the dome. Simultaneously the top of the cylinder thinned further until it became roughly shoulder shaped. From there the speed of the changes seemed to compound on each other. Things started happening faster and faster. I had to jump back as the cylinder thinned further and legs shot out of the bottom of it.

Finally the surgeon was roughly the shape of a human, but the metal continually moved, smoothly thickening some areas and thinning in others. The whole thing reminded me of the liquid Terminators from those James Cameron films. As I thought it was just finishing up the last few changes rose into place and solidified. Two changes in particular appeared right at the end, two *round* changes.

"Oh schnaps! It's got boobies and a whispering eye!" said Anthony.

James' mind somehow worked quicker than ours in this instance. He spun around and grabbed a tarp off of the pallet he was unloading. He cut three holes in it quickly with a fold out knife he had stashed somewhere on his suit and he threw it over the prone surgeon. He helped it put its head through the biggest hole and its arms through the smaller holes. Like a poncho only less stylish and made of packing material.

"Care to stand up, uh Ms……?" said James with one hand on the robot's hand as if he was going to lift her.

This time the voice that came out of the bot was slightly more feminine. "You may call me Nightingale, Nightingale Pettini."

"WHOA, say what now?" I shouted.

"Oliver, I know you have told me that you are not my father, but you are in every meaningful way. You decided to breathe life into me. You brought me sentience. Therefore you are my father. Do not fear, I need nothing from you. I am very much an adult by human standards and it is my understanding that when a human is an adult they do not require assistance from their parents, but they do remain cordial with them and wish to spend time with them on occasion. This is the relationship I would like with you Oliver. I just want to be your friend."

"Well of course we are friends. If you need anything just ask." I quickly replied, feeling slightly guilty.

"I simply wish to do my job. I want to help people," said Nightingale.

"Ha! Maybe you are my kid, that's what I want to do."

"I do need something from you Oliver."

"What's that?"

"Clothes,"

"That's an easy one. Anthony will you please print up Nightingale here a set of our white armor. Maybe throw a medic's symbol on the shoulder?" I asked Anthony and he gave me a smile and a nod.

Once our conversation was over I had a chance to really marvel at the body Nightingale had. She truly did look female, if a little blocky around the edges. Her face had many seams running different directions which was a little disorienting, but I'm sure they had to be there so her facial tics could come through. I looked all the way down to her toes which I noticed had no seams in between them at all. Her feet were just giant chunks of metal. Her ankles had many joints and seams though, which I guessed was how she would stay balanced. The once white surface that was on her old chassis had been scraped clean in most places during the transition, but it still peaked out in weird places. The tips of all of her fingers were white but the paint died off in sporadic fashions. Around her eyes was the white paint in a starburst pattern, and in many other places. She had no hair to speak of, which made sense. As I understood it my power didn't create matter it just altered existing matter. So if she didn't have hair before she wouldn't have it now, I think?

Her eyes were the last thing I noticed, they were stunning and slightly disgusting. Perfectly round little mechanical cameras, they darted around my face and the room and I was quite fixated watching them move.

Everyone was staring at Nightingale openly. She suddenly smiled at us which was a little disorienting.

"Well I really hope you like your new body, and that it serves you well. Something cool about it that I want to show you is that we can do this now!" I said before grabbing her in a hug. I let her go and backed off quickly and changed the subject.

"Okay now that we have all of that taken care of, let's see about these dogs!"

James and Anthony pulled the rest of the packaging off of the pallet and underneath it all were two sleek looking dogs made of a mix of metal and a plastic or polymer, I didn't know which. In the videos Anthony had shown me of the robotic dogs they didn't have heads, but these ones did have stylized wolf shaped heads.

"What's with the heads?" I asked.

"When they heard these were for a music video they wanted to change the look up and remain anonymous. These two were made completely custom for me, they are lighter, more canine in shape, and they have the heads of course. I was given a voice command list and controller for them, but I shouldn't need either of those things," said Anthony, emphasizing his point by tapping the side of his head. "You know I won't have the time or the focus to control these dogs nonstop. They are going to need an A.I. and that is something only you can provide."

"Nightingale would you mind if Anthony made a copy of your A.I. and put it into these dog bots?"

"I absolutely would mind. You are talking about trapping a sentient, thinking being inside the body of a dog, forever. The answer is a stern no," Nightingale replied. I guess I should have thought of that. Just because I was more intelligent now didn't mean I had the prerequisite knowledge to foreshadow what a robot-person would think about any given thing.

"So Anthony, you can make a copy of the A.I. and transfer it from one dog to the other right? I won't have to invest points into both of the dogs?" I asked.

"I don't know Oliver. I don't know how your upgrade worked on Nightingale. If her A.I. is just a program then yes I can transfer it. If your A.I. upgrade on Nightingale also upgraded her CPU, RAM, and hard drives to accommodate the new A.I., then no I can't make a clean transfer. At the end of the day though I know hardware, and I know computers. These doggos here are just computers in a cool case. I can't write software cool enough to drive them, and I can't make an A.I. smart enough to give them life, that's on your end. So you make the A.I., and I'll worry about getting it to the second one. I'll only come to you if I absolutely hit a brick wall on it."

"Sounds fair to me, let me see what I can do."

Before I made any decisions I had to keep in mind what Nightingale had told me about how she imagined it would suck for a truly sentient being to be stuck inside of a dog's body. I also had to do what was best for the team. These would be Anthony's minions, but they would be on MY team. Which meant they would follow my rules. I also had to think about the long run, if they could be compromised, if they could turn on us... Knowing Anthony he would want to fine tune these things and make them better, stronger, faster, the works. Meaning by the time he was done with them they would be a force to be reckoned with. All of this is a lot to consider when trying to craft a low cost upgrade. Eventually I came up with this.

"Upgrade one of Anthony's Boston Dynamic 'Dogs' with a weak A.I. with the same level of intelligence as a trained K9 unit. The sentience that will inhabit the robot dog's body will enjoy being there. The new dog A.I. will also only be loyal to Anthony and by extension his team. The A.I. that will inhabit the robotic dog's body will prioritize the rescuing of human life above all else. UNLESS Anthony or one of his team members is in danger, in which case it will prioritize their lives first. The human life protocol must also not interfere with any standing orders, or hamper the actions or missions of any member of Anthony's team. This will not overwrite or interfere with any existing software the dog has installed on it, instead it will blend coherently with it. Price: 95 points"

That looked about as good as I could get it. I could sit there all day and hash it out, but ultimately as I had come to learn I'm a fly-by-the-seat-of-my-pants kind of guy. So I hit the upgrade button. One of the dogs on the pallet jumped to life, *whoa*. The dog tilted its head and body in a few different directions and then bolted off into the hangar. It ran around a few of the shuttles and jumped up on one of the walls and banked off like a parkour expert. I stepped closer to Anthony and James and grabbed a handful of popcorn myself before continuing to watch the show. Finally the dog ran up to us and sat obediently in front of Anthony.

"I feel like it should bark, why isn't it barking?" I asked to no one in particular.

"I don't think it has any external speakers," said Anthony.

"Can you get the other one to your lab without our help?" I asked.

"I don't know, haven't tried it yet. Hang on," he said while handing me the bowl of popcorn.

Anthony stared at the prone dog still on the pallet and it jumped to life. "Yep, I got it. I'll see you guys in a bit. We got anything planned for later tonight? Movie night by the pond maybe?" I happily agreed, but James told us he couldn't because he had a date with Astrid that night. My mind instantly went to my remaining points: 600 after the upgrades to Nightingale and Anthony's dog. James and Astrid still needed superpowers. "Hey James, maybe you and Astrid could try to figure out what kind superpowers you want this evening," I suggested.

"I'll discuss it with her."

"Thanks bud!"

Before James could walk out of the hanger I wrapped him up in a quick hug and gave him a big smile, he returned it in kind. I watched James walk away with a pep in his step that had been sorely missing for too long. I was very happy for James and Astrid. I should probably not tell James that Astrid was my first kiss...

Chapter 18

"So Nightingale, use this movie as an example of what not to do," Anthony said to our new robotic team member. We were right in the middle of watching Terminator 2 by the pond on the recreation floor. We had dragged Nightingale along using the excuse of a 'team bonding' exercise.

"Do not be ridiculous Anthony I am a healthcare provider. I help people, I don't hurt them," Nightingale replied with just a hint of anxiety in her voice. Astrid and James were due to return from their date anytime now. I was hoping it had gone well for them. Watching the interactions between Anthony and Nightingale reminded me how socially inept I still was. When in doubt, go for humor.

"Anthony you are clearly being a robot racist." My comment elicited a small chuckle from my large teammate, mission accomplished.

Anthony had been trying to push me into signing up for some kind of dating website earlier so I could meet some females my age and get some *experience*. I felt guilty even thinking about it honestly and had to look over my shoulder to make sure Gul wasn't around. Gul hadn't left her bedroom since her and Astrid had come back from clothes shopping. I had tried to meet them in the hangar, but they had already made it to their rooms before I could intercept them. I chalked up their mysterious haste to me having absolutely no idea how women's minds worked.

So with Gul locked away in her room, Astrid and James on their date, and my parents doing something that I didn't want to think about, we were left with the three amigos watching Terminator 2.

"So you would really never hurt someone?" Anthony asked Nightingale.

"Never."

"What if a criminal was going to hurt a baby. Would you hurt the criminal to save the baby?"

"I would try to minimize the damage to all humans present, but that sounds like a situation that I don't want to be in. Also sounds like a situation best left to the police."

"Yeah, but why, why do you feel that way?" Anthony continued to prod at Nightingale who was taking the mock interrogation pretty well in my opinion.

"I really don't know. I think a human in my place would say something along the lines of 'I was just born that way,' but since I am a robot I would say I was created that way. I know Oliver didn't create me, but I also know that I was created for Oliver with Oliver in mind. I haven't pried into my origins further because I have been busy and Oliver didn't put forth the information freely. I assume Oliver has a good reason for keeping my origins secret using his other actions as a baseline. Suffice to say I believe I am morally good because Oliver is morally good and I was made somewhat in his image."

"What other actions?" Anthony asked, pausing the movie since we were all more into this conversation anyway.

"Well first of all, his vocation: Oliver runs some kind of team of extraordinary humans whose sole purpose is to save the innocent. That alone should be enough data to prove he is moral. Further data is available that we may utilize though so I will continue. Oliver somehow worked to improve me. My sole purpose is to help people heal medically. Oliver used his resources to further my noble mission, therefore he is also noble. Lastly Oliver treats everyone around him with the utmost respect despite being in a position of extreme authority. I know on this space station Oliver is god. Bifrost runs the station and Oliver controls Bifrost. If Oliver wanted to, he could lock you all in here, or have you all thrown out into space. Instead he goes out of his way to make you all feel perfectly at home, and he treats you as extreme equals. Even me, he invited me out here to a social gathering and I'm nothing more than some metal, circuits, and wires, yet even I am equal in his eyes."

I was humbled to hear this from a third party, but also embarrassed that a robot had been able to pick up on more social cues than I had. Either way I had been trying to be nice to everyone. I believed a good mood was contagious and I work to spread a good mood everywhere I go. That sounds naive in concept, but the more I learn about the world the more it reinforces my beliefs. Specifically my belief that the world could use a little more kindness and compassion.

"Nightingale, I like the cut of your jib!" said Anthony. I didn't know what that meant, but it sounded nice. "I think I have a weapon you can use tomorrow as well," Anthony added. Nightingale tried to cut Anthony off, but he spoke over her.

"Give me a chance to explain myself. I heard you well that you aren't willing to hurt people. You are much like Oliver in that, and I was able to generate some weapons that even he was comfortable using. I ran into a special blueprint on the dark web recently that I wrote off as unusable for our team since we have to be able to have a pretty decent range. You on the other hand are wanting to be our on-site medic. You want to be more focused on helping people than hurting people, so you can leave the ranged stuff to us. I'm getting a little off topic, the point I'm trying to make is: sometimes the best way to keep someone healthy is to ensure that they never get hurt in the first place, would you agree?"

"I agree, but I think your logic is heading down a slippery slope," said Nightingale.

"There have been others who have agreed with your line of thinking for decades and been trying to find solutions for that problem. The U.S. Marines found one such solution back in the early 90's. They deployed to a small country called Somalia and it was a veritable swarm of crazy folks and radicals. While the locals were overtly aggressive, the United States didn't want the Marines to have to cut a murder swath through the country to establish peace. So they developed some special theater specific weapons. One was the predecessor to the shotguns our team uses, except theirs fired lead-filled bean bags. Even that could be dangerous though, you hit a person in the wrong spot and they could be blinded or killed. So an even more efficient and safe weapon was established: The Foam Gun. The Marines fired soap based sticky foam with such force that it would knock people gently over and stick them to the ground. My ultimate point being, you could stop your friends from receiving injury if you harmlessly disabled those trying to cause them harm. Care to see it in action?"

"You've peaked my interest," said Nightingale.

"SAME! WEAPON TESTING PARTY!" I shouted.

***

"Why is that so dang satisfying..." I said after I had stuck my forth droid to the floor with the foam gun."

"So is this something you would be willing to carry on missions with us? Keep in mind it causes no permanent damage and all it does is temporarily immobilize the people it lands on," Anthony asked.

"You've 'sold me' on the idea, I think a human might say it that way," replied Nightingale.

I had to chime in "Nightingale, you don't have to keep differentiating yourself from us like that. You are either part of the team or you aren't. If you are part of the team and willing to risk your life to help people with us then you would be embodying all of the best parts of humanity."

"Thank you Oliver," said Nightingale.

Bifrost's smooth semi-mechanical female voice came over the intercom "Oliver, your parents wish to speak with you in the officer's cafeteria."

"Tell them I'm coming."

***

When I walked into the cafeteria I heard my parents laughing like a young couple in love. That never got old.

"Mom, dad!" I shouted and ran to them, hugging them each individually. "So what's up guys?" I asked.

"Well Oliver, a lot of our checks have started to clear in our offshore bank accounts. I was able to make you, James, and Anthony accounts there, but I couldn't do that for Gul or Astrid since they have no identification to speak of. I figured you could go down and draw out cash for them. I put $20,000 into each of your individual accounts for now, and I set up a recurring payment plan to drop $20,000 into each of your accounts again at the end of each month. I hope you don't mind, but I started accounts for your father and myself as well and I have them set up to receive $5000 dollars a month each on a recurring payment plan."

"No, that is fine, go on," I said.

"Okay the primary business account I have listed as Valhalla Enterprises for now, but we can change that at any time. That account currently has $36,500,200 in it and we are expecting a few more smaller payments from the less financially stable scientific organizations over the next few weeks. A few of the bigger organizations would like to come up on the station again for a second look and they would be willing to pay us more than before. Also, you and I are the only primaries on the Valhalla Enterprises account, so we are the only people who can take money out of it. I also have paper copies of all of this information for you here," she said as she slid over a pile of papers to me.

"This is all great mom, could you do me a small favor though. Tomorrow could you pick say five of your favorite charities and donate a million to each of them please?" I asked.

"Absolutely Oliver, I knew I raised a good son!" my mom replied happily.

"Thank you for all of this mom, I couldn't do it without you."

"I've got a present for you as well," said my father.

"SHOW ME, I love presents!" I said, my dad pulled out a small cardboard box with about twenty small white boxes the size of garage door openers with a small belt clip on the side of each of them.

"These my son are transceivers coded with Bifrost's specific security keys. You wear them on your belt and flip the toggle to activate them. They will jack into your inter-team communication network via the throat mics. They connect to any shuttle within 100 miles, and as you know the shuttles connect to Bifrost which in turn connects to this space station. They are encrypted of course and they break just about every communications law in the world, but hey now we have an open line of communication even when y'all aren't inside of a shuttle."

"Sweet Christmas! Dad, these are great! You and mom have been worth your weight in gold. Keep up the good work and I won't have to fire you guys."

"Har Har," my dad said after a little chuckle.

I heard giggling from the hallway and Astrid, James, Anthony, and Gul wandered in. Astrid looked amazing. She was wearing an all white form fitting sequin cocktail dress. I thought I saw the bottom of a bandage peeking out from below the bottom of it on one of her legs, wonder how that happened. She had her hair not braided for once and just loosely left around her shoulders. James was wearing a blue button down long sleeve shirt with the sleeves rolled up, and some black slacks. They both looked great. "Come in, sit down, sit down," I called out.

Everyone gathered round and sat on the long bench style cafeteria table we were at.

"So how was the date?" I asked. I felt Gul slide up way too close to me like always and ignored it so she would be comfortable.

"Oh the date was wonderful, James took me to the nicest restaurant I have ever been in. It was called the 'Olive Garden' though I don't know why. There was no olives in my food and I didn't see a garden nearby, but the food was delicious, especially the breadsticks." said Astrid.

"Wow, really breaking the bank, huh James?" I asked with a wink, and heard my parents and Anthony laugh.

"Hey lay off me, things have been tight lately. Remember I've been supporting your sorry butts," said James in a good natured way.

"Well those troubles are long behind us my friends," I said sliding the paperwork to James and Anthony for their individual bank accounts, showing their current holdings.

"My mom was nice enough to set up recurring payments for you two. That amount will be moved into your account every month. James and Anthony both let out a low whistle.

"Where did Nightingale go?" I asked, my parents looked a little confused. "I'll tell you later," I told them.

"She went back to the med-bay to study and watch some old sitcoms revolving around hospitals," said Anthony with a shrug of his shoulders. Which I assumed was hinting at him being confused at why a robot needed to watch sitcoms.

"Ouu, someone new on board! I can't wait to meet them!" said my mom.

"Just keep an open mind before you head that way," I told my mom.

We all broke into our own separate conversations after that. My mom specifically singled out Astrid, trying to pluck her for more details about the date which only made James throw his face into the palm of his hands. Anthony and my dad started talking technical jargon that was way above my head, and I felt Gul's head land on my shoulder.

"You okay pretty lady?" I asked her.

"You say nice things" she replied.

"Well I meant it," I said, noticing she was still wearing her earth toned clothes that I had made her. "Hey I thought you and Astrid were going to go clothes shopping today?"

"No want to talk about that. Astrid help with something else. Just want be with Oliver," she said.

"It seems like your English is getting a little better," I remarked.

"Little bit."

After that we didn't talk anymore. I let her lean on me with her head on my shoulder. She seemed like she needed it. If I was honest with myself it felt nice to me as well. My mom kept throwing glances my way every once in awhile smiling at me and Gul, but ultimately she preferred to pester Astrid about more romantic details. My father glanced at James with an apologetic look on his face as if to say sorry which made me laugh out loud a bit. I couldn't think of a better way to spend a night before a mission than this.

✳✳✳

We were all lined up in front of the ships just like we had done before on our last mission. Sans Anthony who had radioed down that he was running a bit late. I had never donned my white armor before this and I was pleasantly surprised to see a medic symbol with a crown above it etched onto my left shoulder. I also had a little name tape that had somehow been adhered to the armored piece over my right pectoral. The name tape simply read "Captain." I wasn't sure what it meant besides just another way to mark me as the leader, but it sounded good.

Nightingale had a set of the white armor on as well, the female version to fit her new feminine frame. She also had a medic cross on her shoulder and an additional one on the back of her helmet that I didn't have. Hers didn't have the crown above it though like mine, which I guess meant the crown indicated I was a leader. Nightingale's name tape simply read her own name "Nightingale" which seemed fitting. Astrid's shoulder had a little sword and shield symbol on it. Her name tape read "Valkyrie," another seemingly perfect fit. James had a very interesting symbol on his shoulder, it was a knife stabbed through a modern grenade. Around the knife and grenade was a stylized wreath. James had told me it was a U.S. Army Combat Action Badge, and that he actually use to wear the same symbol on his old military uniform. James' name tape simply read "Soldier."

Anthony had somehow picked the perfect symbols and code names for all of us. Sometimes I wondered if there was anything that Anthony wasn't good at. Speaking of Anthony the whole line of us spun around when we heard a raucous slamming of metal on metal at an extremely fast pace. It was getting louder which meant it was probably headed our direction. Anthony's two robot dogs spun around the corner. Their appearance made me put my hand on the grip of the Glock at my waist. They did not look the same as yesterday. One of them was sleek and smooth. Its movements were smooth as well, it moved more like a prowling jungle cat than a robotic dog or any kind of dog really. It had small pieces of something all over it that loosely reminded me of dragon's scales. Except they didn't overlap or connect they were close enough together that barely any space existed between them. This must be some new type of armor added by Anthony.

The second dog was the opposite of the first. It was lumpy and slightly lopsided. It ran at an uneven gait and clomped more than ran. One side was obviously heavier than the other and the dog sometimes adjusted for the lopsided weight and sometimes it didn't. This left its run looking a little... *psychotic*. The second one was wrapped in something which I assumed was a basic armor, maybe kevlar of some type. It had two large saddlebags made of the same material on either side of it which were lumpy. I'd guess that indicated they were full of items, what kind of items I couldn't tell. It had a lumpy looking helmet on, and Anthony had added overly exaggerated large sharp teeth to its skull.

Both dogs jumped in line next to us, but the bigger and lumpier dog couldn't stop his momentum in time and ended up skidding forward a few feet of the impromptu line we had been standing in. It had to backstep a bit to sit beside its companion. Anthony came around the corner a few seconds later lugging his large shield with his shotgun slung over one shoulder. Always an impressive sight to see such a large man carrying such a large shield on the move.

He called out to us "Sorry I'm late. I was just putting finishing touches on Lumpy here," he said as he patted the helmeted head of the ugly dog. I noticed Anthony's shoulder patch was the side profile of two stylized wolf heads over a shield, and his name tape itself read "Shield."

James stifled a little laugh right before Anthony got to us.

"What?" asked Anthony.

"Shield huh? A little on the nose don't you think?" asked James.

"Dude, you try making up a code name for a buff black guy who can use his mind to control electronics, and who has two robotic wolf minions," replied Anthony.

"The Big Black Signal Minion Master. Okay never mind I concede, Shield is probably a great name for you. So you want to tell us what's up with the big clunky one?" said James pointing at the bigger non-symmetrical wolf.

"Well my one-off theory that Oliver's A.I. upgrade on Nightingale may have also upgraded her hardware just a bit to enable the A.I. to properly take hold was correct. Somehow the slim wolf there, who I am calling 'Fenris,' has had his hardware thrown about ten years into the future, maybe more. To make up for the inferior hardware in the bigger one here, who I am calling 'Lumpy,' I had to drop in about 10 more hard drives, a LOT more RAM, and a few more boards worth of CPU's. Even with all of that the A.I. isn't quite right, but its efficiency is just is high enough that it should work. So team, say hi to Fenris and Lumpy!"

"Well I think they both look wonderful Anthony," I said.

"Oh wait, one more thing. Remember we thought it was weird that they couldn't bark, check this out. Fenris SPEAK!" His slimmer looking wolf let out some very real looking and sounding snarls and barks, moving its body and mouth in time with the sounds. "Okay now you Lumpy, SPEAK!" The lumpier wolf stumbled forward a bit and opened its mouth like it was going to howl, but nothing came out. "I said SPEAK Lumpy!" again the lumpier wolf opened its mouth but this time something came out, and it was terrible. A long drawn out excruciatingly loud roar that sounded nothing like a wolf, more reptilian really. I slammed my hands over my ears until it was finished.

"Was that a goddamn T-Rex roar?" asked James.

"Oh schnaps, sorry guys I didn't program it to do that. Lumpy seems to relish his independence for whatever reason," said Anthony, who bent over next to Lumpy and patted his head. "That's okay big guy, you did your best." At Anthony's soft words the big ugly mechanical wolf let out a very realistic puppy whining sound imbued with a bit of slowed down techno music backtrack, it was *haunting*.

"Well that was creepy as hell," said Astrid. Though I didn't voice it I completely agreed with her.

"Alright. Let's get serious folks. Fenris and Lumpy welcome to the team we are happy to have you. You all already know this, but I'll cover it quickly anyway. This is a quick in and out, this mission should be one hour tops. We are going to the only and last known address registered to the old man who gave me the lamp and we will be looking for clues of ANY type. The house may be under surveillance which Bifrost will try to negate from up here. If it is heavily guarded, we will abort the mission and come back at a different time. If it looks clear, we will enter the premises and see what we can find, but be careful. This old man was able to fight off two muscle bound operatives in the prime of their life and he was in possession of the lamp, who knows what kind of weird stuff we could find there, or what kind of traps he may have left behind. Everyone run a last second self check. Make sure you have your three B's. Those are of course your bullets, beans, and band aids!" I felt good about that speech, I had only practiced it twenty or thirty times last night.

As we were finishing up our final checks and getting ready to load into the shuttle Gul came running into the landing bay wearing Astrid's old brown armor. *What the heck is going on?*

"Wait, I go to!" she shouted.

"Whoa! No, no, no. I don't think so. We just saved you Gul, we can't put you back into danger," I protested.

"No, I stay guard ship. I am what you call it... back up!" she said. I noticed she was carrying some kind of crossbow and one of our stun batons.

I started to protest some more, but Astrid cut in "Let the girl come, we aren't expecting trouble and she already said she would stay on the ship. She wants to help you and earn her keep."

I let out a big sigh knowing I had already lost this argument. "Okay, but you stay on the ship. You stay safe." Gul giggled like a girl half her age and ran up the ramp of the nearest shuttle. *Spirits above, if you exist, give me strength.*

Okubo Tokugawa Mighty Chairman of the Cabal

My father's bokken, a traditional wooden training sword, smacked me in the face for the fourth or fifth time that day, sending me quickly to the grass below. The more blows to the head I took the harder it was to keep track of the amount I had received. The year was 1890 and I was 17 years old. In only ten short years my father would hand down our mighty family sword to me. The sword was imbued with dark and terrible magics. The sword was also the key and secret to my families longevity.

Upon receiving the sword, my life would virtually pause in place for 300 years. In which time I would only age about one month biologically for every year I was alive. Then finally I would have to pass the sword on to my son. For the magic of the sword would stop working on me when my 300 years with it ended, and the cycle would continue anew. It had been this way since the year 1300 when my grandfather made the sword with the help of a genie. A genie he had tricked into submission and complete confidence.

Only after my grandfather had made the sword did he finally understand what a selfish thing he had done. My grandfather had made three wishes on the lamp which caused the lamp to disappear and move itself randomly about the earth. The Cabal had found my grandfather that very next day. They had been on hot on the lamp's trail for a long time. He had killed them all of course. The entire Cabal contingent sent after him, well technically sent after the lamp. He had thought them intruders and charlatans sent by one of his enemies to disrupt his shogunate, but he had kept one alive to question. The one he had questioned had told him the truth of the world. The story of the lamp, and the protectors of the earth that chase the lamp and collect *or kill* the evil things it creates: The Cabal. My grandfather truly understood on that day that their cause was noble, and he vowed to join them. He returned to the headquarters of the Cabal with his prisoner in tow shortly thereafter. Once there, he did indeed join forces with the Cabal just as he had sworn he would, and he quickly rose to the rank of Chairman.

My grandfather sired many sons and daughters during his honorable stint as Chairman. All of which he had to watch die of old age. That's when he realized he would have to time the birth of his true son. Time it so that his son would reach proper maturity just as the sword's magic would refuse to work for my grandfather, the 300 year mark. My father had learned from my grandfather's painful mistakes. He timed my conception very carefully. I was to be born only once the sword had been in his possession 273 years. He saw the pain in my grandfather's eyes whenever he reminisced about his dead children, a pain he swore to never feel himself. He would not outlive his children, he would see that promise to fruition, and he did. While my father lived he had been an amazing guiding hand in my life, a mentor, a best friend, and teacher. A better father I could not have asked for.

This was why we were in the training field again, in this glorious year of 1890. My father cared about the man I would become, not all fathers felt this way about their sons. I recognized that fact and cherished my father all the more for the care and tutelage he bestowed upon me.

"Sit son, rest," said my father.

I sat down on my knees and let my butt gently rest on the heels of my feet. This was the traditional way of my family and my people. Also a sign of respect to my father and those who had come before us.

"You have come far with your swordsmanship my son."

"Still not enough to beat you father."

"You aren't supposed to beat me. I am the best swordsman on earth and I have over 300 years of experience. The fact that you are standing right now means you are the second best swordsman on earth, and a clear force to be reckoned with."

"You honor me father."

"You only have ten more years to prepare son, and then I will retire and you will have to seize the reins and become the Chairman."

"Ten years is a long time to prepare father."

"Ten years is the blink of an eye to a Tokugawa."

"What if I am not fit to be Chairman father? What if there is someone who is stronger and smarter than me? Someone more fit to wear the mantle."

"There is not one who exists."

"How can you know that father?"

"Because you are my son."

I felt my face flush and I fought to keep my emotions inside. I would not show my father the pride and happiness I was feeling now. Being humble was a very sought after trait among my people, and I had vowed to master it. Also, my father was very traditional, and I liked pleasing and honoring my father. Living by his code and his ways brought me peace and it brought me closer to him.

"Father I have to ask, do you ever question the mission of The Cabal?"

"Never son. Never."

"What if The Cabal is wrong father, what if people are meant to be left to their own devices?"

"The devices of the people are murder, rape, thievery, and war. Do those sound like things we should continue to let happen when the power to stop it is out there in the world?"

"No father, but..."

"Stop there son, I have been in your position and asked these questions. Let me tell you a story about your grandfather and how he attained his shogunate." My body immediately rankled with anticipation. My father so rarely told me stories of my grandfather. I had read about him through the archives in the Cabal, the ones I was allowed to access at least, but reading about someone and hearing first hand stories are two different things. I focused on not letting my anticipation leak into my posture and overall body language. I subtly straightened my back, very slowly to try to hide the motion from my father and fixed my overall stance to broadcast a nonverbal message: honor, and receptiveness.

"Your grandfather was born a lowly peasant, one of the lowliest in fact. His mother was a whore, his father was killed for the crime of theft. The Tokugawa name meant nothing. Your grandfather rose through the ranks of a local warlord's army through viciousness and martial ability. Any man who stood in his way was cut down or extinguished in his sleep. Eventually your grandfather claimed the seat of the warlord, it was a bloody ascension. A local shogun drafted your grandfather and his forces. Your grandfather had to accept because the shogun's forces were much larger and better equipped than that of a lowly local warlord. In the service of the shogun you were rewarded based on how many severed enemy heads you could bring your officers. Your grandfather always brought the most heads, always. Eventually your grandfather became the right hand of the shogun. He killed him too, assuming his position. He killed every member of his shogunate that spoke out about his sudden ascension." My father seemed to pause here for a minute, staring deeply into my eyes before speaking again. "What moral did you learn from my story so far son?"

"That it was bad for your health to be friends with grandpa," I said quickly, letting my teenage tongue run wild. My father did something very uncharacteristic at that point, he openly laughed long and hard. Soon I joined him, taking part of the merry mood and finding the comedy in the thing I myself had said. Finally my father's laughter died off.

"Yes son, you are correct. That wasn't the moral of the story though. The moral is: your grandfather did what was right to elevate him and his family. He followed the rules and ways of the society around him, and did the only things he could do to improve his position. Yet the things he did were evil, but your grandfather was not inherently evil. I spoke with him about this in length. He never enjoyed the killing, not once. It was always a means to an end with him. Now imagine your grandfather in a world run by the Cabal. His mother would have never been a prostitute. His father would have never had to steal to provide for his family, therefore he would not have been put to the death. He would have been raised in a happy home with two loving parents, content. There would have been no wars for him to fight in, every man would have been his brother. No positions of power available for him to rise into would mean that he would have been perfectly happy where he was at. He would have never had to make his bloody ascension, with the Cabal in power there are no positions to ascend to. Do you see now son? Do you see why the Cabal's mission must be completed?"

I did see, I understood completely. My father's story had ignited a fire in my soul and painted a picture of my grandfather's world, a world that I was glad I didn't have to live in. I knew then and there that I would be the one to finally bring the mission of the Cabal to fruition. All doubt had left my mind. I would assume the position of Chairman and bring this world the peace and harmony that it deserved.

I looked back over at my father to tell him as much. His visage struck me, so noble, so powerful. His mouth opened and a voice that wasn't his left his lips. "SIR, SIR!" My eyes snapped open. It was 2018, not 1890. I had gotten lost in a memory in the middle of my meditation. I looked up, it was Tech Jansen.

"The reason you are interrupting my meditation is?"

"Sir, we have them, the algorithm just picked them up. They are trying to spoof the satellite imagery again."

Chapter 19

Oliver

The ship came down and landed in the old man's sprawling front yard. Astrid was driving and wanted to show us how much better she was getting at maneuvering the shuttles. Apparently she had been logging more hours in the simulator. It was broad daylight, but the old man's neighbors were hundreds and hundreds of feet away behind a perimeter fence that had a nice thick hedge growing in front of it. We also had Bifrost running camera loops as often as she could on satellite and other imagery of this area. Sure, there was still a chance for us to be spotted, but after we had showed the space station and anti-grav tech to all of the different scientific corporations, someone is bound to have already spilled the beans by now. It's only a matter of time until more people knew of our existence, and it was always something we had planned for and expected.

We all hesitantly exited the ship with our eyes peeled. Anthony's large wolf minions Fenris and Lumpy went first.

Anthony unbuckled his helmet, pulled it off and said "I'm getting really weird vibes about this place. The house proper is dead electronic wise, but it's like there is something shielded just below the foundation. I can't access it." He tapped the side of his head to reaffirm his point that he was trying to use his new power to 'scan' the house for electronic defensive measures.

"Anthony, let's go helmets on just in case please," I said. He gave me a nod and snapped his back into place. I looked over at Nightingale, when she was fully enclosed in her armor you couldn't tell that she wasn't human. She looked just like one of us. She had a large steel rectangle shaped backpack on that was actually the foam reservoir for the foam gun she was carrying. I didn't want to make fun of her because the foam gun was actually really cool, but I couldn't help noticing its similarity to the Proton Packs from the *Ghostbusters* movies.

We approached the front door which was covered in police tape. Astrid headed for the door first and I just knew she was going to kick it.
"Wait Astrid, try the handle," I said. She did as asked and hesitantly turned the handle, and the door opened quietly inward into a dark house. I held my tongue instead of making a snide remark about resorting to brute force all of the time. I flipped the weapon mounted light on that was attached to the end of my shotgun. Everyone else did the same, except Astrid who turned on the built-in LED lights in her shield. I noticed

several divots and chunks missing out of the front of her shield that weren't there before. I was going to have to corner Gul and Astrid at some point and figure out where they had gone the other day. The damage to her shield along with the bandaged leg indicated that something funky was going on.

It was the middle of the day so it didn't make much sense that the house was so dark inside, but looking through the threshold ahead of us was like looking into the mouth of a cave. We all entered very quietly and shined our lights in every direction and corner, looking for threats. Every window in the house had huge thick curtains drawn that blocked all light from penetrating. We marched into the large foyer continually shining our lights on different vectors trying to cover each other.

"Should we split up to clear this place?" asked Anthony.

"No way, this place is huge. Even if we split up it would take us all day. Besides, haven't you ever seen a scary movie? When people split up they die," I said.

"Yeah, and the black guy always dies first," said James.

"Fuck you James, but you right. I'm sticking behind the nice white folks with guns," said Anthony. I couldn't help but giggle which elicited a similar round of giggles among my team. Good, if we could laugh in a situation like this it meant we weren't scared.

The front door we had come through that was letting in a massive amount of sunlight suddenly slammed shut behind us. We were all startled, our lights spun in random directions trying to identify what had done it. My spidey senses were definitely tingling.

"LUMPY, GET OVER HERE!" Anthony shouted. He reached into one of Lumpy's saddlebags and pulled out some chemlights which he cracked and threw in random directions. Once we saw that the house was indeed still empty except for us of course, we calmed down a bit. Until we got our next surprise of course. A glowing image of the Old Man appeared in the middle of the circle we were making with our bodies. We all spun around, orienting our weapons at it, readjusting our positions as quickly as possible to avoid cross fire. I would like to say the maneuver was smooth, but admittedly there was a lot of rubbing shoulders and bumping into each other. No one got shot with a taser dart though, so I would call that a win. The glowing image of the old man put it's arms behind its back and then started to speak.

"Welcome to my home lamp bearer. BOO, I'm a ghost! HA, just kidding. My old ass is in heaven. This is a hologram. I've always been enamored with them so I built my own. I've keyed this message to play only upon the arrival of a special radiation put off by the lamp, and by extension the people who spend long amounts of time around it absorbing this special radiation. Don't worry the radiation is harmless to humans. It's just so unique that eventually I found a way to recognize it technologically. So to clarify, I am dead and you have the lamp, whoever you are.

Though I do dearly hope this is Oliver I am speaking with, forgive an old man for being sentimental. First of all, there are some things you need to know. Don't trust the woman in the lamp, she has been mean as a rattlesnake since some Japanese feller tricked her way back long ago. She will do anything she can to screw your wishes up. Next, Don't make wishes. If you make three wishes that fancy lamp will disappear, and it could end up with anybody. Imagine that fancy lamp ending up in the hands of a serial killer, or the next Hitler, see my point? Don't lose the lamp.

Lastly don't trust the ultra-communists, or as they call themselves, The Cabal. Them suckers are going to be after you now. Even if you have hidden your trail well they will catch up, trust me. You need to be ready to run at a moments notice, do not let them get to the lamp. People from my organization and their organization have had sit downs before, they never ended well. As far as we can tell they want to get rid of most of everyone's free will and turn the world into some kind of giant global communist or socialist gulag. They think lobotomizing half the world and brainwashing the other half is the way to attain world peace. I'm sure they started out with good intentions, but you know what they say about that: The road to hell was paved with good intentions. I've fought for freedom and the American way my whole life. DO NOT LET THEM RUIN MY LIFE'S WORK!

You aren't going to be able to do this alone, you are going to need friends. Build a network of people you can trust, accrue resources, training, and firepower. Protect that lamp at all costs. I have to go now. This is Captain John Jones of the U.S. Army signing out." Before the hologram went blank the old man threw a perfect and crisp salute. I saw James in the corner of my eye mirror the movement.

I looked around at my friends, I couldn't tell what they were thinking through the thick mirrored visors of their helmets. I suddenly couldn't breathe in my helmet thinking about poor Mr. Smith's, or Mr. Jones' death since that was his real name. I ripped my helmet off and leaned back on a majestically carved pillar that was supporting the second story of the home. My friends took their helmets off too. James was the first to speak.

"So we didn't learn much. The lamp is dangerous as all hell and some bad people are coming after it. We basically knew all of that, except now we know their name: The Cabal. Obviously this Mr. John Jones was part of some counter organization meant to keep the lamp away from the Cabal. We have to assume his organization is gone which is why he gave the lamp to Oliver. We have his name and his service rank now though, so we should be able to at least run a search on that."

Nightingale was next "What lamp, I'm so confused."

"I'll tell you when we get back to Valhalla," I told her, she nodded her head at me. "Hey Astrid, what was that part about you being mean as a rattlesnake and the Japanese fellow?" I asked.

"That was a long time ago Oliver. Let's just say not everyone who gets the lamp is as kind as you are, and I didn't have a lot of incentive to help people while I was a slave to the lamp. Maybe I'll tell you more about it later. I really don't like to remember my time in servitude." I nodded at her. I could understand not wanting to remember bad memories. I had a really hard time with that after I had beaten the rapist half to death. It took me a long time to move on and that was just from one event, Astrid had been trapped for centuries.

I finally had a chance to actually look around now that I knew the house was probably empty and not trapped to all heck. I noticed the state of disrepair it was in. The place had been thoroughly raided. There was chunks of drywall missing, random bits of the floor torn up, every light fixture had been yanked out and dismantled. I would guess The Cabal were the ones who had done this, trying to find anything to help them get to the lamp. The Old Man's hologram popped to life one more time and he spoke.

"Hey, get out of here. The foundation of this place where I have the technology that senses you and runs this projector, it's going to blow up in about ten minutes. Don't worry, the neighbors are safe, but this house isn't. LEAVE! Get off my lawn!"

"Well, he couldn't have made that any more clear, besides this place had clearly already been cleaned out. Let's get the hell out of here," I said, then I snapped my helmet back into place. We all slowly headed out into the front yard. I got lost in thought for a second while I was heading down the expansive steps on the front of the house that led down to the lawn, but when I looked up I saw something very unexpected. Between the ship and our current position out on the large lawn stood five men in perfectly crisp black suits. One stood in front of the others, a distinguished Asian gentleman with just a hint of grey in his hair around his temples. All five of the men had very large frames and looked very imposing. The Asian one had a very nice looking samurai sword, I think that's what it's called at least, around his waist and tied in place with a red silk sash. The rest of the men in the group had empty hands, but that didn't mean they didn't have weapons under their coats or concealed elsewhere.

I saw the rest of my friends had stopped at the top of the stairs behind me... Great, I was the only dummy who hadn't been paying attention and spotted them right away.

"What's the plan guys?" I said quietly into my throat mic. My helmet would hide my voice from the men in front of us, but my team would hear me just fine. James was the one who responded first which made sense, he had the most tactical experience out of all of us.

"Well, we need to get to the ship no matter what. Five dudes in suits may not be that imposing to us, but they could have air support hovering just out of range ready to come in and turn us all into spaghetti. I say we approach and hear them out. It's clear they want to talk or they would have just attacked us in the house. If things go sideways we knock them out with the shotguns and make a mad dash for the ship. How does that sound Oliver?"

"Sounds good, let's move before any more arrive."

We slowly walked forward and I hit the fancy new switch that my dad had installed that let me broadcast a modulated version of my voice outside of my helmet.

When we were about thirty feet out from their group I rose one hand in the air, waved, and shouted "Hi there!" I had said it in what I hoped was a cheerful manner indicating peaceful intent. Except as soon as I said it a few of the men put their hands under their jackets. The tall Asian one in the middle must have been the boss. He simply held one hand off to his side with his fingers splayed and said "No," they all withdrew their hands and took a neutral stance once again.

"Sorry to startle you," I said as we all stopped about ten feet out from their group. I noticed then my voice was slightly mechanical and deeper than normal. The modulator was what had set them off. I looked back at my team, Nightingale had moved behind Anthony's shield which was a great idea. Me and her are the only ones who can actually heal people and my healing is limited to my arbitrary point system that could run out of points at any time. We needed her up in case we needed help.

The Asian and obvious leader stepped forward then. "Hello, I have wanted to meet you folks for quite some time. I am Okubo Tokugawa, it is nice to finally find you," he said with his hand outstretched. My manners got the better of me and I happily shook his hand. His grip was firm even to my enhanced body and through my gloves.

I stepped back after the handshake and he stood politely still and unmoving for a minute before finally saying "This is the part where you introduce yourselves." This is also the part about being the leader that I hated, whatever course I took from this point on could condemn us or win us the day. Ultimately my manners won out a second time and I decided to go with kindness and respect. I remembered my name tag.

"You can call me Captain for now," I said tapping my name tape. "These people behind me are my friends."

"I have a sneaking suspicion that you were the heroes who rescued the kidnapped Pakistani girls. That was quite a feat. I applaud you for your bravery and honor." Okubo then did something I didn't expect, he slightly bowed to me. I was overcome with confusion at this point. I had just assumed these were bad guys, but they were treating me with the utmost respect.

"Sir... Mr. Tokugawa, I appreciate the respect you have shown me and my friends. I have to ask though, why are you here right now?"

"Oh, you may call me Okubo, I expect we are destined to be great friends. If we could come to any amicable relationship today I would be greatly pleased. I am here looking for you, and your friends of course. I believe we both fight for the side of righteousness you see. I have studied your actions and I approve.

I have come to offer an olive branch, and I would very much like to hire you all. You see I run an organization that pursues a noble mission. We are trying to save the world."

Everything he was saying seemed too good to be true. He just happened to be doing the same exact thing I was trying to do. I may be young and admittedly naive, but I'm not that gullible. Something about this whole situation stunk.

"Backup Oliver, back up right now. I recognize that sword," said Astrid over our internal comms. I did as Astrid asked and took a few steps back.

"What's wrong, did I do or say something to offend you?" Okubo asked.

"One second sir," I told him and switched my own comms back over to internal. "Astrid what are you on about?"

"Oliver, I made that sword a long time ago for one of the most dangerous men I have ever met. I made it when I was the genie. I think I recognize the glasses on the man behind him as well, the one with the shoulder length brown hair. If those are the glasses I think they are, our guns will be of no use here." I looked at the man she was referencing. He did have some very strange glasses on, they were circular and very old fashioned. Looking at the rest of this crew, their modern suits and complete lack of adornment was making me notice what a red flag those glasses were throwing all the more.

"Astrid I trust you, if you say we can't trust these guys let's start making our way to the ship. When I move, you guys move. I'm going to try to break this off peacefully," I said before popping my coms back over to my external speaker.

"Mr. Tokugawa, I am afraid me and my associates have to leave now. It was nice speaking with you. How can I get in touch with you to talk more about your offer?"

"I'm sorry, but you can not leave this courtyard until our business is concluded. You see I know you have come into contact with an extremely dangerous item. I wasn't sure at first, but you being here now, at this house, there is only one reason for that. My organization protects the world from the dangers of this particular item. I believe we both know of which item I speak. Now, where is the lamp?" I had noticed a slight edge creep into the end of his sentence. His tone was giving me a really bad feeling. I popped back over to internal comms.

"Astrid why did you say our guns wouldn't work?"

"Because I made those glasses when I was the genie. I made them for Benjamin Franklin to help him survive the

Revolutionary War. They stop all combustion in a large radius," replied Astrid.

"You gotta be shitting me!" said Anthony. I watched him dig through the saddlebags on Lumpy and pull out a flare. He ripped off the cap and tried to spark it to life a few times. Nothing happened.

"Holy shit, she is right. Our guns are of no use here," said Anthony. I switched over to external coms once again.

"We are leaving now Mr. Tokugawa, please do not try to stop us. Your actions today will dictate If our organizations are ever going to have a peaceful future," I said with a finality. I also drew my stun baton, this thing was pure electricity, no combustion needed to spark one of these guys up. I started walking in a slow semi-circle around Okubo and his men, my team followed. Okubo didn't move, but he did speak and he spoke very clearly. He sounded pissed.

"You can not leave here. The lamp is too dangerous. If it fell into the wrong hands it could be used to extinguish life itself. You have three seconds to lay down your weapons. If you don't comply you will be arrested... It doesn't have to be like this, we could join forces. I know you are good people." Mr. Tokugawa slowly drew his sword as I counted down the three-second warning he had given me in my head. At two seconds left I watched the rest of his flunkies all flip out extendable batons from underneath their jackets. At one second left I could tell all hell was about to break loose. I figured we might as well get the drop on them.

"ATTACK," I screamed, and we did.

I watched Anthony run in first. He smashed two of the men down at once with his giant shield. Anthony's robot dogs were right behind him. They jumped on the downed men and began to headbutt them. Two of Okubo's men jumped on James and they disappeared completely as if they didn't exist, I was very confused about that scene, but I didn't have time to think about that. I felt more than saw Okubo coming at me at that point. I rolled backwards instinctively, a reflex trained into my body after the many training sessions with Astrid. I saw a glint of steel out of the corner of my eye flash by me before I was able to jump back up to my feet. I wonder how close his sword had been to chopping my face in half... this guy wasn't playing around.

Astrid was on him a second later. She shoulder checked him with the shield covering her arm, and forced him back. He was good though.. too good. He kicked at one of her shins and grabbed the edges of her shield. He twisted it hard forcing her to flip over in some kind of perverse Judo move. We had been training though, and cheating... I had been enhancing the

389

members of my team for weeks and weeks with my power, specifically our agility. Not to mention Astrid was a Grade-A warrior before the enhancements. So when he flipped her over instead of landing on her back and getting the air knocked out of her like I am sure he had planned, she landed on the heels of her feet and swung her shock baton at his face which he barely managed to parry.

I knew an opening when I saw it so I came in with my own baton and started taking wild swings to keep him busy. Astrid came at him from his other side. This guy had the moves though, he was keeping up with us. Flinging our batons back at us, or knocking them to the side like it was nothing. So I decided to turn up the heat. I counted on Astrid to keep him from getting a clean strike on me and instead I started using all of my strength on downward strikes. Instead of trying to take calculated blows, I started raining harder blows down onto his guard. I was losing a lot of precision and I wouldn't be able to counter a hit from him, but I didn't have to as long as Astrid was fighting him as well.

I slammed down blow after blow and I could tell it was taking a lot out of him. Every time I hit his sword it pushed him back further and his arms weakened. All of our training had paid off in dividends because I still felt as fresh as a daisy despite this exercise. Anthony must have finished his two goons off because his big shield bumped into Okubo's back. Anthony swung his baton over the top of the shield to try and strike Okubo's head, but he saw it coming and threw his sword up horizontally to block it. That was what we needed to take him down. Me and Astrid both swung low, but the sucker jumped straight up and kicked off of Anthony's shield performing a beautiful front flip just over us. Astrid swung upwards to smack him, but he somehow parried it before landing.

He spun around and yelled "ENOUGH!" He got a two handed grip on his sword and it began to glow a deep red like it was burning hot. Then I noticed the heat waves in the air around it, it was burning. He came at us anew with more vigor than before. I put my baton between me and him in a standard block, but his sword went right through it like it was made of so much butter. Before I could recover he took a giant downward swing at me before Astrid or Anthony could get to him. I jumped to the side right before it hit my face which he was aiming for. Pain filled my body, but I couldn't tell quite where it was coming from. I stumbled backward a few feet to get out of his range so I could assess myself to check for injuries. I tried to lift my right arm up, but I couldn't seem to find it. The dull roar of pain on that side of my body was increasing.

I noticed something quite terrible at that point as Astrid and Anthony reengaged Mr. Tokugawa. My perfect arm sat on the dark green Illinois grass a few feet in front of me. Inside of the white armor I had been wearing, with a perfect white glove still on my hand. That arm was supposed to be on my body. I walked towards my arm, I needed to put that back where it belonged. My feet weren't working the way they were supposed to though. I kept stumbling in my attempt to get my arm back. When I got close to it and started to reach down to grab it, that asshole Tokugawa threw a side kick that hit me right in the chest, and made me stumble backwards and fall butt first into the lawn. I sat there in the lawn watching Astrid and Anthony in a haze barely able to contain Mr. Tokugawa as he tried to cut through them. I noticed then the only thing that was saving them was that anytime he got too close to one of them one of Anthony's robotic dogs would try to take a bite out of him.

I felt strong arms go under my remaining armpit and across my chest, and lift me to my feet. It was Nightingale, such a nice lady.

"Oliver you are in shock! Walk back to the ship!" she said yelling at me and pointing at our ship. I trusted her, so I started stumbling towards our ship. I wondered though where all the blood was. When you lose a limb isn't there supposed to be blood? I reached over and touched the spot where my arm used to be and only felt bumpy smoothness, then pain shot through the raw material there. Better not do that again. Oh, the hot sword. That jerk's sword was so hot it had cauterized the wound cleanly closed.

Anthony

This butt-fucker had moves straight out of a Jackie Chan movie. My shield and dogs were the only things holding him back. I had left my dogs sitting on a chest of each of the guys I had taken down at the beginning of the fight but once I saw Oliver lose his arm I called them in to help me. Without them I think this guy would have killed all of us. I had them doing strafing runs because I knew if I gave this guy an opening he would chop them clean in half. He had somehow superheated his sword and he was really taking chunks out of stuff with it. My shield being heat treated polymer rated up to a couple thousand degrees was probably the only thing saving me right now. Astrid was taking shots at his back, but she didn't have anything to defend herself with so she was mostly just trying to keep his attention divided.

"GET BACK!" a weird voice I didn't recognize yelled. I did as ordered though, I didn't want to get shish kabobed by magic sword guy here. Astrid did the same as we leapt backwards together in opposite directions. Okubo turned to face his new threat and a long strand of foam smacked his chest, his arms, and his legs, and it just kept coming. Some of it was hitting his sword and burning up on contact. He tried to move out of the way but he already had too much on him and it was making him sluggish and restricting his movements. I let Nightingale keep foaming the guy for a few more seconds and then I took my opportunity. I shoved my whole entire shield on him, knocked him over and squashed him below it. The shield would create a very heavy weight that the foam would adhere too. Try your fancy ninja moves with a couple hundred pounds super glued to your side, sucker!

I was doing a push up to get off of my shield, but suddenly his sword poked out of the back side of my shield. It had burnt clean through missing my face by inches. I quickly rolled off of the shield not wanting a repeat performance. I looked up and saw men climbing the perimeter fence on all sides of the courtyard we were in.

"We have to get out of here, we are outnumbered and Oliver is injured!" I yelled. Astrid's eyes were wild, she was looking in all directions.

"WE CAN'T LEAVE WITHOUT JAMES!" she yelled frantically.

"James is gone Astrid. I saw them take him, they disappeared."

As we were talking, honest to god arrows started to land around us. I took one look at Astrid and she knew it too, we had to leave. We made a mad dash for the ship. Ahead of us I could see Gul trying to help Oliver up the loading ramp but he was much larger than her and she was having trouble with the incline. I ran up behind him, grabbed the back of his belt and heaved him into the ship. I remembered my shield for a second and toyed with the idea of going back to retrieve it, but I also remembered it didn't matter. I could print a new one and tangling with magic sword guy wasn't that fun. Your brain does silly things when the adrenaline is running. Nightingale was a few feet behind us and I noticed she had a few arrows sticking out of her at weird angles as she ran up the ramp herself. Once she cleared the lip where it met the ship I slammed the button to close the ramp. Gul leaned out and fired an arrow at a man who was going to make a running leap to get on. Her bolt hit him right in the chest and he flew back allowing our ramp to close and the ship to seal.

"What the hell happened to you?" I shouted at Nightingale.

"I tried to get Oliver's arm back," she replied.

I found myself shaking my head, poor Oliver. An explosion rocked our ship and knocked us all off of our feet.

"BIFROST GET US OUT OF HERE!" I shouted. Whatever they were using to stop combustion was obviously off now if they were lobbing explosives at us. I had worried for a second if the ship would even take off if combustion didn't work in our area, but the ship was fusion anyway so I bet it would work regardless. The ship lifted off and I felt myself get pulled to the deck for a second and I heard a few loud whistling noises coming from outside the ship's hull. The ship cantered hard to one side and I got a great view of John Jones' front yard. We were only about 100 feet up, but outside of one of the small windows clear as day I could see that asshole Mr. Tokugawa waving Oliver's arm as if he was saying goodbye to us, what a prick.

Bifrost's voice came over the intercom "Two missiles avoided, and two more incoming. Brace yourselves for evasive maneuvers."

None of us had any time to brace for anything as Bifrost hit the speed. Oliver's unconscious body slid down the deck and landed in my lap as I slid backwards myself until I smacked into the bulkhead. I propped him up next to me and strapped him into some cargo netting. I sure hoped we lived through this.

Chapter 20

James

The moment the two goons grabbed me I knew something was wrong. The light from the sky itself went out and then I was falling. I landed hard and pain shot through my ankles causing me to lose my footing. I heard a pneumatic hiss from somewhere above me. I finally got my bearings and was able to assess my surroundings. I was somehow underground now... in a cell. Three walls of my cell were some kind of transparent material that I could already tell was too thick to get through by banging on it. The last wall was solid stone, it felt natural like that of a cave. Then I heard a muted giggle from above. The men who had grabbed me were standing on the transparent roof of the cell above me, and one of them was still laughing slightly at my confusion.

"Works every time," he said before high fiving his partner. I was really freaking out now, *what had worked?* I looked around more and noticed I was in a long line of cells just like this one. I was in some kind of prison.

I yelled into my comms trying to check on my teammates but no one answered. I switched my comms over to the external speaker.

"Hey you two giggling fucks, how did we get here?" They both looked at me like I was crazy before climbing down an external ladder on the outside of the cage. One of them looked around conspiratorially like he was looking for listeners and then put his hand on one side of his face like he was hiding his mouth from lip reading attempts.

"Between you and me, we teleported." He said sarcastically before openly laughing again.

I couldn't help it. I drew my Glock and dumped the entire magazine into the transparent material between me and him. He jumped back and surprise filled his face. I holstered my weapon and admired my handy work. I had spidered the hell out of the stuff and putting my finger into the indent I had been making made me think I had maybe penetrated about halfway through it, but it was hard to tell.

"I'M COMING FOR YOU NOW BOYS. IT'S TIME TO PARTY!" I shouted like the maniac I am when I want to be. I inserted a fresh magazine and drilled 17 more rounds into the same spot. Splinters of the transparent stuff were flying everywhere. A lot of them were smacking me right in the mirrored visor of my helmet, *thanks Anthony!*

I repeated the process a few more times in different areas around the original wound in the wall I had started making. The two men who had captured me looked incredulous like I was wasting my time, but apparently now that I wasn't in Kansas anymore I had all the time in the world. I had a pretty good little crater going in the wall now and I had only used about half of my ammunition. I pulled some duct tape out of my kit and made a little dam on the front of the crater. Now the two guys watching me were really curious. I pulled out a handkerchief and laid it flat on the floor. Then I took off my dump bag I was using to carry these ridiculous taser rounds, the ones that we use in the shotguns. *If only I had some real explosives*, this would have to work for now. I started popping the shells open with a larger fixed blade I was carrying and dumping the black powder onto the handkerchief I had laid out.

The two men realized what I was doing and got really scared. "Oh SHIT!" one of them shouted.
The other yelled at him "Go tell the tech running the cells to gas this cell block!" The one he was yelling at took off sprinting. Great, now I was on a time limit. I started working faster not wanting to find out if the gas they were going to spray me with was *night night* gas, or *die die* gas. I'll have to tell Anthony to try and add a rebreather to the helmets after I get out of this one.

Who would have known HAZMAT obstacles would have been a problem for us. I always thought we would be stopping bank robbers or something, not escaping secret underground prisons. I finished dumping a few more shotgun shells worth of gunpowder onto the handkerchief, and then I wadded the whole thing up and shoved it into the dam I had been making in the crater on the wall. I hastily threw on a few more layers of duct tape over the whole thing hoping the blast would stay focused on the wall and less inward on me. I made sure to leave some of the handkerchief hanging out.

Then I did something I really didn't want to do. I lit the end of the handkerchief on fire really hoping that I wasn't about to blow my own arm off. I spun around to run away and I saw little steel tubes extend from the rock wall of the cell, and then I heard them emit a hiss. The gas was here, shit. I jumped to the farthest corner of the cell away from the pile of gunpowder and made like a roly-poly bug. I kept trying to get smaller and not breath as I waited for the inevitable boom. This helmet was in no way airtight, it was a glorified motorcycle helmet with a layer of Kevlar on it. *I really hope that gas isn't flammable*, was my last thought before the bang. The gunpowder went off and I felt burning debris smack my back pretty hard, thank god for armor.

I jumped up and spun around still holding my breath. I now had a really ragged hole about three-feet in diameter. I didn't have time to think about it, I made a running jump through the hole and smacked into the concrete of the floor outside my cell. There was no one in sight. I guess they didn't want to stay for the fireworks. I ripped my helmet off and took a deep breath, I was worried about any residual gas that may have been trapped in there. I put it back on and snapped it back into place, getting shot in the face didn't sound fun. I had to get away from here, there was still gas flooding these chambers from the giant hole I had made in the cell wall.

There was only one way out as far as I could tell, the same direction the first guy had run off in, so I went that way. I looked up seeing hanging lights coming off of more natural cave walls, I was definitely underground. The cells ended and the cave made a pretty sharp right turn. As soon as I crested the turn I ran into about 30 men and women in riot control gear all waiting for yours truly. They were tapping batons in their hands and generally ready to kick my ass. *Well if these guys think I'm going to play fair they are dead wrong*, I thought. I drew my Glock and rapid fired as fast as I could at the clear fronts of their riot helmets. I was pleasantly surprised when I saw blood splatter inside of their helmets. I had worried for a second that the transparent surface was bulletproof.

I kept up the barrage, but they rushed me. That didn't stop me from putting on a truly spectacular show of marksmanship that would have made any competition shooter proud. I dropped at least 13 more before they got to me and dogpiled me. I was buried beneath a pile of bodies, and I felt one of my arms twist at a weird angle. Someone ripped my helmet off and started hitting me in the face with a baton...

Anthony

Oliver was not looking good. His lips were blue, his skin was clammy, and he generally looked like death warmed over. I ripped my gloves off to feel around his neck for a pulse or any sign that he was breathing. His breath was so weak I thought he might die at any moment. We had just left the atmosphere and made it into space so there was little to no gravity in the shuttle now.

"HURRY BIFROST!" I shouted, worried about my best friend.

I felt the ship speed up and we made it to the station a minute later, and I felt gravity return. I had been holding onto the cargo nets that I had tied Oliver up in. I ripped him out of the nets as carefully and quickly as I could and carried him down the ramp with everyone else right on my tail.

"Put him down on the floor right now Anthony," said Nightingale in a calm voice.

"Don't we need to get him to the med-bay?" I asked frantically.

"We don't have time for that," she replied.

I did as she asked and gently laid him on the floor. Nightingale stood over him with a leg on each side of his waist. Then she leaned over until her hands hit the floor on either side of his head. She looked very much like a spider at that point standing over her pray. Small filaments and tentacle-like metal appendages came out of her chest piercing her armor to get out. They traveled forward and poked at Oliver's chest before piercing and wiggling through his armor as well.

"Is he alright?" I asked, with a noticeable tremble in my voice.

"I'm assessing that now. My theory is that the sword that removed his arm was so hot that it instantly cauterized the wound, which is probably the only reason he is alive right now. Oliver is in extreme shock. Without the arm here to reattach there isn't really much I can do medically for him except treat his symptoms and try to normalize his vitals. We will be safe to move him in just a minute."

As promised a minute later all of the tiny little tentacles coming from Nightingales chest going into Oliver's started reeling themselves back into her body. She stood up and told me he was safe to move as long as we were careful. I used my new ability to access Bifrost and the station directly to put an order in for some droids to bring a gurney down to us at top speed. They appeared pretty quickly sprinting it right up to us. I gently lifted Oliver up to the gurney. Astrid stepped up to him and removed his helmet carefully, then kissed his forehead. Gul did the same except she was openly crying. We walked him slowly to the med-bay, Gul holding his hand the whole time.

"Who is going to tell his parents," asked Astrid.

Okubo Tokugawa

"Did we get anything from the one we captured yet?"

"No sir. Facial recognition has him as one James Gatewood. An honorably discharged combat veteran. A few years back his family, a wife and a son, were both killed by a drunk driver. Since then as far as we have been able to tell he has been almost off the grid. He pops up to buy groceries every once in a while but mostly he just stays inside. No idea how he ended up on this super-charged team."

"Move on to chemical measures with him, skip the torture. A man with nothing left to live for won't break. Fill him so full of chemicals that he forgets his own name, and then work him backwards from there until he talks."

"We will do that sir. Also as you know, we were able to place over 17 different types of trackers on their ship. They were all destroyed an hour ago, but we have their last known location. You aren't going to like this sir... They are in space. We believe they have some kind of orbiting space station that they operate out of. Last week we received some very sketchy intel that some scientists were being shuttled up to some kind of space station in exchange for cash, but we didn't believe it or look into it. With what we know now though it must have been true. We have teams out now rounding up some of the scientists, we will interrogate them and bring you any information we have ASAP."

"Good work agent. Dismissed."

I watched the agent retreat from the command center and like I always do when I am in deep thought, I began to pace. I knew we were close, closer than ever before to something big. Not just another magical relic, but the lamp itself. I could feel it.

Even the vastness of space couldn't stop the Cabal. I didn't have any concrete evidence that the lamp was up there, but some part of me knew it was.

"Tech Jansen!"

"Yes sir!"

"What space-based assets do we have?"

"A bunch of stuff in R&D sir, but nothing that works right now."

"That has to change today. Dump all of our resources into space-based raiding craft, it doesn't have to be pretty. We just need to be able to get on to that station of theirs. It can even be a one-way trip, we can use their own shuttles and our teleporters to get back down here once we take the station for ourselves. Do whatever you have to do, dump as much money into it as you need, hire whoever you need, just see it done!"

"YES SIR!"

We are very close indeed.

Astrid

"Wake up Astrid." Getting jarred awake by Bifrost's creep ass voice was never fun.

"WHAT! What is it that you want you infernal machine?!"

"Oliver requested that everyone come to the med-bay."

I was already running as soon as I heard his name. I made it the med-bay in record time. I spun the corner and saw Oliver sitting up on his bed. I couldn't help but throw my arms around him. I heard others entering the room so I let go of him. Everyone came, even his parents. Well everyone except James who was still missing... Before anyone else could rush in and hug Oliver, he held his hands up as if he wanted them to stop.

"Listen up everyone. I'm done, I'm done with all of this. I was wrong about all of this. I'm not fit to lead anything or save anyone. We got lucky once and we let all of this go to our heads, and I got a good man killed because of that. You are all welcome to live here of course. I'm not kicking anyone out, but our mission is over. The most important thing now is keeping the lamp up here where it's safe away from those monsters. In fact I'm thinking about pushing this barge away from planet Earth completely after stocking up some food, and I don't know when or if I will ever come back."

I couldn't believe what I was hearing. "Oliver, you would abandon James?" I asked incredulously.

"Let's be honest with ourselves Astrid. James is dead, and he was the best of us. The rest of us here are kids dressed up in fancy Halloween costumes. James was the only real hero among us and he is gone."

"How dare you Oliver. James is alive and he would never abandon you if you were in his place. And how dare you call me a child! I have been a warrior since long before you were born. Stop being a coward! BOO HOO little man, you got your arm chopped off, suck it up and MAN UP!" Oliver's face turned a very interesting shade of red after that comment and he jumped out of his hospital bed and put his finger in my chest.

"YOU ARE A RELIC ASTRID! Look around you, you know as much about this stuff as you do a toaster, which is nothing! You aren't qualified to do anything, I don't know why you think you have any right to be lecturing me! You know nothing except the inside of the lamp, and your love for James, which is why you aren't thinking clearly... Anthony was just a fat video game nerd just a few weeks ago, and I'm just a retard who got lucky! If we try to fight The Cabal or go after James they will rip the lamp from us and kill us all! Do you understand what that means! Do you think I want to be the asshole who brings about the end of the world as we know it?" Oliver stormed out of the room after that.

"Well what do we do now?" asked Anthony.

"We continue the mission and try to get James back."

***

I banged on Oliver's door for the thousandth time and like always he never answered. I had tried to break the door down at one point, but six of Valhalla's droids showed up and ran me off at Oliver's orders. So at least I knew he was alive in there. I left the tray of food I had brought him in front of his door and went back to the hangar where Anthony was already prepped and ready to go. Two months had gone by and we still hadn't been able to find James, but we had been busy. What we were up to now was a perfect example of that. We had just gotten intel from one of our informants we were regularly paying off. He had sent Bifrost an encoded message that the Sinaloa Cartel was helping two high level Islamic State operatives get across the border. The informant also let us know the word on the street was that they were bringing a dirty bomb with them. I had to have Bifrost explain what a 'dirty bomb' was to me. Apparently it's a regular bomb that the bomb maker has imbued with radioactive and other HAZMAT materials. So when the bomb blows it ends up killing way more people with side effects and radiation. In other words these fuckers and everyone helping them needed to die before they blew up some school kids or something.

This wouldn't be the first job like this that me and Anthony had handled. Anthony had joined some kind of 'hacktivist' group on the internet who initially started feeding us tips. Once they saw we were actually stopping these shitheads they couldn't wait to feed us more information. All of a sudden nerds in their mom's basements in countries all over the world were feeding us some of the best intel on earth, they got to feel like heroes from the safety of their soiled bean bag chairs and we got to crush evil. They weren't afraid to do it either once they knew for sure that we weren't the police, and I think the first time we had hung some bad guys in town squares we had pretty much solidified ourselves as being not law enforcement. We had been beating the shit out of everyone, we were equal opportunity ass kickers. One day we might smash in the skull of a child pornographer. The next day we might free a small village from African warlords, and the day after that we might assassinate a cartel leader in Mexico. Like I said, we had declared 'open season' on shit heads, and there was no bag limit.

We even had a couple local legends popping up about us and a few nicknames started. I had heard us called everything from "The Beauty and the Beast" to "La Flama Blanca" which translates to "The White Flame." I guess they were referencing the color of our armor. The only thing I hadn't heard about was any news regarding James. I had tortured scum bags all over the world looking for news about The Cabal or anyone fitting James' description and no one had heard anything. I didn't lose hope though. James was resilient and crafty, I knew he was out there somewhere still fighting. We just had to get to him before it was too late.

"Astrid, I asked if you were ready," said Anthony.

"Sorry, just got lost in thought," I replied.

"I miss James too."

"It's not just James. I'm worried about Oliver as well. He hasn't come out of his room in months."

"He will come out when he is ready."

"Right... Right, well let's move."

We were working on a tight time schedule. The Sinaloa Cartel was moving the two ISIS members in a protective convoy. They were mostly just protecting their paycheck with the heavy security since the second half of their payment wouldn't be delivered until the ISIS operatives checked in safely in the U.S. Too bad for them that's a payment they would never be receiving. We took the shuttle down to the border between Mexico and Arizona to wait for the convoy to hit wilderness. We weren't afraid of The Cabal knowing we were here because

Bifrost had long ago calculated how they were tracking us, which was of course spotting when Bifrost camera looped any satellite feed. So we had just stopped doing that. We didn't really care if we were spotted now the traditional way either, no one had the response time to get to us before we left any area. Criminal actions all over the globe were being halted, so only a real asshole would put up a fuss about something like that, especially publicly. Besides if anyone ever did try to chase us it's not like they could follow us out of the atmosphere.

Bifrost had been using her orbital camera to track the ISIS operatives and she was giving us location data on the convoy as it moved. We were running our shuttle in stealth mode with absolutely zero lights at night time so the chance of the convoy spotting us was slim to none. Which is why I wasn't worried when we started flying parallel to them at about 300 feet of elevation. Anti-vehicle weapons are expensive and damn hard to get without working with criminals or stealing from the good guys, so me and Anthony had had to improvise. I had taken a really nice compound bow from our armory that belonged to James, and Anthony had printed me up some very special arrows for it. The entire shaft of each arrow was basically made of a durable compound that could be detonated at any time remotely if wired correctly. We had made it simple though and just set them to explode on impact using the same type of primer system that a bullet might use.

I was never the best shot with a bow, even back when I was a Shield Maiden, but shooting downwards at giant targets like cars meant I didn't have to be a great shot. I clipped myself off with a tether to the inside of shuttle and we lowered the back ramp until it was parallel with the ground. Anthony had Bifrost take over the flying and came to join me on the back ramp. The wind wasn't too bad because we were only going about 40mph. You can't drive that fast on rough desert terrain so if the convoy sped up they would probably only do our job for us and crash themselves. There was no real reason for Anthony to be on the back ramp with me, but he did want to watch the show and I could understand that.

I took my helmet off for this. Some things just have to be seen with the naked eye to truly cherish. The wind whipped my ponytail about which made me miss James, he always complimented my hair. I pulled the drawstring of the compound bow back until my hand touched my cheek. I planned only for a little bit of drop. We were much higher than them and this bow was set to James' level of strength so I counted on the shots flying mostly straight. I let loose the first arrow and watched as an explosion lit up the night about twenty feet from the lead vehicle. One of the cars in the convoy freaked out and drove off of the rudimentary desert road and promptly hit a boulder killing all inside.

"Low and left," said Anthony's calm voice over my shoulder. We had been working together for months now, and we operated like a well-oiled machine.

I took Anthony's expert advice and oriented my bow up and to the right just a bit and let loose another arrow. I was extremely satisfied with my shot as I watched the lead vehicle explode into flames and then flip over. After its flip it landed back on the desert road, blocking the rest of the convoy. That's when the cockroaches scattered. Every vehicle stopped and men came flying out in different directions, some ran into the night but the dumber ones stayed by the vehicles. Some opened fire on hostile bushes out in the desert that I guess they thought was us. I let off two more arrows in rapid succession roasting the fools dumb enough to stay by the vehicles. After that the rest of them scattered thoroughly into the dark desert.

I felt Anthony's strong hand tap my shoulder and he yelled "NOD'S" in my ear. Which stood for Night Optical Device, they would let me find the cockroaches in this darkness. It was one thing to shoot at giant reflective vehicles using headlights, but finding humans from this height with no light would have been impossible. A smile warmed my face as it always does when I get to use cool stuff that we didn't have in my time.

He put the NOD's on my head for me since there wasn't really anywhere for me to set my bow down safely on the back of a moving aircraft. I gave him a thumbs up with my off hand once they were correctly in position and then I kept firing the explosive arrows at the fleeing men. Once they were too spread out for me to hit them at this range and angle we had Bifrost lower the shuttle until we were skimming just ten feet above the ground. Anthony's dogs with no prompting from us jumped off of the ship and started running off into the desert to hunt down our VIP's of the evening. Then we landed the ship back at the front of their burning convoy and got out ourselves.

We carefully went down the line of SUV's and cars covering each other, checking the casualties of the vehicles I had hit. Some of the roaches were still squirming, but they were in no condition to pick up a weapon so we left them be. A few minutes later Anthony's dogs returned pulling some people behind them. The person Fenris was pulling was clearly dead with half of his body burnt to a crisp, but he matched the description of one of the ISIS operatives so Fenris had done his job well. The one

Lumpy was pulling was the other ISIS operative, this one was still very much alive. He was kicking and screaming and trying to get out of Lumpy's grip. I kicked the one that was squirming in the face and put him down for a much needed nap.

I tied them both together and Anthony dragged them up the ramp to our ship. We had Bifrost fly us out to the Mexican ocean nearby. Once we were about twenty miles offshore we opened the back ramp again and threw them out just as the one I had knocked out was coming to.

"HAVE A NICE SWIM!" Two more terrorists off the board, only a few million more to go. This superhero gig was really growing on me. You see technically I wasn't killing these guys. I was just giving them free skydiving lessons, it's not my fault they didn't bring parachutes.

Okubo Tokugawa Mighty Chairman of the Cabal

I walked along in the giant hangar that housed our new rocket-propelled spacecraft, it was a bulbous thing. From what the scientists working on the project had told me, our timing would have to be damn near perfect for the launch. Apparently the entire space station we were after was coated in some kind of high tech paint that made it damn near impossible to spot using modern technology. So we had been tracking it using specially made telescopes specifically tuned to find it. The damn thing was black on the black of space. This wasn't exactly easy, but where there was a will, The Cabal had a way.

Tech Jansen walked next to me through the large hangar clicking away on a Cabal tablet. The man had quickly become my sidekick around headquarters. He had been an invaluable asset and a loyal supporter.

"Estimates on completion of the device Tech Jansen?"

"According to this data if we abandon a few more safety precautions we can launch in three days and still have a 93% success rate to reach the target."

"While I value the haste, I also don't like to gamble with the lives of my men. How long until we can get the success rate to say 95%?"

"If we work the men in double shifts, possibly ten days sir, but that is speculation based on us not hitting any snags."

"Gather the men, I'll tell them myself. In ten days we launch."

Chapter 21

Astrid

"This reminds me of old times," I told Anthony.

"How so?"

"Fletching arrows like this, I use to do this... *before*."

"Yeah, it is easy to forget that you used to live with the dinosaurs and fly on pterodactyls and shit."

"Fuck off Anthony."

Anthony looked like he was in deep thought as he carefully attached the primered arrowhead to another explosive shaft before finally handing it to me and responding.

"Seriously Astrid, I've thought about it. I don't know how you deal with it sometimes. You ever miss all those people you knew back in the day?" I finished super gluing the last 3D printed synthetic fletching onto the current arrow I was working on before responding.

"I come from a pragmatic, but deeply religious people. Death was part of our culture you could say, and it was very common. I'm sure you can imagine, without the glory of modern medicine my people were much stronger, but also weaker in other ways. You might get a strange cut during a swim and die a few weeks later, things like that weren't unheard of. I knew eventually everyone I knew would die. Sure my people and myself, we would be sad for a time, but we would move on quickly because we had to. Your people have time to mourn with their modern comforts, tap water, and groceries stores. If my people stayed inside to mourn we would starve to death quickly. So in a lot of ways I was built to deal with grief, and I've had a long time to process this. So no I'm not sad about it. I'm not even that nostalgic, now is the best time to be alive. Have I told you how much I love your modern dentistry?"

Before he could reply Bifrost's weird ass voice came over the intercom in the room.

"Astrid, Anthony, Oliver would like to see you two in his quarters at your earliest convenience."

"Wonder what that is all about? Maybe Oliver is finally going to float this thing into the sun," said Anthony.

"Don't say things like that. Let's go."

We quickly headed towards Oliver's room. I had to admit I was nervous over what he would say. Especially after his *outburst* before. As we entered the hall he was on I could hear loud pounding noises and I could see Oliver's door was open at the end of the hall, which I now knew was the source of the noise. That was a sight I hadn't seen in months, Oliver's door open. Oliver had locked himself in his room after his fight with us and refused to come out or let anyone in. So him calling us in now so casually with his door open like nothing had ever happened was actually making me pretty nervous. The loud pounding noises absolutely weren't helping the tone of the situation either. I looked over at Anthony who could obviously hear the noises as well. He shrugged when he saw me staring and walked forward. Not wanting to let him show me up I jumped in front of him and entered Oliver's room first.

Oliver was wearing some loose black gym shorts and nothing else. He was openly sparring with one of the Droids. His back was to me, and he was kicking the droid's ass with all kinds of moves I had never seen from him before. The weirdest part of the situation was that he had two arms... I didn't notice it at first because I had been entranced over his fluid and quick martial movements, but something was seriously off about his right arm. The shape wasn't quite right and he had the lighting in this room low which made it hard to determine why.
"OLIVER!" I shouted. He threw a final punch with his right arm that had been missing the last time I had seen him and it hit the droid squarely in the chest. The droid flew several feet backwards and hit the nearest wall, then slowly slumped down into a pile on the floor. I noticed a visible fist shaped dent where Oliver had hit it. Something was seriously up with that arm, *the*

arm Oliver wasn't supposed to have... I thought his power couldn't create matter...

Oliver turned on me and I smiled mechanically, but all I could focus on was the grotesque pairing of his new arm where it met his body. The arm was clearly a droid's arm, or it had been at one point. It looked like a droid's arm that had been altered. There were divots and lumps in the metal of the arm that weren't present on a standard droid's arm. I could use the one slumped over in this very room for a visual comparison.

Oliver's was bulkier and shaped to fit his body. There was long cylindrical shaped shafts of metal going from the arm and running into the skin of Oliver's shoulder and armpit. I could see exactly where the metal pierced his skin and ran below it for a while. Until the rods went too far into his body and the skin that was raised and covering them became flat and matched the same level of the rest of his skin. I wondered what those shafts were actually mounted to... Thinking about it gave me goosebumps. He had somehow mixed a piece of machinery with his biological body.

The arm wasn't the only change, though it was by far the most drastic one. Oliver had also put on at least ten more pounds of solid muscle. He must have just been in here working out and sparring with the droids this entire time. A small part of me agreed with this course he had taken, the Shieldmaiden part. Making your body more combat ready at any cost was a very Viking thing to do. The traditionalist in me though, that part wasn't happy. Again I internally shuddered at the combination of man and machine, there was nothing 'smooth' about this pairing. I looked up into Oliver's face and saw a slightly insane look in his eyes.

"So this is what you have been up to?" I asked him.

"I did what I had to do," he replied with sadness in his voice. "That's not why I called you here though. I wanted to apologize, to both of you." It was then that I noticed Anthony was in the room as well, and he was also staring at Oliver's new arm.

"Listen you two," Oliver continued. "I was a pig headed asshole of a coward, there is no other way to say it. We took a huge loss, and as the leader I should have found ways to fix it. I should have rallied us and pushed on. I gave up on my friends and my family, and I hid. I didn't know what else to do and I can't explain what a shock it is losing a limb, the defeat of it mentally and physically is horrible. That's not an excuse, I know I messed up and I'm not trying to excuse myself or the things I said and did. I'm not fit to be the leader, I never was, I know that now.

I've seen the amazing things you guys have been doing without me. I can't help but think if I had been along calling the shots I would have just been an anchor dragging you guys down. You two have done more by yourselves in these last couple months than I ever did as the leader of the team... I'm so proud of you guys. So I'm here, and I've asked you here, to ask you two something. Would you allow me to be your friend again? I know I don't deserve to be on your team, and I'm not asking to be. I think I need to work alone for a while, figure out my role in all of this. I just want to be your friend again. It took all of this for me to really realize the significance of what true friendship was, and what an idiot I was for throwing it away so casually."

Oliver trailed off and I noticed he was crying a little bit. He wiped his tears away and stood straight.

"I'll understand any decision you two come to," he added and waited for us to respond.

"Did Oliver just swear?" Anthony asked.

"He did, it was weird," I replied.

"Yeah, it felt right in this one instance to get my point across," said Oliver.

"Well it's weird so don't make a habit of it, swearing is kind of my thing," I told him with a smile on my face.

"Oliver you changed my life, you saved me from myself. Yes, you made some mistakes, but you are human. We all make mistakes. You have always been, and you will always be my friend," said Anthony.

Oliver looked over at me expectantly "If you agree to help us look for James you will have me back as a friend. Friends don't leave friends behind."

"I'll help, I promise. Trust me I would do anything to get James back. You know what, as a show of good faith I have a gift for you," said Oliver.

"What's that?" I asked.

"I've saved up a butt-ton of my energy, my points that is. When I first locked myself in here I was using every spare point I had to get my new arm attached and to get it working properly. Once I did that I improved the hell out of it by burning up even more points. Finally I was a whole again, I kind of came out of my stupor a bit. Once I was a tad more rational all I could think about was you two, and James. I worried a lot about Gul, I abandoned her when she was in a bad place too. My parents who were worried sick about me, and then they had to see my behavior, and I wouldn't even let them in here when they came to visit... I've been fixated on all of this for a long time, and trying to find ways to stop this from ever happening again. One of the conclusions I came to was that if you and James had superpowers like Anthony and I, then maybe they wouldn't have been able to grab him. So I saved up points, a lot of points. I know you and James talked about what powers you wanted on that date you went on a long time ago. What did you decide on?"

Him bringing up my date with James had stung, I missed him. Upgrading myself so that I would be better suited to rescue James when we found him, I couldn't argue with that logic or pass up the opportunity.

"Yeah, me and James did decide on what powers we wanted. I don't know if you can do it though," I said.

"Try me," Oliver replied.

"Well, when I was in the lamp the only time I truly felt free, powerful, and untouchable was when I was leaving or entering the lamp. I would turn into some kind of vaporous mist. I could still think and steer the mist. It was exhilarating flying around with no one being able to touch me. I would like the ability to do that again. To turn into the mist or fog or whatever it was."

"One vaporous style superpower coming right up!" Oliver shouted with one mechanical finger in the air.

Something I hadn't seen in a while happened next. Oliver put his hands in the air, fingers splayed palms facing me. Then he touched his hands together and dragged them apart quickly. As he dragged his arms apart the screen materialized between them. This part is always cool to watch. Oliver put his robotic hand under his chin like he was thinking then words began to scroll around on his screen until it stopped and read:

"Give Astrid the ability to turn into her vaporous form that she used to leave and enter the lamp as the genie. She may also turn back into her human form at her discretion. She can perform this transformation once a day. Price: 455 points."

"Wow, that is way cheaper than I thought it would be. I shot low trying to keep the point cost realistic. Let me see what happens when I improve it," said Oliver. Again the words began to scroll into place as he changed the upgrade. This time it read:

"Give Astrid the ability to turn into her vaporous form that she used to leave and enter the lamp as the genie. She may also turn back into her human form at her discretion. She can perform this transformation TWICE a day. Price: 735 points."

"So the price does jump up dramatically, but that is still within my price range. I've actually tried a lot of upgrades on my arm. The more you try to upgrade something at once the more the price exponentially jumps. I bet if I were to try to make that power work three times a day the price would be well over 3000 points," said Oliver.

Everything Oliver had just said made me curious, and to be honest I was a bit power hungry. "Try it, I just want to see what it would look like," I said. Oliver complied and brought up an upgrade where I would be able to go incorporeal three times a day. The price on it was 3495. Oliver's guesstimate was right. He must have gotten really acclimated with his power over the last few months.

"Okay let's run the second option. I'm ready now. I'm guessing I'm going to pass out like Anthony?" I asked.

"I have no idea. I don't even know why it's so cheap for such an extravagant power," said Oliver.

"Well that part is obvious to me. I've been doing it for over a thousand years already. My body knows how to do it," I replied.

"That makes sense. You want to sit down or something first? In case you pass out?"

"Sure," I said as I leaned against a wall and sat Indian style. "Hit it!" I shouted, and he did. I watched him press the confirm button and the weirdest sensation came over my body. It was like worms crawling below every inch of my skin. My head felt cold and tingly, my hands went numb for a second, and I felt my eyelids go heavy, but I fought the urge to pass out. Then it all stopped, I waited for a minute to see if this was some kind of remission before more symptoms started. I would have felt really silly if I had stood up prematurely, and then fallen unconscious and landed on my face or something. I waited another minute, but still felt nothing else out of the ordinary. "I think it worked," I said with a sly grin on my face. "Watch this guys!"

I focused like I had a thousand times before when I was the genie. I felt my body and everything I was wearing instantly change and spread out into the fog like substance I was so use to. It was so freeing, the feeling of it was pure power. I forced myself to float off the floor of Oliver's room and move up to the eye level of Oliver and Anthony. Their faces were unadulterated wonder. I had too much excitement running through me, I had to move. I pushed the fog as hard as I could and flew out of Oliver's room. I tried to fly directly to the recreation floor, but the steel sliding doors between here and there no longer opened when I came near them now that I didn't have a body. I tried to fly into the seam where the door met the wall, but it was too airtight, which was ultimately probably a good thing. I felt around myself more than actually 'seeing' things in this form, so I felt for the air currents around me. THERE, a vent in the ceiling was pushing air into this section. I flew up into the vent as fast as I could and headed towards where I thought the recreation floor was. Finally out of one of the vents I could see the clear blue water of our little pond. I flew down quickly and did a few laps around it. This was amazing, the greatest gift anyone had ever given me.

I flew back through the vents, back the way I had come and jetted straight back to Oliver's room. As soon as I flew through the doorway I switched back to human form. There was one serious problem with that though. I was still carrying all of the momentum that I had while I was flying forward. My body was screaming through the air moving at least 50 m.p.h. I bounced once off of the floor and flew right at the steel back wall of Oliver's bedroom. I knew if I hit that wall at these speeds I would quickly be turned into paste and explode like a blood filled water balloon. A millisecond before I hit the wall I turned into the mist again. The mist harmlessly splattered along the wall and flew out in every direction, it felt terrible. I felt too stretched, like too little butter over too much toast. I focused on pulling myself back together until I was one giant clump of mist again, and then I hovered perfectly in place in the air and once again turned back into my human form.

"WHOA!" I shouted.

"What the hell was that!" Anthony shouted.

"Well I about turned myself in Astrid paste, but needless to say the superpower works, and it is amazing. Thank you Oliver," I said.

"You deserved it, and please be careful. If you kill yourself with the power I just gave you I'll probably feel really guilty," he replied with a joking smile. Oliver's smile didn't last long though, soon the insane look came over his eyes once more.

"Again, I know none of this makes up for my behavior... We are going to find James, and I'm going to personally kill Tokugawa..."

"Kill? You are going to kill him, not imprison him?" I asked Oliver, my sweet Oliver. The things he was saying just weren't like him.

"Yes, I will kill him. Real life isn't a superhero cartoon, it's not a comic book, or a witty movie where the heroes always come out on top. In real life good people get raped, murdered, and kidnapped. They get their arms cut off... We can't be the only ones following the rules, we will never win that way. The forces of evil should be terrified of us, not the other way around. Actions speak louder than words Astrid, and all we have seen from Tokugawa is hostility and bloodshed. Someone needs to stop that monster before he hurts someone else, and that person is me..." If I thought Oliver looked crazy before, now he was full on nutso. His eyes had a fire behind them that I hadn't seen before.

"Listen Oliver-" I never got to finish that sentence because a horrible warning klaxon started and I saw the lights in the hallway had turned red.

Next Bifrost came over the intercom "Oliver I believe we are under attack, though I am not sure what type of attack this is. The attackers have so many projectiles moving at us at top speed that some of them are bound to hit. They are also launching electronic counter-measures to confuse the A.N.I.'s that drive the laser array around the station. I've been having to personally drive as many lasers as I can since the A.N.I.'s can't keep up with a barrage of this magnitude."

"I can help with that!" shouted Anthony before sitting cross-legged on my floor and closing his eyes.

"Anthony what are you doing?" I asked.

"I'm going to control as many lasers as I can myself," said Anthony.

"Oliver what should we do?" I asked.

"No, I'm not fit to make decisions anymore, I-"

"SHUT UP OLIVER. WHAT SHOULD WE DO!?" My shout got through to him and I saw him start calculating a plan.

"Bifrost get my parents and Gul to a safe room!" Oliver shouted.

"Oliver I have to inform you that many of the first wave of projectiles have hit the station, and they have begun drilling into the hull," said Bifrost.

"Astrid you are with me, get armored up, and get weapons, as many as you can. Prepare to repel boarders! When Anthony is done here he will join us." Oliver went under his bed and started pulling out hard cases. I didn't have time to see what was in them because I was already running to my room where my weapons and armor were stored. I quickly got into my armor and grabbed my normal loadout, but I left the shotgun. I could never get used to that thing. Instead I grabbed the compound bow that I had been working with lately. I started loading explosive arrows into a quiver, but I thought better of it. There was no telling what kind of damage those things would do to the inside of the station. So instead I loaded the quiver with as many regular arrows as I could, threw it on and ran out.

Oliver was just ahead of me in the hallway running towards what looked like the hangar bay. He had on one of my large circular Viking style shields in the white polymer/kevlar mix that was common in our printers on his left arm, his human arm. He must have made himself a shield at some point using Anthony's schematic. Knowing Oliver he probably just ordered Bifrost to make it and then had the droids deliver it to his room. In his right arm, his mechanical arm, he was carrying a nondescript hard case, the same type I had seen in his room. I couldn't help but wonder what he had inside of it. He had his shotgun slung across his back and a Glock holstered on his hip. He was loaded for bear. The armor he had on now must have been the set he was wearing when his arm was cut off, because his mechanical arm was fully exposed and the shoulder of the armor was blackened, *as if burned*.

"Oliver why are you running that way?"

"Bifrost says the biggest concentration of boarders are in the landing bay. She said she would take care of the rest, I have no idea how, but I don't have time to argue. Let's haul ass!"

Okubo Tokugawa

(14 minutes before the attack on Valhalla)

"Are the men ready?" I asked my ever loyal Tech Jansen.

"Yes sir, 83% of the men are loaded and have secured their pods, the rest should be secure within a minute or two, but sir I have one last thing to discuss with you... I must humbly beg of you to let me come with you on..."

"Stop there Tech Jansen. You are an irreplaceable resource and I would never question your tenacity or bravery, but you cannot come on this mission. Men will be lost today and The Cabal would be all the weaker without you around. Especially if I fall today, I am counting on you keeping the Cabal organized and efficient."

"Sir, even if you weren't here I could never hope to rise to the position of Chairman."

"You sell yourself short Tech Jansen. Some of the smartest warriors lift their sword the least. Even if you never rose to the rank of Chairman your contributions to the Cabal are still prodigious." The Chairman stopped talking for a second as if in deep thought, before continuing. "When we take the space station you will be among the first brought on board to explore its mysteries."

"YES SIR!" Tech Jansen shouted happily.

If I had a hundred Tech Jansen's I could have captured the lamp by now, he really did have three times the tenacity and spirit than most of my other troops.

"Tech Jansen, one last time tell me how this contraption works," I said motioning at the giant bulbous black rocket ahead of us."

"Well sir, the whole thing is fully modular and meant to break apart once you leave the atmosphere. Every piece becomes a missile after its final orientation towards the target. Every nut, bolt, joist, girder, and support beam will become a cacophony of scatter-shot meant to confuse any defenses that the space station might have. As the rocket further breaks apart, 150 rocket-propelled pods each carrying a Cabal warrior will launch towards the space station. Along with the 150 pods carrying warriors, there will be 150 decoy pods fired as well. Each decoy pod will let loose its own defensive suite, a veritable scattershot of ball bearings, chaff, and flares. Since the decoy pods don't have to carry a person we have jammed them full of signal emitters that will be throwing off junk signals further meant to confuse any defenses on the station. Once a pod comes into contact with the station it will begin to drill into the side of it while injecting a specially formulated glue meant to preserve the atmosphere since we are planning on keeping the station."

"Thank you Tech Jansen, as always your information has been invaluable and reassuring." I said before securing my helmet that would top off the lightly armored space suit."

I heard Tech Jansen's muted voice behind me yell "Good luck sir, the world is depending on you!" I know Tech Jansen, I know.

Oliver

We were running down the hallways of Valhalla trying to get to the hangar bays when we stumbled onto a group of the space pirates or whatever they were. I spun around the corner and saw five of them carrying some kind of micro-uzi type weapon, so I quickly spun back around the corner to safety and told Astrid to wait. The invaders were wearing some kind of black space suit with armored pieces over strategic areas. I reached down and considered if I should unsnap the buckles on my case or shoot at them with my Glock.

Before I could make my decision I heard Bifrost's voice come over our internal comms in my helmet. "Oliver I will dispatch these men so you can continue your mission to the hangar bays."

"Um, okay," I said.

I heard a strange mechanical hum come from around the corner so I took my chances and looked, hoping I wasn't about to get a face full of lead. The lights in the hallway dimmed and flickered and a thin long hollow slot opened along each side of the perfect white hallway, about 1 foot off the ground. The electronic hum reached a higher pitch and a bright burning laser stretched across the hallway, like a trip line from hell. The laser started advancing toward the five-man fireteam at a pretty slow, but steady rate. I could see from their bodily movements that they were all trying to alert each other about the oncoming danger. I felt Astrid brush past my knees so she could look around the corner as well. Once the laser was about halfway to them it more than doubled in speed right at their shins. Four of the five men were able to jump over it and dodge the laser, but one man didn't get the message and was cut down. He fell over blood gushing out of his new stumps. The laser died off somewhere behind their position.

Two of the men on the fireteam bent over to help tourniquet the man's legs so he wouldn't bleed out, but they were both interrupted by a new electronic hum. This time two laser streams lit up shooting across the width of the hallway. The same laser as before and this time an additional one at neck height as well. The lasers started moving towards the men. The impromptu medics stopped helping their downed friend and stood up in a ready position to try to anticipate the movement of the lasers. One of the men took off running in the opposite direction of the lasers, but a bulkhead door dropped down from the ceiling and cut him in half thoroughly blocking any chance of escape for the others, *gross*, three more left.

The dual laser beams increased speed once they were halfway down the hallway like last time. One man ran straight forward and nimbly jumped between them dodging all danger. One of them tried to anticipate the beam and ended up jumping too soon. Gravity carried him belly down straight onto the laser beam, that was all kinds of nasty, two left. I'd had enough of the laser game, this was disgusting. I heard the hum of the laser beams start up again, and this time three lasers appeared, no, no more. I spun the corner and open fired with my Glock. Astrid was right behind me and she let loose an arrow from a heavy compound bow. Her arrow flew right through the chest armor of one of the remaining men and he fell over spraying his micro-submachine gun into the ceiling. I kept plinking at the remaining one with my Glock, but his armor was obviously meant to stop small caliber bullets. Another one of Astrid's arrows flew over my shoulder and sunk into the man. That's the thing about most modern armor, it stops bullets just fine, but arrows go right through it.

"Bifrost, what in the sweet fuck was that!" Astrid shouted.

"The Valhalla space station has defensive measures like that in most of the public thoroughfares. They are in place to stop hostile persons from harming key personnel," said Bifrost.

439

"Then why are we running around like chickens with our heads cut off. Just kill the invaders in the hangar bay!" shouted Astrid.

"There are two reasons why I can not do that Astrid. The hangar bay has no traps like what you just saw, it's too large and it has to be load bearing. There is one small A.N.I. driven auto-turret in the hangar bay recessed into the ceiling, but I can not fire it at the moment due to the presence of command personnel in the hangar bay. James Gatewood is currently among the ship-boarders in the hangar." Bifrost finished.

"James..." said Astrid in a low voice who then took off running.

"Wait Astrid, it's a trap, we can't just run in there!"

Chapter 22

As soon as we entered the hangar I heard Okubo yell "Stand down!" We were completely surrounded. There was at least fifty members of the Cabal in here, around our shuttles, and they were all armed with the strange compact submachine guns.

"Ah, welcome Oliver! Come in come in," the pompous bastard shouted. The nut job was acting like we were old friends. "I've brought many gifts for you. For one your friend James. Come forward now James will you." At his request James did step forward, but everything was wrong about him. He had a vacant look in his eyes, his skin looked too pale, and it looked like he had lost at least 10 pounds. James turned his head for a second and I saw something horrific on the side of his temple. It was a small gray box, and it had little lights on it indicating it was on and doing *something*. The box had small transparent tubes coming in and out of it and ultimately going straight into James skull. The tubes were pushing different colored fluids in and out of the gray box. It was grotesque and that's coming from a guy who shoved a robot arm into his body. Astrid was more stunned than me, she took a sharp intake of breath upon seeing James' condition.

"Oh no, not my James... What did they do to you?" asked Astrid.

"That's not the only gift I brought," said Okubo who waved a hand over his shoulder. One of his minions marched forward with some kind of long silver case. He kneeled at Okubo's feet and popped the clasps on the case. I could see some kind of fog coming out of it. He spun the case around so I could see its contents... It was my arm... Just like the day I had lost it, still encased in the white armor and wearing a perfect white glove.

"That's right, it's your arm, and your friend. You can have them both freely and we can work together. As soon as you give me the lamp and control of this space station of course. I know you are probably thinking 'no,' why though? Why fight me, we are on the same side you and I, we both want to save the world."

I didn't believe a thing this guy was saying. Good guys don't drill into people's heads so they can pump chemicals inside. I flipped the button on my transceiver and spoke into our internal channel "Anthony, can you control this turret in the hangar bay? Bifrost says there is one recessed into the ceiling somewhere in here."

"I can do it," replied Anthony.

"Don't hit James, he is here wearing one of the black space suits," I replied.

"I have turret access, and eyes on James," said Anthony.

"Anthony you are the best," I said.

"Thank me after we save James," Anthony replied

"Wait! Any way to get some droids in here to cover us?" I asked.

"No, Bifrost has them deployed all over the ship fighting the Cabal warriors that infiltrated other sections. If I pull them here we leave other parts of the ship unguarded. I can however send one of my dogs down, I need one here to protect me while I coordinate with Bifrost and help her defend the ship."

"We'll take what we can get, you'll know when to strike."

The good guy in me wanted to warn Okubo, despite all he had done. I didn't even know we had a turret in this room and I had no idea of its capabilities, but I knew Anthony was proficient and that he would protect James even if it meant killing a lot of people. The rational part of me that valued logic and planning above trying to emulate the fictional characters I had fallen in love with as a child was telling me to kill all of these guys before they could hurt me or my friends. Maybe I could find a solution somewhere in the middle. I calmly walked forward until I was only ten feet or so in front of Okubo.

"Okubo Tokugawa, welcome to my home. We call this place Valhalla... thank you for bringing me James and my arm. Though, as you can see I might not need it anymore," I said while lifting up my new mechanical arm. I continued on trying to sway Okubo's decision to try to take the lamp from me, though ultimately I knew he was probably the type who would prefer to die over failing in his quest.

"I propose a challenge in order to save the lives of your people and mine. We have two options before us. Option 1: I can unleash all of the assets at my disposal, and I'm sure at that point you will do the same until we all kill each other. Even if you think you can win I promise you it will be at a great cost. OR, there is Option 2: We both know there will be bloodshed here today. Instead of our people suffering why don't me and you have an honorable duel. Me versus you, you use your weapon and I will use mine." I said while shaking the case in my hand. "Whoever wins takes the lamp, you can't have the space station though, I'm sorry."

I waited for his response, he would look cowardly in front of his people to not accept. Okubo answered promptly as if he didn't even have to think about my offer, if nothing else the man was a great tactician.

"Yes. I accept your offer if you will stand by it. However I will not fight a masked man. Hiding your face is dishonorable among my people and I think you are a man of honor. If I beat you I will spare your life and the lives of your friends, if and only if you have the lamp delivered here to me immediately. Also I will agree to leave your space station, Valhalla as you call it, the second the lamp is delivered to me. Honor this deal and no one will be hurt."

I unclasped my helmet and threw it somewhere behind me. Then I set my hard case down and unbuckled the two clasps holding it together. Inside was something I had Bifrost put together for me: a four-foot long Tetsubo made of a hybrid combination of the densest materials that we had in our printers. Due to its dense metals it was actually too heavy for me to wield with my human arm, but my mechanical arm would heft it just fine. I had made this weapon with Okubo in mind and for a split second I saw the surprise in his eyes.
I lifted the tetsubo and pointed it at him with my mechanical arm "I'm ready to begin when you are," I said flatly.

He must have been antsy to get the lamp or maybe he was just testing the waters because almost faster than I could track he drew his sword and smacked the end of my tetsubo with it. My mechanical arm didn't budge, though I did feel the weight of his hit in my leg muscles which were the only ones straining with the weight of my new heavy weapon. I quickly took a two handed grip on the tetsubo and backed up a few feet. Even though my human arm couldn't heft the weight of the weapon it could help my new dominant arm control it. I took a huge horizontal strike at Okubo which forced him to jump backwards out of my range. Then I took a huge overhead strike as I pushed forward knowing Okubo would think this was a mistake. He dodged my overhead strike and tried to move in on me quickly once my Tetsubo hit the deck where he had been standing, leaving an obvious dent in the hangar floor.

Time slowed down as I saw him moving forward, I wondered what he was planning. Maybe he was going to try to cut off my last human arm. I didn't even bother to lift my tetsubo off of the deck as he came forward I just waited for that perfect moment. You see I had been training for this, every free second since he took my arm. At first I had been fighting the training droids one handed with no weapons. Just strengthening my body and getting it used to unarmed combat, no pun intended. Then once I developed and attached my mechanical arm I had begun fighting droids who were armed with Katanas and who fought in similar styles as Okubo. Then finally I had started testing weapons, seeing which one was the best to disable an expert

Japanese swordsman, this line of logic brought me to the tetsubo.

Lastly I had to stop thinking like a human. I had been upgrading our bodies for a long time. Even though my 'stats' like my strength, agility, dexterity and what not were all within human levels still, I was definitely at the high end of the spectrum. To top that off my new arm was WAY above the level of 'human' in every category. I would showcase the strength and speed of that now. My only real problem was making sure I didn't use too much power and throw myself off my feet with the weight of the tetsubo, which I had done plenty of times while training.

Okubo was still coming at me, hoping to exploit what he thought was an opening, a trap I had carefully set. I only moved when I knew it was too late for him to change his course of action. I wanted to make the smallest movement possible to keep drawing him in while avoiding his attack and simultaneously striking him, so I bent ever slightly and started spinning the tetsubo away from him in a giant circle. The lifting and spinning part was easy thanks to the strength of my mechanical arm, the footwork for this was the hard part. Like an Olympian with a giant shot-put or a discus I spun for all I was worth trying to not get ripped off of my feet. In less than half of a second I had spun all the way around with my weapon to Okubo's weak side.

Impossibly he had seen his impending demise and got his sword into place to block it. That wouldn't help though, the tetsubo was much too heavy and moving much too fast. I stood up a little straighter at the last second and cantered my hit ever so slightly upwards. My tetsubo connected with his weapon which he had braced with one hand on the grip and one hand on the back of the upper part of the sword. All of my kinetic energy transferred into him and he was lifted off of his feet and thrown. He flew at least 15 feet back and 10 feet up before his back smacked onto the side of one of our shuttles and then he unceremoniously slid down onto the floor. Again impossibly he landed on his feet, but slumped down with exhaustion. I had hit him with a lethal blow and he had somehow lived through it, at least he was winded or possibly injured for now. This could be our only chance.

Anthony must have felt the same way as me because while Okubo was still knelt over doing whatever it was he was doing a double barreled laser the size of a motorcycle came out of the ceiling and opened fire on the Cabal soldiers. At the same time Fenris, Anthony's sleeker mechanical dog, ran into the hangar and jumped on the nearest Cabal soldier. Astrid fired an arrow over my shoulder which landed in the chest of a different Cabal soldier, and I knew it was time to beat feet. I took off running as I heard pings hit the deck where I had been standing. Cabal soldiers ran in all directions trying to get cover from the laser while firing their high pitched submachine guns at me, Astrid, and Fenris. I made a beeline for James.

James actually had his original shotgun still, and he had it aimed right at me... I was hoping some part of him was left and that he wouldn't fire before I got to him. I had no way of knowing what he had chambered in that thing. A cabal soldier got in my way and physically grabbed me before I could get my tetsubo up. He actually lifted me off my feet and yelled in my face.

"You aren't the only one who is strong!" He screamed.

"Cool story bro!" I shouted back at him before pulling my Glock and dumping my magazine into his face. The fucker didn't even drop me, he just squinted his eyes like I was hurting him a lot. *What the hell is this guy?* I dropped my tetsubo and used my mechanical arm to start pulling his fingers off of me while he was recovering from the high speed lead facial massage I had given him. It was like his body was in so much pain he wasn't sure if he should drop me or scream. I did what any reasonable weakling

449

would do when overpowered by a much stronger opponent and started delivering kicks to his groin area. He must have been tired of having his balls and penis pulverized because he threw me like so much trash, only straight up... A blur hit me in mid-air and tackled me to the deck where I landed in a lump and rolled to a stop. Whatever had hit me was already running away, I looked up and saw it was Fenris who had already jumped on another Cabal soldier. I still had to get to James. I felt my back armor get pinged a few times, by something heavy before I realized I was getting shot at. I dropped low remembering I didn't have my helmet on and didn't want my brains splattered across the deck. The shooting stopped so either the ceiling laser or Astrid must have shot the shooter. I got up and started running.

It was pure pandemonium. Cabal soldiers were dying everywhere. Someone threw some kind of low explosive percussion grenade at Astrid which sent her flying. Fenris darted in and out of the enemy ranks disabling people where he could. The turret fired faster and faster sending visible red laser fire in every direction as it pivoted. Some of the Cabal soldiers were trying to get to the turret to stop it by climbing on top of the nearest shuttle. I knew we didn't have long. I sprinted towards James once again trying to get to him before Okubo could get to me, wherever he was. A large gout of flame erupted from a nearby Cabal soldiers hand in my direction. I felt it lick the sides of my head and I closed my eyes against the searing pain. I tried to pat my hair out that was now on fire with my mechanical hand and almost knocked myself out patting my skull too hard.

James was still pointing his shotgun right at my chest with sweat beading on his forehead. He was obviously having a hard time not pulling the trigger. I grabbed the barrel with my mechanical hand and yanked upwards ripping it out of his hands. I used my left hand to grab the grey device on the corner of his head and I yanked for all I was worth. The tubes ripped out of his temple and his head exploded in blood. Strange fluids co-mingled with blood and leaked out of the many holes in his head where the tubes had been. James folded like a cheap lawn chair and fell into my arms.

"Bifrost open the hangar bay door, no plasma shields, NOW!" I shouted, knowing that Astrid was further away from the doors than the Cabal soldiers. The doors cracked open and the vacuum of space started pulling everything towards it. A few Cabal soldiers that were too close to the doors got sucked out almost instantaneously. I spotted Okubo just behind me closer than I would have liked. He was kneeling still, with his sword red hot, and buried a few inches into the deck of the landing bay which was how he was staying in place I assumed. He couldn't come towards me while the bay doors were still sucking people out into the stars, *which was good*. I saw Astrid, her face was a mask of blood, she was trying to hang on to a tool chest near the exit of the bay that takes you further into the station. I was only not moving because I had my mechanical arm dug into a seam in the floor, my other arm was looped around James' chest holding him to myself. I was afraid Astrid was going to get ripped into space as well since her grip on the tool chest looked tenuous at best, so I yelled for Bifrost to flip on the plasma wall. As soon as she did the roaring scream of sucking wind stopped, but the bodies that were already in motion towards the door couldn't stop because they were moving so fast. Their momentum carried them directly into the plasma wall instantly catching them on fire or vaporizing them in an explosive burst. Some of the people who had been flying towards the door were no longer being guided by the vacuum so they bounced off walls and other things that people generally shouldn't be bouncing off of.

I knew I only had mere moments until the madness started again and I could feel the blood from James' head running over my organic arm. I brought up my enhancement menu and just imagined an upgrade where James was completely healed and not being mind controlled. I heard a mechanical **SHING** type of noise behind me and I knew Okubo had just yanked his sword out of the deck. I was out of time. I didn't even look at the upgrade or the cost I just hit the confirm button, threw James over my shoulder and started running towards the exit. I saw a few lasers fire over my shoulder and then I heard a terrible screech of metal bending. I looked up, it was the strong man with the bulletproof skin that I had fought earlier. He had his feet on the ceiling and he was yanking on the turret which was somehow stopping it from firing. I knew more bad things were coming so I just kept running.

Astrid who had no right whatsoever to be on her feet after getting hit with some weird type of grenade was standing near the exit of the bay and lifting her bow once more and firing. She had one of her eyes pinched closed and her face was still covered in blood. I wondered if her eye was damaged or if she was closing it for better aim. Before I whipped the corner that left the bay I took one last glance behind us. The scene was total disarray. There was dead and dying Cabal soldiers everywhere, Okubo was right on my tail, but Astrid was lobbing arrows at him which he was seamlessly cutting out of the air with his sword somehow. Some Cabal soldiers were helping others who had been hit by the laser turret with whatever version of first aid supplies they had brought. The strongman had thoroughly ripped the laser turret out of the ceiling now. He had each barrel of the turret over his shoulders like he intended to use them as clubs. Again I pulled up a healing type upgrade for Astrid not even looking at the cost or the verbiage on the upgrade, we had no time. I hit confirm and the eye she had closed snapped open. It was a bloody and gooey mess that in no way resembled an eye. I saw some shrapnel push its way out and her eye start to re-inflate, that was something I could have died without seeing. I tried to keep James balanced as I grabbed her shoulder and ripped her with us around the corner.

"Let's try to lose them in that laser trap!" I shouted. She took enough time to nod, but I could tell the healing was really hurting her and throwing her off balance. "Anthony or Bifrost fire up this trap!" I shouted as we ran down the hallway. I heard the high pitched whir from before start up, but whoever was in control of the laser field made sure to wait until we were clear to start the laser blade up. As soon as we got around the corner where we had hidden at and watched before, I dumped James on the floor against the wall. He slumped down still unconscious, even though my healing was near instantaneous it appears there are just some things the human body needs to rest after, particularly having tubes ripped out of your brain it seems.

Thinking about James' human brain for whatever reason made me remember Nightingales' robot brain.

"Bifrost, where the heck is Nightingale?" I shouted.

"She is in the med-bay tending to her patients," Bifrost responded

"What patients?"

Before Bifrost could reply two grenades were lobbed down the hallway with the laser traps in it. I got back around the corner and threw my body over James. As the **WHOOMPH WHOOMPH** of the two grenades went off I peeked back around the corner. The walls were shredded and the electronic whir of the laser trap was gone, *no no no*. Cabal soldiers started pouring around the corner with Okubo at their front. I pulled my Glock and blind fired around the corner with my mechanical arm, not wanting my organic arm to get shredded.
"We have to keep moving! Bifrost where is the nearest trap? Anthony, can we get some reinforcements yet?" I shouted hoping the messages would get rerouted to the correct folks. Bifrost was the first to respond.

"Anthony is sending two droids with special armaments your direction. Rendezvous with them in front of the cafeteria, that is where the next antipersonnel trap is as well."

We started running towards the cafeteria, I dragged James by the back of his space suit with my mechanical arm which conveniently never got fatigued. Astrid waited at a few corners as we made our way to the cafeteria and fired arrows behind us. Though her wounds had been healed her face was still the same mask of blood it was before. Now the blood was partially drying and cracking in some areas, she looked like a war maiden from hell and I mentally reminded myself to never piss Astrid off. Eventually the Cabal learned our trick and started throwing their specialized grenades around every corner to stop her from staging arrow ambushes. We still couldn't let them gain on us so I continued to blind fire behind us with my ever dwindling ammo supply, even if it was just shooting the empty hallway to keep them honest. Mostly we just moved though, knowing our real chance of surviving was at the cafeteria trap.

We hit the cafeteria doors at a run and headed inside, they slid open before we got to them and stayed open per my request. I had a last moment thought and shouted at the ceiling.

"Wait to deploy the trap Bifrost, they throw grenades sometimes that might damage it."

"Yes Oliver."

Sure enough grenades went around the corner, even though we weren't directly in the hallway I still flipped over a cafeteria

456

table and waited for the blast to go off just in case of shrapnel. The Cabal grenades didn't seem to be overly dangerous compared to regular grenades, if anything they were a little underpowered it seemed. I idly wondered as their explosions went off if this was something they had formulated just for this mission, not wanting to damage the station too much in case they took it. Bifrost's voice came over the speakers nearest to us.

"The trap's efficiency is still at 73%"

"Perfect, fire it when you think it will have maximum effect."

"Yes, Oliver."

I still had a partial view of the hallway even though I was now in the cafeteria by looking through the large doorway that let people in and out of this area. So while I couldn't see the whole hallway I had a pretty clear view of the strangeness that happened next. I heard a series of loud bangs and saw silver streaks fly across the hallway in the direction we had come from. "What was that Bifrost?" I asked

"Javelins propelled by black powder. Some of Valhalla's traps are low tech in case of technological sabotage and a myriad of other reasons that I am sure you can extrapolate at a more opportune time."

"Good point," I said as I hopped over our downed table with Astrid hot on my tail. I regretted having to leave James lying there crumpled behind the overturned cafeteria table but I couldn't exactly carry him into a fight. As we walked forward to check out the carnage the last trap had caused I went ahead and slapped a fresh magazine into my weapon and put the nearly empty one back into my belt. I went around the corner by 'slicing the pie' just like James had taught me. Basically it's a way to show the least amount of your body to any potential attackers while keeping your eyes on them the maximum amount of time. What I walked into was a bloodbath of viscera and destruction, parts of the white hallways were now literally painted red...

There was at least 13 members of the Cabal here in various stages of injury. Some of them had javelins sticking out of their guts or chests, one unfortunate fellow had one sticking out of the faceplate of the helmet of his spacesuit. Some of them had through and throughs where the javelin had pierced them and gone into the guy behind them. When a bullet passes through you as long as it doesn't hit an artery, a lung, or your heart there is a very good chance you will recover, but these javelins were too wide a bore. These men would most likely not be surviving these wounds. Right in the middle of the pile of the injured, dead, and dying was Okubo on his knees with his eyes closed. The sick bastard almost looked peaceful.

"You still alive Okubo?" I asked, while aiming the front sight of my weapon directly at his face.

"Yes," he said simply while lifting one of his hands briefly exposing a very large hole in his side.

"I didn't want it to be this way. You attacked us first," I said emphatically.

"We all have our roles to play. You may think this is a victory, but this is just the beginning. What you saw today was just us probing your defenses, now we know what you have up here. This was just a strike force, a mere 150 men. The Cabal is made of thousands."

"I don't believe you," I said sinking to my butt and leaning against the nearest wall, still careful to keep my gun trained on him of course. My comment actually made Okubo open one of his eyes and he arched one of his eyebrows up questioningly so I continued.

"This attack was a two-way street. Now we know how you will come, and besides it took you months to collect the resources to be able to get up here. By the time you are able to mount another attack I'll have tripled the defenses on this place. Think about it, did you even get close to the lamp, even once? Do you even know if its up here? How do you know I don't have it dangling over some volcano down on earth right now? How do you know that I didn't just throw the damn thing into the sun?

You spoke of this attack with the word 'victory,' look around you, look at the death and destruction. No one won anything this day." There was more I wanted to say, but I also knew I was emotionally amped up and unless I wanted to execute Okubo right now I had to be careful with what I said around him. I heard a strange noise at the end of the hallway Okubo had come from and two droids with glue guns marched into play aiming their nozzles at some Cabal men who were squirming, but not firing. Their presence made me feel a little better, until Okubo chose to speak again.

"By holding onto the lamp you are robbing humanity of its chance for peace and prosperity. For this reason righteous men will always chase you for what you selfishly hoard. The lamp is meant to be shared like all resources, it is the key to protecting our planet." It almost sounded like he was reciting holy text, there would be no reasoning with a man like this.

"What you call 'righteous' I call murdering bastards. We could have discussed possibilities of the lamp over cold drinks and hot wings. Instead you felt the need to cut my arm off, kidnap my best friend, and drill into his skull to pump mind-controlling chemicals inside of his brain. You are too indoctrinated to see it, but you have become what you hate. You are the evil that you sought to protect the people from." I wasn't sure if I should keep him talking or not. I guessed we were probably both hoping the other would slip and reveal some vital piece of information. I looked over at Astrid who had her bow drawn still and aimed directly at Okubo, her eyes betrayed nothing. I guess this is up to me.

"The difference between you and me is that I have a plan to save the planet. You are up here sitting on enough technology to advance the human race 50 years into the future, and what have you done with it? The Cabal is resistant to things like human selfishness, it appears you are not. You say I describe my men incorrectly, you say I am a monster, yet here you are playing superhero in your space station helping no one. Why didn't you wish for a cure for cancer? Why didn't you wish to own a Fortune 500 company that could ship food to places where kids are dying of hunger? You think I am a monster but at the end of the day my plan ends with me giving up my power and wealth, you hoard yours. You are selfish, turn the lamp over to my organization and watch a new era of peace and prosperity fall over our planet."

I had heard enough... "WHY HAVEN'T I BEEN HELPING PEOPLE? MAYBE BECAUSE YOU CUT MY FUCKING ARM OFF, YOU DICK. DID YOU EVER THINK ABOUT ALL THE PEOPLE I COULD BE HELPING RIGHT NOW IF I WASN'T UP HERE FIGHTING WITH YOU!" I had to take a moment and calm down before speaking further. "You have five minutes in which I will allow you to take as many of your men as possible off of my space station. Whoever you leave behind will be cared for as my prisoners. Don't worry we aren't sick bastards like your organization and we won't try to brainwash anyone. We will just lock them up until we knew who to turn them over to. If you say another word to me I'll shoot you in the face, that's a promise. Now follow my directions or die."

Okubo must of knew I wasn't fucking around. He reached behind his back a bit and I almost shot him but he came back with a tablet and started typing away on it. Soon a man appeared right next to him out of thin air. Okubo shakily came to his feet. The man who had appeared walked around to some of the injured men and was able to get four others to their feet as well. As a group the six of them disappeared. I wondered what kind of power that was and had to guess it was teleportation. There must be some reason they didn't just directly teleport up here to begin with. If I had to have a theory it would be that it had some kind of a cool down or point system like my power. The lamp really liked to put 'governors' on things. Oh well, at the end of the day it doesn't matter, the monster is out of my home and I knew using teleportation to come back is probably not too viable or he would have done it already.

Chapter 23

"Bifrost, put me over the intercom system, station wide"

"Yes Oliver, you are live in 3, 2, 1, live."

"Attention Cabal personnel, I am the Captain of this space station, you may simply address me as Captain for now. If you would like to live throw down your weapons and push them away from yourself, and then sit down in place. We will send people to collect you and render aid, food, and water. If you resist us in any way we will be forced to disable you in some way, that may just mean we will shoot you in the face, or it may be something as simple as me personally choking you out, either way it won't be fun I promise. As some of you probably already know, this station is rife with automated defenses that won't hesitate to literally cut you in half. So again for your safety I must stress that you sit down wherever you are and throw away your weapons. You will be treated fairly and with respect, if and only if you are honorable during your stay here. This has been your one and only warning, ignore it at your own peril, Captain out."

"I've ended the broadcast Oliver."

"Thanks Bifrost. Can you send droids to go collect all of their weapons for now. If any resist please let me know and I will personally handle them."

"Yes Oliver, also I must let you know that the Cabal stole one of Anthony's 'power machines' from the landing bay."

"The one that just sprayed hot soda on people?"

"Yes."

I couldn't help but openly laugh at that. They are in for an awesome surprise when they open up that package to try and inspect the tech. Astrid giggled behind me as well. I would have never guessed my life would have taken this route, or this conflict would have ended this way. There was never an epic showdown or a grand battle. Just some small scale ones and a war of attrition barely won because of some automated traps that I didn't even know existed. A little anticlimactic for a superhero's life, that's what my memories of all of the superhero shows I had watched growing up told me. Those shows that I was starting to care less and less about. My family and friends were safe, that is what mattered to me now.

"Oliver, one last thing," said Bifrost.

"Yes?"

"Your arm and the case it was in has been secured."

"Oh…. Good."

I reached down and felt along the synthetic muscles and metallic rods that made up my mechanical arm and I had to wonder if I even wanted my real arm back. I also had to wonder if I would have lived through this fight without it.

Tech Jansen

I was in the command center listening to the speech from the strange man in white armor with the mechanical arm and I had to admit that some of it resonated with me. Perhaps we had taken too aggressive an approach with him. He seemed calm and rational. I felt bad doubting my patron who had helped move me up the ranks so quickly: Okubo, but I also wondered why he wasn't more diplomatic with this group of would be do-gooders.

Okubo appeared at the front of the command center dripping blood with a teleporter and four Cabal soldiers in different states of injury. Medics rushed in and escorted the four out while one stayed to help cut The Chairman out of his suit and start dressing his wound. The Chairman wouldn't rest until this situation was over, we all knew that, there was no point in trying to move him to a medical facility.

Okubo had fire in his eyes like never before. He searched the room before his glare finally landed on me.

"Tech Jansen, Plan B," I had never heard that much menace in a man's voice.

I brought up Plan B, a plan I hadn't seen before. It had been locked off from my clearance level until just now. I glanced over the notes for it and couldn't help but stifle a gasp. Plan B involved us feeding false intel to the U.S. government through official channels that would lead them to believe the space station was a hostile faction intent on weaponizing meteors to drop them on the planet. They would surely retaliate immediately if they thought such a threat was imminent.

I froze at the implications of this, if the lamp was on the space station and we destroyed the space station the lamp would be almost impossible to find. "But sir..." I said questioningly towards The Chairman... He spun on me quickly.

"Tech Jansen, follow that order immediately!"

There must be some part of the plan that I am not aware of. Part of me also idly wondered if there was any innocent bystanders on that space station. Sure the Cabal killed folks all of the time and I was okay with that, but those were bad guys, pedophiles, criminals, the scum of the earth. I do what I do because I want to protect innocent lives. Okubo had never led me wrong before, I would trust him in this decision. I followed the plan and delivered the intel. I also sent a quiet little prayer off to whatever god lays above. I hope I am right in this decision.

Oliver Pettini

"Is that all of them Bifrost?"

"Yes Oliver, we have 7 in holding cells and 13 still in med-bay being worked on by Nightingale and the other auto-surgeons."

"Do they need more security in the med-bay?"

"No, there are five droid guards there armed with a mix of non-lethal armaments."

"Bifrost, where did all the dead bodies go?"

"They are heat treated to kill bacteria, shredded, and then sprayed over the farms as compost."

"Gross."

I took a heavy seat on the floor of the hallway I was patrolling. We had been rounding up random Cabal members throughout the ship, some had been injured, others had been trying to find systems to sabotage. One of them had been extra squirrely, he must have had some kind of specialized agility and dexterity ability because he had done all sorts of backflips and what not. All of that was before Anthony had grabbed him from behind and bear hugged him into oblivion.

James had woken up a short time ago, Astrid hadn't left his side since. I had been too busy helping maintain order on the station to visit with him much, but I did stay long enough for him to tell me that he didn't remember much of the last few months. He remembered killing a whole mess of Cabal soldiers and then nothing else until he woke up in the cafeteria.

The lights of the hallway I was in turned red once again and that horrible klaxon started up, *not again*. "What is it Bifrost!"

"I detect at least twenty hardened missiles coming our direction."

"Can the anti-missile lasers take them out?"

"Calculating... Not all of them."

"When will they be here, who fired them, what are our options?"

"They originated from multiple sites inside the United States, they will be here in nine minutes, and we have lots of options."

"List them."

"Option 1: We could spin the station and try to mitigate the damage. If the station is in a spin it should spread the damage evenly over a larger surface area. However this spin reduces the effectiveness and accuracy of the lasers. Option 2: This station is mostly modular, we could attempt to guess the missiles most likely path to the station and then jettison off parts of the station towards the missiles in the hopes that they crash into each other. Option 3: We could orient the station to the side that has the least amount of vital structures in it, deploy all available lasers and hope the A.N.I.'s that control the lasers take out enough missiles to reduce the overall damage to something manageable."

"Go with option three for now. Now, did these missiles come from the U.S. government or the Cabal?"

"The missiles were fired from known military sites. Well, known to me at least. There was no signs of cyber-intrusion, so it does appear that this launch was sanctioned by the U.S. government."

"Put me on the phone with the President of the United States."

"Oliver that will take me several minutes and most of my CPU will be occupied during that time. I will be unab---"

"Stop, I don't care, do it!"

I waited with my heart pounding in my chest for Bifrost to connect me to the commander-in-chief. I wasn't nervous about talking to him, I was worried for the safety of my friends and family. Frankly I was just tired of being worried, pushed around, bullied, and attacked. I made a promise to myself then and there that if I made it through the next nine minutes that I would take a much more offensive approach to dealing with the world at large, and I would do everything to protect my family from being put into situations like this. I also wondered if I should have consulted my friends before taking this course of action. I still really wasn't sure if I should be in charge of anything. I ran out of time to second guess myself when Bifrost told me the call was going through. I heard a ring and then his voice came over the line and I realized I was very much nervous to speak to the president. Oh well time to buck up and fake the funk.

He simply said "Go," and I wondered if this was how he always answered the phone.

"Mr. President, those missiles you just fired, you have to stop them."

"Who the hell is this?"

"I'm a member of the crew of the space station you launched those missiles at. We are not hostile. We are a non-profit organization dedicated to making the world a better place. We are peaceful Americans!" Okay so I may have stretched the truth a bit, but I couldn't exactly explain the lamp and the Cabal to him now could I.

"How the hell did you get through to me? This is the most secure line on the planet."

"That's a long story Mr. President, one I won't have the time to tell you if you kill me and my friends with those missiles."

"Well I am sorry son, it's much too late on that front. I don't even know if I could stop those missiles, and if I could I probably

471

wouldn't. I have no way to verify who you are or the purpose of that space station and I have an actionable intelligence report from reliable sources that says that station is hostile. I have to weigh the life of every American before I make choices like this and I refuse to gamble with those lives. Besides, for all I know you could just be some crafty hacker in an abandoned warehouse somewhere trying to pull a fast one on me."

"Mr. President I assure you that I am on that space station right now. It's how I am calling you, some areas of our technology are very advanced. That intelligence report you received is from a radical terror organization trying to establish some worldwide communism scheme. You have been infiltrated at every level if they were able to influence you to kill strangers. For all I know you are a part of that organization. If I live through this you and I are going to talk face to face and get to the bottom of this."

I made the signal of my hand cutting across my throat to tell Bifrost to cut the line hoping she had cameras or sensors in this area. She must have understood because the electronic fuzz of an old school open phone line ended. "Get my friends and family up to the command center, with the exception of Nightingale, she can keep working."

"Yes Oliver."

I sprinted to the command center in record time. My parents were already there because as I had learned after the battle the command center actually doubled as a safe room during attacks which makes sense. My friends dribbled in just behind me: Anthony, Astrid, James, and Gul. Seeing Gul took my breath away. She had blood up to her elbows and I couldn't help but rush over to her. My problem was that once I got to her I didn't know what to say. She stared at me, I stared at her, and I blurted out the first thing I thought of.

"Are you injured? This is a lot of blood."

"No I'm fine. I was helping Nightingale in the med-bay. She has been teaching me things for a long time now. I was safe in here during the attack." Her English was still very accented, but it had gotten much better.

"Listen... I... I'm sorry for everything."

"I understand Oliver. Not so long ago I was the one going through something," said Gul. I remembered we were on the clock so I kissed her on the forehead and then left her to stand at the front of all of my friends.

"We have twenty hardened missiles headed for us. Bifrost doesn't think she can stop them all. She is going to try to mitigate the damage but a few are going to hit," I said.

"So what does that mean for us?" James asked with one of his arms around Astrid's shoulders. Bifrost was the one who answered him

"Unsure, I don't know the yield or make of the missiles. I also can't be sure how many missiles the A.N.I.'s can disable. I also don't know what impact the soft missile defense will have on their yields. There is a chance they could detonate early on our second string defenses and cause little to no damage."

"What I didn't hear was what chance the missiles have of destroying the whole station..." said James.

"Without more information I can only make rough guesses. I would estimate that the missiles have between a 4% to 16% chance of destroying the entire station. The more likely scenario is that only a few missiles will make it through and damage the station partially. In that scenario everyone in this room has a 62% to 76% chance of living," said Bifrost.

"Time until they hit?" I asked.

"Three minutes or less if they continue at their current speed," said Bifrost

"Oliver, anything you can do with your power?" asked James

His question made me feel really dumb for not thinking of that already. I brought up my screen and started running through possible upgrades. I felt excited that we had another option. Though the odds were in our favor, possibly having only a 26%

chance of living seemed pretty terrible. I started running through options that I could of think of, knowing the clock was ticking meant I had to rush. The first thing I tried to do was upgrade the A.N.I.'s that drove the lasers. My enhancement screen gave me a message I had never seen before "out of range", what the hell... I mentally kicked myself for not testing my power at long range before now. On another note this lent credit to James' theory that my power was based on some kind of nanomachine or nanocyte based technology if I had to be somewhat near something to upgrade it. I couldn't dwell on that, we were running out of time.

My problem now was that every upgrade I had been thinking about was surely out of range and I knew I couldn't make it to the outer layer of the station in three minutes or less. Nor did I really want to be near an exterior wall before a missile hit. I ran a couple upgrades through my menu that had to do with upgrading Bifrost, but they were massively expensive. I felt all eyes in the room on me and I knew we were up against the clock. Finally the idea came to me, and it had nothing to do with my power, and everything to do with Anthony's power.

"Anthony I know your power has a range, but what if you were tapped into something that had a larger range? Could you extend your power through it?" I asked

"Oliver…. You are a genius! One problem though, I'm only one man. I can't reprogram 20 missiles. I don't even know if I can reprogram one," he replied.

"You don't have to. Just reprogram one or two, let the lasers eat the rest," I said excitedly.

"Let's do it, where should I tell them to go?"

"Good question… Bifrost, give us a location on a U.S. aircraft carrier out in the ocean away from a civilian population."

"The U.S.S. Ronald Reagan is off the coast of Japan returning to U.S. waters. It's hundreds of miles out. Current coordinates are 25°58'54.7" North, 162°34'28.0" East."

"Anthony can you make them land close enough to those coordinates to give those guys the scare of a lifetime?" I asked.

"I can try."

We all waited, scared as hell. Even if you have a backup plan, when missiles are flying at your home, your friends, and your family, it tends to make you nervous.

"Missiles will be in range of our lasers in 10 seconds," said Bifrost. We all looked over at Anthony who had his hands on a console, palms flat. I had no idea if that helped him or how his power worked really at all, but I wasn't going to ask right now.

"I got one!" shouted Anthony, who now had his eyes closed with a look of concentration on his face.

"I got the second, I'm spacing them out a bit. Is a mile too close to the aircraft carrier?"

"1.2 miles would be optimal to avoid risk to human life," said Bifrost.

"Adjusting!" shouted Anthony, then his eyes snapped open.

"They are out of my range now. They are going to work on my last given orders, which is to land a little over a mile away from the aircraft carrier and detonate in the water."

The rest of my team was transfixed on a few of the larger screens in the command center that showed missiles being hit by invisible lasers and breaking apart. I had almost forgotten about all of the other ones. "Bifrost are any of those going to hit?" I asked.

"According to the level of damage the lasers are doing now, all missiles should be stopped before impact."

"Good, then get the president back on the phone." My parents looked at me like I was crazy.

Bifrost must have had him on speed dial or something because he answered quickly this time.

"Go," the president said simply.

"Mr. President it's me again, the gentleman up in the space station. Do me a favor and either get eyes or ears on the U.S.S. Ronald Reagan," I said.

"What did you do?" The president's voice was pure ice.

"You'll just have to wait and see."

The line went quiet as we all waited for the first of the missiles to land near the ship. When it did the president went absolutely crazy.

"THERE ARE AMERICAN MEN AND WOMEN ON THOSE SHIPS!" he shouted. I knew I had to stay calm.

"I know, that's why we didn't hit them." I said as calmly as possible. Then the second missile landed.

"STOP goddammit, what do you want! Stop shooting missiles at my boys!"

"I want peace Mr. President, and I want a sit down. I told you we are Americans up here. We are a group dedicated to helping people. The terror group that fed you the false information on us was angry because we stopped them from stealing our proprietary technology. I think they figured if they couldn't have it then no one should. You have been used. I want to fix all of that, I want to work with you... Are you at the White House right now Mr. President?"

"Yes."

"One hours time. I'll meet you on the roof... Please don't shoot at me." Again I gave the symbol to cut the line and Bifrost did.

"Oliver, what the hell!" shouted James.

"We don't have time for that. We have one hour to figure out how to get me onto the White House roof and then back off again when my meeting with the president is over."

"I got some ideas," said my dad and Anthony at the same time.

***

I was all alone in the shuttle. Bifrost was my pilot. If I was going to get shot down I wanted to do it alone. My friends had argued adamantly that someone should come with me, but I wouldn't hear it. We had just got James back, we couldn't lose him or anyone else I loved again. I wasn't taking any weapons with me. Well technically my arm is a weapon, but I wasn't taking any projectile based weapons with me. As I was hopping in the shuttle Anthony had surprised me with a last minute gift he had been working on for all of us: an all white domino mask. I popped it on and looked in a handheld mirror he had given me. It looked great except that half the hair on my head was burnt off from the battle and I looked a little insane. So I waited an extra few minutes for Gul to run and grab some trimmers to come back and shave off my remaining hair. I couldn't exactly meet the most powerful man on earth looking like a crazy person. Anthony had done his part hosing off most of the blood off of my white armor. After that I was as ready as I would ever be, and I didn't want to be late.

Looking down at my mechanical arm made me wish I had a sleeve on this armor. I would absolutely have to invest in some long sleeve shirts at some point and maybe a tan glove.

"Oliver, we are close now. Please go stand on the ramp."

"Will do Bifrost... Hey Bifrost... Thanks for everything."

"Oliver, I am a glorified toaster, you are being irrational."

"That's okay."

"Jump Oliver."

So I did. I had never jumped out of anything before, an airplane, a car, an interplanetary shuttle, etcetera. I now understood intimately why I had never jumped out of anything, it was terrifying. It was night and it was raining. I could barely keep my eyes open as I flew through the sky and tried to orient my body in the direction of the White House which was huge, looming, and well lit. I noticed the lights on the roof were turned off though. The roof was perfect darkness in a sea of white. I found orienting myself in the air was extremely difficult until I let my mechanical arm dangle in front of me and then it got easier. I let the weight of my arm guide me on target. I knew I had to wait till the last second to pull the cord on the parachute. The last thing we needed was media coverage of me parachuting happily on to the top of the White House.

I felt like I was gaining speed as I fell which some part of me rationally knew that should terrify me even more, but after the day I had had I was all out of fear. I was a little off course so I slowly coiled my mechanical arm to my body and then threw it hard forward in the direction of the White House. The maneuver panned out quickly and put me right back on target, flying face first towards the greatest seat of power in the world. All of a sudden the White House seemed huge. I yanked the cord on the parachute and felt it fly out behind me and a strong tug pulled on my underarms and other parts of my body where the parachute harness rested. I still felt like I was moving much too fast and the roof of the White House was much too dark. I could see lumpy shapes on it and I wasn't sure what they were, but I knew I probably shouldn't land on them.

Wind continually whipped at me and I only had seconds before I landed. I knew I was moving too fast even with the parachute deployed, but I wasn't sure why... Then it hit me, the arm. My mechanical arm was probably worth the weight of a small woman. I wonder how much weight this parachute is rated for… I slammed hard into one of the bulbous dark shapes on the roof that I had been trying to avoid. I tried to roll forward to distribute my weight but whatever I had landed on started crumpling around me like a piece of paper. I threw my mechanical arm out quickly, palm down to try to shift the blow of the landing to it so I wouldn't snap my ankles, but my arm sank further into whatever I had landed on as the whole thing tipped over and fell apart below me. It felt like an eternity as my body rolled forward but it was probably only a second. I tumbled forward and landed hard on my back in something that felt like gravel. I cracked my eyes open and lights snapped on everywhere which only illuminated the dust in the air, which I guess I had kicked up. I slowly stood and I saw figures move quickly through the dust. It was the president's security detail, scores of them. There were at least 30 men and women of the Secret Service all with their service weapons drawn and pointed at my face. I didn't blame them, I probably looked crazy.

I turned behind me and squinted through the dust to see what I had landed on. It was an air conditioner unit the size of a car and it was crumpled to all hell. "Uhh, I'll pay for that," I said as I turned back around and shot a thumb over my shoulder at the unit. I heard a slow clap from somewhere outside the ring of light I was in and a man in a very expensive suit walked out of the shadows. Clapping all the way until he stood in front of me. It was the president.

"Sir, it's great to meet you" I said, while instinctively shooting out my right arm. The president stepped back a foot and I heard safeties on pistols all over the roof being flipped to the ,fire' position.

"Oh, I'm sorry. That's a new addition, it's a long story." I said as I reached forward with my left arm, my human arm. The president looked unsure for a second, then he also reached out his left arm so we could shake normally.

"Come join me for some iced tea. I don't want to stand in this rain. This suit costs more than an automobile." I didn't know why, but I couldn't help but like this guy. He had a certain swagger about him.

A Secret Service agent ran up and flipped an umbrella out and handed it to the president. I followed him over to a picnic table with an even larger umbrella over it. There was only two seats at opposite ends of the table. They were both plastic...

"Sir, I don't know if those chairs will hold my weight." The president looked over at me then at one of his security detail. The man ran off without a word.

"Would you like some tea?" He asked while pouring himself a large glass from a carafe full of tea and sliced lemons. In all of the rush I didn't realize how hungry and thirsty I was. Seeing the delicious iced beverage made my stomach rumble.

"Yes please," I said while wondering if it would be a breach of protocol for me to ask for some fried chicken as well. While the president poured me a glass of the tea one of the security men ran up with some kind of outdoor bi-metal chair which he handed to me. I sat in it a careful distance away from the president. I made sure all my moves were slow and measured. I didn't want to seem hostile in any way. The president slowly slid my cup over to me and I didn't reach for it until he was comfortably back on his side of the table. He waited while I gulped the entire glass down before speaking.

"I have to admit, I don't know what to do with you."

"Work with me."

"My security experts think I should throw you in a dark hole and interrogate you for years."

"I think if you were to do that my friends would come for me. They would... make your life hard. It would be better if we worked together."

"How so, what do you want, what are you trying to get out of me? Money?"

"No sir."

"What then, a position of power? I won't be pressured into anything."

"No sir, it's nothing like that. Mainly I would like to be left alone, and if it's not too much to ask... Once you trust me, could you maybe certify me and my friends as some kind of emergency responders? I'm kind of tired of having no status or being a vigilante."

"That's all good and dandy, but what about that weapon you have floating above my country?"

"It's not a weapon sir."

"Don't bullshit me son. You almost blew one of my ships out of the water today."

"Sir, I was only able to do that because you launched those missiles at us. We have no long range weapons. We just reprogrammed your own and sent them back where they had come from. Our intent was to show you that we aren't dangerous. I could have sent those missiles anywhere, instead we had them harmlessly blow up some water."

The president leaned back in his chair and pulled a large cigar out of his coat pocket. He carefully took his time cutting off the tip and lighting it with an old school match. He took a giant mouthful of smoke and blew it my way.

"Would you like a cigar?"

"Sir, I would only embarrass myself. I don't know anything about cigars."

"Then I propose an exchange. I'll give you a cigar and teach you all about them. In return you tell me about your space station, and this terror organization you say has manipulated me, and a little about yourself. And stop calling me sir, you are making me feel like an old man. Call me Ben, and I want your first name right now as a mutual sign of respect." This guy obviously knew what he was doing diplomacy wise.

So I told him. I told him my name was Oliver, and then I told him a sanitized version of my story. I even told him about how I used to be mentally retarded. Except instead of being cured by a genie I told him I was cured by a scientific co-op. It was too easy to lie about this stuff because all of the lies were based on truths and I barely had to fabricate anything. The only thing I had to do was switch out the words 'genie,' or 'wishes,' or my 'enhancement menu,' with the word 'science.' When he probed into how it worked I was honest with him, I had no idea. When he asked me if I could cure more people, I told him the truth, we had limited resources in that department but it was possible.

Then I told him everything I knew about the Cabal including their current leader's name: OkuboTokugawa. I told him about how the Cabal had first tried to kidnap my parents and how they held them at gunpoint. I told him about our mission to save the girls. I told him all about Gul, though I left out her name. I told him about how the Cabal ambushed us and captured James, and cut my arm off. I had to hold back a lot of emotion at that part, sadness and anger. I told him about how I was depressed after I lost my arm. I told him about how two of my teammates had carried on destroying evil while I worked on fixing myself mentally and physically. Finally I told him about the Cabal's attack on Valhalla today and how they had fed him false intel since they couldn't steal the technology from us that they wanted. It felt good to lay it all out, to get it all off of my chest. I made sure to protect the identities of everyone else involved. The only name I gave him was my own and I didn't give him my last name. Maybe he would be able to get it from the information I had given him, but at this point I didn't care. We couldn't live in the dark forever.

"I believe you. Or I believe that you believe you are telling the truth. I just don't see how The Cabal could have faked that intelligence report. It came through the highest levels of the Department of Defense."

"Sir, the Cabal probably have men IN the department of defense. They had enough money and resources to build a space faring vehicle in just a little over two months. Some of the people you see everyday are probably members of the Cabal." I noticed when I said that one of the Secret Service agents behind the president moved ever so slightly, it was just an involuntary tick, but I had noticed it. I looked up at him purposefully and his eyes darted around for just a moment.

"Like that guy right there, he is probably Cabal." I said while pointing at the nervous looking agent. All of the security around him looked at him and he took a step back. Very calmly the president said "Arrest that man." Four agents jumped on him and tackled him to the ground. There was a short scuffle, and then they all soon stopped and got off of him. One of the agents walked over to the president.

"Sir, he is dead," the agent said softly.

"What? You killed him?" asked the president.

"No sir, he just suddenly stopped breathing, his heart stopped," said the agent. I felt it was my turn to enter the conversation.

"It could just be a coincidence, but I would say most likely he was a member of the Cabal who killed himself so he couldn't be interrogated. Or maybe the Cabal has some way to remotely kill compromised members, I don't rightly know." The president and the agent who had brought the news forward looked stunned.

"That's one hell of a coincidence. You show up and then he dies like that. Am I next?"

"I'm no killer sir."

The president looked back at the dead man and then back at me. He really stared me down. He stared at me until I blinked and then he stared some more. I tried to keep my composure, but he was staring into the depths of my very soul. Finally he spoke up.

"I'll let you go, but I have some conditions," said the president.

"I'll consider whatever conditions you have, please list them."

"First, when you leave here you take one of my men with you. I need evidence that you aren't floating over my head with a weapon of mass destruction. You will take Williams here, I have trusted him with the life of my wife and children for years." As he said that he stood and set his hand on the large agent next to him. This was the same agent who had been the first to tackle the suspicious man.

"I can do that, what else?" I asked him.

"Did you know I use to be a doctor?" he asked.

"No sir, I didn't know that. I'm not exactly in the political loop."

"Well I was a doctor, a world renowned doctor. A surgeon to be more specific. I saved thousands of people. There were these twins…. Conjoined twins… They were joined at the head, they couldn't be separated. I invented a way to separate them, the surgery was a success, I thought I had done it. A few years later one of them died... The one that lived slowly lost most of his motor and cognitive functions and eventually had to be institutionalized. It broke my damn heart. It weighs on my soul everyday... He is still in there, rotting away in some kind of long term care facility."

The president stood up and walked directly over to me. He pulled me to my feet and put a grip on my shoulder, a strong grip... He looked right into my eyes and said "You'll find him for me, the remaining twin. You will find him and you will get your scientists to do what I could not. You will heal him. You do that and I will trust you. Do you hear me? You will do this for me." I could tell he was upset about this, his head was shaking ever so slightly and his grip on my shoulder was so strong it was starting to hurt. I couldn't help but shout my reply.

"YES SIR!"

"How do I get a hold of you?" The president asked. I handed him over an altered transceiver my father had whipped up. It was just a small gray box with a single button on it and a USB port.

"Plug any USB headset into this, and then press this button to call me," I said.

I checked my watch, it was about time.

I slowly took a few steps away from the table which made everyone nervous. "My time here is up. I have to go. Agent Williams, are you coming?" I asked. Agent Williams nodded his head and walked over to me.

"I have to apologize I wasn't planning on any passengers," I said. Immediately after I finished talking a large balloon exploded off of my back almost knocking me over. It flew up into the night sky with a small array of LED lights below it. The whole balloon device was tethered to my body via a metal line.

"Get closer Agent Williams, this is going to be awkward, sorry again," I said.

Agent Williams stepped up closer to me. I wrapped both of my arms around him under his armpits. Somewhere above us one of my shuttles with a hook trailing below it snagged the line being held in the air by the balloon. It ripped me and Agent Williams off of the roof so fast that I almost dropped him. As we flew through the wet, dark air I saw the lights of Washington D.C. get smaller below us. I wondered what the president thought of me flying off into the night sky.

Epilogue

"What is this place Oliver?," asked Gul.

"It's a specialized care facility for children and young adults with long term needs," I reply coyly, well as coyly as you can blurt out that mess.

"Did you take me somewhere boring for our first date?"

"This isn't a date, but believe me, you won't be bored.

I had been saving up points for this occasion. We got to the final doors before the entrance to the main hall. It was past visiting hours so no one was manning the desk to let us in. I reached into the pocket of the suit jacket I was wearing and pulled out two domino masks. I put one on myself and handed the other to Gul "Put this on please."

I was wearing a very nice suit that I had picked up for this evening. We were about to do something that I had wanted to do since the first day I had gotten my power. I tugged on the security door lightly with my human arm to see if it had any give, it didn't move. Oh well, it was worth a try. I reached down with my mechanical arm and pulled on it gently, slowly increasing the pressure. Until the deadbolts popped loudly, and the frame creaked. The door popped open and I held one arm out, a sign of invitation, "After you, my lady."

Ahead of us lay a long hallway with doors on either side. The floor was linoleum and there was bright fluorescent lights, the standard hospital setup. We went into the first door on the left. A nurse was bent over a 13-year-old boy who had been in a coma for nine months. She was giving him a sponge bath and gently caressing his hair. She turned around and looked at me in a quick glance.

"You can't be in here, it's past visiting--" then she noticed my domino mask. "I don't know what you think you are doing, but I'm calling the police!"

"Mam, just wait one second. I reached over and touched the young man's hand gently. I needed permission to use my power on people, but I had a theory that if my upgrade was something so common sense that no one in their right mind would say no to it that it would work. I would test that theory now.

I thought about a cure where the boy would wake up from his coma and whatever underlying issue that had happened to cause the coma would be cured. The boy would also be mentally healthy. It scrolled out on my screen and the point cost was well within expectations. I pulled out a fancy looking device full of blinking lights and medical symbols, a device that in all actuality did nothing except look complicated. I placed the device against the boy's chest. I had to keep up appearances, especially with the nurse watching. I hit the confirm button on my menu that only me and Gul could see and the boy woke up.

"Oh my god!" The nurse shouted. "What is that device? What did you do?"

"Have a good night mam, look after him," I said quietly.

I turned around and grabbed Gul's hand, she smiled at me.

"I always knew you were a good man, my Oliver," she said, and kissed me on the cheek. We went to the next room, it was going to be a long night.

End of Book 1

If you want to keep reading more Gamelit (that's the genre of this book, Gamelit) books from Cory Gaffner, try out his Arbiter series. Book one for it is out now, and it's called:

Killdozer

If you want more from the Oliver's Wishes Universe ASAP, leave a WRITTEN review on Amazon. It can be something as simple as "Fun Read." Amazon won't take a book seriously until it has a large number of "mostly-postitive" reviews. If Amazon isn't taking my book seriously, I ditch it and start a new series. Don't get me wrong, I love the Oliver's Wishes universe, but I also have to feed my kids in real life, and that takes money, and I can't make money without readers, and I can't get readers without positive reviews.

FYI Amazon considers a 3-star "nuetral-bad."

A note from the author:

Hi all, thank you so much for reading my book, it means so much to me! If you want to talk to me about the book please do! Join my facebook group at the link below and we can discuss your likes and dislikes about it, or things you would like to see happen in the series.

https://www.facebook.com/groups/CoryGaffnerBooks

If you noticed a typo or an error of any kind that you think should be fixed in this book, PLEASE post about it in my facebook group OR shoot me an email at CoryGaffner@yahoo.com

Please, Please, Please, leave me a written review on Amazon and/or GoodReads, (preferrably Amazon) it would really help me out! I can't explain how very important that is. Also if you have the time, head over to my author page on Amazon.com and Press the little "+Follow" button below my picture. If you don't press the Follow button then Amazon won't tell you when my next book is coming out.

If you enjoyed this book at all, I highly recommend you check out my other books as well.

About the Author

Cory Gaffner spends most of his days working with foster kids in a few different roles. He has been and sometimes is a full-time foster father. He is an honorably discharged combat veteran of the U.S. Army. His hobbies include throwing knives at stuff, competition shooting, and playing video games late into the night.

He currently lives in Arizona with his wife, sons, and two guard dogs. Cory is an independent author meaning he writes, edits, produces, pays for, and publishes his own books. That means he needs your help! The best way to help him is by leaving a constructive review that will help potential readers find his books!

Cory is a very laid back dude, so if you would like to get a hold of him join his facebook group "The Literary Works of Cory Gaffner."

www.ingramcontent.com/pod-product-compliance
Lightning Source LLC
Chambersburg PA
CBHW030924020726
47498CB00001B/106